Other books by Linda Chaikin

Arabian Nights
Lions of the Desert

VALIANT
Hearts

Linda Chaikin

ALABASTER

BOOKS

VALIANT HEARTS
Published by Alabaster Books
a division of Multnomah Publishers, Inc.
© 1998 by Linda Chaikin

International Standard Book Number: 1-57673-240-1

Cover illustration by Artworks/Paul Bachem
Cover design by Brenda McGee

All Scripture quotations, unless otherwise indicated, are taken from
The Holy Bible: New King James Version (NKJV) © 1984 by Thomas
Nelson, Inc. Used by permission of Thomas Nelson, Inc.
All rights reserved.

Alabaster is a trademark of Multnomah Publishers, Inc.

For information:
Multnomah Publishers, Inc.•PO Box 1720•Sisters, OR 97759

Library of Congress Cataloging-in-Publication Data
Chaikin, L.L. 1943—
    Valiant hearts/by Linda Chaikin.
        p. cm.
    ISBN 1-57673-240-1 (alk. paper)
    1. World War, 1914-1918—Medical care—Fiction   2. World War,
    1914-1918—Egypt—Fiction. I. Title
PS3553.H2427V3 1998
813'.54—dc21   98-13065
                                                                          CIP

Now and then a writer is privileged to work with the best.

This book is dedicated to Karen Ball,

senior editor of Alabaster books and the editor of

Lions of the Desert and *Valiant Hearts*.

Thanks, Karen.

PART I

CAIRO

Who through faith…quenched the violence of fire, escaped the edge of the sword, out of weakness were made strong, became valiant in battle…

HEBREWS 11:33A–34

ONE

>━┥◆>━◇━<◆┝━<

In the Valley of the Kings

THE WIND MOANED THROUGH the towering ruins of Karnak temple near ancient Thebes, sounding like a thousand temple priests paying homage to the pharaohs. Gusts, like invisible fingers, clawed the beds of sand as though trying to unearth the ancient, imprisoned dead.

Nearby, a solitary listener in a dark Prince Albert coat stood entranced by the sights and sounds—his concentration broken only when he noticed a group of tourists on camels approaching in the distance. No doubt they were coming for a moonlight tour later that evening. Their voices floated toward him—female laughter, masculine excitement. His mouth thinned. *Tourists.* His lip curled. *Fools! All of them! How can they appreciate these awesome mysteries!*

He slipped like a shadow behind a great aged stone, then disappeared into the windswept sand, his silent footsteps retreating, leaving not a trace as the grains blew.

In his wake, the setting red sun threw a menacing shroud upon the tombs of the once powerful pharaohs.

~ ~ ~ ~ ~

On the Train to Zeitoun

The shrill wail of the train filled the air as the low rumbling of the wheels echoed over the iron track. Allison Wescott sat in the sun-baked, dusty tram en route from Cairo to the isolated junction in the Egyptian desert. Allison had an obscure notion that perhaps one or possibly even two other passengers were aboard in the stuffy, hot shadows—although from where she sat toward the back, she could not see them. Which was just as well, for her intense meditation left little room for studying strangers.

She was staring out the dusty window, where, above the flat, endless desert, empty as far as she could see, the broiling orange red sunset scrawled ominously across the vast sky.

Back in Cairo, the murder trial of her mother's cousin, Sir Edgar Simonds, and his son, Gilbert, was ticking toward its bleak end. She had heard that those who frequented the Gezira Club for British officers were secretly wagering on the verdict. The consensus so far? "Death by hanging for Gilbert." But the fate of his father, Sir Edgar, stood shrouded in uncertainty.

"He's a sly one, all right—he'll get by with murder," many of the officers were saying. "Whoever heard of the chief inspector of the Cairo police dangling?"

The wheels clamored, and the stark gusts buffeted the train's sides. Allison winced. Yes, her cousin Gilbert would hang, but she worried more about her sister. If only she could understand the compulsion that drove Beth to her recent behavior. "How can she insist Cousin Gilbert didn't kill Sarah Blaine?" Allison folded her arms with conviction and looked about the empty seats as though speaking to a jury. "Of course he did! Beth was even with me in the brigadier's study when Gilly confessed. He admitted he killed Sarah for the Egyptian treasure."

The only response to her words was the clacking of the wheels.

Allison turned her musings back to three months ago, to the Egyptian treasure piece that she and Colonel Bret Holden had discovered beneath the sundial in the foreboding rose garden of the Blaine house. The heat and dust of the tram faded as she found herself lost in the memory of humid rain on moldy, dead leaves; of wind ripping through the overgrown oleander bushes like tentacles reaching toward her....

She had found the body of Professor Jemal Pasha concealed under those tangled branches.

Shifting position in the warm seat, she felt the harsh, cracked leather beneath her perspiring palms. The treasure... It consisted of a priceless gold statue of Queen Nefertari, which was now secure in the Cairo Museum, but there had been something else: a map—or at least what Bret had told her was a map. And no ordinary map, either, but one leading to a royal burial tomb in the Valley of the Kings. As far as she knew, it remained with Bret, unknown to higher authorities.

She blinked several times, forcing her mind away from Bret, back to her sister.

Beth was just plain wrong about Cousin Gilbert's innocence and she must know it. Why, then, was she making herself ill over it? Allison frowned. What if, by some thread of possibility, Gilbert had not killed Sarah Blaine? The question then was who did?

Sir Edgar denied it flatly, and what's more, he had an alibi that Bret said was as solid as the Rock of Gibraltar. "He's guilty of smuggling rare Egyptian pieces through Constantinople into Berlin," Bret had confided three months ago, in December, "but not of murdering Sarah."

"How did he smuggle them? How was it possible?" she argued.

"Easy." Bret's tone had been lazy, even bored. "The Berlin-Baghdad Railway runs to Constantinople, across the mountains of Bulgaria, and straight into Berlin. We're still watching it. We've reason to think others may yet be involved."

Others? Were they involved in smuggling, or in the death of Sarah Blaine and Jemal? She shook her head, frustrated. Why hadn't she inquired more fully at the time what he had meant by that cryptic comment? She supposed the people working at the mysterious merchant shop in Old Cairo were a possibility. She recalled several odd happenings there since 1914.

Bret's words replayed in her mind like Caruso's record on the gramophone. *Others.* Professor Jemal couldn't have killed Sarah since he'd been killed in the rose garden shortly before her…but what about his son Anwar? He had posed as the chauffeur, after all. Still, like Sir Edgar, he'd denied killing Sarah. To the end.

Anwar had been found dead in his cell two weeks ago. Suicide—or so the final reports had said.

Someone else, then. But there *wasn't* anyone else, she told herself firmly.

A faint shiver walked across her skin as delicately as the legs of a wind spider, and she upbraided herself for her unease. "You're worse than Beth! Your emotions are cracking. Whom do you expect to see in the shadows? Sir Edgar? He's fast behind prison doors. And even if he wasn't, what do you have now that he'd want? That anyone would want? Baroness Helga Kruger has Nefertari, and Bret has the map."

Allison shook her head as if to rid her mind of the noisome hum of unrest. Drawing a steadying breath, she closed her eyes and recommitted her runaway feelings to the Lord.

She had told herself before leaving Cairo that she wouldn't think about the past on the trip out to Zeitoun. "Forgetting those things which are behind, reaching forth unto those things which are before," the Scriptures stated. Soon she would be in the good company of Oswald Chambers and Biddy. Soon—

"Going far?"

Allison turned, startled. Her head lifted, and she looked at the passenger standing in the aisle. Her imagination might have convinced her that she'd conjured him up out of the desert wind, but she recalled that someone else had already been aboard when she entered at Cairo. He must have been sitting closer to the conductor.

He stood, keeping his balance to the rhythm of the train by holding onto the rail. He smiled down at her, and she thought him a pleasant-looking man. He was perhaps in his late twenties, with an unruly thatch of dark gold hair and eyes as frosty as a frozen lake in the Alps. She had seen him before—or had she? Perhaps his features only reminded her of someone she knew.

"I'm sorry, did I startle you? I can see why. It appears we're the only two passengers aboard. I take it this is not a popular route for travelers. It's just as well. Tourists can be rude and selfish." He smiled again. "I hope I am neither. May I introduce myself? I've been watching you since Cairo. I would have spoken before, but you appeared so deep in thought I didn't want to interrupt. I am Paul Kruger," and he gave a smart nod of his head that contrasted noticeably with his otherwise casual appearance.

13

Kruger! She stared at the man, stunned.

Yes, there was a marked resemblance to Baroness Helga Kruger, but unlike the baroness, this man's speech bore no hint of a German accent. He was tall and slight, but he looked strong and as suntanned as the desert soldiers she saw at Zeitoun. For a confused moment Allison thought he was just that, a soldier, until she realized that if he was related to Helga, he would not be stationed in Egypt because he would be a German citizen. Nor would he be dressed as a tourist. He was wearing desert clothing of the expedition sort: a tan-colored canvas shirt with a half-dozen pockets—all crammed with things—and rugged walking trousers bloused into dusty boots. He carried a canvas toppee with a metal rim. All he needed was to be biting on the end of a pipe to have convinced her he was a British professor of some sort.

"I'm sorry, I didn't mean to stare. You're related to Baroness Kruger?"

He grinned, a crinkle at the corners of his eyes altering his aristocratic face. "You know her? I'm amazed!"

She doubted his astonishment, though she wasn't completely certain why. "I've known Helga for several years. She was gracious enough to open her home to me at Christmas."

"Ah yes, a reprieve from the murders taking place at the Blaine house. I read about them in the papers. A nasty business. I meant to be home for the holidays but got fouled up on the way from London. The war, you know," he stated soberly as if he needed to explain.

"The baroness is…your aunt?"

He laughed. "My mother."

Allison tried to conceal her shock, but he must have seen through the attempt, for he grinned again in apparent amusement. "I admit she looks young. Helga is a striking woman. I recall she made quite a stir in Berlin when I was a boy. I haven't seen her in five years, but I imagine she's kept up her appearance. I decided it was past time. Life is too short you know. She'll be quite surprised to see me. She doesn't know I've come."

"Yes, I think she will be." She barely stopped herself from saying that Helga had never mentioned having a son. He might take the omission as a lack of warmth on his mother's part. "You've come from Berlin, Mr. Kruger?"

"Paul, please. No. Merry Old England. I wouldn't dare show my face otherwise. May I sit down?"

He was amiable enough, and Allison was curious. "Yes, do. I'm Allison Wescott." She held out her hand, but rather than briefly shaking it, he proved his Rhineland manners by bending over it. He looked down at her soberly. "I've a confession to make, Miss Wescott. You'll forgive me, but I knew who you were the moment you got on board the tram at Cairo."

On guard, she leaned back in the seat. He explained casually, "Actually, I was expecting you."

Her brows lifted. "That doesn't really explain anything, does it?"

He removed a rumpled packet of cigarettes. "No. Do you mind?" He used a gold lighter, and she analyzed the line of his face as the flame sprang up, wondering what it all meant. Then she noticed the cigarettes were Turkish.

"That you expected me is rather unnerving," she admitted as the train rumbled.

His smile vanished. "After the Blaine house, yes, quite understandable." He gave her a comforting smile. "Nothing sinister lurks in my mind, I assure you."

"Assurances mean very little to me these days."

"Rightly so. I have the best credentials to verify my pristine character. A friend of yours showed me your photograph and suggested I meet you when I came to Egypt."

A friend? "Let me guess; Helga sent you my photograph."

He smiled. "No, but I wish she had."

She ignored that.

"The mail from Cairo has been rather sluggish so it wouldn't have done much good anyway. No, it was a mutual friend in London who told me I might look you up and say hello when I got here."

She watched him lean his head against the high-back seat and his cigarette glowed in the dimness as he drew on it, watching her. "I hope you don't mind his suggestion?"

"That depends on the character of the friend. It's been years since I was in London so I can't imagine who this man might be," she said evasively.

"Colonel Bret Holden."

For a brief moment Allison felt stunned. "Bret?" She recovered smoothly, surprising even herself. To gain time she repeated, "Oh. Yes, the colonel. I didn't know he was in London again."

"We met last year. I'm not certain where he is now. I thought you might know."

"No. I've not seen him since before—" The words lodged in her throat like stickers. "Since just before Christmas eve. I don't think he's serving in Cairo now."

Paul studied his cigarette. "I see. Well perhaps I should drop in at Cairo Intelligence and leave a message."

So he knew that Bret worked in intelligence.

"Quite an interesting but unplanned adventure, how we met." Paul studied her, a glint of something—humor? speculation?—in his cool eyes. "The incident nearly cost us both our lives. I was muddied down in France, so to speak, unable to get back to London. My vehicle had been struck by a German

16

machine gun—is this upsetting you?"

"Oh, no. No, not at all. Please, go on." *Bret!*

"Naturally, it wasn't my intention to get trapped. I was visiting friends in Paris after many years working in Tanzania. But, to make a long tale shorter, Colonel Holden and I happened to meet at the same precarious moment in the midst of gunfire. I do believe he was on some rather interesting business for the government when his vehicle, like mine, was riddled to a standstill. Unfortunately the colonel's aides were killed. Poor chaps. We both made it back to London on foot, thanks to him and that precious Luger. You might ask him sometime where he got it." He smiled. "I'm surprised he didn't mention me to you."

"No." Her voice was thin. "There is much about his private life he doesn't tell me. So he showed you my photograph?"

"He said you were Neal Bristow's cousin. I met Neal in London, a little over a year ago."

Allison forced a smile to her lips. "Well, any friend of Neal's is one of mine. Especially when he also happens to be the baroness's son. What were you doing in London, if you don't mind my asking? Do you have relatives there?"

"No, no relatives. They are all in Berlin, except Helga, of course. I was in London on the lecture route. I'm an archaeologist." He smiled at her surprise. "It seems to run in the family. Small world, as they say. And the world of archaeology is even smaller. Mr. Hedding of the British Museum introduced me to Neal. I'd recently come from Africa where I worked with associates there. When Neal realized who I was and how I was coming out to see my mother in Egypt, he mentioned your avid interest in archaeology and that I'd most likely run into you at one of Helga's club meetings. The last one, if memory serves me right, was in Aleppo just before the war?"

17

Allison didn't answer right away. She was still wondering about Bret. So he had showed Paul Kruger her photograph. That was surprising; she didn't know Bret carried a photo of her. Where had he gotten it? Not from her. Then all this with Paul evidently had happened before she had seen Bret last September, near Kut in the Arabian Desert. Yet, Bret had never mentioned it. She tried to recall if he'd said anything about Cousin Neal....

"I believe Neal is due to return to Egypt this year."

Allison nodded. "Yes, that's true." As was the fact that Neal was overdue. The family had expected him at Christmas. For some inexplicable reason she felt reluctant to mention this. "As you say, the mails are abominably sluggish so I suppose passenger ships are as well."

"German U-boats. A hellish device." He shook his head, frowning at the end of his cigarette as though it were to blame.

"So you were an archaeologist in Tanzania?"

"For nearly six years. I left when the war broke out. There's nothing like tragedy to prompt one to seek his roots. I realized I wanted to see Helga again."

"Then I suppose I needn't inquire whether you'll be attending her two-week retreat in the Valley of the Kings. She's secretary of the Cairo Archaeological Club."

"I wouldn't miss the opportunity. A brilliant woman, my mother, when it comes to Egyptology. You won't mind my saying so." He leaned forward in his seat and spoke in a lower voice, "I tell you, Miss Wescott, this matter of Queen Nefertari is decidedly astounding. The questions, of course, are whether she is genuine, from which royal tomb was she stolen, and where the burial entrance is located."

Allison pondered Paul's choice of words. *Stolen.* Interesting that he should say so.... She inclined her head. "Perhaps the greatest discovery in a century is upon us."

He gazed off toward the desert. "My mother must be decidedly enthused about the queen—and rightly so—yet we must be careful. Some will believe the bizarre circumstances surrounding the find only validate the theory of the pharaoh's curse."

"I don't believe in such things. Besides, the funerary piece may prove unworthy. It may be no more than the error of someone's greed, of jumping to conclusions. Some archaeologists believe we've already located all the royal tombs that haven't been destroyed or looted."

He smiled. "Perhaps so. Nevertheless, I feel Helga must be careful in this matter. My emotions are drawn in two directions. When I arrived to hear of the discovery, I was excited as any archaeologist would be, but between you and me, Miss Wescott, I should like to see it returned to its rightful abode and the matter forgotten."

"Coming from an archaeologist—" she began, but his wry smile interrupted her.

"Yes, I know," he agreed, "but I'm in a position to know there are those who feel differently. Archaeologists who think they have the right to perform any act of profanity to discover what they are not entitled to know are deemed criminals and intruders of the worst sort."

There was something about Paul's statement that made her stare at him. In the silence, the rumble of the train grew progressively louder.

After a moment, Allison shrugged. "It will be left to an expert to make the final judgment on whether Nefertari is genuine."

His eyes were sober. "You mean Count Roderick."

So that was his name. Allison hadn't been told. Information on the expert who'd been called in to evaluate the piece had been limited to a few people in Helga's sphere of influence and to her friends in the intelligence department. Paul was either boasting that he had found out on his own in the short period of time he'd been in Egypt, or he was casually letting her know that he was trustworthy. At the moment she wasn't sure which she believed. He seemed honestly worried about his mother. Was that the reason he had come?

Three months…yes, it was more than enough time for him to have heard the news of the discovery and come to Egypt out of concern for his mother.

"You have met the German—Count Roderick?"

She might have admitted she hadn't even heard of him until just now, but something kept her from wholly trusting this man. "It's not been my good fortune, but if he's the expert that everyone is expecting to come to Cairo, I find it quite exciting. I take it, you have met him?"

"On occasion." He grinned. "When I was a boy in Berlin. He came often to the house to dine with my father and other associates."

Other associates. Her interest caught. "I didn't know your father was into archaeology."

He leaned back, shrugging lazily, his emotions once more ebbing away. "My father was into everything. He had a great mind. A love for invention, for country—unfortunately, the Fatherland became all important. I grew up amid interesting discussions covering most every topic, from the Berlin-Baghdad Railway to a possible invasion of France. Needless to say, my parents were at odds. Mother was totally against the schemes of the kaiser."

Allison knew about Helga's husband being dedicated to the cause of German world power, but in actuality she knew little about Helga's life in Berlin before the baron's death. Still, it would seem Paul had been pulled between two strongly opposing viewpoints while growing up.

"And Count Roderick was a friend of your father's?"

"No, actually. He was mother's friend. The count," he stated, "is aggressively against the kaiser."

Did Paul know that his mother was a British agent? Allison decided he did not since it wasn't something Helga would openly discuss, even with members of her immediate family. Besides, Paul had been away for several years.

"Have you come to Egypt for long?"

He met her curious gaze. "To stay, if Helga agrees."

The idea was an odd one…why wouldn't his mother agree?

He seemed to read her mind. "I haven't seen my mother since my father was killed. Until nearly two years ago I worked in Africa. When the war broke I returned to England to do tours. It was only on my arrival here a few weeks ago that I learned of the unfortunate demise of Helga's Turkish assistant, Professor Jemal Pasha. I don't wish to sound presumptuous, but I hope to fill the position he left open. If she agrees, that is. Mother is not one to make sentimental judgments when it comes to archaeology. She will want the best."

"And you hope to prove yourself at Luxor."

He smiled. "Yes, not that I've the expertise to match Jemal's skills."

Despite his self-effacing words, Allison had the impression Paul believed he did have those skills and should have the vacated position.

"I'll be seeing Professor Gamal al-Sayyid of the Cairo Museum next week," he said. "If he approves of my credentials, he'll approach Helga."

Sayyid was Helga's friend. It would be difficult for him to turn down the son of the baroness. Allison thought that Paul knew that as well.

"If things go as I hope, it will be exciting work. Neal has told me so much about Aleppo and the digs out at Carchemish. It's lamentable the war is hindering further excavation there, but at least it should be safe enough at Luxor since no German or Turkish soldiers are running about. When will you be leaving for Luxor?"

"Not for a few weeks. There's to be a meeting at the museum in Cairo on Thursday to discuss the dates of our departure."

"An auction as well, I'm told."

"Club members will bring some items to sell. The proceeds go to the club's work."

The train was slowing, coming to its destination. Allison remembered Sarah Blaine and her concerns over bringing something to the auction.

"Then I will see you again in Cairo." Paul smiled, apparently pleased at the prospect, as he stood and prepared to get off the train.

Her eyes slid away from his bright blue gaze, aware of some obscure uneasiness. "Yes, good-bye." She caught up her kit bag from the seat beside her as the wheels were shrieking to a halt on the track.

Why had Helga never mentioned having a son...especially one that was interested in archaeology? But then, when had the baroness ever discussed her personal affairs? All Allison knew about Helga's husband was that he'd helped finance building the Berlin-Baghdad Railway for the kaiser. The baron—Allison did not even know his name—had died in a rail accident somewhere in the frozen mountains of Bulgaria. Died, in fact, on the railway he had helped finance for Kaiser Wilhelm.

As the train pulled away, leaving Paul behind in the shadows of the platform, Allison realized the encounter had brought her far more questions than answers.

Two

⊱━◈━◦━◈━⊰

WITH A HUFF OF GRAY STEAM, the small train came to a grinding halt on a section of lonely desert track some six miles northeast of Cairo. The sunset held its glory as Allison disembarked alone, carrying her military style kit bag containing her well-worn Bible, some sermons of Oswald Chambers she had print-ed in Cairo to pass out to the soldiers, and her Sunday clothes for tomorrow's worship service. The train chugged its way out of the station.

Dry wind blew against her, and she reached to hold her canvas hat in place. The last wail of the whistle swept across the desert, which was painted with purple shadows. The train, now a dark blotch in the distance, gathered speed on its route back to Cairo.

The solitary expanse of the Egyptian desert swallowed Allison. Her ankle-length cotton skirt flitted outward as the white sand pummeled a smoothly worn tan rock. A lone lizard with beady eyes lifted its head, then whispered away to shelter. The sand blew across the wooden platform, the tinkling sound only serving to amplify her sense of aloneness.

The boards creaked, sounding almost like footsteps. Allison glanced about. The wind?

She turned to face the long platform constructed of weather-worn timber and dried date palm branches for roofing. Shadows loitered in the corners and behind some crates used for benches.

Was it possible that someone had disembarked with her without her noticing him? She supposed so, if the person had gotten off at the back of the tram.

Her eyes searched the lengthening shadows. Nothing moved but the sand, and the only sound was the wind and the creak of parched wood cooling as the sun went down.

She decided she was alone after all and walked across the platform to the edge, the boards making dull hollow sounds beneath her shoes. She scanned the distant desert for sign of a motorcar. Wade Findlay expected her tonight, but whether or not he could borrow a vehicle to pick her up was another matter. More often than not she ended up walking the mile to Zeitoun.

Unable to win the war of nerves or dismiss the tingle that chased her spine, Allison snatched up her kit bag and left the rundown depot, starting off across the sand. As long as she walked in the wide, open space she needn't think about shadowy figures.

The soft, hot sand sank beneath her sturdy high-button, brown shoes as she trudged forward.

So Helga had a son who was an archaeologist. Based on the fact that he had come from a lecture tour in London, he must be a good one. So why hadn't his mother done a little parental bragging?

She frowned. That was almost as bothersome to her as the fact that Bret had befriended him in France, yet never mentioned Paul when they were together or with the baroness. It simply made no sense. Was Paul telling the truth?

There was no way of checking up on his story about France since Bret wasn't around to ask.

At the thought of him, an image floated into her mind...Bret, darkly handsome and rugged in his colonel's uniform, with that impossibly suave yet cynical expression that refused to give way even to the most determined scrutiny. The uniform, those enigmatic blue eyes, the unrelenting personality

26

that was Bret Holden—it all fit his military calling in British Intelligence well. So well, in fact, that his dangerous occupation had caused her father, Sir Marshall, to explode into fury when she had quietly told him she wanted to marry Bret on Christmas eve.

She lifted her left hand, noticeably bare of an engagement ring, and unwelcome memories washed over her....

"You *what?*" her father had said in the half-finished office at the British Residency.

Allison, masking the fact that her hands behind her back trembled, had tried to affect calmness. "We've decided to marry before Christmas and...um—honeymoon at Helga's Riviera before Bret moves out to Palestine." She'd been pleased that her tone was not far different than when discussing what was planned for supper.

"Helga's Riviera! I return from Bombay and this is the first I hear of such serious intentions?"

"Well, it was a bit unexpected—"

"A bit unexpected, she says! Ho, ho!"

"Daddy, please—"

"Posh! And what's wrong with the poor and godly Wade Findlay I ask? Hardly out of his hospital bed, and you up and desert him for this cynical rogue who can shoot a German 'tween the eyes faster than—"

"Father, I won't be talked down to like a misbehaving child. I'm going to tell Wade and—"

"Oh. She's going to tell Wade." Both bushy brows shot up like a porcupine. "And were you going to tell your poor mother so she might at least attend this Christmas eve ceremony? And her hardly out of her coma—"

"You're not being a whit fair. Bret wants to talk to you and Mum both."

"I should hope so."

"But, well—" she wrung her hands, which was a mistake. He saw her weakening and pounced.

"Oh, he does, does he? Send him in! The scoundrel! Stealing my sweetest rose beneath my nose!"

"He's not here."

Her father's eyes widened, then he threw back his head and laughed. "Of course he isn't. He wasn't serious about marriage. And better he escape now than not show up at the ceremony."

"You don't understand, Daddy. He doesn't even know I've come. He'd be against it if he knew. He wanted to speak to you first. He said you wouldn't accept the idea. He was right!"

"Smart fellow in some ways. Marry? Before Christmas?"

She faltered in desperation. "All right—Valentine's Day."

"Valentine's Day! The colonel?" He had pushed himself up from his desk, leaning there with both palms as if he needed the support. He turned pale, then ruddy with temper. "Have you gone mad? You haven't answered my question about the goodly lad, Wade."

"Father! I love Bret, and he's in love with me."

"War does crazy things to young people with stars in their eyes. If you think to try anything so harebrained, my girl, I'll have him transferred to France so quickly his heels will spin!"

She gasped.

"Oh, don't look shocked. It happens all the time. Some foolish romance sprouts between an official's daughter and a soldier—"

"Bret is more than that and you know it. Cynthia Walsh is going crazy trying to get him."

"Yes, he's more than a soldier to me. That man is my ace, my favorite spy, but I fear it will one day cost him his life for his country and his king. And I'll not see my beloved daughter expecting his child and standing over his grave!"

She stared at him, aghast. His words seemed so brutal, not only toward her, but toward Bret. "Is that all he is? An expendable piece of property for the London Foreign Office? Well, I'm sorry, Daddy, he's a lot more than that to me!"

"Posh. You won't go wheedling my conscience, nor troubling your ill mother about this nonsense of marriage. Why, lass, you hardly know the man. Marry him in two weeks? I think not!"

"I've known him for nearly two years. We met the summer of '14, remember? We've been through so much together. He's saved my life more than once."

"Hah! All because you go traipsing about meddling with German agents."

"How was I to know there was a German spy in the family?"

"Your mother's side of the family," he corrected. "The Wescotts are known for military valor and Victoria Crosses."

"Oh, Daddy!" She turned away.

He came out from behind his desk and began to pace in tense silence. Allison folded her arms.

"I can't allow it, my girl. He's up for a job that's the most dangerous he's been involved in. He doesn't know it yet, maybe that's why he's talking of marriage before he leaves. But he'll understand it's not fair to you once I speak with him about it. I'll see him this afternoon."

She had looked at him with alarm. "You don't mean that. What dangerous mission? Daddy, you've got to do something to stop it—"

"You see? My ace becomes a coddled piece of delicate china once involved with my daughter. That's why I warned you from the moment I arrived to stay away from him. You have to admit I was fair with you. I told you at the house in Port Said.

29

So I won't be browbeaten into feeling guilty by the look you're giving me now. Nor will you bring this matter up to your mother, who's still hovering between life and death in that wretched hospital." He opened his cigar box, but it was empty. He began searching his desk frantically. "It's enough Beth is still mooning over that nincompoop Gilbert!"

Allison stared at him, her hands in fists, fighting back frustration and anger. "You're unfair, Father. You're using guilt to come between Bret and me."

He found a cigar and looked at her. "Aye, I am indeed, and I'll not feel a whit sorry about it either, not if it works. So what do you think of that?"

"I think you're being horrid."

"I'll agree to that, too." And he reached for a match, pointing it at her. "But you won't go marrying the colonel before Christmas. Nor anytime soon. If you love him, leave him be, Allison."

"How can you say that?"

"Because he belongs to the intelligence department, to this war." He sank down in the leather chair behind his cluttered desk, chomped off the end of the cigar, and struck a match. It flared hotly. "And if he loves you as he says—" he grumbled, blowing ill-smelling smoke that made Allison wrinkle her nose— "he'll leave you alone, knowing he's likely to end up blown to pieces or shot by some German in France."

She stormed to the window and threw it open, then turned and faced him. "Daddy, I can't believe you'd care so little for a man who has given everything for his country! He's not just a spy—"

"Close that window. There's spies as thick as Egyptian cockroaches."

"By now the kaiser's heard, you've been shouting so loudly."

He ignored that. "Yes, he's expendable. We're *all* expendable! But my family won't be."

"You wouldn't be so horrid as to send him to France, Father!"

"Oh, wouldn't I?" He turned in his chair and looked at her where she stood by the window. His stern gaze convinced her otherwise.

Tears stung her eyes and her heart thumped so hard she was breathless. Her cold, shaking fingers twisted together. "You're using extortion on me! On your own daughter."

He smiled unpleasantly.

She lifted her chin. "I won't be intimidated by your unfair expectations. I'll tell him what you're trying to do."

"He'll know by my own mouth this afternoon. I intend to make it quite clear to him."

"I'll—I'll marry him anyway. I'm of age."

"When I'm through talking with the colonel, he'll be much too wise to sweep you off to Helga's little retreat."

She was afraid he was right.

"And don't think to trouble your mother or Aunt Lydia— and don't think tears will soften my heart. Now, my girl, don't start crying on me!"

"I'm not crying." She sniffed, taking out her handkerchief and blowing her nose.

He rushed from behind the desk and took hold of her shoulders. "Be sensible, now."

"I don't *want* to be sensible. I want—"

"I know what you want. That rogue! You're a soldier at heart. You know the meaning of sacrifice. Ah, did I not tell you how proud you made me serving at Kut?"

"Flattery won't help!"

"Your mother was upset, of course, but I knew courage ran

in your veins. Wescott blood, that's what it is. Warrior blood! Can't you see Bret is needed for his country? If you marry him, I can't in good conscience send him on his next mission."

"So that's it. Duty before love, duty before family, duty before—"

"Now, now, let's not be disagreeable—"

"You're all unfair to him. The CID included. How many times must he risk his life? What will you give him, another brevet? I want him for myself."

"And in that, lassie," he said with a sigh, "lies the entire dilemma your father's all mucked up in. Why can't you love Wade Findlay? Such a nice lad."

"Oh, Father! You're exasperating!" She turned away.

"Now, now, nothing good can come of quick decisions in time of war."

"Bret? A quick decision?" She laughed. "He resisted to the bitter end! Neither Bret nor I are rash, emotional children."

"Of course you're not," he patted her arm awkwardly. "You're sensible, intelligent, and patriotic—just like the colonel. At any other time you'd make a fine couple."

She walked away and sank onto a chair. "If patriotism means I must give up the man I love to the Turks—"

"Germans," he said calmly. "My dear, please. Bret is an important agent. We want him badly."

She studied his face and was certain he would have Bret transferred out of Egypt if she persisted.

"Ah, daughter, can't you see? There's nothing I can do now. Orders have come from London. It's out of my hands. Try to understand—look! After the war, yes, after the war we'll all sit down like reasonable folk and discuss the issue."

After the war. A million years away.

"Now," he said as though they'd come to an understanding.

"You wouldn't go worrying your mother about all this, would you? Not so close to Christmas? Not after all she's been through? And with her cousin Edgar and his son, Gilbert, facing murder charges. No, of course you wouldn't. That's a good girl. I knew I could depend on you. You're just like your father. You and me, my girl, we're alike. And when I speak to Bret this afternoon, I'll make it clear the decision to wait was none of your idea, but all mine. I'll tell him if he still feels as strongly about marriage after the war—well…"

She looked at him.

"We can come to a decision then. Now, it's all settled, and I'm sure Bret will understand—"

Oh, yes, there was no doubt about it. Colonel Bret Holden had understood.

Allison clenched her left hand, experiencing the emotions all over again as she trudged through the loose sand. The sky above her seemed awash with fire.

Yes. He had understood all right. He had accepted the opposition to their marriage with more restraint than she would have expected. She had thought he would demand that she choose him over her parent's wishes, reminding her she was of age, that if she really loved him she would pack her bag and leave with him at once for Helga's Mediterranean hideaway, that they would marry on the way.

He had not.

Perhaps the disciplined restraint he had shown was due to his line of work: he'd learned to accept dangerous missions without emotional display, to show indifference to possible death each time he left his superior, who also portrayed little if any emotion. Or perhaps—who knew what her father had said to him?

The wedding plans they'd so briefly discussed in December

had been packed away with the Christmas decorations. Her relationship with the enigmatic colonel was, to say mildly, dormant in its cocoon. The New Year of January 1916 had dawned dull and emotionally cold, and Allison's heart had retreated into hibernation.

Not long afterward, Bret had received new orders from his superior in the intelligence department and had been sent from Cairo on urgent military matters. She suspected her father had much to do with the assignment.

While Bret did return for short periods to report to his superior and to her father at the British Residency, matters were so arranged that she rarely saw him alone. And when she did, the old casual aloofness was back. She suspected he blamed her more than her father, and it was this that hurt the most. He considered her, as the old adage went, "Tied to Mama's apron strings," only this time it was to Daddy's plans. Without his telling her so, she suspected he had second thoughts about becoming vulnerable to what he now considered a young woman under the thumb of her overbearing family.

The sand blew around her shoes. She stopped, hitching her kit bag to her other shoulder before trudging on. With the depressing murder trial and a host of other unfinished matters weighing on her heart, marriage to Colonel Bret Holden seemed as far removed from reality as an English rose garden in the Sinai desert.

THREE

❧ ⬩❦⬩ ❧ ⬩❦⬩ ❧

IT WAS ANOTHER MILE ON FOOT to Zeitoun, where Oswald
Chambers, who had arrived in October, was serving as secretary of the YMCA Hut. The Hut was located near the small
missionary compound of the Egypt General Mission.
Surrounding the compound was the sprawling base detail
camp, which housed some twenty thousand newly arrived
Australian and New Zealand soldiers.

Biddy Chambers, Oswald's wife, and their small daughter,
Kathleen, had joined Oswald soon after Christmas. Allison had
been recovering her health from an attack of malaria that hit
her several months earlier. She'd been serving with the British
Nurse's Corps at a field hospital near disaster-ridden Kut-al-
Amara, close to Baghdad. Since her return to Cairo, she had
been coming to Zeitoun twice a week to do two things: help
Biddy with the "free teas" given for the soldiers, and to work
with Wade Findlay, who recently had begun his own Bible lecture with some rowdy troopers of the Australian Lighthorse.

Since Allison and Wade had been two of Oswald
Chambers's students at the Bible Training College in London
before the Great War, it was a special delight for them to be
with him and Biddy Chambers again, doing work that honored
Christ among desperately needy soldiers.

Allison slung the canvas kit bag over her shoulder and continued walking across the desert sand, reminding herself that
Oswald Chambers walked this route nearly every day of the
week! Besides going for his evening lecture in the Hut in the

Zeitoun camp, he also walked many miles each day in the blistering heat to visit the various hospitals and convalescent homes in and about Cairo. At every stop, he spoke of Christ's love and forgiveness to the wounded soldiers and spread good cheer to the nurses.

Recently Chambers had begun a new Bible lecture on Sunday evenings, where he spoke in the open square around Ezbekiah Gardens in Cairo to hundreds of soldiers who came to the blackboard lessons. Allison always attended, taking notes and soaking in the Word of God. Last week she had been able to talk her Jewish friend, Marra Cohen, into coming with her.

Marra had served with her at Kut, and as yet did not accept Jesus as the prophesied Jewish Messiah, but Allison kept Marra's name, along with David Goldstein's, on her prayer list.

The Jews and Jerusalem were much on her mind and heart recently, for Bret had told her that there likely would be a military advance into Palestine sometime this year to capture Jerusalem. She almost believed herself to be part of a special plan of God's, one that was opening a door for his people to return to the land he had sworn to Abraham, Isaac, and Jacob. With that in mind, she hoped to rejoin the Nursing Corps again before the advance into Palestine began.

In the meantime, she had much to occupy her time, including her work with Wade at Zeitoun before the troops moved out. Just when that hour would strike, no one knew, for it was a military secret.

The distant roar of a motor carried on the wind. Allison stopped and shaded her eyes. Soon a military vehicle, probably from Zeitoun, came into view. She watched the driver steer around some dunes and, bumping along a narrow track, drive in her direction. She didn't have to walk all the way after all.

She stopped and waited, smiling thankfully. In her romantic fancy she imagined it was Bret coming to find her, to tell her how sorry he was that he had pulled away from her, that he couldn't live without her, and that he would wait forever if necessary. As the motorcar neared she could see two people in the front seat. One, a woman, called and waved; the driver squeezed the horn in a loud greeting. He rolled up and put on the brake. It was David and Marra.

"If we'd known you'd left Zeitoun, we'd have driven to Cairo first," called Marra, a tall, willowy blond in her twenties with bobbed hair and a boyish figure. She threw open the side door and scrambled out. "But I at least got to meet your friend, Oswald Chambers. You were right—he's a jewel in the king's crown." And she added with a touch of characteristic wryness: "One of the things that impressed me is how he's never without a flyswatter." With that she swept off her beat-up hat and swished at the annoying pests.

"Now you know how old Pharaoh must have felt." David's tone was filled with amusement as he got out from behind the wheel. Allison smiled at him, feeling, as she always did when she saw him, a bit of amazement that this handsome, seemingly carefree young man was actually a Jewish activist deeply involved in working for a Jewish homeland in Israel. A scar on his cheek bore unpleasant witness to his incarceration in Jerusalem by the Turks the previous year. He now served Bret in some unique military fashion in the intelligence department, which allowed him, as it did the colonel, to come and go with a measure of freedom—not at all like the typical Tommy serving in Egypt. He wore khaki pants, leather boots, and the traditional helmetlike expedition hat made of canvas. Allison noted the pistol in his holster as he trudged across the sand toward her.

"How many times has Bret told you you'll get bit by a scorpion one of these days, and who will find you on this lonely stretch?"

She smiled. "It was you who lectured me, not Bret. I haven't seen him in months, and you know it. Besides, if—"

"Yes, we know, no need to say it."

She ignored him. "If Oswald Chambers can trudge the sands of Egypt to serve the Lord, so can Allison Wescott."

David grinned at her, then reached down to toss her satchel onto his shoulder.

She laughed. "You're just in time. My feet are swelling."

"Then into the car, Lady of the Mystic Nile. We've got to get back soon or we'll miss dinner at Mrs. Chambers, and you know what a tragedy that would be for a man of my appetites." His brown eyes smiled at her.

Allison noticed that Marra watched her and David closely. Quickly she walked ahead of her friend. "Don't worry about supper," she called to him. "Oswald and Biddy never have the luxury of dining until after eight. They're too generous with the soldiers at the canteen to leave them." She opened the side door and waited until Marra scooted into the middle beside David.

"I would have expected Wade to come with you to meet me." Allison regarded Marra curiously. "He's not ill, is he?"

"You worry too much about him," Marra said. "If Wade didn't have nerves of steel under that frail exterior he'd have succumbed before now. He's doctoring one of Kathleen's many pets, is all. She's got a new one—a miniature donkey, cute as a bug's ear. Wait till you see it." She settled back into the seat as David turned over the motor. "Biddy's asked us all to stay the night. In the morning we'll bring you back to Cairo."

"I promised Wade I'd stay a few days and help out with one of the Bible lectures."

"Maybe you'll change your mind when you know why we've come," Marra said with confidence. But when Allison looked at her for an explanation, her friend merely gestured to David. "Ask him. He'll explain."

For some reason, Allison's heart began to beat faster.

David steered the motorcar around on the track of sand and drove toward Zeitoun camp. He reached in his military jacket and handed her a sealed envelope. "From the baroness."

"Helga! Now this is a surprise. You'll never guess whom I met on the tram from Cairo." She took the letter. "A man claiming to be Helga's son, Paul Kruger. Ever heard of him?"

David pursed his lips. "Nope. Didn't know she had a son."

"Neither did I. He's an archaeologist, too. He's been working in Africa and is fresh out from doing a lecture tour in London. He told me he'd met Neal and Bret. Interesting, don't you think?"

"Very. When did Bret and Neal sport him about London's circuit?" David's eyes were thoughtful.

Allison tossed her hat into the back and let the wind blow through her hair. "A good question. He says he met Bret in France amid German machine-gun fire. Bret got them out and to London." She frowned. "Did he ever recount a story like that?"

"Bret has told me quite a few," David confessed, "but he's never made much of that one, if it's true."

Marra looked at him, her head tilted. "Why wouldn't it be true?"

David shrugged. "I'm not saying it isn't. It might be. Since the colonel is nowhere to be found, I wouldn't be one to hold Kruger to the fire to talk."

"Anyway," Allison mused, "Paul is here to see Helga and hopes to stay and work with her. He's heard about the open position left by Professor Jemal and wants it."

"Jemal, the mummy digger?" Marra asked.

"Yes, but he dug for more than mummies," Allison said wryly, thinking of the Egyptian treasure map. She looked down at the envelope David had given her from Helga. Odd. What was so important that couldn't wait until she returned on Monday?

Baroness Helga Kruger, secretary of the Cairo Archaeology Club, was preparing for the annual meeting. This year it would be held in the Valley of the Kings. Bret had told her back in December that Helga would also be meeting one of the most skilled professors in Egyptology on the matter of the Nefertari piece. The man was to make a professional judgment on the genuineness of the artifact, which was supposed to fit the period of King Tutankhamen. From her meeting with Paul Kruger on the tram, Allison now knew the esteemed professor was Count Roderick, and she wondered if Bret knew this as well. But then, it could be that Bret was no longer involved.

Before Sarah Blaine was murdered, Allison distinctly recalled someone saying that the expert who was coming to look at the piece was also an international dealer for the world's museums. Did this fit with what Paul had said about his mother's friend, Count Roderick?

"I'm surprised Helga's still in Cairo," Allison said, opening the envelope. "The last time I saw her was over a week ago and she was already packed for Luxor."

"She must have had reason to change her schedule," Marra said. "Perhaps she had wind that her son was coming."

"I wouldn't say so." David's frown was thoughtful. "As for

Luxor, I rather got the idea she was reluctant to go there this year."

"I don't know why you say that," Marra said. "She didn't seem reluctant to me when we were all at her house staying over for Christmas. Luxor was all she talked about. Being no archaeologist, or into this mummy stuff like you and Allison, I found it all rather trying."

"This 'mummy stuff,' as you call it, my poor, dear girl, is worth millions of British pounds," David teased.

"As I was saying—" Marra continued.

But Allison stopped listening. She was reading Helga's letter, which was dated two days earlier.

I was pleased to learn from your mother, Eleanor, that you intend to vacation with the club again this year. After all we've been through recently, we need it! We should have an interesting group in attendance, and it should be much more peaceful than the debacle at Aleppo in '14. We have a few new members, including several soldiers, who will be on leave and, when in London had expressed an interest in archaeology.

I met up with your mother a few days ago at Ezbekiah Gardens for tea. Eleanor tells me she is convalescing well from the injury taken last December at the Blaine house, but that she is quite concerned about Beth. However, I don't need to tell you how badly your sister is taking the trial of your cousin Gilbert Simonds. Doctor Spencer Howard has suggested to Eleanor that she leave the city with Beth since the crowded conditions of both Cairo and Alexandria are most trying. England or even India would do, but Sir Marshall won't hear of it, and I can't say as I blame him. He fears the activity of the German U-boats is at an all-time high.

My home in Alexandria would be a perfect place for your dear mother to vacation with Beth, but I've already offered its use to General Murray for the recuperation of British officers from the Gallipoli front. Bringing Beth there would make matters worse. Therefore it was suggested to me that Eleanor and Beth vacation with the archaeology club at Luxor.

Allison paused. Suggested by whom? Doctor Howard? She read on.

Housing in Luxor is full, so I'm offering my houseboat for Eleanor's use. Unfortunately, it does need fixing up— I'm afraid it's been neglected. While I'll be in the vicinity of Luxor several weeks before the members of the club begin to arrive, I'll be taken up entirely with official business for the Cairo Museum. Would you mind terribly coming early and preparing the houseboat? Naturally, you'll have all the help you need from my assistant, Omar, who will escort you. The boat will need a fresh coat of paint, and other miscellaneous repairs. But it is large enough for separate rooms for the three of you. Everything you need can be bought at Luxor on my account. I'm leaving today, which is Friday, so if you could explain all this to Eleanor it would be appreciated. Baroness Helga Kruger

For the baroness to lend her houseboat was generous, Allison thought. She was sure her mother would find the offer quite workable.

"I think it's an answer to your dilemma about Beth," Marra said a short time later after Allison explained the letter. "It was jolly of Helga to come up with it."

"It wasn't initially her idea." Allison thought for a moment. "She said someone had mentioned it to her first. I wonder who it was."

Marra shrugged. "Probably Doctor Howard."

"Yes, maybe you're right." And yet, though she couldn't explain why, Allison couldn't quite rid herself of an odd sense of unease over the question.

"I haven't heard you mention Doctor Howard before." David looked at her, curious. "What happened to Morrison? Wasn't he treating Mrs. Wescott at the hospital?"

"He was transferred to Alexandria," Marra explained. She'd begun serving at Bulac Hospital and knew the staff. "There's a hospital ship coming in from the Dardanelles soon with hundreds of wounded. We first met Howard after the battle of Kut. He looked after Allison at the temporary camp before we came to Port Said. Didn't he say he was a friend of your father's and that he came from Bombay, Allison?"

Allison thought back to that tragic hour at the camp when she had first thought Wade Findlay was a captive inside Kut...when Bret had gone back to search for him. She'd been ill with malaria then and had worried about Bret as much as she had Wade. She recalled Doctor Howard, a tall man with a walrus mustache—but she remembered him mostly because he had implied, in a rather obscure way, that he had known Sir Edgar in India.

"Yes, Doctor Howard said something then that I thought was curious," Allison said. "But not knowing Edgar at the time, I couldn't fathom it."

"Oh?" David glanced at her. "What was that?"

"Just that he was surprised a man like Sir Edgar would be chosen to fill the vacancy as Cairo's chief inspector."

"Well, he was right, wasn't he?" Marra stated tartly.

"I wonder how he knew?" Allison folded the letter and placed it in her kit bag.

"He must have heard about him from your father."

Allison wondered if David was right. "I'll ask him next time I see him. That, and if he was the one to suggest to Helga about sharing the houseboat."

"The boat? Does it matter?" But while David smiled, she noticed a glimpse of subdued concern in his eyes.

"I suppose not." She looked back out across the desert—the sun was nearly set, and a strange reddish glow covered the sand for miles in all directions. Helga had said Bret didn't want her in Luxor, but it seemed Helga—and someone else—did.

"So you're going? That should please Doctor Howard. That's just what he apparently wants," Marra said.

David looked at her sharply. "Why do you say that?"

"Because he obviously is the one who suggested it." Marra raised her brows. "What's bothering you?"

"Nothing quite at all, except both you and Allison seem to be trying to create a mystery about all this when I don't believe one exists."

"Well, listen to him. Sounds a bit defensive, don't you think, Allison? Maybe it was David who suggested the houseboat to the baroness."

He smiled at Marra. "Do you think I'm conniving to get Beth on Helga's houseboat so I can visit her?"

"That hadn't crossed my mind," Marra replied flatly. "Are you saying you're going to be in Luxor?"

"We both are," he said airily. "I went to the club meeting at Aleppo in the summer of '14."

He glanced at Allison, but she didn't reply, lost as she was in her own troubling thoughts. He went on. "I was there when Leah Bristow was murdered by Rex Blaine."

"Yes, you were there," Allison said, but she knew he'd only gone to meet Bret.

"I didn't know 'we' belonged to the archaeology club," Marra said. "I'm not interested in Egyptian mummies. I keep thinking of that Turkish professor who was murdered—what was his name again?"

"Jemal," David said, frowning as he drove.

"Yes, that was it. But I keep thinking of what Rex Blaine called him…the Egyptian mummy digger." She shuddered.

"Don't be silly, darling, there's much more to archaeology than mummies. Biblical archaeology, for instance, is what Allison and Neal Bristow are interested in. Isn't that right, Allison?"

"Quite, so let's not talk about mummies. Anyway," Allison said brightly, "I think the idea of Beth getting out of Cairo until after the verdict is wise. I'll try to convince my father it's the best we can come up with since a sea voyage is risky."

She was relieved David and Marra would be going to Luxor. The idea of being there alone with Omar was unnerving. She thought back to Aleppo, to the summer before the war. As David had said, her cousin Leah had been found murdered in the desert sand. No one knew that Leah had been an agent, not even David. She didn't think he knew yet, since Bret would have had no cause to tell him. Leah's brother, Neal, had been working with her.…

Neal. When would he return to Egypt? From their conversation on the tram, it was clear Neal's arrival was a topic that interested Paul Kruger as well. But why?

"Maybe Helga's work at Luxor will have something to do

with the gold miniature you and Bret found at the Blaine house," Marra commented.

Allison nodded vaguely, only half listening. It was nearly dark now and the silence of the desert was profound.

"Odd, isn't it?" Marra continued quietly, folding her arms and staring toward the sunset.

David looked at her briefly. His voice turned quiet too, as though he felt compelled to join the mood hovering over both Allison and Marra. "What's odd?"

"All that time the treasure was hidden out in the garden beneath that sundial with the broken cobra head. Ugh. It's enough to make one shiver. I hate snakes, even metal ones. I wonder who else might have known there was treasure there beside Sarah Blaine and her husband? Did the mummy digger know?"

David shook his head. "Jemal stole the Nefertari from some French archaeologists before the war. He may have killed them and buried them in the sand, but later he didn't know where Rex Blaine had hidden it."

It, and the map. But then, no one seemed to know about the map except she and Bret, thought Allison. The others who *had* known were now dead.

They drove in silence.

"I wonder if there isn't still more treasure to be found," Marra said after a while.

"I suppose there is." David glanced her way. "After all, think of all the tombs in the Valley of the Kings. I'd settle for a mere gold scarab." He grinned. "When the war is over I'll cash it in and settle on some Caribbean isle."

Marra looked at him wryly. "I thought your heart was set on a Jewish homeland."

David laughed. "Fair enough. I'll settle for a mere vacation in the Caribbean, then. After that, I'll build a house in Jerusalem."

Caught up in the teasing banter, Allison's mood cheered. Surely Helga's houseboat would prove a pleasant place to stay, even if it did need a bit of fixing up. Who knew? It could be exactly the kind of break Allison herself needed to feel more rested...more at peace.

She would return to Cairo first thing in the morning to broach her mother on the plan.

FOUR

DAVID PULLED INTO ZEITOUN CAMP as the last glow of sunset was fading into a starry night. The sight held such depth of expanse from the Creator that it, combined with the warm desert breeze, brought the greatness of God's presence even closer to Allison's heart. As she climbed out of the vehicle and felt the sand crunch beneath her feet, she took a moment to look up into God's awesome universe. "How wonderful God is!"

Marra's mouth thinned. "Tell that to the thousands of soldiers wounded and suffering in the jam-packed hospitals." Before Allison could respond, she walked away toward a tall, lean man who was waiting for them. Wade Findlay.

David came around the motorcar and in the starlight a smirk showed on his tanned face. "Don't mind Miss Sourpuss. She's still mad at God for allowing the guy she was going to marry to get killed in Belgium." He shoved his hands into his trouser pockets and looked up at the gleaming stars. "As if her tantrum disturbs his sovereign throne," he mused. "He's too great for that. I doubt if he even knows we exist."

"God knows when a sparrow falls." Allison laid a gentle hand on his arm.

"A sparrow? That little piece of brown chattering fluff?" He smiled.

"He takes care to clothe the fields with grass which grows today and tomorrow is scorched by the sun. I know you've been rather busy recently, dear David, but have you taken a moment to look at the spring roses?"

"You received the bouquet I sent, didn't you? Oh, and don't tell Marra about that."

"Yes, and they were beautiful…but the last of the petals got tossed this morning, before I left the house. Just think, David, God took all that care to create a rose with such sweet fragrance when it only lasts a few days. He dresses the lilies of the fields with matchless beauty—why, not even your Jewish king Solomon was arrayed like one of those. Think how much more the Lord cares about you, or about Marra's pain and bitterness? He knows, he loves. All day long he stretches out his hands to draw us to himself. We can come to him with the faith of a child running to a loving parent, or we can rebel like a spoiled child because not all we demand is given."

David looked away, and she bit her lip. She should have known better than to try and engage him in a theological discussion. Yet, this time, just before he shut her out, she thought she saw somewhat of a wistful smile on his lips, and a touch of sobriety reflected in his tired eyes.

His words confirmed that impression: "Lovely words, Angel, where'd you get them?"

"About God caring for sparrows and the lilies of the field?" She smiled gently. "They are not only nice, but divine. They're not mine. Yeshua spoke them. Oh, David, you should read the words of Christ in the Gospel of John—or maybe Matthew, since it was written with your Jewish people in mind. I just paraphrased some of the words Jesus spoke."

He threw an arm around her shoulders and walked her toward Wade. They were wrapped in the stillness of the night. "Maybe I will one day, Allison. If I was convinced he cares about the Jews—about people like Rose Lyman and her little boy, Benny…." He took hold of her shoulders and turned her around, his handsome face intense. His fingers tightened, digging into her flesh until she wanted to wince. "They're in danger now...in Jerusalem. Bret has gone there secretly to try and help. Does your Jesus care, Allison? Can you really expect me to believe he cares when my people are out of the land that the very Bible you believe in tells me he gave to us?" He looked toward the stars. "'If I forget you, O Jerusalem, let my right hand forget its skill!... If I do not exalt Jerusalem above my chief joy.'"

"Yes, he cares," she said fervently. "He is your King. And one day he will reign from Jerusalem unto the ends of the earth!"

Marra stood some distance away in the darkened sand. She called with mild irritation, "Hey, lover boy, she already has two men casting lots for her heart. Doesn't anyone care about mine?"

David's hands dropped from Allison's shoulders as the emotion and seriousness of the moment ebbed away. "No," he called to her. "Men aren't attracted to sour grapes."

"Why you—!" Marra stooped, picked up a small stone, and halfheartedly threw it at him. He ducked as it landed harmlessly.

"Hey, Wade!" David called as the young man walked toward them from the missionary bungalows. "Look what I found wandering the desert floor! A lily!"

"A lily with thorns," Allison countered, walking to meet Wade. In the growing darkness she might have mistaken him for Oswald Chambers, for they were very alike in build: six feet tall, brown hair, blue eyes, and *very* British.

"Hullo, Allison, bring the printed sermons?" Wade called.

"I've got them right here. Are we in time for Chambers's nightly lesson?"

"Just in time. We'll put the sermons on the table with the rest of the free materials."

Wade had been released from the military hospital a few days before Christmas. Allison knew he was still recovering from the serious injuries he'd received when he was trapped near Kut. Bret had gone back for him after the Turks had over-run the British camp—a fact that had left Allison terrified for both of them. Thankfully, Bret found Wade wandering in the desert, wounded. He'd brought him out alive, but Bret had been wounded as well in the process. Because of his bravery, Bret was up for a brevet—though Allison knew the honor meant little to Bret. He'd simply done what any good soldier—and friend—would do.

Both men had recuperated, but Wade still bore the telltale signs of weakened health. Yet, like Chambers, he had been quick to deny himself and had come to Zeitoun in the middle of January.

"The spiritual needs are simply too great to pamper myself," he had said when Allison had protested, asking him to wait a few more weeks. "Death doesn't wait," he had stated matter-of-factly. "Where these young men will spend eternity weighs in the balance. We just can't afford to wait. For such a time as this what else can we do?"

For such a time as this. She knew those words had been taken from the book of Esther, when the Jewish queen had risked her life to save her people from extermination. Oswald Chambers felt much the same way. He believed they had been born for a time of great need and peril, and it was imperative to lay one's life on the line in serving Jesus Christ. She knew his fears were valid. Tomorrow, many faces in the Zeitoun camp would no longer be there.

Wade always seemed to shine the light on the seriousness of life, and it had so moved Allison that she felt the Lord wooing her to become involved. And so she had followed him to Zeitoun.

As she walked with him now in the starlight, something her father told her rang in her memory: "You see, my girl? Wade's the man the Lord has for you. Look at the good spiritual influence he is on you. You may not realize this, but most of your decisions to sacrifice for God and country have been inspired by Wade Findlay and Oswald Chambers."

"And does that also mean Mr. Chambers and I are meant for each other?" she had half joked.

"Now, now, lass, I admit Colonel Holden is a good-looking fellow and a daring soldier—but he'll get himself killed with his daring, and you'll end up a war widow instead of a war bride."

"And which one of his superiors sends him on all these dangerous missions, risking his life?" she had asked, frustrated, but her father merely lit his cigar and changed the subject.

So Bret was in Jerusalem…

Wade was smiling down at her, dragging her heart back to the moment. He removed his small, round spectacles and wiped them on his sleeve—an action Allison had come to equate with this man she so respected and loved. For love him she did, just not in the same way she loved Bret—

"You two coming to the Hut?" Wade asked David and Marra casually.

"Marra ought to go," David said too seriously. "It will do her good."

She stood, hands on hips. "Oh, yeah? Well, for your information, I *did* go with Allison to Ezbekiah Gardens last Sunday night. I enjoyed it, too. What do you think of that?"

"Your rabbi brother-in-law will be weeping onto his matzos

until they turn to matzo-ball soup."

"I'll go anyway." Marra turned toward Allison with a firm look. "Just to show David he can't boss me." And she sauntered ahead of them toward the Hut.

"See you two later," David called, and he walked toward Wade's hut. "Got any coffee, old fellow?"

"Waiting. And don't eat all the cookies before we get back," Wade teased.

Allison walked beside Wade toward the Hut. Lights glowed and she could read the sign that Chambers had put out front:

STUDY HUT
YMCA
9 A.M. — 9 P.M.
Open for reading, writing, & study
A blackboard lecture
each evening at 7:30 P.M.
except Wednesdays and Sundays
Subject: Religious Problems Raised by the War

Zeitoun was absolute desert, but as Oswald Chambers joyously commented when the heat, flies, and sandstorms made life a trial, it was also a "glorious opportunity" to minister to the troops.

When it came to Chambers, Allison could not recall a time when she had heard him complain, although she could see how much he had aged just since arriving in Egypt. The deep lines on his face, browned now to the color of walnut by the burning sun, told their own story of his long hours. While others took their needed rest between noon and 3 P.M., Oswald Chambers was out speaking to the men of their need of Jesus Christ.

"I'm worried about Chambers," Wade commented as they walked across the sand toward the Hut. "During the hottest time of the day, when even the troops rest from the heat, Chambers is out hiking, visiting soldiers in the outlying hospitals."

Allison had heard that he had begun a series of talks at the dermatology hospital in Abassia, where all the soldiers were being treated for venereal diseases. The men had been abandoned, for even the missionaries tended to look upon them as worse sinners than all the rest. While the missionaries didn't say it, they implied by their absence that these particular men had gotten their just reward. It wasn't until the Reverend Douglas Downes, a Church of England chaplain serving in Cairo and a friend of Oswald's, asked him to give a series of talks at Abassia that the door was open to speak of the forgiveness and mercy of Jesus Christ.

Allison, too, when coming to Zeitoun, soaked up his teaching like the desert sand receiving precious water that had spilt from a canteen. The meeting place, the "Hut," was a seventy-foot by forty-foot wooden frame, covered on the outside by walls of matting made from native rushes. To Allison, it was a "shadow in a weary land," a "fortress," a "high tower."

Inside the Hut, she and Wade walked to the wooden benches that were set on a floor of sand. There was enough seating for four hundred listeners. Wade smiled at Allison. "I remember when Chambers first came here in October. He announced on the first night that a prayer meeting would be held, and all the men got up and left except two or three." He glanced about the large room. "Now he has an overflow crowd, with men standing outside the Hut. Men who have never prayed before are coming to believe in Jesus."

The joy in Wade's voice moved Allison. She listened raptly

as he told her of a tough old Scot by the name of Mackenzie. "The man was sarcastic and as hard as nails. But the other morning when Chambers went to where his bunk was, he found Mackenzie on his knees, and Oswald's book on prayer was open on the cot."

"How wonderful!"

Wade nodded. "Mackenzie told Chambers, 'It's you and your life that's made the difference.'"

Allison looked at Wade and saw his eyes shining with pleasure over all that the Lord was doing in the camp. Once again respect for him washed over her. No wonder her parents wanted her to marry Wade.

A few minutes before 7:30, soldiers began to drift in and take seats on the benches.

At one end of the Hut stood a raised platform from which Chambers spoke; at the other end there were two small rooms, one for Chambers and the other for an assistant. There was a long table against one side of the Hut, and Allison opened her kit bag and removed the stack of printed sermons and placed them on that table with the other free materials. The YMCA provided free paper and pencils for the troops to write home and distributed other items as the Red Cross and other private charities provided them. In the Canteen, post cards, stamps, and cigarettes were provided at a minimal cost. Allison disapproved of the tobacco, but the first time she had visited Zeitoun and quietly inquired about it from Wade, he had explained that nothing could be done about it.

"It's the YM rule that servicemen are provided with recreation and help in time of war. The canteen is separate from the Hut, but you can be sure we use every opportunity to make Christ known."

Oswald Chambers had omitted motion pictures and concerts in the canteen in favor of Bible classes. "The other secretaries heard about it and came out from the other camps to have a look. They told him he could never get the troops to stand for it, but he did. You know how much they respect him, even though he has strong convictions about observing the Lord's Day and, on Sunday, closes down the canteen and allows nothing to be sold. The secretaries said the soldiers would never permit that either."

"What happened?" Marra asked, joining them. She picked up one of the printed messages from the stack Allison had placed there. She looked at it with a disinterested air, turning it over in her hand.

Wade looked at her with a smile. "Nothing happened. The men appreciated Oswald's stand. Said it outweighed the complaints. The Bible classes are growing, as is the group listening every night."

Allison glanced around. "Maybe I ought to go so there's more room—"

"No need. We've opened up another tent that seats three hundred. Now Chambers has started nightly classes on biblical psychology."

Allison nodded. It was so wonderful the way the Lord was using Oswald and Biddy Chambers as a watershed of blessing. She looked around the room again, smiling. The presence of the Lord was here. Soldiers were coming to believe and follow Christ. Others, who were already Christians, were learning how to pray and to read the Scriptures on their own. And Wade had told her that even soldiers who were bitter in their hearts—over the war, the interruption to their lives, or the death of their friends—were responding favorably to Chambers's class on the problems the war brought. Men were learning to walk by faith and trust in the goodness of God.

"They are learning that God has a plan for the world that will one day put an end to war, suffering, and death." Wade's words rang with a glad conviction.

Marra looked at him. "You really believe that don't you?" There was a trace of awe in her voice, and Allison could see there was no mockery in her eyes.

Wade nodded. "I believe it because the Scriptures teach it, not because I see the evidence yet. There has not failed one good word of his promise. And that's why Allison and I both also believe the Jews will one day be returned to the land that God swore to Abraham, Isaac, and Jacob."

Marra's eyes glimmered at the thought. She fingered the printed sermon and absently folded it and placed it inside her canvas bag. "If I could worship in Jerusalem at the Wall, I know I could have peace," she murmured.

Allison wanted to say that Jesus had broken down the wall, that there was no longer a separation between mankind and a holy God, but she felt constrained, and so held her peace. She would continue to wrap Marra in prayer.

"The lecture is about to start," Wade said. "Here's Chambers now."

They had taken a bench toward the back as more soldiers drifted in, some carrying New Testaments. Chambers took his place behind the podium and began. He spoke for an hour, using only a handwritten outline.

Allison glanced toward the back entrance of the Hut to find Biddy Chambers was arriving. Like clockwork, each night after Biddy's duties were completed and her daughter, Kathleen, was in the care of her assistant, Miss Mary Riley, Biddy would come to her husband's talks. Biddy cast a smile toward Allison and Marra, then quietly entered the Hut and seated herself on one of the benches. She took out a notepad and pencil and, for the next forty-five minutes, transcribed her husband's talk.

Allison knew that tomorrow Biddy would type out the message and, when she had a goodly supply of her husband's talks collected, would send them off to England to be printed. They were then sent to family members, Bible students, and Oswald's friends.

Biddy Chambers had become a kind of mentor for Allison. She was devoted to Oswald and was sacrificial to the soldiers. Oswald had built her a modest bungalow, and Biddy had turned the place into a home of spiritual beauty and warmth. Soldiers flocked there by the dozens just to be around her and baby Kathleen. Many times Allison had seen a soldier's hardened heart touched by the child's innocence, as well as by Biddy's generosity in serving the cakes and cookies she tirelessly baked for the soldiers to enjoy with a cup of good British tea.

Even in unbearable heat, with flies everywhere, Biddy maintained a composure that Allison admired. Watching her now, Allison shook her head. *Lord, if only I had that meek and quiet spirit of trust you say is so precious in your sight!* Yet she often felt frustrated over foiled goals, about who and what she was meant to be. And about Bret. She hated it that their relationship, despite their love for each other, so often was replete with closed doors and obstacles. More and more she wondered if things would ever work out.

Why can't I trust you about everything, Lord? About Bret, about my own personal failures to be all I want to be for you?

The only answer she received was silence.

After the Bible study, Allison, Wade, and Marra joined a group of soldiers who had gathered at the Chambers's bungalow. Allison helped serve refreshments amid laughter and conversation. She enjoyed repeating one of Oswald's favorite sayings, "I refuse to worry." And his summarization of a good evening's teaching in the Hut and elsewhere: "Well, we had a famous meeting tonight!"

No one could find any reason to disagree with his analysis of the Lord's blessing, for his optimism was contagious.

Allison watched as Oswald stood, his arm around his wife, talking with one of the men.

"I hope I find a man one day who loves me as much as Oswald Chambers loves his wife."

Marra's wistful words brought an understanding nod from Allison. "That's one of the things I like best about him—his devotion to Biddy and his fatherly care for Kathleen."

"I know what you mean," Marra said. "Did you know that anytime he has a little extra money, he takes them into Cairo for dinner at Groppi's, or tea and cakes at the Shepheard's Hotel?"

"He does more than that," came Wade's voice from behind them. "I've known him to buy Biddy a new hat, or take Kathleen to a beauty parlor to have her hair washed and curled."

"Now there's a man who understands his women," Marra said. "Which makes him as rare as snow in the desert in summer."

Wade chuckled, shaking his head. Allison glanced at the Chambers family again, longing to know such contentment and love. *Someday, Lord? With Bret?*

A phrase repeated in her heart…it was something Oswald Chambers often said to Allison when something remained uncertain: "Trust God and do the next thing."

She did not know everything the Lord wanted her to do with her future. She wasn't certain about how things would turn out with Bret. But she did know enough of the Lord's will to walk by faith with him today and to trust tomorrow's questions to his sovereign purposes. And prayer was a gold key to unlocking the storehouse of God's peace.

Wade had told her of the prayer list that Chambers kept in his journal. "I saw it by accident," he had told her on one of her visits. "He has names of men he's brought to believe in the Lord. When one dies in battle and Chambers receives word, he opens up his journal and writes beside the man's name, 'With Christ.'"

With Christ. Allison saw the faces of untold thousands of soldiers blurring and merging together. Too many died about whom that could not be said. *Father, use me as a vessel to bring your message of salvation to those who don't know it.*

She drew a deep breath, feeling a sense of purpose—and contentment. The heat, the flies, the long, trying hours, the personal turmoil that needled her...all this was a small cost to see that the soldiers had at least one opportunity to be forever "with Christ."

The next morning before returning to Cairo, Allison helped with Biddy's Sunday free tea. As many as seven hundred soldiers usually showed up, and Biddy, Miss Riley, and others—including Allison and Wade—would see that the men consumed fried eggs, sandwiches, cakes, and gallons of tea and coffee. Contributions arrived from the members of the Prayer League and friends in England. When the soldiers found out about the need for contributions to buy food, they, too, dropped offerings into the inconspicuous "Donations welcome" container to keep the enterprise going.

On this morning, Allison helped place the clean white tablecloths that Biddy insisted they use, while others placed flowers in vases from the gardens in Cairo, all in preparation for the men's arrival. After the tea, Oswald headed off to Cairo for his weekly meeting at Ezbekiah Gardens. Upon his return that evening, Allison saw a dozen new soldiers with him, all of whom were brought to supper—which started, as it usually did, shortly after 9 P.M. All who came stayed for family prayers. Following supper, Allison took a breath of fresh air with Wade outside the bungalow. As they walked, she told him about her planned trip to Luxor and the upcoming Archaeology Club meeting.

"How swiftly the days have flown by." She sat on the front step beside Wade. "I don't know when I'll get back. Maybe not until the troops move out into Palestine." She touched his arm. "You're going with them, aren't you?"

"The military has asked Chambers to go, and I'd like to join him in the work."

She understood. "I'm thinking of requesting to serve with the field hospital again, along with Marra. These two months I've come out to help here at Zeitoun have been precious."

Wade scooped up a fistful of sand and let it seep through his fingers in the starlight. "However we look at life, Allison, our days are few and precious. Whether we die in the war or live to trim our rosebushes in London at age ninety, our journey begins only to end. And those like Chambers, those few who have poured out their lives as drink offerings for Jesus—they will have truly lived."

Tears stung her eyes. "If it's a choice between being a princess draped with diamonds and being like Biddy Chambers, spending my days and nights with few possessions, I would choose this." She looked about the desert sand, the myriad soldiers' tents beneath the starry, black sky.

She turned to Wade, and their eyes held for a moment. He opened his mouth as though to speak, and she stood quickly, smiling. "Come! I hear Biddy's piano."

His smile was enigmatic as he rose and they went back inside the bungalow.

David and Marra showed no concern as Oswald mentioned closing the night's fellowship with family prayer. Afterward, with Chambers playing the small foot-pump organ, they commenced with the evening singing.

"Let's sing the evening hymns," Biddy said, and Allison automatically turned to one of Biddy's favorites. As the words to "God Be With You 'Till We Meet Again" played out in the warm desert night, Allison's thoughts wandered to Bret.

"Till we meet again..." She remembered the way he had looked at her as they had waltzed at Helga's Christmas Ball, the feel of his arms around her. The future had seemed so bright back in December, when a Christmas wedding seemed to be in the making. And now...

A lump in her throat kept her from singing, but Biddy's and Oswald's confident voices filled the bungalow. Allison could not even look at Marra or David. She just kept her head bent, as though looking at the words she knew so well.

Soon they were all saying good night. Oswald and Biddy went for their usual ten o'clock walk in the desert night, drawing close, a couple bound by their love and their devotion to serving together in a spiritual battle.

Allison and Wade joined David and Marra as they strolled back to Wade's little hut. He and David moved out to a tent, providing Allison and Marra quarters for the night.

Going inside the hut, Allison went to her cot, then paused suddenly, frowning. There, on her cot, was a single white rose.

"Where did that come from?"

Allison turned to see Marra peering at the flower from behind her. "I don't know," she said, moving to pick up the blossom. Its

63

sweet fragrance drifted about her, and she inhaled deeply.

"Hey, there's a note." Marra reached down to grab up a small piece of paper. She started to read it, then paused, looking at Allison. "Perhaps you'd rather I didn't…?"

Allison wondered at the suspicion on her friend's face. She shook her head. "No, it's fine." She smiled. "I've nothing to hide from you."

Marra's cheeks flushed. "Well, of course you don't. But—" She broke off, shaking her head. "Never mind. Let's just see what this says, shall we?"

She opened the slip of paper and read, her forehead creasing in a frown of confusion as she did so. "What does that mean?" she asked.

"What?" Allison moved to look at the note.

Believe.

That was it. One simple scrawled word.

"'Believe'?" Marra met Allison's gaze. "What does that mean?"

Allison shook her head. "I'm sure I don't know." She looked at the note again. The handwriting was unfamiliar.

"Well," Marra remarked shortly, "cryptic as the message may be, one thing is abundantly clear."

"And that is?" Allison lifted the rose to breathe its fragrance again.

"You have an admirer."

Allison blinked, then met Marra's narrowed gaze. "I wonder who it is?"

Marra looked as though she was going to say something, then she pressed her lips together and gave a tight shrug. "I'm sure I don't know. You have an entire camp of men to choose from."

"I don't care to choose any of them," Allison replied with a small laugh.

"Perhaps not," Marra said, and Allison wondered at the catch in her voice. "But it would seem one of them cares a great deal about choosing you."

Unable to sleep, Allison tossed, beating her pillow to try to get comfortable.

A flood of light lay along the windowsill; it grew wider as the moon moved lower in the sky.

Finally Allison gave up trying to fall asleep and went to the window, listening to the camp becoming silent. The long, sandy path leading to the soldiers' distant tents glittered, silent and deserted; the rising wind brushed it free of footprints.

Marra sat on her bunk, smearing cream on her face, insisting it "seeped in" better overnight. Her golden head glinted in the moonlight. "All right, out with it. You're worried about more than Bret this time."

"What?" Allison looked across the small hut.

"Something's troubled you since David and I picked you up near the junction."

"I didn't think I wore my heart on my sleeve."

"Worried about Bret?"

Allison hesitated. "David said he's in Jerusalem."

Marra tensed for a moment, then shrugged. "Yeah, well, you know how closed-lipped the military is about what they're doing." She obviously was trying to lighten the moment. "David's like that, too. He tries to play wise guy, but he's anything but indifferent. About Palestine, that is. He wants to get back to help Rose Lyman. I found out he requested to go instead of Bret, but Bret put a stop to the orders. If I didn't know better," she added wryly, "I'd think David's interest in this Jewish gal named Rose was based on more than interest in Jerusalem."

"Trust me, it's not that. Rose is old enough to be his mum. I'm worried about her too. She was at risk before the war broke. I was there when the Turks came to arrest every Jew who was even faintly suspected of being a Zionist. Now, with the war worsening every day—" They both knew what she meant.

"Is she a British spy?" Marra asked bluntly.

There was no reason to hide it from her. They didn't come more loyal than Marra. "Yes, and I can't bear to think what would happen to her if the Turks found out. She's a brave woman to have stayed behind."

"She probably had no place to go. Jerusalem is the last stop."

That was what Rose had implied when Allison begged her to come back to Cairo with her the night she and Bret escaped the Jewish city.

"What bothers me is why Bret would risk going there to see her now," Allison said quietly.

"You mean, maybe something went wrong?"

"Yes. Rose's contact—whoever it is that relays information between her and Bret—I wonder if he was caught. If so, then Bret may have felt Rose was in danger. She has a boy, he's about fourteen now."

Marra sighed and shook her head. "That's always the worst part isn't it? When the enemy has your child—"

"Let's not think of it. Maybe we're jumping to conclusions. I wonder how much David knows that he isn't allowed to tell us?"

"You mean he may be in touch with Bret?"

That was exactly what Allison was thinking.

Marra blotted the excess cream off her face with a cloth. "I don't know. He has seemed restless, even upset the last week or so. I could ask, but he wouldn't tell me. He doesn't confide in me the way he does—" She broke off, but Allison caught the gaze she cast at the white rose by her bed. Allison had put the still-fragrant bloom in a cup beside her cot.

"With others," Marra finished.

So Marra thought the flower had come from David? Allison opened her mouth to deny it, but swallowed what she'd been about to say. In truth, she didn't know *who* had left the rose for her.

She wished she did. She really did not want yet another mystery to figure out.

Allison realized she'd been rubbing her ring finger. She shoved her hands inside the pockets of her robe and walked over to the bunk and sat down on the edge of the lumpy mattress. "Bret isn't the only reason I've been a little worried. I told you about the man on the train from Cairo."

At her words, Marra's eyes locked on to hers.

"The one who claims to be Helga's son?"

"He returned to England when the war broke. He claims he knows Bret and Neal. That both of them suggested he look me up when he came to Egypt to visit his mother."

Marra looked thoughtful. "That Helga has a son surprises me. Did she ever mention him?"

"Never, but that doesn't necessarily mean she hasn't got one."

"True, but I see your point about having concerns. It's obvious the two men who he claims can back up his story are both absent."

"Helga's here, though."

"No, she isn't," Marra reminded her gravely. "She's gone on

ahead to Luxor. She said so in her letter."

Allison frowned. "You're right, but Paul plans to go there with the club. If he were lying, we'll know it soon enough. He can't very well hide his identify from a woman he claims is his mother."

"Then what worries you about him? That he's German?"

"He seems very British. No, I don't think it's that." Allison rested her chin in her hand. "I really can't put my finger on it. There's just something about him that makes the skin prickle on the back of my neck."

Marra winced. "After what happened at the Blaine house, remind me to stay far afield of him. And to think I promised to go with you down to Luxor to get that houseboat ready for your mother and Beth."

Allison smiled and crawled into bed. "And you're not backing out, either."

Marra whispered, "You know, even Helga seems rather odd to me, spy or no spy."

"What do you mean?" Allison stared at the open window where the desert wind rattled the pane.

"Like you said about this guy, Paul—it's hard to put your finger on it. There's just something unsettling to me about Helga Kruger, despite all her outward friendliness."

"But look how much she's done for the club and the museum. And look how she opened her mansion to all of us last Christmas."

"That's what I mean," Marra said thoughtfully. "She does so much—just like now, offering her houseboat to your mother and Beth. Yet what are her reasons? Does she honestly care, or is there something else driving her?"

"Not Helga," Allison insisted. "Bret trusts her implicitly."

Marra was silent. After a moment Allison raised herself to

an elbow and peered at her in the moonlight. "You're not convinced."

"I noticed that when she looks at anyone, her eyes are lifeless. And despite her handsome appearance and meticulous grooming, she seems cold and without real affection."

Allison pondered this. "Yes, but that's her personality. I admit we know next to nothing about Helga, what she was like in Berlin, her family, et cetera. But that doesn't mean we need to be suspicious of her. She's just guarded."

"Perhaps you're right. Maybe she has real concerns, reasons why she must be guarded. Oh, well…" Marra sighed and yawned. "Luxor can't possibly be worse than the Blaine house. Come to think of it, the prospect of several weeks' vacation on a houseboat grows more pleasant the longer I think about it."

"Yes, let's not ruin it with forebodings because of the past. This may be one of our last opportunities to enjoy ourselves before we move out with the field hospital team."

"I'm sleeping in late tomorrow and going swimming in the Nile."

After a moment Allison laughed.

Marra looked at her. "What's so funny?"

"You. Swimming in the Nile of all things!" She laughed again. "I can see you now—screaming your head off with a crock on your tail. And David won't be there to rescue you."

Marra threw her pillow at Allison.

The next morning, after an early breakfast, they walked to the motorcar for the drive back to Cairo.

"If we don't get back to Cairo soon, I may be court martialed," David called good-naturedly.

"Coming," Allison cried, and she turned to Wade. "If you change your mind about Luxor, you know where to find the club."

She left Wade standing in the hot morning sun among the windblown, flapping tents...and wondered when she would see him again.

FIVE

THE CAIRO RESIDENCY, sometimes called Government House, was a large, white, rambling building with several floors containing numerous offices. These belonged to high-ranking officials serving the London Foreign Office. Because Allison's father, Sir Marshall, was temporarily filling the post of chief consul, half of the house was given for private family use. Even so, the government offices were so arranged that Allison was apt to meet up with some ambassador or chief military aide at any inconvenient moment, for even the private section was filled with people coming and going. What was more, the structure was still undergoing refurbishing, and the sound of hammers and saws went on from sunup to sunset.

Beth, in particular, had hated the noise. "This is the most wretched place I've ever lived," she'd complained early one morning as she, Allison, and their mother were sitting in the garden, trying to find some peace and quite. "I was in my morning robe on my way to bathe and met a positively horrid young soldier rushing up the steps to deliver a message to some military aide. He nearly knocked me down, then had the *audacity* to ask me if I normally wore a robe at noon. I was *so* embarrassed!"

"That will teach you to get dressed instead of lolling about all day in your pajamas," Allison had teased, but clearly Beth was in no mood for humor.

"Even the Blaine house was better than this." She rose in a huff.

"Oh, no," their mother scolded, her somber, green eyes upbraiding her younger daughter.

"I'm going to get the biggest deadbolt I can find in Cairo and put it on my door," Beth called over her shoulder as she'd stormed away. "And if anyone tries to come in, I'll—I'll *shoot* 'em!"

"Beth! Don't even talk that way!" Mother had said, but Beth had run back into the house and up the stairs. Mother had sighed heavily and rose to leave the garden to go after her. "I can't allow her to get by behaving so rudely."

Remembering the incident now, Allison sighed, troubled. Her mother was still painfully thin and weakened easily. She simply hadn't fully recovered from the severe concussion she suffered in December while at the Blaine house. Knowing this, Allison was distressed to see Beth troubling their mother so. Still, Beth's emotional state was in such shambles that Allison found room to make excuses for her behavior. She'd been trying to get her sister to attend the weekly Bible meetings Chambers was conducting at Ezbekiah Gardens, but thus far Beth had flatly refused.

"I asked God to help Gilly, and he didn't. So why should I pray to him anymore?"

"Cousin Gilbert has to be responsible, too. He has a mind and will of his own. God doesn't break down the doors to our hearts."

"Lectures!" had been Beth's only response. "What good are lectures when the man I love is going to jail? Or worse?"

When Allison had arrived at the Residency from Zeitoun early that morning, the incessant hammering and sawing was still going on. Dread filled her over how much of Beth's complaining their mother must have had to listen to....

Dimly, she heard a woman's voice resonating from the

vacated ballroom, followed by a man's low but somewhat impatient reply. *Mother,* Allison assumed, smiling faintly. *I'll wager she's giving last-minute orders to the foreman of the work crew about some detail she wants them to include in the refurbishing of the ballroom.* The foreman, she had heard, could be difficult. Her mother, or "Lady Ellie" as her father sometimes affection-ately called her, had always been socially conscious and was the perfect first lady to represent England and serve at the side of the chief consul. Now that her mother was beginning to regain her health, she had taken on overseeing the redecorating project—but Allison wondered if that might not be consuming too many of her waking hours. Well, at least it kept her mother's mind off worrying about the trial.

She walked toward the ballroom, aware the hammering had ceased. The workmen must be quitting to take their noon meal.

"Hullo, Mum! I'm home early."

Allison walked across the wide foyer and through the divid-ing archway. "I'm famished, what's for luncheon?" She entered, expecting to see her mother, but the mammoth ballroom, which had been built to entertain international dignitaries, was empty. Allison frowned. She was sure she'd just heard her mother talking with someone.

She turned to look across the spacious floor, breathing in the clean fragrance of new lumber. She walked forward, step-ping on wood shavings and sawdust.

This was a ballroom where one would expect to see British and Egyptian royalty, garbed in the world's most expensive gowns and gold-braided uniforms. When the family had first moved into the Residency, Eleanor had informed Allison and Beth that officials from around the world had danced here. "World policy is more likely to be worked out here over a goblet of wine than over treaties signed in the offices of kings and presidents."

"So *that's* what's wrong with the world," Allison had jested. "They don't have their minds buttoned on straight."

Her mother had laughed at her, but Beth had frowned.

Across the ballroom another archway opened onto the garden, and the sun was shining through a tall window that ran down one side of the newly painted cream walls. *Mother must have gone into the garden,* Allison thought.

Except for the echo of her footsteps, it was quiet in the big room. The entire house appeared to have suddenly drawn inward like a garden snail pulling into its shell. Beyond the wide window, the garden seemed to have fallen into slumber.

Allison walked toward the garden, coming to three sets of marble stairs that led down in differing directions to a vast lawn edged with rare botanical flowers and other greenery.

A movement caught her attention, and she paused and turned away from the garden. A dining room, containing the largest mahogany table she'd ever seen and a tall, gilded ceiling with four chandeliers from Switzerland, led off from the ballroom into the west wing of the house. Allison swept through the door. "Mum?"

A long and lean Englishman in short shirtsleeves came from the dining room and into the ballroom. He was carrying a wide-brimmed hat and a jacket slung over his arm. His urbane face was burnt brown, enhancing the wide, reddish brown mustache. Deep set, amber-colored eyes looked out with reflective scorn born from an impatience with those in authority who were inept. Beneath his sometimes self-righteous attitude, he was a physically attractive man of some thirty-eight years; yet for reasons that remained ambiguous to Allison, everyone, including herself, looked upon him as the "cranky old British

Doc." She supposed it might have come from the fact that he'd spent eighteen years in medical service in India and Burma. Seeing her, Doctor Howard cracked a smile. "Uh, Hullo, Allison. Sorry to intrude."

"Not at all."

She had first met Doctor Howard on his way out from India. She had since learned that he had stopped off in Arabia soon after the evacuation at Kut to see Major General Crawford. While there, he'd treated Allison for malaria. Since that fateful day last October when the British under Crawford had suffered a tremendous defeat—one that Bret believed was unnecessary—Dr. Spencer Howard had taken up practice in Cairo, serving as a respected physician in the military department among its chief officers.

Allison believed that Doctor Howard had known her parents well in both Egypt and India. He seemed an especially good friend of her father's. It followed, then, that he would know Sir Edgar as well. It was Doctor Howard who first mentioned to her, when she met him in Abadan, that her mother's cousin was coming to Egypt to become chief inspector of the Cairo police. "Rather a surprise, considering," he had remarked, then had stopped as if he had said too much.

Upon returning home to Egypt, Allison had mused over that simple comment. As it turned out, Doctor Howard had been right, but what did he know about Sir Edgar that had prompted such a comment? Dr. Howard hadn't testified at the trial. No one seemed to think he even knew Edgar Simonds. Perhaps he didn't. Perhaps he had only heard things about him. She had intended to ask him about his knowledge of Edgar in India, but the right moment had never arrived.

"The serving woman Zalika told me Eleanor was in the ballroom giving orders to the workers," the doctor said, glancing about the large, empty room. "But Eleanor seems to have disappeared."

Then it hadn't been his voice she'd heard replying to her mother. It must have been the crew foreman.

"I'm afraid Father isn't here." Allison said, noting he had come from the direction of the west wing where her father's office was located.

"Still in the Dardanelles, is he? A ruddy bit of business, thanks to Kitchener." Doctor Howard seldom had anything positive to say about the secretary of war. "He should never have gotten us involved there. It's a losing battle."

Allison inclined her head. Bret had said much the same thing.

The doctor went on. "These politicians don't know what they're doing half the time. Ought to send them all on a slow boat to China, if you ask me. But I didn't stop by about that. It's your mother, bless her soul. Between Marshall and Beth, Eleanor's worrying herself into a frazzle. I thought I'd see how she was recouping. How is she?"

"I really can't say. I just returned from Zeitoun earlier this morning, so I haven't spent much time with her." She glanced around. "She must have stepped out into the garden. Won't you stay for luncheon?"

He glanced at his watch. "I shouldn't, as I've a patient to see, but I was concerned about Beth as well. The trial coming to its end and all that. A nasty affair."

They came down the marble steps and turned onto the flagstone walkway, passing the rosebushes. Allison was still thinking of her sister as she glanced toward the window of her father's office and saw Beth wearing a fashionable hat. For a moment, Allison almost thought she was glimpsing Cynthia Walsh, the sophisticated young woman who had come to Cairo with self-made plans to become engaged to Bret. Allison's gaze met her sister's, and Beth stepped back from the window quickly, as though not wishing to be seen. Allison was amused. Beth was always getting into their mother's wardrobe and trying on her new hats and gowns. And there were an abundance of them, for their mother, as wife of the chief British consul, attended the myriad of political functions in Egypt.

Allison directed her attention back to the doctor at her side. "I've wanted to ask you about your knowledge of Sir Edgar. You knew him in India?"

He looked insulted, his nostrils flaring. "Simonds? Great Scot! Never met the atrocious fellow. What makes you think I did?"

"Oh, well you did say—" She'd been about to remind him of his passing remark when they were near Kut, but the spark in his amber eyes convinced her it wasn't wise to insist. He was a self-righteous man and easily offended, as though the merest comment somehow became an accusation of some wrong-doing. "I don't keep company with murderers, young lady," he lectured stoically.

"No, of course not," she hastened. "Um—I think Mother may be having lunch on the gazebo. This way, Doctor."

The overgrown banana trees crowded the path with their drooping leaves, and Allison pushed them aside. Her mother's favorite spot, a newly constructed green and ivory gazebo, was just ahead. Allison didn't see her mother there, but the pale table was set for lunch. She mounted the short wooden steps with the doctor and came under the shade of the stylish little roof.

The Egyptian servants had already set the meal and tea was poured, as though her mother had been there but left again. Allison noticed a second place setting, with the cup of tea partially consumed and the white napkin ruffling in the breeze.

Beth, of course. Who else would it be?

Allison walked to the opposite end of the gazebo and held the rail, looking off into the large garden area. The usually relaxing fragrance was charged with an unknown tension, or was it only her own emotions she felt?

Silent noontide shadows edged the wandering path into more thickly grown banana trees. Allison held back a shiver. She must remind her mother to have the gardener trim them.

"I don't seem to see her—" she turned quickly toward Doctor Howard to find him staring back toward the house. It was his expression that startled her, filled with anger, and she left her words unfinished, wondering what had come over him.

He must have felt her gaze and turned toward her. "Don't see Eleanor?" His usual somewhat cryptic expression was back in place, as he walked up beside her and shaded his eyes, looking toward the rainbow patch of carnations, hollyhocks, and delphiniums.

It had all happened so quickly that Allison wondered if she hadn't imagined the doctor's anger.

In the silence the one noticeable sound came from a lone bee that buzzed near the uncovered platter of sweet buns with blueberry filling, but Allison didn't find the lazy drone pleasant. Summer days no longer existed in her heart.

"Isn't that her?"

Allison followed his glance, but seeing her mother standing near the blue delphiniums, stiff and frozen like Lot's wife, did nothing to ease her inner tension. "What in the world is she doing—?" At first she was difficult to make out, for she was attired in a silk dress of the same color as the delphiniums. But then the breeze blew away her lacy hat and her smooth, red-gold hair streaked with gray caught the sun's rays, glinting like copper in a field of blue. Her mother was bent over the tall flowers as though meditating.

"Mother?" she called down from the gazebo.

Eleanor gave a start and straightened. She turned toward the gazebo and looked up.

Allison could not see her mother's expression well from this distance, but even so, she sensed strong emotion emanating from her. So convinced was she, that she looked from her mother to the tall flowers, half expecting someone to step out from among them. And, indeed, the tall delphiniums moved, but it was Tigret, the family cat, that meandered out. The animal sauntered off to look for a spot of sunshine in which to curl up and nap without being bothered by snooping humans.

The doctor sat on the edge of the rail and called: "Hullo, Eleanor! Am I interrupting anything?"

"Hello, Spencer! I'll be right up!" She stooped, gathered up a reed basket overflowing with heavy-headed delphiniums, and came hurrying up the path toward the gazebo.

A moment later Allison's mother came up the steps and entered the round display, and while she wore a perfunctory smile, the evidence of both physical and mental fatigue was visible in her otherwise porcelain-smooth face. She was an exceptionally attractive woman for her age. Many had told Allison that her mother's beautiful hair and face could be seen all over again in her, except that, unlike her mother's light green eyes, her own were a deep sea green. A most uncommon color, or so she'd been told.

Bret had said her eyes haunted his memory when he was away.

Well, they most likely didn't send his pulse rate climbing now, she thought cynically.

She went to meet her mother. "Hullo, Mum, why so many flowers?" She wrinkled her nose, rubbing the end as though she might sneeze. "Reminds me of a funeral."

Eleanor's mouth curled, and she whispered: "Don't even hint of it," as she gave her daughter her customary brief kiss.

Turning toward the doctor with a warm smile, Allison's mother said, "So good to see you, Spencer," and she quickly set aside the flowers, tossing her gloves into the basket next to the shears. "You're just in time for luncheon. You, too, Allison. You're home early. I didn't expect you until Wednesday. Wade with you?" she glanced about the gazebo as though looking for him, though it was evident that he wasn't there. Her mother seemed breathless. Her somewhat wide eyes came back to Allison. "Nothing wrong out at Zeitoun?"

Allison laughed wryly. "You can see our present state of mind, Doctor Howard. Whenever the family meets, the first thing we ask one another is whether anything is wrong. No, Mum, everything is peaches. Wade stayed to work with Mr. Chambers, is all. Troops may move out again soon, and the work must press on. But I'm not inclined to be so sacrificial at present." She looked at the doctor with a smile and explained, "I'm an archaeology bug. I can't leave it alone. And this year the Cairo club is planning a two-week holiday at Luxor."

"Don't blame you at all. If I had the time I'd join Helga's club just to take in the lectures. The Valley of the Kings has always interested me with its profound history. One could say it's godlike. The British don't seem to appreciate the majesty of this ancient culture! Disgusting, really."

"Godlike" was a bit extreme to Allison, and she looked at him to find his expression intensely—and curiously—sober.

He looked at Eleanor. "Can't stay long. I've a patient in a bad way, though I'm afraid there's little more I can do for the chap." As Eleanor went to speak to the serving man, Doctor Howard tossed his hat and coat onto a wooden bench. A stony mask descended over his face. "Nurse Phillips succumbed to heart failure a week ago," he stated in a low voice.

The abrupt change in topic was jarring. Allison looked at him blankly.

"I take it you didn't know her."

"No," she admitted. "I haven't been working in any of the hospitals since Arabia. I'm sorry about her, though. The military is in desperate need of nurses."

His mouth twitched. "Especially the ones that are qualified. Many are woefully inexperienced, or else they spend their time coquetting with the soldiers. I won't have that sort working at my elbow! Nurse Phillips was collected. Very calm. No hysterics when the guns were going off. I shall miss her. She was loyal and adept. Served with me in India for a year in the midst of battle." He fixed her with a steely gaze. "I took the initiative of looking at your record. Should you ever want a nursing position, Allison, you have but to mention it. General Murray and I play chess together in the evenings. I think you could fill her place. I can have you with me in Palestine when the general gives the word to move out."

Allison blinked in surprise at the suggestion, but managed to say, "Thank you. I'll remember your offer."

Eleanor finished speaking in low Egyptian to the serving man, telling him to remove the place settings and bring fresh utensils. No mention was made of what appeared to have been a luncheon already in progress, or why Eleanor had suddenly left to gather a basket of delphiniums.

"Tea, Spencer?" she was asking as another boy pulled back a chair for him to sit.

Doctor Howard was frowning. "Eleanor, you're looking

more pale each time I see you. Why didn't you tell me the headaches were returning?"

"Oh, it's nothing." She waved aside his concerns, then poured tea into fragile china cups with pink rosebuds and gold leaf. "It's Marshall I'm worried about now."

"Those headaches are nothing to ignore," insisted Spencer. "I'm going to write a new prescription before I leave. Take one before you retire tonight."

"Oh, all right, I will, but I'm sure they have nothing at all to do with what happened to me at the Blaine house."

Remembering the attack on her mother, Allison set her cup down after barely sipping her Darjeeling tea.

"It's this wearisome murder trial," her mother went on.

"You know my professional opinion on that. The wisest thing for you and Beth to do is leave Cairo until it's over."

Allison thought her mother looked uncomfortable as she squeezed lemon into her tea. "Inspector Mortimer has reason to think the Germans are increasing attacks on civilian ships. There's no possible way to leave for a holiday."

"Oh? Julian into dabbling in intelligence, too?"

Allison looked from Spencer to her mother. "Julian?"

Her mother met her curious gaze. "Julian Mortimer, the new chief inspector. He's taken the position of—of Edgar. I thought you'd met him, dear, two weeks ago at the dinner ball given in his honor."

Allison remembered something about the ball, but she hadn't attended. There was always some dinner or ball or garden social in Cairo to flatter certain officials of all nationalities.

"I didn't go."

"A sound decision," Spencer said. "A person could spend one's entire life fulfilling social obligations. Nor is it necessarily safe."

82

What an odd remark. Allison looked at him. "Not safe? What do you mean?"

Her mother looked as though she would try to detour him from answering, but Spencer frowned as he cut sharply into his broiled chicken breast. "I'm speaking of what happened last night at the French ambassador's house."

Allison realized she was clutching her fork and relaxed her grip. "What happened?"

Her mother's face went colorless, and she remained silent as Spencer jabbed the piece of chicken with the prongs of his fork and turned with weary eyes to state, "They found a corpse in the garden."

Eleanor made a little sound, something like a sigh, and slumped back against the chair, but Allison sat rigid.

"Another—heart failure?" she found herself inquiring foolishly, "like—like Nurse Phillips?"

His lip curled. "Hardly. The man was murdered."

"Now, Spencer, don't upset her. We don't know that for certain," Eleanor argued. "Julian Mortimer doesn't think so."

"Julian, my dear Eleanor, knows much that he isn't speaking. He's a poker face, if you know what I mean."

"Do they know who the man was?" breathed Allison. "And how did he die?"

Her mother was silent, but Spencer showed little reticence. "Some little known French diplomat."

"His name was Vautier," stated Eleanor.

"It seems he had a headache, went out for a stroll amid the garden roses, and didn't come back. Everyone, including I, thought he'd gone back to the Shepheard Hotel. He was due to sail for Alexandria this morning for his return to France."

Eleanor looked at her gravely. "Monsieur Vautier was found

at dawn by the French ambassador's security guard when he made the morning rounds."

Spencer emptied his cup and set it down too carefully. "He was stabbed—with a dagger."

Allison breathed deeply, fighting the sense of panic growing in her. "Did they find the weapon?"

"No, but I wouldn't expect them to. The murderer would be a fool to leave that sort of evidence."

Allison sat still, her heart pumping so fast she felt weak. Another murder. But surely—oh, *surely* this didn't have anything to do with the past! "Robbery?" came her hopeful question.

"Yes." Eleanor's tone echoed with the same hope. "Julian Mortimer said Monsieur Vautier had been searched."

"Everything was taken," Spencer agreed. "Even the man's clothing and shoes."

Yes, robbery, thought Allison again. *That's why the thieves took his clothing.*

Spencer didn't appear to notice the stifling silence that descended around the table and went on in a brisk tone as though the subject was now satisfied and a new topic must be unearthed. "Any word from your nephew, Eleanor?" Allison looked at her mother and thought she looked anxious to change the topic, even if the subject of Neal Bristow was nearly as troubling. There was still no explanation for why Neal's ship hadn't arrived as expected at Christmastime. Bret had done what he could to find out the cause for the delay and the ship's whereabouts, but before anything definite was known, Bret, too, had all but disappeared from Cairo. Then Allison had met Helga's son on the train from Cairo to Zeitoun.

"Marshall has hopes Neal may arrive soon," Allison's mother said.

Allison was about to mention Paul Kruger and his knowledge of Neal being delayed, but to discuss it meant she would also need to explain about Helga having a son…and for some reason she was loathe to do that.

"I can quite understand why Marshall's digging in his heels about not letting you and Beth voyage to England," Spencer said. "I read in the paper that another civilian ship was sunk, this time off the coast of Scotland. Terror is a weapon the Germans use well. If they can instill fear into civilians, it will reduce the number of supply ships."

"German terror or not," Eleanor said wearily, "I'd leave tomorrow if possible. Anything to get Beth away from this dreadful trial." Her mouth tightened. "Gilbert is sure to hang."

Allison held back a shudder. It was too horrid to even contemplate. If only Gilbert's heart could have been reached for God before he—

"But there's Marshall—his gout. Poor dear. I can't bring myself to simply leave him while he shoulders the burdens of Egypt! The work is just too important."

"I wouldn't worry so about Marshall. He's doing better than you are, if you want to know the truth. He's quite able to handle the present situation in Egypt, even if political unrest over the new sultan erupts in riots from the independence party. General Murray has troops enough to squelch any trouble."

Allison understood little about the tension surrounding the inauguration of a new sultan since she hadn't kept up with Egyptian politics. Nor did she want to ask now, fearful that Doctor Howard might go off on a long tirade. Her mind was too full of the problems at hand. What mattered to her now was that her father was due back in Cairo to oversee the sultan's inauguration. Sir Marshall had been away for nearly two months, but it felt more like two years to Allison. Although she did not see eye-to-eye with him over the matter of marriage to

Bret, he could handle Beth when no one else could.

"I thought Father was to return from the Dardanelles by Sunday."

"The military changed plans. It seems Intelligence feared that word had somehow gotten out to the German U-boats."

"You mean there could be an attack?" Allison cried.

"It's all right now, darling," her mother quickly soothed. "I was assured only this morning of your father's safety. He's on a French war vessel, which one I don't know."

"French!" Spencer said. "Bravo to the chap who thought of that. They'd naturally be surveying British ships coming in from the Dardanelles. Don't tell me the French ship is docking in Alexandria?"

"They aren't saying, and I didn't ask. I didn't want to know so I wouldn't let it slip out."

"Most likely Alexandria," Spencer said. "That can hardly be a secret to the enemy."

"Perhaps," was all she would say. "You know how ship movements are never discussed openly."

Especially if someone of importance is aboard, Allison thought. She'd been disturbed over her father's going when first told about the secret fact-finding voyage into the Dardanelles. That particular strip of waterway had provided Constantinople's security for many centuries, and it was once again a bulwark for Turkey. From the time of the ancient Byzantine Empire, the city by the Golden Horn had been protected from countless attempts of foreign invasion by its secure geography.

Sir Marshall had gone to the Dardanelles at the request of Secretary of War Kitchener to gather firsthand information on how well the evacuation of British troops from the area was progressing.

"We've blundered the Dardanelles badly," Doctor Howard stated harshly. "England's involvement was an error from the beginning. And now we're paying the cost—the lives of thousands of young British soldiers."

Allison recalled Bret having said much the same thing in December when the first evacuation of troops had begun. Later a second war front in the Dardanelles was opened to keep the Turks from extending their military presence on their border with Russia. But high, impregnable cliffs guarded the narrow straight where the British landed.

"Just a few Turks can dig in with machine guns and hold off thousands of our soldiers indefinitely," Allison stated, quoting Bret and looking thoughtfully at Spencer Howard.

"Too bad Kitchener doesn't have your military expertise, my dear," he said dryly.

"Those are the words of Colonel Holden," she confessed. "Like you, he was angry with the ineptitude of the government."

"He'd better watch himself. The top brass do not approve of smart colonels detecting their blunders."

She remembered Bret's difficulty with Major General Townsend over Baghdad. Now, Townsend and some eight thousand soldiers were held up at Kut in a siege that continued to drag on with little hope of escape.

"And the war in the Dardanelles drags on with thousands of losses. All because of a plan to try to help Czar Nicholas of Russia! Did Holden also tell you they're stuck in miserable frozen trenches, left to endure the elements?"

"Yes, and unable to either advance with success or to retreat to the exposure of the beach."

London was being criticized in the newspapers for failing to get supply ships to the Dardanelles, where there was a desperate need for winter clothing and food. Some men were without boots and growing ill with disease.

"And if that weren't enough," Doctor Howard continued. "They're getting scarce medical help."

Hospital boats were on the way, but tragically late. Allison, in reading about the troops, had been frustrated enough to seriously consider signing up for service on one of the ships, but her mother's health and the problems rising over Beth had deterred her.

With luncheon over, they stood and moved toward the gazebo rail where the doctor picked up his jacket and hat from the bench.

"If Father doesn't arrive soon, I'll need to start for Luxor without seeing him." Allison had thought she might leave on Saturday. Then she remembered what Helga wrote in her letter about someone having suggested that her mother use the houseboat. Watching Doctor Howard, she mentioned Helga's offer of the houseboat to her mother. "At least you'll be away from Cairo until after the trial," she finished.

"I heartily agree," Spencer said. "Wouldn't mind coming myself if I had the time. I may yet get down there for a few days if Helga can make room for me."

"Well," Eleanor began reluctantly, "I suppose Luxor is better than staying here."

Spencer took hold of her arm, "Doctor's orders, Eleanor," he said soberly. "Pack your bags and Beth's. Marshall is sure to agree. And Allison is right. You'll be away from Cairo until the worst is over. That's what matters, isn't it?"

"Yes, yes, Spencer, I know. And I want her away, too. But I'll need to wait to discuss things with Marshall."

"If you can get Marshall to join you for a few days of rest, even better. Well, ladies, I must be off. Thanks for the luncheon, and Eleanor—" he paused, going down the steps and looking back at her—"I don't want to be an alarmist, but it's expedient that the child be taken out of all this before her emotions snap."

They watched him walking away down the flagstone path back toward the Residency, his energetic stride in keeping with a man who enjoyed long and rigorous hikes.

Allison found at least one blessing to be grateful for amid the tragedy striking her family: her parents' marriage appeared to be on the mend. The war seemed to have brought her mother and father closer together. That her mother felt more concern for her father than she did for her own plans of leaving Egypt showed marked improvement from the days before the Great War. Her mother had gone to India the previous summer to offer Marshall an ultimatum: either resign his position and leave Egypt to retire in the English countryside as he'd been promising to do for years, or she would leave without him, taking Beth with her to be schooled in London.

Yes, much had changed. Allison noticed pride in her mother's eyes as she discussed her father's work for their country. There was even a deeper concern for Egypt and its people. Her mother was showing interest in the convalescing soldiers and had suggested to Allison that as she regained her strength and completed the refurbishing of the Residency, she and Beth might help out at the YMCA. not in Zeitoun, but at the busy Benha railway junction.

Two of Oswald Chambers's previous BTC students, Kathleen Ashe and Gertrude Ballinger, had recently begun to operate a Christian work at Benha, where the YMCA Hut was located on the train platform.

Tragedy and trial, mused Allison. *Could they be blessings in disguise?* Beautiful roses had their thorns—a reminder that the whole creation was still groaning and travailing together until the redemption. And in her own family it appeared as though the sorrows were bringing them closer to one another, and to the heart of God.

Still, she wrestled with these truths in her mind as her heart swelled with the doubts and fears she could not seem to overcome. Bret...her mother's health...Beth's frail mental state...it was all simply too much to take in.

And so she did what she'd been doing for months, she pushed it all away, refusing to think about it—and hoping she'd find a way to deal with it before it completely overwhelmed her.

Six

"I DON'T SEE WHY LONDON WAITED so long to begin the inevitable evacuation from the Dardanelles," Allison protested. "The wounded and sick soldiers number over sixty thousand in Cairo alone, and that doesn't include the overcrowded hospitals in Alexandria."

Her mother looked strained as they stood together at the gazebo railing looking after Dr. Spencer Howard until he disappeared around the shrubs.

"There were sound reasons. The Intelligence Department was against it. They feared a withdrawal now would free the Turkish army to be sent to reinforce the siege of Kut. We're trying to arrange a relief army to be sent. But if we abandon the Dardanelles—well, you see our difficulty. It may already be too late. The thought horrifies me. So many vulnerable men!"

With a stab of guilt, Allison recalled the more than eight thousand British men who were trapped inside the Arab town of Kut. Any new Turkish soldiers sent there from the Dardanelles would make the task of saving them utterly hopeless. "What about Colonel Holden? You haven't mentioned him. In December he wanted to go to India to try to raise support for a relief army."

Eleanor's gaze dropped to her plate. "Darling, I think it best we not discuss the colonel now. I shouldn't even have told you about your father."

Allison caught herself, steadying her nerves and staring into her mother's anguished eyes.

Eleanor walked over to the table and lowered herself onto a chair.

Allison followed, tense and waiting. There was silence. She sat down, holding the edge of the table. "Is father really in the Dardanelles?"

Eleanor lifted her teacup and stared at the brew as though it contained poison.

"Mother?" she pressed.

She sighed. "No."

Allison considered. "You didn't want Doctor Howard to know?"

Eleanor waved her handkerchief as though the question were irrelevant. "It isn't just Spencer. The information is secret. There's nothing to fear from Spencer, I've known him for years."

"Which means nothing nowadays. Sir Edgar is our cousin. And what of Rex and Sarah Blaine?"

"Yes, I know. But I wouldn't have said anything no matter who had luncheon with us. Lives are at stake. As you say, one can't be too careful. Your father would be outraged if he knew I was discussing this with you."

"I've already been involved in espionage with Colonel Holden in Arabia—the Constantinople Papers, remember? And we all know Cousin Leah was murdered because she was involved in such things. And Neal—"

"Hush, Allison!"

Allison's cold fingers twisted about each other. Then her father was on secret business for the government. And Bret—who knew?

After a moment, her mother said in a low voice, "With the British soldiers being evacuated from the Dardanelles, Intelligence has spotted new Turkish troop movements in Arabia. General Townsend in Kut will have no choice but to

92

surrender to the Turks. If they do, it's likely to end in a death march to Anatolia. The Turks are not known for humane treatment of their prisoners of war."

Allison recalled what Bret had told her about the Christian Armenians who had been forced to march into the icy mountains far from food and water, dying by the thousands. If tragedy also awaited the soldiers at Kut, Bret was likely to know, since he had cared so deeply about them. Why was he so silent now?

Allison's sympathy for London increased as she realized the dilemma. So much was interlinked—a policy in the Dardanelles could effect the lives of British troops elsewhere. No wonder people said War Secretary Kitchener had aged drastically since German guns had first sounded in Belgium.

There was so much to think about, to worry about, to hope and pray about, that Allison found her mind pulled in ever-widening directions. What must it be like for Secretary of War Kitchener to have the weight of the nation on his mind and heart? She reminded herself of her responsibility to pray for those in positions of authority, that they would have the wisdom and courage to make right decisions. She found it easy to be critical, but difficult to simply bring the leaders before the throne of grace in intercession. Oswald Chambers was right in his instruction to "Pray for our national leaders." She needed to do that. To pray for her leaders…and for Bret.

Allison bit her lower lip. "I see." She looked at her mother's tense face. "Then when will Father be back in Cairo?"

"That I don't know, but what I said to Spencer earlier is true. I was told by General Murray this morning that he was safe on a French ship and soon to arrive in Egypt."

There was some relief in knowing that. "And you can't tell me what Bret is doing?"

Her mother lifted a hand and tiredly rubbed her forehead as though a new headache were coming on. "I can honestly say I don't know. He's been away for weeks now. I think he's on—leave."

"Leave?" she whispered, confused, and noted that her mother avoided her eyes.

"Darling, you mustn't breathe a word of this to anyone."

"No, Mum, of course not, but—"

"We mustn't talk about it anymore." Her mother set her cup down quietly but firmly, showing the matter had come to an end. Allison knew her mother well enough to realize she would receive no more information.

The afternoon sunlight painted the flame trees a warm orange, and the breeze began to murmur like low voices. Allison remembered something and looked at her mother curiously. "Who were you having lunch with before Doctor Howard and I arrived?"

"What? Oh. Beth. She left to visit with one of the McAllister girls. They'll be having dinner together at Ezbekiah Gardens."

"That's odd. Beth told me she wasn't getting on with Hedda McAllister. The trial, and all that."

"It's true. Beth is insecure, and their criticism demoralizes her. She needs a wider circle of friends. I fear she depends on their acceptance too much."

Allison, too, had experienced the curious and sometimes morbid stares of others, but she tried not to allow the incidents to make her unhappy. Her mother had always taken great stock in social reputation, and to have such a scandal on her side of the family was particularly galling.

"It seems many are intrigued by the fact that we have a relative about to be executed for murder."

Her mother looked at her with restrained consternation.

"Isn't it horrible! Sometimes I can't accept what happened. I tell myself there has to be some mistake, that my cousin and nephew could not do such a thing. Somehow I can accept the propensity for evil in other families easier than I can in my own." She looked at Allison. "Something Lydia said the other week stays in my mind. Do you suppose we're trying to deny what the Scripture says about our fallen natures being incorrigible?"

Allison stirred uncomfortably. She thought she knew the verse that Aunt Lydia had referred to. "It's in the Old Testament, in Jeremiah: 'The heart is deceitful above all things, and desperately wicked; who can know it?'" She looked at her mother. "It's not very flattering to our egos, but when clearly realized, it can make us flee to Jesus."

Eleanor leaned back into her chair and tapped her chin, musing. "Mmm, you're right, but that doesn't make me feel any the better about Edgar and Gilbert." She sighed. "If only your father could have done something to have the horrid trial moved to another town in Egypt. Instead we have to bear the brunt of wagging tongues and even see it spread all over the papers."

Allison smiled ruefully. "Father doesn't worry about gossip, and being inside government, you can be sure he's getting plenty of it."

"Of course," her mother agreed briskly. "The men go home in the evening to wives who can't wait to learn the latest muck about how the chief consul is bearing up with a wife whose cousin is about to be hanged for murder. But you're right about your father. He has skin as thick as a crocodile—nothing seems to bother him. I wish I could develop a hide like his."

Allison gave a brittle laugh. Her father had proceeded with his duties as though Sir Edgar and Gilbert did not exist. She

believed his attitude had something to do with having had suspicions about Edgar long before he arrived in Cairo. She wondered if her father had said anything to her mother about
deliberately placing Sir Edgar in the police department in order
to trap him.

"And you're also quite right about Beth and her friends,"
Eleanor mused. "I was surprised she would want to dine with
Margaret's daughter tonight, or that Hedda would even ask her
to the birthday party at Ezbekiah. It's the first time Beth's
shown interest in getting out since this dreadful business
began." Her eyes lifted absently toward the garden. "I've been
so concerned about her. I mentioned it to Helga when we met
the other day." She looked back at Allison. "I suppose that's
what motivated her to offer the houseboat. It was kind of her."

This seemed the proper time for Allison to mention meeting
Paul Kruger on the train. As she did so, her mother appeared as
surprised as Allison had been when Paul first introduced himself.

"A son? I wasn't aware Helga had children. And an archaeologist at that. One would have expected her to speak of him
with some pride since archaeology means so much to her."

"Exactly what I thought. He hopes to stay in Egypt and
apply for a position at the museum. He was working, so he
said, in Tanzania."

"Rather interesting, considering."

"Considering what, Mum?"

"That Tanzania is as close to becoming a German colony as
Egypt is to becoming an English one."

She wondered what her mother might be hinting at. "He
claims to disown Germany's militaristic ambitions."

"I would think he must if he were Helga's son. Her reputation for favoring the Allies over the Central Powers is well
established in Egypt."

Allison refrained from mentioning that Helga was an agent, though she suspected her mother knew—as she was sure she knew a good many other secrets to which she herself wasn't privy. "What about staying on the baroness's houseboat?"

"I simply *must* get Beth out of Cairo, for all that she's not likely to want to leave. Though she may want to avoid gossip, she'd be prone to feel she's abandoning Gilbert. Our Beth may want to be in the audience until the day he's sentenced—she'll feel as if she's being loyal to him."

Allison believed her mother was right. It was depressing to think of her sister emotionally bonding with a young man so devoid of character. What was more troubling, though, was that Beth didn't seem to notice Gilbert's deficiency. Her lack of discernment was hurting her more than it would ever help Gilbert.

"If I know Beth, she'll likely end up fainting at the end," Allison warned.

Her mother groaned and, picking up her fan, swished it, closing her eyes she leaned her head back against the chair. "What a great stir that will make in the newspapers. I can see the headlines now: Cousin of Murder Assailant Faints at Verdict." She snapped her fan shut and straightened her shoulders. "That settles it. We'll go to Luxor and stay on Helga's houseboat. You go on ahead and get the boat ready. When your father returns, I'll talk him into bringing us down to join you." A wistful tenderness came to her eyes. "Maybe I can even get him to stay a few days on vacation. He needs some time to rest. We all do."

"When's Aunt Lydia coming from her plantation?"

"I don't know she will anytime soon. She rather likes it out in the country. She's found new interest in using her medical and missionary endeavors with the Egyptian workers, though she still hopes to receive official permission to get back control of *The Mercy*."

Aunt Lydia had been trying for several months now to gain permission from General Murray to take her medical mission boat back on the Nile, this time toward the Suez.

Allison finished her tea and began to make mental note of all the things she would need to bring with her to Luxor. At the top of the list was a pair of desert walking boots since her one decent pair remained locked up with her trunk at the Blaine house. She was calculating whether her private funds would also allow her to add a few other items to her shopping list when her mother's serving woman, Zalika, arrived from the Residency carrying the afternoon mail in a decorative reed basket.

"Oh, my, how lovely."

Allison looked up to see her mother holding a white rose, to which a small envelope was attached. She felt her mouth drop open, but before she could think of anything to say, her mother went on.

"It was on top of the mail," she said, looking at the small envelope. Her smiling gaze came to rest on Allison. "It's for you, my dear."

Allison sat unmoving for a moment, then slowly reached out to take the flower from her mother. She opened the envelope and pulled out the small card. Her eyes widened as she read the printed word.

Believe.

"Who's it from, Allison?"

She looked at her mother. "I—I don't know. There's no name."

"What does it say?"

Allison looked at the word again. "Believe."

Her mother's forehead creased in a thoughtful frown.

"Rather an odd message, don't you think?"

Allison shook her head, not sure *what* to think. Who was sending the flowers? Could it be, as Marra so clearly suspected, David? Was he trying to encourage her to believe in herself? Or in Bret?

Her mother smiled tenderly. "Well, whatever it means, the flower is lovely. Why don't you go get a vase to put it in, dear."

Allison nodded numbly, and rose to do as her mother bid. When she returned, she set the vase in the center of the table. As she sat down again, Eleanor lifted an envelope from the stack of mail and passed it to her. "Here, Allison," she said, then went on sorting.

She handed over several other uninteresting pieces and, as Allison collected them together, intending to look at them later, the sender's name on one of the envelopes commanded her interest.

The letter was from Gamal al-Sayyid, the chief curator at the Cairo Museum, an associate of Helga's. He was the one who was also arranging the club's two-week holiday at the Valley of the Kings. It was Mr. Sayyid whom Paul Kruger would have to seek out to submit an application to fill the position vacated by the late Professor Jemal Pasha.

Allison looked at the envelope and saw Sayyid's name in the upper left corner, but no postal mark on the stamp. Her eyebrows raised. So the envelope had been hand delivered.

Using an ivory-and-silver letter opener of carved Egyptian design, she slit the waxed seal. She couldn't imagine what Mr. Sayyid wanted. It must have something to do with the museum auction to be held later that week. Allison wondered what she might bring—she'd been so preoccupied recently that she hadn't given it much attention.

However, Mr. Sayyid's short letter, dated that morning,

informed her that the late Mrs. Sarah Blaine's house and possessions were to be retained by the authorities until her will was executed. Mrs. Blaine had left instructions with her lawyer that her house and possessions were to be sold, with the proceeds going to the museum and the archaeology club of which she was so fond. He wanted to complete these matters promptly, therefore, would Miss Wescott be so kind as to come and collect her personal belongings, which had been locked up in the guest bedroom since the "unfortunate demise of Mrs. Blaine in December." He would appreciate it, so he wrote, if she could come this afternoon since he would be there at 4 P.M. to show the property to an interested buyer.

There was also another matter of import that he wished to discuss with her that was best not put in writing.

Allison stared at the letter in her hand. A matter of import? That was best not put in writing? What could it be?

Thoughts of Sarah Blaine filled her mind, bringing back the memory of that rainy night in December when Allison found Jemal's body lying under the oleander bushes. The idea of returning to the Blaine house, where murder had been committed, and walking up those stairs to the bedroom next to the office of the late Major General Rex Blaine, brought Allison a shiver.

A silence crept over the garden gazebo. The cool shadows that only minutes earlier seemed pleasant after the afternoon heat now seemed to conceal some new menace. The fragrance from the basket of flowers was carried away as the blue delphiniums nodded in the breeze, which touched the hem of Allison's skirt like a disturbing whisper.

She had a mind to forget her trunk. She never wanted to see the Blaine house again, least of all to look at the closed door leading into Sarah's bedroom—a room that stood empty and deadly silent, perhaps concealing secrets unknown to Allison or anyone else. In her mind's eye she could still see Sarah's frightened expression as she insisted she was afraid someone was going to try to murder her.

Allison squeezed her eyes shut. Sarah had been right. Terrifyingly so. Allison could envision the house as it had been in December, sitting back amid trees and garden, overgrown and silent. She saw Sir Edgar Simonds in his white suit and white broad-rimmed Panama hat, walking silently toward her on scuffed white shoes, his eyes feverish and bright. Had he killed Sarah?

"Allison!"

Her mother's voice broke through the tumult of thoughts whirling in her mind.

"What is it, darling, bad news?"

Allison's voice sounded thin and watery, even to herself. "N-no, Mum, just a letter from the museum curator is all."

"Gamal al-Sayyid? A nice fellow, I think, but his assistant is rather odd." Eleanor frowned to herself.

"His assistant? You mean Mr. Rahotep?" Allison smiled, thinking of the short, round Egyptian who was always in a flutter.

"Yes, that's the chap."

"Why do you say he's odd?"

"I met him at a charity tea last week for the museum. Seems the nervous sort. Reminded me of a twittering bird. His fingers were constantly moving." She shook her head, as though dis-missing the man. "So, what does Sayyid want? I suppose the letter has something to do with the club meeting?"

"Oh. Nothing much. Sarah's will left everything of value to the museum. It's all to be sold, with proceeds divided between the museum and the archaeology club."

"That was generous of her. Having no children or close relations, her action is understandable, though I doubt Rex would have been pleased." A wry look came to her eyes. "He would have preferred it left to his gin-drinking chums at the polo club, I'm certain. Did you expect Sarah to mention you in her will? You look disappointed."

"What, Mum? Oh, no. Not at all. It's just that I've been asked to come to the house this afternoon to collect my things. After the—the incident in December, the police wouldn't permit any of us to take our bags. You remember. Marra's things are still there, too, and I think even Bret had left a military jacket in—in Rex Blaine's study."

"We all left bags. Why is he only asking you to come?"

Her mother's question was indeed a good one, and Allison hadn't considered it until this moment. "Mr. Sayyid has not notified any of the others?"

"No. And if I recall," Eleanor said, "only Helga was permitted to remove her things, and most of those only because they were valuables connected with the museum."

"Well, I suppose he wants to speak to me about the museum auction this week. And the club will be leaving soon for Luxor."

"Or perhaps Sarah left you something in her will after all. If you'd like, I can accompany you. What time do you need to be there?"

"This afternoon, but you needn't go, really. There's nothing to it I'm sure. I can handle returning to the house—just a brief return—especially since Mr. Sayyid will be there showing the property to an interested buyer." She offered a ghost of a smile. "Anyway, I do want to get my things. I've left a good pair of desert boots; I was going to buy new ones. And Marra was inquiring about her trunk just last week. She has some old letters from the soldier she was going to marry and wants them back...for sentimental reasons. I should take care of it before they're misplaced."

"Well, then, you might as well bring back what belongs to me and Beth. Have the driver take you to Old Cairo so he can load the back of the motorcar." She fixed Allison with a concerned look. "You're certain you don't mind going alone?"

"No, I may even stop at Ezbekiah Gardens to see how Beth is doing renewing her friendship with Hedda McAllister."

"You might talk up the holiday on Helga's houseboat. It will be more pleasant for us all if Beth wants to go." Her mother walked to the bench and picked up the basket of delphiniums. "All right, then. I've got to run along. I'll see you tonight after dinner."

Her mother's brisk footsteps died away on the flagstone walk.

Allison glanced at the crystal clock on the table. 1:55 P.M. She had plenty of time for a little shopping before meeting Mr. Sayyid. She must return to her room and collect her handbag before she called her mother's driver to bring her into Old Cairo to the Blaine house.

But a few minutes later Allison was still lingering over a cup of tea while musing about Gamal al-Sayyid's letter. Suddenly she became aware of a stillness in the garden...the chattering birds had fallen silent, as though frightened away. She looked toward the blue delphiniums. Remembering something curious, she walked over to the gazebo rail and looked out onto the garden where the banana trees waved their leafy stems. Why had she thought her mother was behaving oddly in the garden when she arrived with Spencer?

She stood staring ahead into the garden so intently that she did not immediately see a figure crouched near the tall flowers. Startled, she watched for a moment, wondering if it was the

Egyptian gardener, but his behavior was secretive and so convinced her otherwise. Whoever it was had disappeared. A moment later she left the gazebo and walked through the garden toward the delphiniums.

The path wound around a casual terraced area of blooming pink-and-white asters, where bees crawled happily across the large yellow centers gathering pollen. She came to the thick banana trees. The ground was muddy from a recent watering. A man's footprints were pressed into the soil, and the impressions appeared recent. A blossom was pressed into the imprint. She stooped and loosened it with a twig. The petal color was fresh. Someone had cut across the back of the garden recently....

She walked to the delphinium patch and saw that someone had stepped on the plants. The figure she had seen crouching? Then it hadn't been the gardener; he took great pride in the flowers and would never carelessly step on them. She looked about, thinking...and made a decision. Someone had been looking for something. But who? And what might they have lost, and why?

Allison heard some branches move and turned to glance over her shoulder. She could see the gazebo in the distance and caught a glimpse of a white-clad figure. It was only Dahib, one of the servants, coming to clear the table of the luncheon dishes.

A few minutes passed before she walked back to the gazebo to collect her mail and return to the house for her handbag. The table, she noticed, was still cluttered. Dahib must have been in a hurry, but he had picked up her mail and brought it to the house. She entered the hall and stopped at the table by the stairway, but the basket was empty.

There was another basket sitting nearby, and she looked at it, only to find that it was the container her mother used to carry cut flowers from the garden. The blue delphiniums were still waiting to be put in vases. Allison was turning away to go up the staircase when she noticed something else among the flowers, barely noticeable, because it was half concealed. Had her mother forgotten it was there? Allison removed a soiled, worn leather pouch with drawstrings. At one time it must have contained fragrant tobacco, but it was empty now. The initials K.G. were barely clear, faded from finger use. *It must belong to the gardener,* she thought, and tossed it back in with the flowers.

She heard the carpenters back at work as she went up the stairs to her room to collect her handbag. She saw Zalika coming down the hall from one of the rooms.

"Zalika, did Dahib return my mail from the gazebo?"

"Dahib not here today. Death in family."

She stopped. "He's not here?"

"No, Miss Allison."

Allison told her about her mail, and sent her to ask the other servants whether they had gathered it up and returned it to the house.

Zalika returned some ten minutes later. "None of servants have yet been to gazebo to clear table of the luncheon dishes, Miss Allison. So sorry. You sure you not leave, maybe on bench? I will send again to see."

She thanked her and went into her bedroom, but thought back to the figure she had seen for that brief moment. It couldn't have been Dahib. The white tunic had merely convinced her that it was a servant. It might have been anyone, but who would have wanted her mail? She thought again about the letter from Gamal al-Sayyid...it had contained nothing important. Or had it?

In any case, the incident increased her desire to meet with Mr. Sayyid that afternoon and find out what he wanted.

Of course, the greatest likelihood was that when she

returned from her appointment later that afternoon she'd find her mail in the basket on the hall table.

Allison snatched her handbag from her bureau drawer, caught up her hat, and came back down the stairs to the hall.

Zalika waited with a broad smile. "I came down, and mail is here, Miss Allison. Servant must have brought it a minute ago."

"Oh, grand, Zalika, thank you."

It was all there, including her letter from Mr. Sayyid. She left the other pile on the hall table, slipped Sayyid's letter into her bag, and—satisfied and relieved—went on her way. As she did, passing the flowers, she absently noticed that the small leather pouch was gone. Then it must have belonged to the servant who returned her mail.

The chauffeur was waiting out front on the wide drive with the motorcar. He opened the door, and Allison slid into the seat.

"Take me to Old Cairo, please. To the Blaine house."

SEVEN

ALLISON WATCHED OUT THE WINDOW as the car drove from the western section of the city and edged into the narrow, crowded streets of Old Cairo, avoiding Egyptian peasants, donkey brigades, pushcarts, and camels as they went. The driver squeezed the horn, producing a cranky wail that sent vendors scattering.

Allison caught a whiff of oddly variant smells: the pungent odor of animal urine on sunbaked ancient stone battled with the enticing fragrance of bread still warm from the ovens. The tumult of noise droned in her ears like a nest of busy hornets. It was nerve-racking, yet it held a familiar feel, a sense of home, for Allison had heard such sounds all her life.

Tall, narrow houses with Moslem latticework and domed roofs shadowed the streets. Large, elaborate doors decorated with carvings were barred to keep people out; a glimpse of white robes and immobile faces showed from time to time in the shadows.

It had always been a curiosity to Allison that the Blaines would have a house in this section rather than in the British sector, since neither Sarah nor the major general had Egyptian friends.

At last the motorcar turned off the street and down a narrow lane, away from the shops. On either side were closely spaced houses of stucco and wrought-iron latticework. At the very end, the Blaine house stood back from the street. The surrounding yard was overgrown with stunted bushes, tangled briars, and a fig tree. Everything was just as she remembered it—except in decided disrepair. The spring growth in the garden shrubs emphasized the look of abandonment. Allison's somber mood seemed a perfect fit for the depressing atmosphere.

If only things hadn't turned out so bleakly. But it would be foolish for her to continue wishing for "if onlys." The days marched forward, building upon the unchangeable past, unconcerned with how matters had turned out.

As the driver maneuvered the vehicle up the tree-lined parkway, the tires crunched over dead leaves, neglected since fall. When the sound of the engine ceased, Allison got out and glanced up toward the tall, blue-roofed house. A strange, oppressive silence settled over the afternoon. She looked up at the bedroom where she had stayed. The curtains were drawn shut, just as she had left them. So why did she have the odd sensation that someone was inside watching her. She glanced at the driver. He had walked some feet away and his back was toward her.

She straightened her shoulders. Of course someone was inside. No doubt the museum curator, Mr. Sayyid, had heard the motorcar approaching and was coming out to meet her.

If only that fact would still her uneasy fluttering of nerves and erase the sense that whoever was watching her was not doing so with any sort of good intent.

She deliberately scoffed at her paranoia. There was nothing unusual about Sayyid's letter, nor was there anything odd about the man himself. Yes, her mother did find his mannerisms a little strange. Still, he was just a museum curator. Nothing more. Certainly nothing to cause this dread she felt.

Allison shook her head impatiently. Undoubtedly she felt uneasy because life for the past few weeks had been almost free of the memories of murder and espionage. Now, returning to this house, those awful memories were rekindled. While working at Zeitoun in the wonderful company of Oswald and Biddy Chambers, Allison had felt free of the nightmares of the past. Yet as soon she'd returned to Cairo, the memories had reappeared to haunt her. She had tried to push them from her while speaking with her mother at luncheon, but her suspicions that someone was hiding in the delphiniums and her unease over her mail being moved were evidence enough that fear and uncertainties lurked in the shadows of her mind.

"I don't believe in ghosts." She set her jaw defiantly. "It's only natural to feel strange about returning here, where a friend was murdered. I simply will not allow my imagination to run away with me."

Clenching her teeth, she walked up the gravel path. What if Sayyid wasn't here yet? How would she get inside? There were no other vehicles in the drive. Perhaps he had walked? But what of the person interested in buying the property? Surely they would have come by motorcar…the museum was some distance away. Perhaps it was parked in back. At any rate, she wasn't going to sit on the steps. There had to be a door or window open somewhere.

She approached the house and saw that the front door stood ajar. So, Sayyid *was* here. Either that or he had hired someone to come and air out the house for the prospective buyer.

Allison pushed the door open wider and stepped over the threshold into the musty hall. As she gazed about, a chill raced over her skin. Memories came rushing at her like imprisoned wraiths, anxious to pounce on the first human to enter their domain. The sights…the smells…all played havoc with her courage. She almost expected to hear Sarah's voice ringing out: "Is that you, Allison, dear?"

Her throat tightened. She missed Sarah more than she had thought she would. The woman had been her mother's friend, but since the archaeological club meetings at Aleppo back in 1914, Sarah had become Allison's friend as well. Allison felt a wave of anger over the evil deed performed by either Sir Edgar or Gilbert! How could Beth continue to pine away for Gilbert, as spoiled and immature as he was? And when he was guilty of such a heinous crime? For the first time she felt impatience toward her sister, who seemed more worried about Gilbert than she did about those who'd been ruthlessly murdered! Well, Beth would just have to forget the handsome but empty-hearted Gilly and get on with her life! With her focus on such a creature, it was little wonder Beth was becoming morbid—or that it was affecting her mind.

As it's affecting yours? The wry question whispered from within her. *Making you think people are watching you...people who wish you ill...?*

Stop it! Allison chided herself. *This way of thinking isn't helping anyone.* She pushed her emotions away and walked briskly into the square hall, her heels clicking noisily on the floor. If there *were* any ghosts, she'd disturb them instead of the other way around!

Maybe she should have brought Beth with her. Allison smiled grimly. Surely being here would remind her sister what Gilly had done and show her how foolish she was being in continuing to give the scoundrel her unflagging support.

On the heels of that thought, her conscience smote her. The image of how Oswald or Biddy Chambers would behave toward Beth rose in her mind, and she sighed. The Lord didn't want her to be harsh and critical, she knew that. And if Beth wasn't strong emotionally, she needed Allison's support, not her censure.

She wrapped her arms around herself and glanced about. The house was as she remembered it. Indeed, as far as she could see at first glance, nothing had been removed. The rooms were comfortably but not expensively furnished; large but too silent, and too dark with plants that grew too close to the windows—most of which were dying from lack of water. A drawing room and a smaller dining room looked out on a large garden that lay at the back of the house and that sported more overgrown shrubs and trees near a high stone wall.

Allison tensed. She just couldn't shake the feeling that shadows were coming out from the stillness to watch her. She considered calling out for Mr. Sayyid, but the oppressive silence restrained her.

She walked forward and looked up the staircase leading from the wide hall to a narrow landing. This landing ran around three sides of the stairwell and gave access to two bedrooms, which were separated by an office.

Clamping her jaw, she began climbing the stairs. From the sounds of the branches against the house, the spring afternoon had turned windy. The old house, with wooden lattice shutters and creaking roof timbers, commenced a morbid chorus of its own, as though mourning the death of its mistress.

Allison drew in a quick breath, then rushed up the rest of the stairway to the top landing. Major General Rex Blaine's office door confronted her. She experienced a small revulsion remembering the man, a traitor, then looked toward Sarah's bedroom. That door, too, was closed, the crack beneath as black as ink; the inside drapes apparently were drawn tightly. Allison frowned. Why hadn't Mr. Sayyid sent someone to open all the windows to rid the house of its stale atmosphere? She couldn't imagine anyone wanting to buy the house with the murder trial still in progress! Perhaps there was someone who would find the idea…interesting.

Allison's gaze fixed on the closed door leading to the bedroom where she had stayed during her visit here. Squaring her shoulders, she started forward. While she was waiting for Mr. Sayyid she could gather her things together, as well as Marra's things, which should be on the other side of the house. She could most likely have them ready and waiting in the downstairs hall by the time the curator arrived with his prospective buyer.

Abruptly, she stopped, the back of her neck tightening…a creak sounded from below, but not from the wind this time. Footsteps! Someone was walking carefully, as though not wishing to be heard. Allison listened and she was almost certain the sounds came from below, somewhere in the dining room.

She turned in a sudden panic, fleeing back down the stairs and racing for the front door. She had her hand on the door handle before she got a grip on herself. She paused, breathing heavily. *You're behaving like a scared rabbit!* she scolded herself. *Do you want the driver to see you like this?*

Yes, her driver…sitting outside in the front yard, perfectly calm and trustworthy. The man had worked for her mother for several years. Allison was sure she could trust him. All she'd have to do was scream and he'd come running.

She drew in a settling breath and did as her mother often suggested: she counted to ten. Then, with a forced calm, she turned to call out: "Hello? Who's there? Anyone? Mr. Sayyid?"

A sudden thought hit her. What if the letter had not even been from Gamal al-Sayyid? What if someone else had sent it—someone who thought she might know something? No. Her fears were running away with her yet again. What was there to know? The murderers had been arrested and were about to be convicted. There was no more mystery. Only some

112

trunks to collect and a brief meeting with Sayyid when he arrived with his buyer.

The creaks and groans were only from the wind. She entered the familiar dining room and saw branches scraping against the windowpanes. On her left was the small anteroom that led to the steps up to the room Marra had occupied.

She heard Sarah's old grandfather clock ticking in the corner of the dining room, and her steps kept time as she walked softly to the window and peered out into Sarah's rose garden.

The rosebushes meandered in profusion, while yellow and crimson blooms were dropping petals onto the court. Beside the pond was Rex Blaine's sundial, reflecting the hot, bright sun. Allison could see, as clearly as if it had happened yesterday, the day she and Bret had discovered that the sundial disc was removable. Inside they'd found the golden statue of Nefertari, but that wasn't all...there also was a map...leading, or so Bret thought, to a royal treasure tomb, perhaps of King Tutankhamen.

The map, where was it now?...with Bret in India? Or had he turned it over to the intelligence department?

Allison looked toward the courtyard bench and blinked, startled. Someone was seated there! So she hadn't imagined those footsteps walking softly through the dining room. She left the windows and walked swiftly toward the dining room back door, down the walkway under the wisteria trellis, and around the side of the house toward the rose garden. She paused, staring at the tall, slender brunette seated on the bench. The wind tossed the girl's hair and skirts, and her face was still, as though she were locked in a trance. Dried rose petals scuttled about her feet. Her hands were clasped in her lap, her fingers tightly intertwined. Allison walked up quietly and stopped beside the bench.

"What are you doing here, Beth? Why aren't you at Ezbekiah Gardens like you told Mum? Is Hedda here with you?" She glanced about doubtfully.

"No," came her sister's dull voice. "I don't care anything about her birthday dinner, and her company is too trying."

"Then why did you tell Mum you were going?" Beth kept staring at the oleander bushes. "Because I had to think. I had to be alone. Here. Where it all happened."

Her seventeen-year-old sister lifted intense brown eyes to look at Allison. "I could ask you the same question. What are *you* doing here?"

"It's no secret." Allison sat down beside her, scooping up a handful of rose petals from the stone courtyard. "I received a letter from the museum curator, Mr. Sayyid, asking me to come collect our trunks. I've the motorcar out front. But you didn't tell Mum the truth."

Beth shrugged. If she were troubled by her conscience, it didn't show on her face. "It was just an excuse to get away without her finding out," she admitted. "I knew she wouldn't want me to come here, especially alone. She'd start asking me all kinds of questions about my *morbid* state. I'm not morbid at all. I'm just certain there's more to the murders than the Cairo authorities will admit."

Listening to her sister now, Allison tended to agree that Beth's emotional state wasn't quite as pathetic as she'd been told. "So you lied to her. Do you think that's appropriate? Seems to me you've been doing quite a bit of that recently."

"I told you, I *had* to come. I knew she wouldn't understand. No one does."

For a moment Allison wondered if Sayyid might have asked Beth to show up as well. "What is it Mum wouldn't understand? Were you asked to meet someone here?"

"Meet someone?" Beth shot a cautious glance toward the sundial. "No. Who would ask?"

"There's nothing inside it now. Did you think you might find something else?"

Beth's hands formed sudden fists. "Not in the sundial. Maybe not even in the house. I was just thinking about the possibilities, and especially about that awful night. Oh, Allison!" her eyes were imploring. "Gilly planned to steal the Nefertari, but he *didn't* murder Sarah Blaine."

Allison swallowed back a rise of impatience. She wanted to make Beth see the truth, but she couldn't force it. "We've been over that horrid night a dozen times since it happened. There's nothing left to discover. Cousin Gilbert confessed. Have you forgotten? You were with me in General Blaine's office when he did."

Beth gave her a disdainful look. "I remember what he said. Do you think I'm a ninny? You had those ghastly tobacco tins in hand—" she wrinkled her nose—"the ones with the cobra heads, and we were sitting in the chair thinking Nefertari was hidden inside one of them. Gilly came up behind us and scared us half out of our wits. He came out of hiding when he thought we had found the statue, but it wasn't there." She shook her head slowly. "That's what bothers me. Wouldn't he have known where the statue was if he murdered Professor Jemal and Sarah for the purpose of finding out?"

"Maybe they refused to tell him it was in the sundial."

"Not the way Sarah died…"

Allison tensed. "What do you mean?"

But Beth only looked toward the sundial again as though the answer were still concealed there. Allison, too, found herself staring. A shadow from a flock of birds passed over and the sundial face momentarily flickered.

"Nefertari was hidden inside there all the time," Beth said in a low voice, "hidden in a vault that odious General Blaine had built. It was like him, wasn't it? He thought himself so clever and amusing—how he would laugh if he knew how many people died trying to discover his little secret."

Allison wanted to forget Rex Blaine. She looked at her sister sharply. By the inflection in Beth's voice, she could almost think Beth had wanted Gilbert to locate the treasure. That was absurd. Yet, there had been a trace of something like resentment in her tone just now over Rex's clever concealment.

"Beth," she whispered in sudden rush, "did you know about Nefertari before Sarah was killed? Before Bret discovered what it was that everyone was looking for?"

Beth refused to meet her eyes.

Allison's nerves tightened. "Gilbert told you he was looking for it?"

Beth's brown eyes grew defiant, then unexpectedly wavered, and two bright stains warmed her cheeks. She brushed away a strand of loose hair from her face. "Yes, he told me," came her quiet admittance. "But I had nothing to do with carrying it out."

"Beth!" Allison was horrified. "If the authorities knew—"

"Well, they don't," her sister grumbled. She looked at Allison quickly, suddenly frightened. "And you wouldn't mention it to the new inspector would you?"

Allison's breath escaped. How long had Beth known about Gilbert's plans? And if she had gone to either her or Bret earlier with what she knew, could things have turned out differently? At least for Sarah? The possibility was too unpleasant for Allison to dwell upon. She stared dismally at the sundial.

"You should have told me."

"I know," Beth whispered, wringing her hands in her lap.

"I'll confess something else to you. Remember how disappointed I behaved when Gilly and I arrived?"

"About not being able to spend Christmas at Helga's mansion?"

"Yes. Well, it was planned to divert Sarah. So she wouldn't be suspicious of Gilly. It was his idea. He said they'd expect such behavior from me—not very flattering, but probably true." She sighed. "And it worked, too. Just like he said. I carried on and convinced everyone."

Allison stared at her, disappointment cutting into her heart.

"Oh, please, don't look at me like that. I had nothing to do with the murders. Do you think I actually knew someone would kill poor Sarah? Or even the mummy digger? I didn't even know Jemal. And Gilly was only interested in hunting for treasure. I—I thought it was fun. I didn't realize how serious he was about finding it until the night Helga came with that collection of artifacts from the museum. Then I became afraid, but it was too late. When I went to meet him in the garden, I was going to tell him it had gone far enough—but I never met him. And then everything went wrong and Mum was hit, and Sarah was killed, and Jemal—it was all dreadful! Oh, please don't tell Mum, *please*? She'd be so disappointed in me. And goodness knows she already is. And I don't know what Father would do to me! I've disappointed everyone," she said gloomily. "I'm nothing like you, and they won't let me forget it."

"Feeling sorry for yourself won't help anything. Mum and Daddy don't want a second Allison, they want you, Beth. But they want you to develop the kind character that God intends for you to have, and you seem to deliberately go the opposite direction, as though you want to hurt them."

"I don't." Beth's voice was low, her tone almost raw. "At least, I don't think I do. I'm confused. Sometimes I don't know *what* I want." She looked at Allison and her eyes moistened. "But there's one thing I *do* know: I want Gilly vindicated. I want the real murderer to be found."

"The real murderer?"

"I'm telling you, Allison, Gilly didn't murder Sarah Blaine. Someone else did." Beth glanced about as though she expected the murderer's arrival with the gust of wind.

"Don't be silly, Beth. There isn't anyone else. And you're giving me the creeps. Tell me about Gilbert. What did he tell you about treasure hunting?"

"We were going to find it before anyone else. Like I said, it was sort of an adventure. Then he was going to bring it to some man that he said Sir Edgar wanted to meet. A man who would pay a lot for it."

"Did he say who that was?"

"No, I don't think Gilly ever knew. When I asked him, he said that not even his father was certain. But somehow they thought they could contact him, or knew someone who could." She frowned, looking confused again.

"Go on," Allison urged, her heart thumping. "Who was that?"

"I can only guess, since Gilly never said, but sometimes I sort of thought, well—that it might be Sarah Blaine."

"Sarah? Impossible!" Allison's denial sounded too emphatic, even to her own ears. Still, she just couldn't believe such a thing of her friend. Still, what if Sarah *had* known? She, like her husband and like Jemal, had been silenced, unless...Allison bit her lip. Unless Sarah told someone else? If there was someone else involved, someone who knew more than Rex, Jemal, or Sarah, did he also know about the map?

Beth's words droned on, and Allison stirred, realizing her hands were cold and clammy. She glanced down at the lump of damp rose petals she'd been squeezing tightly in her palm.

"I know," Beth whispered, her eyes widening. "I—I was wrong to do what I did. If I could go back I wouldn't help Gilly. But I don't think he murdered Sarah, and something ought to be done before—he hangs. There, I said the awful word that's been sticking in my throat like a fish bone for months. *Hanged.*" And tears suddenly splashed down her cheeks.

Allison threw her arms about her sister and held her, but no words of comfort would come.

"We weren't going to hurt anyone," Beth sobbed. "I swear we weren't. Someone else did it." She reached over and shook Allison's arm. "And the horrid thing is, I don't think he's been caught. I don't think it was Sir Edgar, either."

Allison's skin tingled as a dreadful silence descended. The oleander bush stirred as the wind crooned uneasily.

Allison shook off the horror. "There was Sarah, the Egyptian maid, Neith, and Jemal. And Gilbert admitted his guilt to us in Rex's office."

"But I know he didn't kill Sarah. Gilly was waiting for you in the general's office to come and locate Nefertari. Don't you see, Allison?"

"No." Allison suddenly felt very tired. "I don't. I think you're twisting things a bit to defend Gilbert and I see no justification for it. We know he's guilty of crimes."

"Yes, but there is another reason, one beyond Gilly—" and Beth's wide frightened eyes looked about. "There could still be a murderer loose. Someone worse than Gilbert or Sir Edgar. Someone even Colonel Holden doesn't know about. It's enough to keep me awake. Because—because I was working with Gilly, and the real murderer may think I know something. And I don't."

By now Allison was feeling genuinely frightened. "Stop it, Beth! Pull yourself together. You're imagining too much. And you should never have come here. Sarah's death didn't happen the way you're thinking."

"Why not?" she challenged. "No one knows for certain! The authorities are only blaming Gilbert because Anwar committed suicide in jail and they have no one else. Allison? Don't you think it strange that Anwar would hang himself in his cell like that?"

Beth's suspicions were more troubling than anything Allison had thought of until now. A murderer that even Bret didn't know about? Was it possible? "Yes," she murmured, "it's strange. But what I wonder is not that he would commit suicide, but *how* he could have accomplished it? For one thing, how did he get rope to do it? Why wasn't he being carefully watched when they knew how important he was to the trial?"

Beth's eyes blazed. "He was silenced. Don't you see?"

Allison wouldn't accept any more. "I don't see why that should be."

"You know what I think?" Beth leaned toward her, a flush on her cheeks. "I think whoever killed Sarah Blaine had Anwar eliminated because he was the one man left who knew who the dealer was. Anwar knew—when Sir Edgar and Gilly didn't—because he learned it from his father, Jemal. And it's frightening because it shows someone has power enough to accomplish Anwar's removal—even inside the prison."

Chilled, though not because of the wind, Allison folded her arms tightly together and stared at the ground below the oleander bushes…the very spot where she'd discovered Anwar's father, Jemal—dead. Yes, if anyone had known what was going on, it was Anwar. And, like the rest of those involved from the days at Aleppo, he was dead. They all were dead…all except her cousin Neal.

"If it wasn't Gilbert—then it might have been Sir Edgar," Allison said after a long pause.

Beth shook her head. "You know he loves Gilly too much to allow his son to hang for something he did. Why are you deliberately refusing to consider what I'm saying, Allison?"

Allison looked at her, surprised. Was she? "So far, all your suspicions are just that. And until I came here, I had a lovely holiday in mind for Luxor. I don't want it spoiled. As for Edgar, why should he confess even if Gilbert is his son? He knows Gilbert will hang for murdering Jemal, anyway, so he might as well do double duty and hang for Sarah as well."

Beth stubbornly shook her head. "I don't understand why you can't see it. It's so obvious."

"Then suppose you explain what it is that's so obvious that everyone, including Bret, has missed it. Everyone, that is, except you."

Beth glared. "Well, if you're going to make fun of me—"

"I'm not, believe me. I'm surprised you thought up all this, really. It's quite good. What Mum took for emotional doldrums over the loss of Gilly was actually some very original thought on your part. I'm sorry, but you can see why I don't want to believe it. But, please, go on."

Beth smirked and stood. She began to pace, her eyes narrowing. "There are two things that convince me someone else killed Sarah Blaine."

"Lower your voice. Who knows who may be wandering about, like the gardener for instance."

Beth didn't appear to hear. "First of all, let's get back to Gilly. It's believed he came into the garden around the same time I left the house to meet him, remember?"

Allison remembered perfectly. "And instead of meeting you as planned, he came upon Jemal and Sarah."

"Yes, near to where we are now. It's assumed they were discussing—or arguing—about the Egyptian treasure. If Gilly killed them both—what was accomplished? He still didn't know where General Blaine had hidden Nefertari. Gilly thought it was in the tobacco tin with the cobra handle."

"Because they didn't tell him where it was."

"So he killed Jemal, then turned and killed Sarah? That doesn't make sense, Allison. Why didn't Sarah scream and run?"

She had wondered that, too.

"Because Jemal and Sarah were not together when Gilly approached." Beth sounded almost triumphant. "I think Jemal was alone when Gilly came. And that Sarah Blaine met someone else." Beth's eyes met Allison's. "The person who killed her."

"Go on. You said there were two reasons. What's the second one?"

Beth turned her dark head and looked up toward the house. Allison uneasily followed her stare to Marra's room. The curtains were still.

"There's something you don't know. Something about Sarah's death."

Allison sat stiffly. "Yes?"

"Something that convinces me more than anything else that Gilly couldn't have done it."

What did Beth actually know about Sarah's death? Bret hadn't actually given Allison any details, but then she hadn't really wanted him to, and he'd known it.

Beth looked at her gravely. "I know Gilly better than anyone else in the family. Better than the authorities who want to see him convicted. I happen to know Gilly isn't brutal. He wouldn't have bruised and battered Sarah that way. He would have—well, it's very distasteful to say, but he would have hit her over the head then thrown her in the pond to drown. But Sarah *didn't* drown. She was dead before she was put in the pond."

Allison stared up at her. It was a moment before she could speak. "What did you say?" she finally managed.

"Sarah Blaine was dead before she was put in that pond—" Beth paled as she gestured across the court. "She was struck many times, with brutal force. As though someone had kept hitting her, trying to force her to tell something that she refused. Gilly—Gilly just wouldn't have done that."

Stunned, sickened, Allison gasped. "No one told me this."

Beth grimaced. "I suppose Bret didn't want you to know. You were friends with her and all. The papers said it was dreadful. You cared about Sarah, and he probably wanted to keep the ugly details from you. But it was all in the papers. That's how I learned about it. I've been keeping up with the trial since it began."

It was true. Allison hadn't wanted to read the details of her friend's death and so had avoided reading the paper or asking questions. She had thought she already knew what it was about. And Bret had told her—

"It *was* someone else. Someone who thinks they've gotten away with it."

Allison stood. "But Bret would have thought of that, too. He'd have seen the discrepancies. He would know it wasn't Gilbert."

Beth's eyes were shadowed. "Maybe he does know."

Allison looked at her sharply. "What do you mean by that?"

123

Beth merely shrugged and sat down again, her head in her hands.

"Look, Beth, what you say is possible. I'll admit Sarah's manner of death doesn't sound like something Gilbert could have done. But he *did* kill once, and he may have snapped by the time he found Sarah. He may have grown desperate when she wouldn't talk, and one thing led to another. That's the way sin is; one small disobedience leads to yet another and another. Ultimately, if it isn't dealt with, it brings death. But even if Gilly didn't kill her, he's guilty, and so is Sir Edgar. I refuse to make myself ill thinking about the horrid details or the upcoming verdict, and neither will you. Mum and I won't allow it. We're leaving Cairo for Luxor, and you're coming with us."

Beth lifted her head quickly, eyes wide. "Leaving Cairo?"

Allison hadn't intended to bring the subject up so bluntly, but Beth's ideas had affected her more than she wanted to admit. If Gilbert hadn't committed the murder, then who? If only she could talk all this out with Bret! But he didn't appear to care to write her from Jerusalem, though maybe he couldn't since his presence there was a secret.

Someone else…was it possible?

Allison closed her eyes for a moment, fighting the emotions that threatened to overwhelm her. She wouldn't dare admit it to Beth, but she wondered if there *may* have been someone else…someone everyone had overlooked—

"Luxor?" Beth repeated when Allison remained silent. "Whatever for? I'm not interested in archaeology, and neither is Mum. That's *your* hobby."

"There's lots to do in the Valley of the Kings besides seeing tombs and attending lectures. Helga has offered the use of her houseboat for a few weeks. You and Mum, and maybe even Father can stay there. It's cool and pleasant on the Nile, and a good rest will do us all wonders. Oh, do come, Beth, please. Mum and I both want you with us."

Beth frowned. "You want me with you? Really?"

"Why—of course." Why in the world would Beth question the idea?

Beth sighed. "I doubt I have any say in the matter anyway. It's *dreadful* being seventeen."

Allison smiled. "Think so? Well, wait until you reach *my* age. You'll wish you were seventeen again."

"How old we sound," Beth groaned. "Old and beaten—both of us losing the men we wanted. But at least yours was a knight in shining armor, and mine—mine—" Her voice cracked and her eyes filled with tears as she looked at her sister.

"Don't cry," Allison whispered, taking her arms. "I've learned that we've got to trust God and keep walking into the future."

"I'm not as strong as you are." Beth's voice was raspy, and she sniffed back tears. "I don't have your kind of faith."

Allison thought of Oswald and Biddy Chambers, and wondered what kind of faith she really had...certainly not their kind, not the kind that could turn bitter waters sweet.

"But I won't go to Luxor until after the trial," Beth insisted.

"You're leaving in a few days. In fact, I'm going down first to get Helga's houseboat ready. Can't you try to make it? For Mum's sake, let's make a fun holiday out of this time, the three of us together. It won't be long before I'll be leaving for the Palestine front. We've got to think of her, too, you know, not just ourselves. She's not as well as she pretends. And she's worrying herself to a frazzle over Father."

"I suppose I should try. I don't mean to hurt Mum. I love her dearly."

"I know you do. Well then, what do you say? Will you cooperate?"

Beth considered, then tried to smile, but fear still reflected in her eyes. "All right. But will you at least mention what I've told you to Colonel Holden when you see him?"

Allison couldn't bring herself to admit she didn't know when she would see Bret again, but she nodded. "Yes, I'll talk to him. Just as soon as I see him next."

Beth seemed satisfied. "I'm glad I could talk to you. I wanted to talk to someone for weeks but couldn't bring myself to do it." She looked about the windy garden. "You know, I came here to just sit and think. Trying to remember anything that might bring some forgotten bit of information to mind about anything I might have seen or heard. I thought if I was actually here, where it happened—I might remember some incident, even a word." She sighed. "Nothing unusual comes to mind except what I've told you."

Allison was anxious to get away. "I doubt if there's anything new either of us could remember. But maybe a change of scenery at Luxor will help. But Beth, I wouldn't expect too much. If there was someone else who murdered Sarah, it was probably Anwar. Maybe that's why he committed suicide. He may have had a friend among the guards who felt sorry enough for him to make it possible."

Beth looked beaten, or perhaps she was merely exhausted. "Maybe you're right. I saw Anwar only once and I didn't like him at all. I could see him being brutal to get his way."

"Yes, and remember, he was capable of killing a woman— an old woman at that, Neith."

"I'd forgotten that. Well, if he did kill Sarah, we'll never know, will we?"

Allison was silent a moment too long. "No, we'll never know."

"What do you think will happen to Sir Edgar? I read in the paper this morning that some people think Edgar will get a few years in prison for smuggling, then be released—but Gilly—"

Allison squeezed her arm. "I don't know. But I promise you I'll speak to Bret about what you've told me when I see him next. And to Father when he returns. And, I hear there's a new chief inspector who took Sir Edgar's place. A Julian Mortimer. Mum's already met him. I'll ask him about Sarah as well."

"Do you think it's wise? I mean, Bret is one thing, and Daddy, too, but what do we know of Julian Mortimer?"

"He's the new chief inspector."

"So was Sir Edgar."

Allison shook her head. "That couldn't happen again. Two crooked inspectors?"

Beth shrugged. "Someone killed Sarah. And until the person's face comes out of the fog, everyone's a suspect."

Allison turned and looked toward the bleak house. She desperately needed a change of subject. "I'm expecting Mr. Sayyid from the museum. He should have been here by now. You might as well wait for me. Did you come by rented *calishe?*" Beth nodded. "Fine. Then we'll drive home together. But Beth, you'll need to admit to Mum where you've been. It's not right to lie to her, no matter how justified you may think your reasons."

Beth nodded. "I know. Maybe she'll forgive me." She smiled ruefully. "Again."

Allison's lips tucked into a smile. "I know she will. Come along. Let's go."

As they came back up the flagstone walk toward the house, Allison cast a last look toward the oleander bushes. "I never did care for this garden. It's always windy and, well, just a trifle spooky, if you know what I mean."

Beth quickened her steps, glancing back with her dark brows in a worried crease.

EIGHT

ALLISON ENTERED THE HOUSE THROUGH the dining room. The door into the drawing room was inched open and a rustling sound escaped. Her heart fluttered, hoping against hope that it was Mr. Sayyid waiting for her, and not something...well, horrible.

She shook her head at herself. All the talk with Beth in the garden had obviously rekindled her ridiculous fears. She shivered. At least, she hoped they were ridiculous.

She stepped into the drawing room and a round man of less than five feet tall with a moon face pitted by smallpox scars bustled toward her. "Ah? Won't you take a seat? Mr. Sayyid will be with you in one moment. He's with another client."

Allison smiled, recognizing Mr. Rahotep, Sayyid's assistant. She glanced across the room to see Sayyid seated, his back toward her, busily shuffling papers, which he then pushed across the polished walnut table to the client. The woman lifted her pince-nez and began to read.

Allison took several seconds to react—it was Lady Edith Walsh, the widowed mother of Miss Cynthia Walsh. Evidently the young and sophisticated Cynthia was not with her mother, unless she was somewhere else in the house. Allison stared at Mrs. Walsh, certain she must be imagining what she saw. Lady Walsh was interested in buying the Blaine house? Somehow it was all out of kilter. This was not the sort of house to enchant either Cynthia or her silver-haired mother.

Mr. Rahotep must have mistook her reaction for disappointment. The round little man in the drab brown robe began to make apologies. "Mr. Sayyid never expected the property to sell so quickly. It proves one must never underestimate the buying public. You are not the only client to be disappointed I'm afraid."

"There were others interested in buying?"

"Oh, my yes. They will be disappointed, too. We never thought there would be such avid interest in this property. Not that the museum deals much in such matters," he hastened. "It must be the prime location. So many Europeans find a house in the midst of Old Cairo culturally enriching."

Allison, born and raised in Egypt and acquainted with both the British and Egyptian mind-set, knew the opposite to be true. While there were always some who found a foreign culture stimulating, most of the British in Egypt lived separate from the natives. There were some rare private dinners where English and Egyptians mingled as friends, but it was primarily politics that brought them together, often in grand and regal garb. The British in Egypt were typical of Queen Victoria's dutiful subjects, and there was always a so-called "Little England" inside every colony where the Union Jack flew.

She recalled at least two occasions when Sarah had told Rex she wanted to move to the British sector. "Nonsense, dear Sarah," he had said jovially. "Think of the rich culture to which we are subject here. And since we are not inclined to give lavish entertainments like the baroness, we don't need to put on the English Dog to influence the snobs—or should I say the German Dogs?"

Shaking off the memory, Allison watched Lady Walsh, who most certainly did put on lavish entertainments, continue to scan the papers. The Blaine house seemed totally unsuitable for such socially-minded bluebloods as the Walshes, and she couldn't help wondering whatever had possessed the woman.

If that weren't enough to seize her curiosity, Sayyid's assistant's assertion that there were a number of others interested in buying the house still nudged at her. Who were they? British or Egyptian?

Allison looked down at the little man again. "Are you saying that Lady Walsh is buying Sarah's—I mean, Mrs. Blaine's house?"

He smiled apologetically. "The house was just what Lady Walsh was looking for. She's spent the last two months searching for the right domicile and was especially taken with this structure."

"Wasn't the decision to accept Lady Walsh's offer rather hasty? From what Mr. Sayyid told me, the house just became available today."

"It is available today, yes, but we have known for some time Mrs. Blaine would leave us the estate. Word reached us that there were interested parties, and we were presented several early bids. I assume," he apologized, "you were not able to participate?"

"I did not bid. Did many English?"

"Oh, yes. An impressive list. Mr. Sayyid did not know that another assistant, Mr. Kadir, had escorted the highest bidder on a tour of the premises early this morning. Lady Walsh is known for making up her mind suddenly." His brown eyes offered sympathy. "Mr. Sayyid will be saddened by your disappointment, er—Mrs.?—" and he lifted a paper from the mound he held and checked the list of names.

Allison leaned over to look. "Um—I don't see my name on the list...."

"The secretary was quite careful in these matters, but..."

and he obliged her by bringing the ledger closer. "They are not in alphabetical order."

Her eyes swiftly scanned the dozen names, but she did not recognize any of them—until she came near the middle of the list and saw the name of Lady Edith Walsh.

Lady Walsh hadn't noticed her yet. When she completed signing the documents before her, she stood with a business-like expression and somewhat hesitantly accepted the hand Mr. Sayyid held toward her.

Hoping to avoid Mrs. Walsh, Allison excused herself from Mr. Rahotep and walked quickly to the stairway.

Beth waited up in the bedroom Allison had used while Sarah was alive. Her sister was standing in front of the open closet staring at the clothes as Allison came in and quietly shut the door.

"What is it? What are you looking at?"

"My clothes—what are they doing in here? I left them in Marra's room. I stayed with her that night, remember?"

Allison waved a hand. "Oh, it doesn't matter. The authorities must have brought them here. Let's get them down and pack our trunks. I just learned Lady Walsh is the new owner of the house, and I don't want her to know I just pretended to be a losing bidder." She pulled her blue trunk from the walk-in closet into the middle of the room and sat down on the edge of the bed, thinking.

Beth turned, her eyes wide. "Cynthia's mum bought this spooky place? Whyever would she do such a morbid thing? Why, I thought the Walshes had *trunks* of money and a grand house in the city of London. They give lavish parties." She looked about. "Ugh, who'd want to come here, except for on All Hallow's Eve?"

"I don't know why she bought it, but she wasn't the only

one interested. And that interests me a great deal, that so many would consider buying a bleak house where three murders were committed! Because, as you say, neither Lady Walsh nor Cynthia are the type to go in for such things. 'Too ghastly!' is the way Lady Walsh put it when Bret and I met her at Ezbekiah Gardens."

Beth stood there, saying nothing, staring off into space.

Allison opened her trunk and began tossing her clothing inside, anxious to get her time in this house over with. "Do hurry, Beth. I hear a motorcar leaving now. That must be Lady Walsh." She rushed to the window and, without moving the curtains, peered below into the drive. The black Mercedes was just turning the tree-lined corners of the drive and disappearing toward Cairo. Had Lady Walsh recognized their motorcar and driver? Allison hoped not.

She spotted Mr. Sayyid standing in the drive, looking after the Mercedes, his assistant nearby. A moment later, both men turned and walked back inside the house. Allison turned from the window to Beth.

"I'll need to go down and speak with Mr. Sayyid. Can you finish my packing?"

"All right, but what about Marra's things?"

"I'll get those after I speak to Mr. Sayyid."

"Do hurry, Allison. This place is giving me the shivers."

"I won't be long."

Gamal al-Sayyid was waiting for her in the drawing room. He was a dignified gentleman, whose short silvery beard contrasted with brown skin and sharp, lively eyes as black as syrupy pools. He wore his customary black coat and turban, and a single clear stone at his throat.

"Miss Wescott, my apologies for keeping you waiting. My appointment with Lady Walsh was unexpected. I trust you have found your trunk?"

"Yes, my sister is collecting our belongings now." She tested her curiosity over Lady Walsh. "Congratulations in selling the Blaine property so quickly. The museum will be very pleased."

"So my assistant, Rahotep, must have informed you of our surprising good news. I confess, Lady Walsh's bid took me off guard. Her generous offer will help the museum greatly. I was concerned the house might not sell for months, perhaps years. There is a natural stigma associated with a house where death has recently played a prominent role."

Allison was certain that Lady Walsh's interest in the house was not motivated by generosity toward the museum. Any more than was the interest of the dozen or so people whose names were on Rahotep's list. Allison frowned slightly at the thought of the assistant. Where had he gone so quickly?

"The sale will benefit the Cairo archaeological club as well. The baroness will be delighted, although it may also be a disappointment." He looked at her. "Paul Kruger had shown interest in buying. You've met her son from Tanzania, Miss Wescott?"

Allison felt the man's heavy gaze resting on her. Paul must have spoken with him about the vacant position at the museum.

"I met him briefly on the train. I believe he has intentions of staying on in Egypt."

"So he told you of his wish to assume Professor Pasha's position? That is a matter to be discussed at length with the baroness." A thin smile of apology showed on Sayyid's lips. "But that is not the reason I wished to see you, Miss Wescott. I shall get right to the matter. Won't you sit down?"

As she did so, he walked to the table where Lady Walsh had signed the papers and removed a document from its folder. He felt in his jacket pocket, murmuring something about having misplaced his pince-nez some weeks ago. Bringing the paper with him, he came to sit opposite Allison in a wing-backed leather chair. He crossed one slim leg over a knee and swung his polished black leather shoe, looking at her meditatively as he leaned his elbow on the armrest. He rested his chin on his knuckles, all the while drumming the fingers on his left hand.

"The attorney informed me of a small change in Sarah Blaine's will. She has left you an item. Something of little real value, but I am sure it has sentimental meaning."

Yes, it would be like Sarah to leave her something as a token of their friendship and shared interests.

"I haven't collected it yet," he confessed. "I have no idea where she would have kept it. You may look for it before you leave, or I could have it sent to you as the house is cleared for the new buyer."

Allison was mildly curious. "I'll take it with me now. What was it she left?"

"A menagerie of items she collected in her travels with General Blaine." He looked at the sheet, squinting. "She mentions a box of collectibles, one of those rather—er, shall we say *inexpensive* black enameled wooden boxes with an oriental design."

Allison started, giving a quick intake of breath. Sarah's box!

Sayyid looked up at her questioningly. "You know which box it is to which Mrs. Blaine is referring?"

Allison sat quite still under his gaze. "Yes," she managed after a long moment. "Sarah collected small pieces from her travels. She and General Blaine were in India for some years, and in Burma, and maybe Constantinople as well. I don't recall. But Sarah enjoyed collecting small ornaments of pottery and glass from various interesting spots."

135

"Ah, yes…like the shop here in Old Cairo."

Allison carefully retained a blank expression. "Yes, something like that."

"Bric-a-brac, I think, is how the British say it?" and he smiled.

"Yes." She hoped he didn't notice the slight breathlessness in her voice, and she tried to slow her pulse. Sarah had left her the box where Rex had hidden the broken cobra head!

He looked relieved and stood from the chair. "Well, Miss Wescott, I am pleased you know what Mrs. Blaine was making reference to. I had feared trying to locate it might be a great waste of time for the museum workers."

"Then this is all you wished to speak to me about?" She stood as well.

"Indeed. We simply hoped you would know what box she spoke of so it would not be disposed of with the rest of the estate. And we do need to get things sorted and sold as quickly as possible."

"It won't take me long to get our things taken care of—" she began, when he collected his coat as if in a hurry to be away.

"Please, don't feel as if I'm rushing you. Do take your time. My assistant will be here to offer any help should you need it. He'll lock up after you." His wide smile looked strangely ominous in the shadowy drawing room, but Allison was sure it was only her mood. Gamal al-Sayyid was a well-known and respected Egyptologist. She had known him for several years through the club. No matter that she had told her mother at luncheon that familiarity meant little when it came to building trust, she did trust Mr. Sayyid.

He finished gathering his satchel of papers from the table. "I look forward to seeing you again in Luxor," he was saying politely. "You will be attending the club meeting?"

"Yes, and Eleanor and Beth will be joining me as soon as they can."

"Ah yes." He nodded sagely. "It is good they will be away from Cairo for the remainder of the trial. They should find the houseboat a pleasant diversion." He smiled again and walked toward the door. "Good day, Miss Wescott—oh, there is one thing more. I'd nearly forgotten. The auction will be held on Friday night. You will attend?"

The auction had been delayed since before Christmas, so it was good to know it was at last scheduled. "I plan to. I believe Paul Kruger will be there as well. Helga will be in charge I think."

"Ah yes, a brilliant woman. She is sure to raise us a generous amount of revenue. Have you decided what to place in the auction?"

She forced a smile. "Nothing rare, I'm afraid. Just a small item I've had for some time. It came from my cousin when he worked for the British museum at Carchemish."

"It should prove interesting, then. Good day," he said cheerily. "I will see you on Friday night."

"Yes, good day, Mr. Sayyid."

The front doors closed behind him. Allison heard his steps fade as he moved down the walk, toward the drive. A few minutes later the motorcar started and drove away.

Allison became aware again of the too quiet house, of the deepening afternoon shadows that lurked in the corners of the rooms. Memories, like unrelenting phantoms, once more surged toward her. She looked toward the windows, at the light dipping behind the distant trees and leaving the garden and the house in twilight. If she was going to look for the box, she must do it quickly. She looked around. Was it where she and Sarah had left it? In the storage closet near the room Marra had occupied?

A creak sounded outside in the hall and the door opened. "Allison?" came Beth's hushed, nervous voice. "What did the curator want?"

Allison left the drawing room and walked into the dining room. She didn't want to alarm Beth by telling her Sarah left her the box where the cobra head had been found.

"Oh, Sarah left me something of sentimental value. Did you collect our things upstairs?"

"Yes, they're all packed. I dragged the trunk into the hall."

Allison walked through the dining room and the open doorway into the shadowed alcove. She looked up the flight of short hardwood steps to the narrow passageway where Marra's room was. She fought a shiver, remembering...

"I'll collect Marra's bags and get the item Sarah left me. Tell Mum's driver he can carry the trunk to the motorcar. I won't be long."

"All right, but I have to get my hat first. I left it in the bedroom." Beth went back up the stairs, and Allison walked into the anteroom. She paused below the short flight of steps to the other side of the house, then, drawing in a breath, hurried up to the landing. She glanced down the narrow, darkened hall.

No. She wouldn't think about that night when she had found the body of the Egyptian maid, Neith, on the laundry room floor.

Instead, she turned her mind to the list of names. Strange how Mr. Sayyid appeared to want her to think that few people had been interested in buying the property. It almost seemed he had been trying to make an excuse for selling to Lady Walsh.

Allison walked past Marra's room to the storage closet. She remembered the awful hour when she and Sarah had searched here, looking for the illusive Egyptian treasure doll.

She opened the door, and darkness and the smell of moth-balls reached out to engulf her. She removed the lantern from the upper shelf and struck a match. A glow filled the closet and Allison's eyes searched. A moment later she saw it—an ornate black trunk of Far Eastern design. In the lantern light the pink flamingos were in flight above the cherry trees. It was sitting on the floor where she had left it.

"The entire menagerie is worth less than five hundred pounds. Hardly anything worth smuggling. Certainly nothing worth poor Neith's life." Sarah's words echoed in Allison's mind as she pulled the trunk out and stooped to lift the lid.

All the odds and ends appeared to be there: ceramic replicas of mummy dolls, some miniature animal idols, a scarab, a frog, a leopard, and a brass cobra with onyx eyes.

It had been here, among these items, that Sarah had come across the broken cobra head that later was discovered to belong to the garden sundial.

Allison stiffened. Her heart began to pound in her temples. She hadn't mistaken that sound—a footstep, soft and furtive, came from behind her! She heard someone breathing unevenly.

She turned her head and caught just a glimpse of some-thing dark surging up behind her. In a second it swooped over her head like the great, beating wings of a fowl. It was heavy, thick, and scratchy—like a woolen blanket. It twisted about her head and arms like the coils of a python, smothering her.

In a panic, Allison fought wildly to free herself. Her strength must have surprised even her attacker, for she nearly broke loose. Someone was gasping, or was it herself she heard in the struggle? Allison managed to drop to her knees in an attempt to drag her assailant down to the floor. For a moment she thought she might succeed, and the breathing became desper-ate. Allison got an arm free from the blanket and reached to grab the person. As she did, her fingers touched a face—

She froze, startled. No! It couldn't be—!

Something fell in the closet, then a thudding blow landed against her forehead. Pain splintered like sparks throughout her skull. She fell backward into the boxes and lay there, her brain engulfed in white-and-red zigzags.

NINE

>─┤─►─○─◄─┤─◄

ALLISON STIRRED, MOANING SOFTLY. Where was she? Why did her head hurt so badly? She managed to raise herself onto her hands and knees. Her head was throbbing. The air was stale and hot and smothering. She stretched a hand in front of her, touching what felt like books and boxes—

It came rushing back—the horrid ordeal of a few minutes ago, or had it been an hour ago? Someone had struck her, knocking her unconscious!

She pushed herself up from the floor, swayed dizzily, and groped for the doorknob, but the door wouldn't budge. Her attacker had locked her inside. No, wait…there was no lock on the outside of the storage room. Something must have been shoved against the door from the outside. Books? Furniture?

Allison pressed a trembling hand to her forehead. Why hadn't Beth heard the noise? Why hadn't she come looking for her?

Allison struggled, using all the strength she could muster to push. At last the door inched open, letting in a ray of light from the outer hall. She managed to slip through the opening, stepping over books as she went. The hall was empty. The house too silent. Had the assailant gone? Had he hurt Beth?

She reached the stairs down to the anteroom. The space below was empty and foreboding. She heard the clock ticking—and remembered the box! The box Sarah had left her, the one containing the menagerie. Had it been stolen? There was no time to go back and look, nor did she want to. She inched her way down the steep steps, feeling nauseous and dizzy.

"Beth?"

The dining room, too, was empty. Through the window the rose garden stared back at her ominously. How long had she been unconscious? Where was her sister?

In the hallway she saw the trunks were still there, waiting to be carried to the motorcar. She started up the main staircase, looking toward the general's office, but could not bring herself to go up. "Beth?"

The house seemed to mock her with its silence as she climbed the stairs. She entered the bedroom, then stopped.

No one was there. Allison looked around, fighting the panic that threatened to overwhelm her. Had Beth gone out to the motorcar to wait for her? Allison's eyes widened in sudden realization. The driver! She would call for his help.

She moved to look out the window. The motorcar was parked in the drive, and she could see the driver darkly silhouetted in the twilight. Mr. Sayyid's assistant, Rahotep, would also arrive. He should have been here before dark.

She turned around and came back down the stairs, walking weakly past the trunks toward the front door. Why hadn't the driver carried them out to the vehicle?

The front door was ajar, and a gust of wind greeted Allison as she pulled it wide open. A wave of relief rushed into her heart. The driver was sitting behind the wheel, but Beth was nowhere in sight.

She came down the porch steps, thinking her knees would soon give way. "Hello?" she called desperately to the chauffeur. The gravel in the drive crunched beneath the soles of her shoes. She tried to hasten her steps. At least the driver was here and could help her. She came around the front hood of the motorcar, her eyes blurring.

"Something has happened," she told him, bending down to peer through the open side window. "There was—someone in the house who attacked me." She touched trembling fingers to her swollen forehead and felt the wet, sticky blood. "Did Beth come out? Have you seen her?"

He sat, unresponsive, staring at the steering wheel.

"Driver!" She grabbed at his shoulder. "What—" she stopped. She drew her hand away with horror and the lifeless body fell against the door. As it did, his cap fell off and Allison saw blood on the side of his head—lots of it. A look of horror was frozen on his face.

Allison backed away, hands at her mouth. A scream clawed at her throat, but it had tightened into silence. She kept backing away until her heels bumped against the large rocks that lined the curve in the drive. She tumbled to the ground in a heap. Her head throbbing and dizziness assailing her, she lay there in the gravel, too stunned to move, to even think.

Twilight shrank away and night descended.

Vaguely, she looked around. How long had she sat here? One minute, or ten?

A star appeared in the sky above the dark, foreboding house, and a sudden thought assailed Allison. Beth!

Her emotions cracked and a sob escaped her lips. She dropped her head into her hands, feeling the horrid swelling across her forehead. "God, help me—" she prayed for the hundredth time. "I—I don't know what to do. God! Help me—"

A breeze swirled around her, lifting the hem of her skirt. The tall, overgrown shrubs along the drive rustled and brought her gaze in that direction. Cold terror gripped her heart, clawing at her. *She's not in there! She's not dead. Not my little sister. Not Beth!*

Out of the night Beth's words stirred in Allison's memory: "I just thought of something. Allison, I know someone else killed Sarah Blaine!"

The thought was too much to bear. Suppose Beth did know something? And what if that "someone" knew it? Had whoever knocked her unconscious and killed the chauffeur been after Beth? She refused to believe it, because the moment she did, she would begin to scream and keep on screaming until she went mad. *Pull yourself together, Allison,* she seemed to hear Bret saying in the back of her mind. *Where's your courage, your indomitable spirit?*

Yes, yes. I must pull my emotions together. Beth is missing—but must that mean she's dead?

Her wide eyes looked back up at the house with its dark, gaping windows staring back at her. Was Beth in one of those rooms?

Another sob escaped Allison. She knew that not all the courage remaining within her could bring her back inside to search those upstairs rooms for Beth. Though she felt sure the murderer was gone by now, the very thought of going back inside filled her with terror.

She struggled to get back on her feet, then looked toward the motorcar where the driver's body was slouched, leaning against the door. She—she might be able to push him to the passenger's seat and drive back to the Residency herself, but even in her emotional state she thought better of disturbing police evidence. She must start back on foot, but that would mean walking alone through the dark stretch of trees farther down the road. She would need to walk for some distance before coming to the narrow street where there were public buildings and people. Even if it was safe, she knew she would never make it. She was feeling worse by the moment and was dreadfully sick to her stomach. She must have a concussion.

The house appeared to tip and sway.

She must walk—she must force herself—

She stumbled along the drive until she reached the bend and the stretch between the tall trees. The moon was not yet out, and the sky not yet black enough to offer light from the stars. That didn't matter, though, for she couldn't even make them out with her throbbing headache. "'Whenever I am afraid, I will trust in You,'" she encouraged herself, quoting from the psalms, forcing herself onward.

Her feet grew heavy, every step more labored. The blood pounded in her temples.

"'Even the night shall be light about me,'" she quoted. "'The darkness and the light are both alike to You.'"

She came to a large stump on the side of the narrow roadway, which was now lined with dark, secretive shrubs and trees. She knew she could go no farther. She slumped to the earth and rested the side of her head against the rough, dead bark of the stump. Her breathing came in short, uncomfortable gasps. The smell of hot earth and thirsty plants filled her senses. Behind her the house stood silent and watchful. Before her darkness crept in like stalking wolves. "'The Lord is my light and my salvation—the Lord is the strength of my life—'"

Allison drew her knees to her chest and sat there, helpless, her eyes closing against her will as the night descended. Only God knew the fate of her sister, and only God could keep watch over her. And if the morning did not dawn…

The motorcar turned down a narrow, dusty street and twisted and turned for some five minutes until the shops of Old Cairo were left behind in the night. Secretive houses shielded with wrought-iron latticework looked down in stilted silence until the road gave way to a grove of trees lining both sides of the dirt road. Date palms, flame trees, and overgrown banana trees bunched together forming even blacker shadows. The hands on the pocket watch dangling on the dashboard moved ominously to quarter past midnight.

Eleanor Wescott gripped the edge of the front seat. She tried to shut out the fears that tormented her. She stared down the road but could hardly see where they were going. Dense foliage added to the possibility of running into wildlife, and she wished Spencer would slow down.

"You're certain they were both here when you left?" Spencer asked again to the passenger in the back of the car.

"Assuredly, Doctor Howard," came the placating voice of the museum curator, Gamal-al Sayyid. "As I told Lady Wescott earlier, I left the Blaine house around 4:45 this afternoon. Miss Wescott was here, along with her sister, gathering their belongings left from last December."

"And you say the Wescott's chauffeur was there at the time?"

"Oh, certainly. He'd walked toward some trees lining the drive. He looked to be resting in the shade, leaning against a trunk and smoking while waiting to be called to carry the trunks to the car. Neither of Lady Wescott's two daughters were left in the house alone," he insisted nervously, as though fearful of being blamed for negligence. "My assistant, Mr. Rahotep, locked up after them."

"We assume he locked up," came Spencer's corrective voice.

"I feel assured he did, Spencer. Rahotep is diligent, though sometimes on the edgy side, but nevertheless dependable. I trust him to lock up after me most every night at the museum. I'm sure he would take the same precaution at the Blaine house, now that it's been sold."

"To Lady Walsh?"

Eleanor glanced toward Spencer, wondering at the slight ironic suggestion in his tone. For some reason unknown to her, Spencer did not appear to think well of Lady Walsh. That she had bought the Blaine house was surprising to Eleanor, but she hadn't given it much thought with her concerns over Allison and Beth. It was trying having two unmarried daughters of their age, both of whom were so attractive they turned the heads of too many men. Especially Allison. Eleanor's neat brows drew together.

Eleanor had waited until after 10 P.M. before she began making inquiries as to the whereabouts of Allison and Beth. When she learned from Hedda's mother that Beth had not shown up at Ezbekiah Gardens for Hedda's birthday dinner, nor had Allison dropped by, Eleanor's natural concerns as a mother had leaped from worry to real fear. She knew Allison had gone to the Blaine house to meet with Mr. Sayyid and so she had inquired of him at once if her daughter had kept the 4 P.M. appointment. When he told her she had and that Beth was with her, Eleanor felt relieved. But after 10 P.M. there were new and more foreboding reasons to worry. Why hadn't they returned home in time for dinner? Did it take six hours to gather a few trunks?

Of course, Allison and Beth may have decided to drive out to Zeitoun to deliver their nurse friend's trunk.... Eleanor frowned. That hardly seemed like anything Allison would do without stopping by the house first to let her know what they were doing.

Eleanor had then sent word to Spencer, who had been at home reading, telling him what had happened and asking him to come to the Residency. Thankfully, Spencer had come at once, bringing Mr. Sayyid with him since the curator had been the last one to speak with Allison that afternoon. Mr. Sayyid had been quite helpful to Eleanor and suggested that it was most likely her two daughters had gone out on their own for some refreshment, perhaps visiting fellow YMCA workers at the Benha railway station. But while Eleanor believed it was possible, she didn't think it likely since Allison had recently come from Zeitoun.

There was only one way to find out, Spencer suggested in his professional tone. "We'll take a jaunt there to find out. If they are not there, I think it wise, my dear Eleanor, that we notify Julian Mortimer at once."

Now, as Spencer's motorcar sharply took the turn in the road, he continued pummeling Mr. Sayyid with questions. Eleanor felt rather embarrassed about it, as though Mr. Sayyid might think they held him responsible for the actions of her two daughters.

"You say Rahotep remained behind to lock up, but you haven't heard from him," Spencer said flatly.

"I agree it is curious," Sayyid said uneasily. "I should have called at his dwelling near the museum."

"You think it's curious, or something else?"

Eleanor looked across the seat at Spencer. "Really, Spencer, we went through all this earlier at the Residency. You're beginning to sound like Inspector Mortimer."

Spencer looked surprised, then a little sheepish. "Yes, I suppose you're right. No offense, Gamal," he called to the backseat. "We're all a bit edgy tonight after what happened at the Blaine house last year."

"No apology necessary, Spencer. We've known one another too long for that. There is reason to be concerned." He swayed to and fro on the backseat as the motorcar raced along. "But we must not rush to conclusions and upset Lady Wescott further—Spencer! For the sake of Allah, look out—!"

Eleanor saw her, too—a woman on the side of the narrow road, caught in the beams of the headlamps. Horror rose to her throat, choking her, as she recognized Allison. Allison on the road, practically in line with the path of the vehicle! She threw herself toward the steering wheel to turn it, a scream dying in her throat. She was thrown forward into the dashboard as Spencer desperately slammed the brakes.

The motorcar slid off the road into the shrubs. Eleanor braced herself with both hands and feet as the force jolted her, snapping her head back. They struck thick bushes, and the engine sputtered and died.

Eleanor sat, unable to move, staring at the leafy green banana trees caught in the beams of the headlamps.

Sayyid stirred from the backseat, groaning, and a moment later she heard him crawling out, calling to her, and then to Spencer. Spencer was slouched over the wheel but beginning to stir.

"Spencer, are you all right?"

"Never mind me! Allison! Did I—hit her? Sayyid! Hurry! Hurry!"

Sayyid was on his feet, stumbling back up the mound. Eleanor struggled out of the car, but the bank was somewhat steep and she lost her balance. She clambered up to the road, her knees so weak they buckled once and she went down. But she was back on her feet again and soon reached the dark road.

"Allison!" she whispered, "Oh God, please. Allison—"

"She's all right, Lady Wescott," Sayyid shouted from ahead of her. "The motorcar missed her by several feet!"

Eleanor slumped back to the dirt, the relief so great her tears erupted. Sayyid ran past her to the edge of the road and called down to Spencer: "She is hurt! Come quickly!"

Spencer climbed the mound, his breath ragged, wiping

sweat and a bit of blood from his face. "Did we hit her?"

"No, but it was close. Could you not see her?"

"Great Scot, man! Of what are you accusing me?"

"Of course nothing, of nothing—"

Eleanor arose and stumbled toward them, finding both men on their knees beside her daughter, who was curled up against the stump.

"Allison, my baby—" Eleanor sank to her knees, gathering Allison into her trembling arms. It was then that she saw the purplish swelling on her daughter's forehead and the dried blood. She sucked in her breath, her heart going cold. Was Allison dead after all?

"She's alive," Spencer said briskly, taking command. "Move aside, Eleanor, let me look at her. Sayyid! Quickly! My bag! In the backseat!"

Sayyid ran back to the motorcar, and Eleanor sat in the dirt as Spencer bent over her. "Looks like a concussion. I won't know yet, but I think she'll be all right, Eleanor."

"A concussion? But how?" Eleanor looked about, confused. "The motorcar?"

"No, no, this is several hours old at least." He turned to scowl over his shoulder. "What's keeping Sayyid? It shouldn't take him this long!"

Eleanor pushed herself up from the ground and started to walk toward the embankment when she heard Sayyid's running feet stirring up the dust. "He's coming now."

Spencer rummaged through his bag. "Odd, I always carry it. But it doesn't appear to be here." He turned, his brown face tense in the moonlight, his eyes scanning Sayyid. "Was my bag open? Did anything fall out?"

Sayyid's sweating face was blank. He looked from Spencer

to Eleanor. "I do not know. I found it and came as quickly as I could. Is—is something missing?"

"Yes, and now we'll need to get Allison to the Blaine house," he said briskly. "I'll also need one of the military medical orderlies to bring me some medications. Do you think you could handle that for me?"

"At once. I'll need to go on foot until I reach Old Cairo. The tire has gone flat. It should not take me long. I am a runner."

"Good. One thing more."

Eleanor saw them exchange glances and her nerves tightened. She guessed what Spencer was about to say—and she was right.

"Better send for Inspector Julian Mortimer. I think we're going to need him."

TEN

><+>•☉•<+><

ALLISON TURNED HER HEAD ON THE PILLOW and grimaced from pain. Through blurred vision she saw a man sitting tall and straight in a wooden chair beside her bunk. He seemed so perfectly still that she thought he must be a mirage.

It's the medication I've been taking. Or maybe he's an angel come to keep watch over me, she thought dully, *to protect me from—*

"But angels don't wear black," she murmured.

"You're quite right, Miss Wescott, though I'm sure they could if they ever needed to. But now that you've spoken and convinced me of your reasoning skills, permit me to introduce myself." He stood with a crisp bow. "The name is Inspector Julian Mortimer. At your service." His mouth twitched with humor.

Allison blinked, and decided the man was indeed flesh and blood. Her gaze studied his sleek, black hair and dark eyes, his somewhat disdainfully long nose with audacious nostrils. He looked to be thirty-five, handsome in a sophisticated and studious sort of way, and sported a rat-tailed mustache that shot straight across the upper lip of an almost effeminate-looking mouth. He was impeccably dressed in a tight-fitting, black camlet coat with gold cuff links; his long fingers deftly lifted a gold pocket watch from his amber water-silk vest as he scrutinized the time. He was the first man Allison had seen in Cairo whose pale complexion convinced her that he had either just arrived in Egypt or he covered himself with shade from an umbrella.

She saw his vital black eyes fix upon her swollen forehead. He made a clucking sound. "Ghastly bump."

"My sister, Beth? Is she—" Her eyes widened.

"Positively safe," he assured her quickly. "And under Lady Wescott's watchful eye at the Residency. Beth is lamenting having put you through a dreadful fright. She tells me she grew quite afraid of some unearthly noise in the dining room and in her own words: 'Hid beneath the bed like a ninny until she was ashamed.' Doctor Howard found her there sometime after midnight when he arrived with Eleanor and Mr. Sayyid. That," he stated sympathetically, "was two days ago."

"I've been here for two days?" She grimaced. "Am I in the hospital?"

"Yes to both questions."

Allison closed her tired eyes, sighing. Beth was alive and safe. That was what really mattered at the moment. Silently offering her thanks to Jesus, Allison felt a wash of relief so great she managed a smile and her eyes opened again. "Smart girl to hide under the bed," she murmured, reaching to touch her forehead. "I should have."

Mortimer looked down at her gravely, his expression implying he agreed. "How is that head of yours?"

"Feels like a swollen watermelon—ready to split."

"Gracious." He winced. "Then I shall keep my questions to a minimum. Are you up to a few minutes?"

She was sure he'd insist even if she weren't. "I think so. Could you hand me that tin of water please?"

He did so, and Allison managed to quench her dry throat while Julian Mortimer retook his seat. *Am I looking at another deceptive Sir Edgar?* She realized with a slight sense of panic that she trusted no one outside her immediate family. If only Bret were here.

Julian interlaced his fingers and wiggled them thoughtfully. "I am new to the Blaine case, but I've been enmeshing myself in all the gory details since I arrived in Cairo. Naturally, I'm keeping up with the trial. I realize you were there at the house when the others were killed, and that Mrs. Blaine was a friend of yours."

"Yes, that's right." She did her best to keep the unease out of her tone.

"You were also in Aleppo when your cousin Leah Bristow was killed."

"Yes—"

"And you were at the Blaine house two days ago when the chauffeur was murdered."

"That's true." Her eyes moved to his. "Suggesting I did it, Inspector?"

He smiled. "No. Suggesting that you are jinxed perhaps?"

There was nothing accusing in his smile and a flicker of sympathy was in his eyes, but that did not assuage Allison's concerns. "I assure you I didn't clobber the chauffeur on the head with an iron club, then drag him back and place him behind the steering wheel. After which, quite calmly I bashed myself in the forehead to cover my crime and earn your sympathy."

His interlaced fingers wiggled again, and his smile deepened. "Aptly put. Why *did* you go back to the Blaine house?"

"Didn't Mr. Sayyid and Doctor Howard explain?"

"It's your explanation I want."

Allison watched him. He was rather pleasant, but she had been wrong too many times in the past to trust that assessment. What was the real Julian Mortimer like? Where had he come from? What was his character, his background? Since he was in the position to ask the questions, there was little she could do but cooperate. Nevertheless she would be cautious and refrain from telling him everything until she talked with Bret.

"They found me on the side of the road unconscious. Doctor Howard brought me to the house—"

"No, no, I mean, why did you go to the Blaine house to meet Mr. Sayyid?"

"I went because he sent me a message asking that I come to meet him. My mother can verify that. And I still have the letter, or at least I did. I placed it inside my bag."

"Yes, I have it."

If he had the letter from Sayyid, then why ask her? She thought she knew why. He was double checking because he didn't trust her.

He looked down into a small black book he had opened and she guessed it contained notes he had taken down from his other conversations.

"What time did you arrive to keep this appointment with Mr. Sayyid?"

"Around four o'clock."

"Did he say what he wanted?"

"You have the letter, Inspector Mortimer."

"I need your answer, Miss Wescott."

She sighed. "Yes, he was going to be there to show the house to an interested client wishing to buy. He thought it was a good time for me to come collect my trunk."

He looked up, his eyes bright. "And was he there at around four o'clock?"

"No. He was late."

"What did you do while you waited for his arrival?"

"I went upstairs to collect my things."

"Was there anything unusual about your trunk?"

Why did he ask that? "I didn't check. I noticed my sister's baggage had been brought there from the other bedroom she'd shared with a friend of mine, Nurse Marra Cohen. I suspect the police moved it there, but it seemed a bit curious."

He was interested. "Why curious?"

"Because they hadn't brought Marra's bags too. It was then I heard what I thought were footsteps below, perhaps in the dining room area. I thought it might be Mr. Sayyid, although I hadn't heard the motorcar arrive and I could see the front drive through the window."

"And Lady Wescott's driver was still out front where you left him?"

She mused. "Yes, I think so. I don't recall if I saw him around the motorcar or not. I went downstairs to the dining room. Through the window I saw Beth in the garden and I was surprised."

"Because she had told Lady Wescott she was attending a birthday dinner with some girlfriends at Ezbekiah Gardens?"

"Yes. I went out to the garden to see why she was at the house. We sat on the bench for perhaps fifteen to twenty minutes until Mr. Sayyid and his assistant arrived."

"And what did you discuss during this interval?"

Had Beth told him her concerns about Gilbert not killing Sarah Blaine?

"We discussed a holiday at Luxor with the archaeological club. And we talked about staying several weeks on Baroness Helga Kruger's houseboat."

He appeared satisfied with her explanation, convincing her that Beth hadn't told him about her suspicions. Allison tottered on the verge of telling him everything, but she held back as a tiny voice raised suspicions of her own, not about Gilbert, but about Julian Mortimer.

Maybe I'm becoming paranoid. I don't trust anyone fully. But should I?

Mortimer went on asking her brief questions in his casual way until she explained about going up the steps to the hall where Marra's room was located. At this point she hesitated uncertainly. She wanted to go on, but there were odd blank spots in her memory.

"Why did you go there?"

"I—I went to collect Marra's bags."

"Anything else?"

"No."

"You're certain, Miss Wescott?"

Why was he staring at her. "Yes. I mean—I think so."

"You think so? What was it that Mr. Sayyid wished to discuss with you? He mentioned the need to talk in the letter."

"Oh—yes—I remember—Sarah left me some bric-a-brac in her will, objects of sentiment. I went after them."

"In Marra's room, among her baggage?"

"No—" She looked at him, alert as her memory began to clear. "In the storage closet. In a black enameled box with pink flamingos on it."

He smiled.

"I went there, found the box, and—and—"

He leaned forward in his chair. "Do you remember what was in the box?"

"A menagerie of glass and ceramic animal motifs, and of Egyptian replicas—mummy dolls, a tiger, and such."

He watched her. "Have you ever seen that box before?"

Careful. Did he know Sarah had found the broken-off cobra head from the sundial in the box? Had Bret written about it in his report? She was sure Bret hadn't mentioned the map yet. But he must have written about the sundial and how he had unearthed Nefertari. He would have mentioned the box.

"I suppose I had seen the box before."

He let that slip by. "What do you think the items in the menagerie are worth?"

"Not much, Sarah implied around 500 pounds."

"You agree with her estimate?"

She shrugged. "Yes."

"Certainly not worth stealing, nor attacking you to run off with? Not like the Nefertari?"

"No."

"I see. Then where are the items now?"

She swallowed, her throat dry, and took a sip of water. "I have no idea. Whoever it was must have taken the box?"

"So it appears. And I am assuming, of course, that you'd found the box and were looking at these items when you were knocked unconscious."

"Yes. Someone hit me from behind and I fell into the storage boxes. When I awoke, I couldn't find Beth. So I went outside and—" She stopped, a look of growing horror on her face as she remembered the shock of finding the chauffeur dead behind the steering wheel.

"Someone could not have struck you from behind, Miss Wescott. Doctor Howard assures us there is no bruise except the one on your forehead."

"Yes, I remember now...I turned to look behind me."

"What made you turn?"

"Footsteps." She shuddered.

He leaned forward watching her intently. "This next question is very important. Were you able to get a glimpse of your assailant?"

"No! No!"

"Anything at all? Like the sound of the footsteps—heavy, light? Male, female?"

"I didn't see him."

"Him? You think it was a man then?"

"No! I mean I'm not sure. He—I mean someone, covered my face with something, and it all happened too quickly."

He leaned back thoughtfully. "From the looks of the storage room, you put up quite a struggle. In all that time, as you fought to save yourself from this someone, perhaps there was something that you might have noticed? The lantern was lit, was it not?"

"Lantern? No, I had struck a match."

He stood and leaned over the bunk. "Whom did you see, Miss Wescott? Whom are you protecting?"

Her eyes were wide, her heart thudding. "No! I didn't see anyone. If I had, I'd tell you!"

His eyes gleamed. "Would you?"

Stunned, she sucked in her breath. A moment of silence passed before she stirred indignantly. "Yes! I have no reason to hide a murderer!"

"So you do know that your someone is a murderer—you just said you didn't know anything about him."

"What do you mean? It must have been the person who killed the chauffeur. I mean—" She stopped.

"Whoever killed the chauffeur need not have been the same person who struck you—unless you know otherwise."

"I tell you, I don't. I don't know who it was."

"You didn't notice anything at all?"

"Absolutely not."

He said nothing for a moment. "You did hear footsteps."

"Yes, yes I did."

"And you turned around."

She closed her eyes tightly, her mind whirring. As hard as she tried to remember, the details were in a fog.

"I must insist we call this to a halt, Inspector!" It was Doctor

Howard, and he was less than pleased. "You've wantonly disregarded my medical orders."

"Wantonly?" Julian laughed in a low voice. "Come, come, Spencer. I treated her gently indeed."

"I told you the girl remains in fragile condition. There'll be no more badgering. "

Relief swept over Allison, and she looked from Julian to Spencer. The doctor stood glowering at the inspector. Julian Mortimer, however, looked unruffled.

"You're quite right, Spencer. I don't want to distress Miss Wescott any more than I need to. We've talked enough for one morning," and he turned to Allison with an apologetic smile. "I'm sorry I had to 'badger' you, as Spencer aptly puts it. It's my duty you know. Perhaps I will drop by this evening after you've had supper, Miss Wescott—"

"I think not," cut in Spencer. "I would advise tomorrow, after luncheon," he added. "No bright and early pounding on the door. My patient comes first."

Mortimer offered a nod of his head. "Luncheon it is." He looked toward Allison, smiling. "Then you'd vow you don't remember anything to help us identity whoever struck you and took that box?"

"I remember nothing."

"Perhaps," Julian said soberly, "it is well you do not. We should hate to leave the murderer thinking you remembered something to identify him with and yet refused to tell it to the police."

As Allison thought about his words, Julian turned to Spencer with a languid smile. "Well, Spencer, you look a bit done in today. How about luncheon at Groppi's?"

Spencer sighed and ran his fingers through his chestnut-colored hair. "You're right, Julian. Serving as a war doctor is one thing, but treating friends heats the emotions. I could use a bit of a break, I'm afraid. I've been taking this in a less professional manner than I normally would."

"Being close friends with the Wescotts, I can quite understand how it is," Julian said consolingly. "Come along then, chap, I shall even brighten your day by paying."

Spencer gave a laugh. "I won't resist that."

Julian turned toward Allison. "I do wish you were well enough to join us, Miss Wescott." He smiled. "Perhaps another time, if luck comes my way."

"Yes," she murmured, still thinking about the inspector's earlier words about not wanting the guilty person to think she might be able to recognize him. "Yes, perhaps," she repeated, trying to be polite. "Thank you."

Spencer leaned over and squeezed her hand, his eyes troubled. "Try not to worry. I've called for Marra Cohen. Pulling a few strings here and there has arranged for her to be your nurse for the next few days. I thought you could use a friend. I could arrange it because they know I'm without my regular nurse."

Allison smiled her thanks.

"Don't worry. You're recuperating splendidly. If you're having a few lapses in your memory, it's nothing to worry about. It's not uncommon in such cases of head injury. And don't allow this bully of an inspector to hound you into a tizzy."

Mortimer laughed. "Don't give Miss Wescott wrong ideas about me, Spencer."

The doctor smiled in his wry, brittle way. "You'd best be warned, Julian."

"Warned?"

"Miss Wescott belongs to a certain colonel."

Allison was too exhausted to feel embarrassed, even when

Julian Mortimer looked at her with clearly unprofessional disappointment.

"Then I assume Mr. Holden will have enough sense to come home soon," was his casual remark. "His armor is becoming a bit rusty—along with his reputation."

Allison closed her eyes, preferring to act as though she hadn't heard the inspector's comment and that she was already dozing off.

"By the way," he was saying to Spencer as their footsteps were fading away. "You've heard he was suspended?"

"A shocking bit of news. I find it difficult to believe about Holden."

"Yes, but the best of men are made of clay. We suspect him of smuggling Egyptian artifacts into Constantinople."

Shock jolted through Allison, and she struggled to draw her breath. Suspended? A smuggler?

Oh Bret, it can't be true! Allison's heart both ached and yearned for his presence—but once again, he wasn't there.

Doctor Howard had seen to it that Marra was able to hang a canvas partition from hooks in the ceiling, giving Allison privacy around her bunk. The hospital ward was overcrowded with wounded and sick soldiers, many in very grave condition.

As Allison grew a little stronger, she was able to climb out of bed and peek through the canvas to see the men. The pitiable sight brought the horrors of Kut back to her again. Most of these wounded and dying were from Gallipoli, and she wondered how the evacuation was going. The sight convinced her she must rejoin the Nurses Corps when she returned from Luxor.

In the days that followed she had plenty of visitors at Bulac Hospital, even Lady Walsh dropped by, lamenting the dreadful and ghastly thing that had happened at her house. "A horrid mistake to buy the property. I'm putting it back up for sale at once. I mean, *another* murder? Wicked spirits haunt the place. What else could it be, my dear?"

Allison had a suggestion but thought better of saying it to Lady Walsh.

Eleanor came each day, assuring Allison that friends at YMCA were praying for her recovery. On one of those visits Beth came as well. Allison understood the little subdued anxious glances Beth cast in her direction. After their conversation in the Blaine garden, Beth was now convinced she was right about Gilbert not killing Sarah. Allison couldn't think about it for long; her head ached too much. She wanted to get well and strong again. Everything else must wait.

"Sorry I was such a dreadful coward," Beth apologized. "When you didn't come back from Marra's room the way you said, I went looking for you, but you weren't there. I went for the driver, but he was missing too." She rubbed her arms and whispered: "I had this sensation that I was being watched from the trees. So I went back inside. It was then I heard all these creaks and groans and the wind came up. I called for you again, but you didn't answer. So I just got frightened and ran back up to the room and hid under the bed."

"Don't blame yourself," Eleanor told her. "There was nothing you could have done. Had you braved the intruder you might have gotten hurt like Allison." She looked at Allison. "I think we've both learned our lessons about going and searching for intruders," she said, and Allison knew she was making reference to the time she, too, had been struck unconscious.

"I wasn't searching," Allison said. "I was in the storage closet when someone came up behind me."

Eleanor laid a calm, restraining hand on her arm. "Yes, I

know. Let's not think about it anymore until you're stronger. Julian is looking into the case. And I've reason to believe your father will be home early next week."

"When will you be coming home?" Beth asked.

Allison could see her sister was alert. She behaved as though she had something to tell her once they were alone at the Residency.

Allison didn't know when she would be released, but Eleanor seemed to think Doctor Spencer had estimated her return for the end of the week.

"What about Luxor?" Beth asked unexpectedly, her eyes bright and knowing. "Are we still going down to holiday on Helga's houseboat?"

"I hardly think so, dear, after what's happened to Allison."

"Oh, Mum, I don't know why not." Allison wanted to get away. "I'm feeling much better, and I don't want to miss the club meetings. It will be a good place to rest before I rejoin the Nursing Corps."

Eleanor's displeasure over her daughter's interest in serving again in a field hospital was evident, but she said nothing. "You know what Helga said in her letter. To use the houseboat we'll need to spend a week or so getting it ready. You can't possibly do that now. And I can't leave without your father. There's the inauguration of the new sultan coming up."

"I can go with her," Beth said. "I'll help get things ready."

"And Marra's coming with me too," Allison pointed out. "I'll have plenty of help, Mum. And members of the club will also be arriving. I'll be in good company."

Eleanor looked at her, but Allison pretended she didn't see the look of concern in her mother's eyes. She was almost sure Bret was in the Valley of the Kings and she simply had to see him. She had the perfect excuse now to go and search for him.

Someone had stolen the box with Sarah's menagerie and knocked her unconscious. The truth remained that whoever it was could have killed her just as easily as they had the chauffeur. The fact that she'd gotten off with a concussion told her that she was not in mortal danger. It was the box they had wanted. Well, they had it now. That should be the end of the matter. But it gave her the perfect opening to retain her pride and dignity and still make the first move to locate Bret.

David came to see her a few days later. Since Marra was now her nurse, thanks to Doctor Howard, she was able to keep Allison closely informed of whether or not David had heard from Bret. When Marra told him what had happened, David came at once.

"Back to your old tricks, are you? Bret's likely to go through the roof when he finds out this one—and that you stumbled across another corpse."

Allison grimaced at the memory, and Marra gave him a sharp look.

"All right, I take it back. I wasn't supposed to say *corpse*. I wonder what the old fella knew that caused someone to want to silence him permanently?"

"Well," Marra said, "maybe it wasn't what the 'old fella' knew, but what he saw."

"Why do you say that?" Allison asked. She was finally strong enough to sit up against a pillow.

Marra shrugged. "Seems only plausible to me. I mean, here this fella goes meandering off into the trees to sit down and smoke. Maybe he saw someone he wasn't supposed to see go in the house. Maybe he went to see what he wanted, or what he was doing there. And then—he meets his bleak end."

Allison wondered. Had the chauffeur seen something—or someone—that aroused his curiosity?

166

"Has Julian asked about it?" Allison inquired.

"Julian?" David repeated with exaggerated surprise. "First name basis doesn't sound good for the absentee colonel."

"Don't be silly." Allison felt the flush come into her cheeks. Did everyone think her that fickle? "Are you working with Julian?"

"No, but he comes in and out of CID. It may mean nothing, where the chauffeur's concerned, but then who knows? We shouldn't let it pass. If there's a chance he may have seen someone, Julian should look into the possibility."

"But who was there to see that would bring about his death?" Allison mused.

"We're not likely to find out." Marra's resigned comment was delivered with a shrug. "But if it did happen that way, then someone was worried enough about having been seen to commit an unplanned murder." She looked at David. "And by the way, how is it you know so much if you're not working with Julian Mortimer?"

David grinned. "Because, little angel, I have access to his reports. Mortimer sends them over to CID."

Marra looked at Allison. "And then Wonder Boy here writes them up." She leaned against a medical cart. "David gets all the latest gossip as well as facts."

"And if a particular CID man knew I was sharing a *bit* of it with two females who are prone to nosy about, I'd be slam-dunked so fast my head would be spinning. It just goes to show how devoted I am to you—both," he added, glancing at Marra. She smirked, and David winked.

Allison didn't believe him. She had the notion he was meant to keep an eye on her to find out what she knew, and that the orders had come from the CID itself.

"Have you heard from Colonel Holden?" Allison asked silkily, sipping from the cup of tea Marra had given her. She took a sweet cake from the plate and tasted it, looking at David, schooling her features to seem as innocent as possible.

David appeared to be taken off guard, then smiled. "Officially?"

"No, truthfully," she countered seriously, her voice low.

David finished his tea and set down the cup, then stood from the corner of her bunk where he'd been sitting. He edged aside the divider of Allison's tiny cubicle and looked out to the rest of the overcrowded ward.

Allison guessed what he was doing. He wanted to know if anyone was close enough to overhear. He appeared satisfied, but she noted a slight hesitation.

David looked back at her, and he wasn't smiling anymore. "This is one ruddy time to tell you, but there's some valid concern. Even the CID hasn't heard from the colonel."

Her hands turned cold and clammy. "Are you saying he's missing in action?"

"No."

He remained frustratingly noncommittal, and Allison searched his sober face. "Out with it, David. You can't bait me and expect me to lie down peacefully!"

"I know I can't." He sighed, then threw up his hands and walked over to the side of the bed. "All right. Take this for what it's worth because it isn't likely to be worth much. Bret's been, well, temporarily suspended from the CID. He's on what you might say is a probation until after the hearing."

Allison couldn't move. She hadn't really believed Julian, but David...

"There, you've gone and done it now," Marra said fiercely. "I could almost think you were dying to tell the bad news."

"Don't be absurd."

"Am I?" Marra goaded.

"What's that supposed to mean?" David's angry question shot out through gritted teeth.

"Just what it implies, dearie."

"Dearie!" he exploded. "Ease the sarcasm, wonder girl, or I'll—"

"Or you'll what? Whack me over the head?"

He stopped, a look of shock on his handsome face.

But Marra was breathing hard. "You're sweet on Allison and you're only too glad to see Bret's armor tarnished. Admit it."

"You maddening female! You *know* Bret's a close friend of mine. The *best* of friends. You think I could be *happy* about his removal?"

"When it comes to two men wanting the same woman—"

"Stop it!" Allison held her head, trying to hold back her emotions as well. "Both of you!" She spoke with labored slowness. "Just—stop—it! I can't take any more." She looked at Marra, exasperated. Marra's face was flushed with internal seething.

"There's nothing romantic between David and me. I would think you'd know that by now, Marra."

"Because of *your* refusal, not his!"

"That *does* it!" David turned to walk out, then spun back to face them and held out an accusing hand toward Marra. "And don't think I'll come around apologizing, either. We're through, kid. It's been one miserable merry-go-round. I'm just glad I got off in time." He turned to stride out, nearly bumping into Doctor Howard as he went.

Spencer was frowning, his bright eyes shooting from David to Marra, then to Allison with alarm.

"Great Scot! Out of here! Both of you!"

"Doctor, I—" Marra began, biting her lip. For the first time

Allison could remember, she saw tears spill from the other woman's eyes.

"You, young lady, are removed from my staff. As of this moment!"

Marra looked at Allison, then after David, then her teeth clamped as she seemed to cram the lid tighter on her feelings.

"As you wish, Doctor." She went past the bunk, where Allison sat trying to swallow her tears, and out the partition.

Doctor Howard removed something from his coat pocket, then reached out to take Allison's shaking shoulders and lay her down against the pillow. "Now, now, enough tears. These ridiculous situations come up in life, and we'll just pretend it was a bad dream for now. It's time to get some sleep, my dear. Tomorrow is a new day. You can think of it then."

Allison was too weary to resist the injection he gave her. She turned her head away to stare at the peeling paint on the wall and allowed her warm tears to spill onto the pillow in silence. It was bad enough about Bret, but to find she had come between two people she loved dearly was heartbreaking.

It couldn't be true about Bret, it just couldn't. There had to be some explanation. What had he done to warrant an investigation? The map? Could it be they found out he had kept it from them?

"You'll be asleep in a few moments," came Doctor Howard's cool voice.

Yes, tomorrow is a good time to worry, she found her numbing brain thinking. *Don't panic, your heavenly Father cares for the sparrows…he cares for you…tomorrow, yes, tomorrow…*

Allison opened her eyes slowly, blinking at the darkness that surrounded her. She was groggy from the injection Dr. Howard had given her, but she had the oddest feeling…

She turned her head on the pillow, feeling as though she were underwater. She closed her eyes, then opened them again, trying to focus. Was it her imagination, or was someone there?

Alarm rose in her when she felt something brush her face. "Who…?" The word came out soft and slurred.

"Shh. It's all right. You're safe."

The whisper drifted to her through the fog in her brain, deep and soothing. Oddly enough, her momentary fear melted away. There was something about that voice… something that made her feel protected, cared for.

Again she had the sensation of someone touching her face, caressing her cheek with featherlight fingers. And then…a kiss, as tender as any she could ever remember receiving, was pressed against her forehead.

"Believe." The deep whisper enveloped her, insulating her, making her feel as though she were being cradled in strong, loving arms. "Believe."

She lifted an unsteady hand—and found nothing but empty space.

"What…?" She turned her head on her pillow. Still no one.

A dream. It must have been a dream. The thought made her sad somehow, and as she drifted back to sleep, she felt a tear trickle down her face.

Sunlight was streaming into the room when Allison awoke the next morning. She raised her arms and stretched, a slight smile on her face.

"My, we look happy today."

She turned to meet the smiling gaze of the morning nurse. "I feel happy," she admitted.

"Happy dreams?" the nurse inquired, and Allison's eyes widened. The dream! She frowned. Or was it a dream? She could have sworn someone was there, in her room last night. That touch—that kiss—had been too real...too reminiscent of—

Her eyes widened again. Only one person had ever made her feel the way she'd felt last night. Bret. But how could that be? How could he have been here last night. He was in Jerusalem...wasn't he?

She shook her head slightly. It must have been her imagination. She'd wanted him there so...longed to be able to talk with him, to hear him tell her everything would be all right. Her need for him must have combined with the sleeping drug she'd been given to create a comforting dream—

"Well, well," the nurse exclaimed, her smile broadening. "I see it's more than just dreams making you smile, my dear."

Allison followed the nurse's gaze—and stared in wonder at the beautiful white rose in a crystal vase beside her bed. A small card was propped against the base of the vase, and Allison's heart pounded. She knew without looking what it said.

"'Believe,'" the nurse read, confirming Allison's suspicion. "What a lovely thing to write." She fixed Allison with a curious, almost envious, glance. "And do you?"

Allison felt the smile spread across her face. She couldn't have stopped it if she tried. "Yes," she said, snuggling down beneath the covers, feeling warm all over. "Yes, I do."

ELEVEN

MARRA HAD DECIDED TO TRANSFER. She explained her decision to Allison as wanting to get away from the overcrowded hospitals and convalescent homes in Cairo, all of which teemed with wounded British soldiers from the Dardanelles. Even so, Allison knew personal issues rather than the harsh working conditions motivated her friend's decision.

This was confirmed when she found out that Marra was transferring to the convalescent hospital at Ismailia, located on the volatile Suez Canal. There had already been skirmishes with Turkish soldiers under German command and with some wild bedouin who kept British soldiers defending themselves from swift and sudden attacks. Marra claimed she wanted to transfer to prepare for the push forward into Palestine.

"Besides, Ismailia is the best location to rejoin some of my old Nursing Corps friends," she told Allison blithely. "It just makes sense."

She had left for Ismailia before Allison had time to tell her good-bye—or to patch things up between them. Losing her old nursing ally from Kut, especially to a misunderstanding like this, was especially painful. Marra had sent Allison a brief letter explaining that she was too rushed to come by before boarding the train with a group of other transferees. *I'll write you when I'm settled in at Ismailia,* she'd written.

Allison let the message fall back to the bedcover and sat staring at her dismal surroundings. Her mind was made up too. She was going home, regardless of what Doctor Howard said. She was going to Luxor to enjoy her archaeology holiday—and she absolutely refused to allow her disappointments over losing Marra's presence and support to ruin it.

She glanced about her at the multitude of beds. Marra had been right about the overcrowded hospitals. Allison was sure that the number of wounded in Cairo—sixty thousand in January—had grown considerably.

Her mother told her there were other concerns, as well. There was the growing fear that Turkey, a Moslem nation, would make a religious appeal to the Egyptian Muslims within Cairo to rise up against the British in a *jeihad*, a so-called holy war.

"There are Muslims among the soldiers from India as well," her mother said. "Many of whom are serving in a new unit sent to help guard the Suez. If they put their religion above their national loyalties and if the Egyptians join with them, there could be no end to the slaughter."

"All the more reason to holiday at Luxor." Allison felt mercifully dull of mind as she answered.

"Your father is to arrive tomorrow," her mother said in a low voice. "He comes none too soon where politics are concerned. Cairo is a powder keg, and the inauguration of the new sultan could provide the spark."

Allison nodded vaguely. She knew there were numerous influential Turks in Egypt among the social aristocracy—and she knew their loyalty greatly concerned the British. She remembered how Sir Edgar had compiled a list of potential spies and enemies, and shook her head. That list had now come to new life through Julian Mortimer, who was gathering the names of those who would be quietly rounded up and sent from Egypt should internal unrest threaten to erupt.

"No point in not being prepared," he'd said during a visit with Allison. He'd made a point of stopping by on a fairly regular basis. "The Germans believe a rebellion from inside Cairo would greatly benefit their plan to take over the Suez using Turkish troops."

"Are they right?" Allison asked.

He shrugged. "Could very well be."

She feared he was right. Her mother had brought her unsettling news during her most recent visit. "I wish your father were home," she said, and Allison had looked at her, alarmed.

"Is there a problem?"

She looked about, then leaned close to speak in low tones. "It's been reported that some one hundred thousand soldiers are amassing in the Sinai for a new attack on the canal."

"Oh, Mother, England can't lose the canal."

"Indeed, not, for that would mean losing our shipping routes to India and the East. I dread to think what a terrible, and most certainly bloody, battle it will be to keep it secure. The Germans have supposedly made a secret alliance with Turkey's leader of the Veiled Protectorate, Enver Pasha, in Constantinople." She sighed heavily.

Allison lay back on her pillows, staring at the ceiling. "It never stops, does it?"

Her mother didn't reply. She didn't need to. Allison remembered her father and Bret telling her that since December of 1913, there'd been a German military mission in Constantinople, headed by General Liman von Sanders.

"Turkey hasn't forgotten that England commandeered two Turkish battleships," her mother finally went on. "The ships were close to being completed in the British shipyards, and because they were built by money from Turkish citizens within Constantinople, I fear the seizure caused great anger in the streets."

Allison pressed her lips together. "Germany certainly was

quick to take advantage of the rift."

"Yes, and what they did was most effective. They rushed two German warships to Constantinople, though how they eluded the British fleet in the Mediterranean is beyond me."

"I've heard the ships—"

"The *Goeben* and *Bresla*," her mother inserted.

She nodded. "I heard they were given over to Turkey's disposal by the German ambassador there, in place of those commandeered in England."

That wasn't all. She'd read that the German admiral had been permitted to use the Turkish fleet to bombard Russian ports in the Black Sea, at the entrance to the Dardanelles. Immediately the British government in Cairo discussed the possibility of annexing Egypt into the British Empire or incorporating it as a Crown Colony. In the end they made Egypt a mere protectorate.

Martial law was still in effect, which meant England alone accepted the sole burden of the war without calling for help from Egyptian soldiers or for financial aid.

"But the *fellahin* are riled because their camels are being taken for the upcoming push into Palestine," her mother told her. "And villagers are being called to dig trenches since they're so good at it. The fellahin are complaining they're losing money digging trenches instead of growing cotton. And they want their camels back."

"What's Father going to do about it?"

"The only thing anyone can do. Promise higher cotton prices and pay for the camels. Let's hope the discontented fellahin don't join up with the Independence Party in Cairo. They're already upset over getting a new sultan. They blame it on us, of course."

"Does Father think a religious war will erupt?"

"It's difficult to say. The majority in the Independence Party says they wish brother Islamic Turkey well in the war—but from afar. They don't want Turkey ruling them anymore than they want England ruling them. Your father and General Murray are depending on just that to keep the lid on things."

Allison hadn't told her mother she intended to leave the hospital. She hadn't wanted to argue the point. When her mother left for the day, Allison dressed herself and collected her meager belongings. She was brushing her waist-length hair and winding it up when she felt a draft and paused. Someone had edged aside the partition.

Slowly Allison turned, then started. "Oh, it's you."

Cynthia Walsh, looking as uncomfortable as a bedouin in a tuxedo, smiled nervously. As always, the young woman was dressed in the height of fashion with not a hair out of place or a flaw in her powder.

"I heard you were much improved, so thought it a good time to come see you. I've been waiting until Eleanor left. I wanted to speak with you alone." Her eyes dropped to Allison's bag. "You're leaving?" Her wide eyes showed her surprise.

"Yes, I can't take another day of confinement."

"Can you leave without Spencer releasing you?"

Allison smiled briefly. "I don't think I'm in prison. Not yet, anyway." At Allison's attempt at light humor, a calculating expression swept Cynthia's face.

"Don't tell me Julian is casting a suspicious eye on you over what's happened recently?"

Cynthia almost seemed hopeful, as though some new possibility was opened to her.

Allison considered ignoring the remark, but shrugged instead. "He's been asking routine questions is all, probably just being conscientious."

Cynthia sat down in the chair, eyeing her critically. Allison was uncomfortably aware that, while the swelling in her forehead had decreased, there were still discolorations that her face powder didn't cover. In comparison to the ever flawless Miss Walsh, she must look dreadful.

Belatedly, Allison also noted that Cynthia called the new chief inspector by his given name. It was true she also called Doctor Howard by his first name, but Spencer was a friend of the inner social circle of Cairo and everyone knew him. Julian Mortimer, on the other hand, had only recently arrived. Where had he come from that Cynthia would know him?

"What is it you came to discuss, Cynthia?"

She sat petting her expensive alligator handbag, but it was clear by her thoughtful expression that she was musing over something. "If you're leaving, I'll give you a ride back to the Residency. My chauffeur is parked outside. How about tea at Ezbekiah first?"

Allison hesitated, then nodded her assent. Suffering through tea with Cynthia might be worthwhile if it helped her ascertain what was on the socialite's mind.

"Naturally I wouldn't want to exhaust you," hastened Cynthia. "There are several flights of stairs."

Allison smiled. "After a week of confinement, it sounds refreshing. I'll be right with you." She finished pinning up her hair, caught up her simple handbag, and—scanning Cynthia with restrained interest—followed her out of the ward.

The overworked hospital staff either didn't notice her or assumed she'd been released, so no one tried to stop her. Fortunately Spencer was nowhere in sight.

"It must have been dreadful coming up against that intruder in the storage closet," Cynthia commented as they left the hospital and walked in the warm sunshine across the hospital grounds.

"Yes, rather." Allison smiled wryly.

"Your bravery astounds me. Being a war nurse is hazardous enough, but that business with Sarah last year was horrid. And now this nasty business of last week. You can thank your lucky stars matters didn't turn out for you the way they did for your mother's chauffeur."

It sounded almost like a warning. Allison glanced at Cynthia, but she was adjusting her stylish hat of black satin and pearls.

How like Cynthia to attribute good fortune to the stars rather than to their creator.

"Do you have all your memory back?"

Allison stared at Cynthia. How had she known about that? Perhaps she was on even closer terms with Julian Mortimer than Allison had suspicioned. In any case, she had the distinct impression Cynthia was probing for information—and Allison had no intention whatsoever of obliging. "Oh, a few gaps still remain."

"Nothing serious I hope? It would be dreadful not to remember about our Colonel Holden, wouldn't it?" She gave a warm little laugh.

Allison ignored it. "Mostly the gaps have to do with what may have happened when I was being attacked."

"I suppose it will all come back eventually."

"Doctor Howard doesn't think so. Things like that happen sometimes. Anyway, I doubt if there's anything to remember. Spencer says I shouldn't try."

The Mercedes was in sight, and Cynthia slowed her steps. "I would think he's right. I mean, wouldn't it be rather too dangerous to have seen who it was?"

Aware of Cynthia's stare and the tucking of her brows, Allison considered the question. Whomever she had come up against would know a short-term memory loss would give temporary cover. If the fog shrouding her subconscious should quickly evaporate, Allison could pose a danger.

"I suppose I shouldn't have said that," Cynthia apologized. They walked on.

"Inspector Mortimer thinks that whoever struck me unconscious may not be the same person who murdered the poor driver."

"An interesting theory. I wonder why he thinks so?"

"It's rather obvious, I think. If someone wanted me dead, they had ample opportunity." Though the sun beat upon her, Allison felt a prickle run along her skin. "I was alone in the house and unconscious. It would have been easy—" She stopped.

"Oh, I see. They could have put an end to you once for all. Yes, that makes sense. Maybe you were lucky this time."

This time?

"I prefer to think it was our heavenly Father, not luck, that was with me. And that he turned this, as he does everything in our lives, to ultimate good."

Cynthia's eyes laughed with restrained mockery. "Everything? Does that include murder?"

Allison refused to be embarrassed. "I believe it includes everything we experience."

Cynthia pursed her lips. "If you want to bring God into all this, why didn't he protect your mother's driver?"

"I don't know. Bad things do happen to all of us, even to God's children. But God works them out for good in the end. The New Testament tells about two of the disciples, Peter and James. The Lord sent his angel to deliver Peter from prison, but he allowed James to die by the sword. To be murdered. Obviously God could have delivered them both. He had a different purpose for each one, but his promise for good was no less true for James than it was for Peter."

Cynthia pondered this, then shrugged. "It's all beyond me. I've never been very religious—though it so happens my chauffeur's name is James!"

They both laughed, and the tension was eased as James opened the door of the Mercedes and they got into the back.

As they drove away from Bulac Hospital, passing convalescing soldiers out strolling across the lawn, Cynthia turned thoughtful eyes on Allison. "Why did you ever go back to the Blaine house?"

There seemed little reason to hide the truth. "Mr. Sayyid asked me to come and collect my things, which I'd left there in December. I had left a good pair of desert hiking boots in my trunk and I wanted them for Luxor. And that reminds me—" She frowned. "My boots are still at the house. Well, I'm certainly not going back there to get them! I have seen the Blaine house for the last time! I'll just ask the authorities to send the entire trunk down to Luxor. It will save me a great deal of unpleasantness."

"I should say so. Quite smart of you after what's happened. And one has got to drive all over Cairo to find a good walking shoe." She looked down at her shiny, strappy slippers. "These will never do. I've got to buy a pair of boots myself. I'm going with the club as well this year," she announced, "with the high hopes of getting relief from this dreadful business going on in Cairo. If Mother hadn't lent our house in Alexandria to be used as a convalescent home I'd holiday there, but I can't bear entertaining more soldiers! It's getting to be too much, really. So inconvenient. Luxor sounds like a charming diversion.

Anyway, dear Helga asked me if I wouldn't come. She wants me to meet her son, Paul. Says he's an archaeologist and quite handsome."

Ah. So Paul was who he said he was, and Helga was aware he was here. So much for the mysterious stranger on the train to Zeitoun! Allison gave Cynthia a relieved smile. It was a splendid idea for her to meet Paul. Maybe then she'd leave Bret alone.

Cynthia, however, was not smiling. Her eyes searched Allison's face. "So that was the only reason you went back to the house? Your walking shoes?"

Allison picked up the slight tension in Cynthia's voice, and wondered at it. What was she getting at? Clearly something was bothering her…. Maybe the inspector had told Cynthia about the menagerie—and how that menagerie had been stolen.

"There was another reason." Allison settled back in the comfortable leather seat. "Mr. Sayyid wanted to tell me about something Sarah left me in her will."

"The missing box?"

So, Allison had been right.

"Yes, but I can't imagine why anyone would go to such lengths for it. I had a good look at its contents. There were only some inexpensive collectibles. Nothing of museum quality."

"Nothing worth being stolen," as Sarah herself had once put it.

"Yes, it is odd." Cynthia gave her a considering look. "Evidently someone didn't know what was in the box. Perhaps they had reason to think there was another great find hidden away, like the statue of Nefertari that Bret found hidden under the sundial."

"Perhaps." Despite her quiet agreement, Allison wondered if it were so simple.

Cynthia looked at her. "I'm glad you're still up to going with the club. When are you leaving?"

"I'm going down early. Helga offered her houseboat to my mother and sister. As you say, this business in Cairo is a bit depressing, especially for Beth. And I'm exhausted with it all. This trip will be my last chance for relaxing. I'm signing with the Nurse's Corps for Palestine."

"I admire you tremendously. My motives are, strictly speaking, selfish." She gave a self-mocking smile, then reached into her alligator bag, removed a gold compact, and powdered her nose and touched up her lipstick. "There isn't a political bone in my body. And I'm just not into the sacrificing spirit. If I had to don desert boots and forego my manicures for longer than a few weeks, well, you understand. *Too* dreadful, really."

Allison smiled, but as she looked at her—actually looked at her for the first time as an individual rather than a threat where Bret was concerned—she noted that Cynthia's face reflected thoughtful intelligence. With just the two of them, there was no need for Cynthia to be batting her lashes—and Allison was surprised to see her eyes were sober and her chin was resolute, showing an inner conviction. There had to be more to Cynthia than her physical attractiveness; Bret would never have shown interest in her otherwise. Allison knew him well enough to be certain he wasn't taken in by the outward appearance alone. Allison began to wonder if Cynthia might not be exaggerating her Lady Vogue behavior. What better way to avoid being taken seriously than to convince everyone she lacked strong views on serious issues?

The foot traffic was slow, and the Mercedes crept along, dodging donkeys and a few camels. When they at last arrived in the European quarters of the city, Shepheard's Hotel was crowded as usual. Allison took a deep breath and looked about at the lush, green Ezbekiah Gardens. She gave silent thanks to her heavenly father for her recovery. Despite the war, the difficulties she encountered, and the uncertainty that dogged her footsteps about her future with Bret, it was good to be alive. How easy it was to forget to thank God for the simple things! The flowers in the garden, growing sweet and colorful in the midst of hot and dusty Cairo, brought a smile of gratitude to her lips.

The hotel, four stories tall with a deep, encircling verandah, had became *the* place for Europeans to meet in Cairo, especially to enjoy lamb stuffed with pistachio nuts and sweetmeats doused in honey.

"We'll be fortunate to get a table," Cynthia said. "Looks like everyone who is anyone is here today." She went to speak in a low voice to the bowing, smiling waiter. Soon he came to usher them past the others waiting to be seated. He led them to a white-clothed table near the terrace overlooking the gardens.

Allison was curious about what Cynthia wanted from her, for she simply couldn't accept Cynthia's visit at face value. By no stretch of the imagination could it be said they were friends, although today they had gotten along much better than Allison might have expected. Thus far Cynthia hadn't asked Allison about her relationship with Bret—save that little remark about Allison getting amnesia over him. Then again, how was Cynthia to know he had wanted to marry her last Christmas? She doubted Bret would have told Cynthia how close he had come to marriage once the door had shut to the possibility.

Allison's optimistic mood spiraled downward again. Had David been right about Bret being temporarily suspended from the CID? She couldn't wait to ask her father about it once he returned home. If anyone knew the details, he did. And she wouldn't admit, even to herself, the main reason she was going to Luxor was to search for him—albeit discreetly, of course.

After they ordered and the Egyptian waiter brought tea and cakes, Allison noted the return of the somewhat apprehensive manner that Cynthia had displayed at the hospital. At times she actually looked frightened, but that couldn't be. What did Cynthia have to be frightened about? After all, *she* had not come up against the intruder in the Blaine house.

Cynthia glanced up from stirring sugar in her tea. As she did so, she looked across the table to the other side of the dining area—and her eyes widened in sudden alarm.

Allison, seated at her right, followed her gaze across several tables of Europeans and toward the doorway. A man had entered, a European, his face shadowed beneath a hat he had not yet removed. He stood and seemed to be looking in their direction. It was more of a perception than a certainty, but Allison had the odd sense that his eyes had left Cynthia and were fixed on her. Had she seen that man before? But why would she think so when his face was in the shadows? He was quite tall and slim, with a rigid, military stance. Just then, a waiter came up to him and led him away, across the large room and through another doorway into the second dining area.

Allison turned quickly toward Cynthia, only to find her reading the menu as though she had decided on luncheon after all. Clearly she didn't want Allison to know she had been alarmed. Allison lifted her cup and took a sip of the bitter brew; her mind worked over the feeling that she'd seen the man before…somewhere….

Her eyes widened. Of course. She was certain that was the same man who had strolled to meet Sir Edgar on the terrace the afternoon she had come here with Sarah and Marra, several months ago. The two men had met on the terrace briefly, as though they were perfect strangers. But Bret had been here that day, too—with Lady Walsh and Cynthia. And later he had told her the man was likely an enemy dealing with Edgar.

She studied Cynthia carefully. Should she confront her over recognizing a man Bret considered an enemy?

She decided it might be unwise.

Cynthia went on as though the momentary incident had never occurred. "I didn't ask to talk with you because of the club holiday in Luxor. There's something else."

"Oh?" Allison, too, was detached. "About what?"

"I'm embarrassed to say, but my worry outweighs my embarrassment. It's about my mother. She's rather unwise about some things. She means well but often blunders badly. I'm afraid that's what she has done this time, and it could be serious for her."

"What do you mean?"

Cynthia looked pained. "Mother's purchase of the Blaine house was not well thought out, I'm afraid. And now I fear her decision to buy the place may have placed her under the harsh scrutiny of Inspector Mortimer."

Inspector Mortimer? Allison wondered if Cynthia used Julian's more formal title for dramatic effect. "I don't see why the inspector would focus on your mother, Cynthia. I admit, it did seem rather odd to me that she'd want the Blaine house. After all, your mother is quite style conscious, and…well…"

"Yes, I know what you're thinking." Cynthia looked away, clearly troubled. "Why would anyone want a house where several ghastly murders took place. Revolting! And I do believe houses have personalities, don't you?"

"Well…no—"

"But Mother bought the house because she mistakenly thought *I* wanted it."

Allison stared at Cynthia, dumbfounded. "You? I would

think you are even more particular than your mother—" She broke off, then inclined her head. "I hope you don't mind my saying that."

"No, of course not. It's quite true, to some extent. But style or not, it goes without saying that large houses in the historical district of Old Cairo are nearly impossible to obtain nowadays. The Egyptians and Turks just don't want to sell to Europeans because of all the mosques there. And the Blaine house could be remodeled into a marvelous abode if done in good taste with a moderate investment. So Mother felt she wanted to buy it and give it to me for a wedding present."

"A...a wedding present?" Allison repeated in a somewhat numb tone.

A half smile showed on Cynthia's lips. "Mother still believes Bret will eventually surrender to what she considers my irresistible charms. Unfortunately, Bret is quite obstinate. But so is my mother. I, for one, well—" She shrugged and nibbled her cake.

Allison took a bite of crumpet and refilled her teacup, hoping her expression didn't reveal her feelings too much.

"So you see," Cynthia explained airily, "it's all a rather horribly mixed-up sort of thing. And now, after the death of your mother's chauffeur, my mother's action does look, well...rather suspicious."

"What do you mean, 'suspicious'? There were others who wanted to buy the house. Why would Inspector Mortimer think anything differently about your mother?" She chuckled. "After all, you can't really see him ever thinking Lady Walsh eliminated the chauffeur!"

"I know, it's quite absurd, isn't it? But Julian is an intense sort of man. He isn't always practical."

Actually, Allison hadn't seen Julian be anything *but* practical.

In some ways, he reminded her of Bret.

"You see," Cynthia went on, plucking at the tablecloth nervously, "I knew Julian—the *inspector*, in England several years ago. And...well, I don't think he's ever forgiven me for allowing Bret to come between us."

Allison stared at her over the gold rim of her china cup. "Oh." She hoped Cynthia hadn't noticed the underlying emotion of that whispered reaction.

She smiled weakly. "Yes, rather sticky and unpleasant, isn't it? To say it mildly, Bret and Julian, well, they don't like one another. And regardless of the colonel dragging his feet on an engagement, Julian would be the last to believe it won't happen. He's rather like my mother. Neither of them can believe I couldn't get the man I wanted, or that Bret prefers—well..."

Her eyes scanned Allison's face, bringing a warm flush to Allison's cheeks. She felt her pride ruffle like the fur on the back of a puppy. "An army nurse who totes a Bible in her kit bag?" The words came out clipped and stiff.

Cynthia smiled, and her delicately plucked brows formed an arch. "Something like that."

"I don't see what I can do about Lady Walsh buying the Blaine house," Allison said flatly. "I don't know Julian Mortimer that well. You need to talk to Mr. Sayyid about it."

"I have. He said I need to speak with you as well."

"I can't imagine why."

"I'll get to the reason in a moment. As for Julian, he's asking a lot of nasty questions about why Mother wanted to buy the house, what her interest in and association with the Blaines was...all *perfectly* foolish, but you can't convince him of that. He's only doing his duty, or so he says." She turned mournful eyes on Allison. "But I know Julian Mortimer. He can be vindictive. And this is the perfect opportunity for him to harass me, to make me sorry for refusing him. But he could easily provoke Mother to a swoon, or worse yet, worry her so that it affects her already weakened heart. Spencer has her on medication, of course. But with all of this, well, she's taken to bed and is worried sick. Julian knows that but doesn't seem to care." She set her cup down with a clatter. "I *loathe* him."

Allison felt a pang of sympathy for Lady Walsh, and even for Cynthia—which was something she had thought she could never do.

"But others wished to buy the house too," Allison protested. "Doesn't the inspector ask them hard questions as well?"

"That's just it. He doesn't. And the reason is clear. He's trying to get back at me. Before I met the colonel at a government dinner in London some two years ago, I was engaged to Julian."

"I see. You think he hasn't gotten over it and holds you responsible for his pain."

"Quite. Julian was very possessive. Nothing like Bret. I suppose that's the reason I was drawn to Bret at once. For once I met a man who wanted to avoid my catching him." She smiled. "It was...intriguing."

"About the house," hastened Allison, not wishing to discuss the elusive colonel. "I still don't see—"

"It's quite simple, really. The others who wanted to purchase the house might, well, feel they were treated badly by Mr. Sayyid if they should find out he gave Mother preference."

"Preference?"

"You did see the list, didn't you?"

Allison noticed the intensity in Cynthia's eyes. She hesitated, trying to gain time to think, trying to decide how much she should admit knowing. She tried to recall the list in her mind's eye.... There had been over a dozen names on it. She couldn't be sure now, but she rather thought Lady Walsh's name had appeared somewhere in the middle of the list.

"The list?" she repeated slowly.

"The list of potential buyers' names." Cynthia's tone was clipped, impatient. "You saw it? When you went there to meet Mr. Sayyid?"

"Oh, that. Well, I paid scant attention since I didn't go there to buy the house. I told you, I went to collect my trunk."

"Yes, yes, I know, but Mr. Sayyid must have mentioned the list of potential buyers to you. He said you had seen it."

"Did he?" She wondered why. She hadn't thought he noticed her speaking with his assistant, Rahotep.

"Sayyid's worried about it too. It doesn't look good for him to have given Mother preference in buying, not when there were others interested who actually had inquired first. He did it for the museum, of course. Mother offered him a thousand pounds more than the others."

"Mr. Rahotep had the list. He mistakenly thought that I was one of those waiting to make an offer. But really, I don't see that it matters."

"It does," Cynthia insisted, two bright spots of color forming on her cheeks. "If Julian learns that others on the list were bypassed to sell the house to us, he will be relentless to make something out of it."

"If he does, I don't see what I can do, Cynthia."

Her eyes burned, and she leaned across the table. "Sayyid hasn't told him about the list yet. He knew you looked at it, but I convinced him I'd talk to you and ask that you might not say anything since it really isn't important to the death of the chauffeur."

"I doubt the poor chauffeur believes that."

"Obviously, whoever killed him was looking for the box

Sarah left you thinking it may provide a key to more royal treasure."

"Yes, that would explain why it was stolen."

"Sayyid has already said he's willing not to mention the
order of the names on the list."

"And you want me to not say anything either, is that it?"

"I was hoping you wouldn't, for the sake of Mother's health.
That's why I told you about me and Julian and Bret, so you'd
understand what Julian is trying to do. He is still bitter, and as
the new chief inspector, he has ample opportunity to get even
with me. Oh, please, Allison, won't you help me?"

"As a matter of truth, I don't recall which names were first
on the list," she said soothingly.

"You don't?" Cynthia's relief was evident.

"I glanced at it, is all, for I had many things on my mind. So
there's little I could tell the inspector should he ask. But by
now Mr. Rahotep will have spoken to Inspector Mortimer
about the list of names anyway."

Cynthia shook her head. "Rahotep won't say anything if
Sayyid asks him to keep quiet. He's afraid of losing his position
at the museum. And keeping quiet about the arrangement of
names is not really important, except to me and Mother. After
all, what's in a dozen names?"

What, indeed?

Cynthia pushed aside her cup, looking more relaxed now.
But her relief was short lived. She glanced across the room, and
her eyes grew wary. "Speaking of Julian, he's coming now."

Allison followed her companion's glance to see the inspector coming out of the second dining area, but it wasn't clear
whether or not he had even noticed them. Nevertheless,
Cynthia gathered her handbag and gloves. "Would you mind
terribly if I scat?"

191

"Not if you really need to escape."

Cynthia stood. "You've turned into a grand friend, Allison."

Allison raised her brows at that. "I really don't see why we can't be, do you?"

"No, and I can't thank you enough. See you in Luxor." Her skittish gaze lingered a moment longer across the room. "Allison, do be careful of Julian. Sometimes I'm inclined to think his mind hangs on a thread over a precipice. I don't know what it would take to snap that thread, but I should hate to be around when it happens. God only knows what Julian Mortimer is truly capable of."

With that, she swept from the room. Allison glanced again at Julian—who stood there, still apparently unaware of her presence—Cynthia's parting comment echoing in her mind: *"God only knows what Julian Mortimer is truly capable of."*

TWELVE

>‑!‑◀▸‑◦‑◂▸‑!‑◄

ALLISON SAT STARING AT THE TABLE. What am I to make of all this, Lord? What could Cynthia possibly have meant—?

"Miss Wescott!"

Allison started. Looking up, she found Julian Mortimer standing beside her table, smiling down at her.

"My *dear* Miss Wescott, I'm delighted to see you up and about. A little surprised, but delighted. I was told you wouldn't be released until Wednesday morning."

"Hello, Inspector." She smiled. "Your surprise is well founded, I suppose. I confess it, I am absent without consent. Won't you sit down a moment?"

He drew back the heavy mahogany chair and seated himself. He was immaculately dressed in black and looked quite striking. He lifted his head, apparently catching a whiff of perfume left behind by Cynthia, and a thoughtful, amused smile lifted his lips. His smile lent softness to what was otherwise a somewhat imperious face. His deep-set black eyes stirred with a commanding energy. They turned back to Allison and took her in with interest. "I seem to have frightened away Miss Walsh."

Allison didn't answer.

"I would be truly disappointed had I frightened you."

She managed a casual smile. "I don't frighten easily, Inspector."

He gave a barklike laugh. "So I have heard, though I daresay that may not always be to your benefit."

From whom had he heard that?

"I thank you for your kind invitation. The very thought of a cup of hot tea cheers me."

"I'm glad you've the time," she said as she lifted a clean cup from the tray and poured. She handed him the steaming cup, noting as he reached out to take it from her that his fingers were lean and strong. *They have the look of a pianist's hands,* she thought absently. His nails were buffed and manicured, and he sported a gold ring with a black stone that looked to be an onyx.

"What an interesting design," she commented of the carving on the black stone. "That's Wadjit, isn't it? The watcher of the pharaoh."

"Ah, you do know your Egyptology. I shouldn't be surprised. In looking over the archaeological club documents last night, I saw you were in excellent standing."

"Oh yes." She kept her tones light, hoping he couldn't tell how little she liked it that he seemed to be checking up on her. "All my dues are paid. I'm not likely to be thrown out yet." What had he read about her and the holiday at Aleppo in 1914?

"I suppose an interest in archaeology runs in your family. I learned your cousin Neal Bristow unearthed some rare finds at Carchemish…from 1912 through 1914, I believe?"

So he *had* been delving into the details surrounding her. But why? Surely he didn't suspect her of wrongdoing? "Yes, he and Leah both did."

"His sister. She's no longer living?"

She suspected he must already know that. "She was murdered by Rex Blaine."

"Her death was gravely unfortunate. Ah! Delectable tea!"

She realized how easily he had switched the conversation

from his ring to the dig at Carchemish. Had the shift of topic been deliberate? But surely there was nothing to hide about the ring. Most every European who came to Cairo ended up with Egyptian jewelry.

"Do you mind if I smoke?" When she shook her head, he took out his pipe. "Thank you. I don't suppose you've remembered anything else that happened at the Blaine house since last we talked?"

"No," she admitted wearily. "Nothing."

"I seemed to have come to the end of the promenade too."

"I've been meaning to ask. What happened to Mr. Rahotep? Where did he disappear to at the house?"

Julian refilled his cup. "He insists he toured the back garden as requested by Mr. Sayyid. He'd been told to compile a list of trees and bushes for a hired gardener to trim before the house sold. When Rahotep returned, the chauffeur wasn't there. He assumed the chap became bored waiting for you and Beth and went for a stroll. Rahotep noticed the front right tire had gone flat. So he says he walked into Old Cairo to send someone out."

It was quite pat. Too much so, to Allison's way of thinking. "Why didn't he inform me or Beth before he left?"

"He claims he tried to, but neither of you answered his summons. He even went up the stairs, so he states, but couldn't find either of you. You had 'vanished into the wainscoting,' is the way he put it. So he scribbled a quick message and left it on the hall table."

She frowned. "I never found it. Was there a message do you think?"

Julian drew in a breath. "There was. We found it just as he had said. Along with his list of trees and bushes for the gardener. Rahotep has a perfect alibi. A neighbor picked him up on the road walking into town. We've checked his story and it rings true."

"I'm pleased to hear it. I rather like him. And he doesn't seem the sort to commit murder."

"They rarely do," he said, biting the end of his pipe. "That still leaves me with two dark, unanswered questions, though. Who *did* kill the unfortunate chauffeur? And why? It seems clear that the death was not premeditated. Perhaps a happenstance meeting with the murderer on a lonely path near the trees. Someone didn't want to be seen or didn't want to have to give excuses later on for being there, I think."

Allison believed the same thing. It was what Marra had said as well. "What about the box Sarah Blaine left to me? Perhaps whomever it was thought it might contain something valuable. Another Nefertari," she said, echoing Cynthia.

Julian placed his palms together and tapped his long fingers. The onyx stone winked in the light. "I think there is something much more involved in all this, but as yet, I've not been able to get a clue."

The relaxed atmosphere chilled to a silence. Then, as though awakening from his reverie, he straightened in his chair and looked at her with a quick smile.

"Ah, pardon, Miss Wescott. I seem to have drifted off." He removed his pocket watch, and his sleek, black brows intertwined across the long aristocratic bridge of his nose.

"I fear I need to leave your delightful company." He gave her a smile. "Unless, of course, you're ready to depart as well?"

She nodded. "Thank you, yes, I am."

"Grand. Then I hope you'll permit me to bring you to the Residency. My car is waiting."

He helped her rise from her chair, and they walked across the room to the terrace. He took her elbow, offering her his strength in going down the flight of stairs.

In the courtyard the doves were cooing in the palm trees, basking in the brilliant sunshine. Allison drew a deep breath—the air was still and thick with fragrances: the scent of old brick, the spicy tang of carnations, the pungent smell of garlic cooking, and the earthy aroma of Arabic coffee.

Julian's meditative silence seemed contagious, for Allison found herself unwilling to speak as they drove back to the Residency. Julian broke the stillness a few times, making comments that required no reply—it was almost as though he was giving her time to ponder whatever was troubling her. When they drove into the paved Residency drive lined with tall shrubs, he cut off the motor and turned in the seat to watch her.

"This isn't going to be pleasant for you, Miss Wescott."

She looked at him, alarmed. He stroked his black mustache thoughtfully. "I need to talk with you about a friend of yours. Colonel Holden."

"If it has anything to do with his suspected loyalties, I want you to know, Inspector, that I reject any such indictment."

"No indictment has been made. Yet."

His calm assurance unnerved her. She had expected less confidence on his part.

"Did David Goldstein already mention the problem to you?"

"He told me there was some mistake, that's all."

"No mistake, sadly. The colonel was suspended from the CID."

She cast him a wary glance, wondering if she could take his seeming sympathy at face value. Yet, despite Cynthia's assertions about Julian, Allison could detect no trace of bitterness in his tone when he mentioned Bret. Still, she knew well enough that his true bitterness could easily be hidden. A sudden thought nudged Allison: could Cynthia have lied for some reason of her own? She didn't have any sound reason to trust Cynthia, did she? But why would she have done so? There had to be a way she could test the reliability of the information Cynthia had passed to her. Bret would be the most reliable source, but, of course, he was not in Cairo. She must get to Luxor. She must find him. Only then would all the answers be forthcoming.

As she stared at Julian she wondered if he and Bret had at any time been at serious odds over the beautiful and mysterious Cynthia.

Allison knew it would be unwise to discuss any past romantic connections between Miss Walsh and the inspector now, but it was all she could do to swallow it back as he attacked Bret.

"Colonel Holden is as loyal to England as they come, Inspector. I think the department knows it too. What are they up to? Why are they saying these things about a man who's been awarded the Victoria Cross? I believe they've been unfair with him all along. They've taken advantage of his honor and devotion to duty. Just as the London Foreign Office has taken advantage of my father, asking him to stay on when he wanted to return to England. But what do they care about any cost to their people? Sacrifice! Sacrifice! That's all the CID cares about—and your department as well!"

Julian remained infuriatingly unruffled—another reminder of Bret. "Did David tell you why the colonel was suspended?"

Allison drew in a shaking breath and tried to calm herself. She pulled at the leather strap on her handbag.

"No," she admitted quietly after a good minute had passed. "I don't think he knew. He'd gotten wind of something and it broke his heart to tell me. But he doesn't believe it either." She turned her head sharply to meet his gaze evenly. "Nor do I care to hear the loathsome details. Because I know Bret. I know him better than anyone else. And all this nonsense is just that."

"Perhaps," he said congenially. "Nevertheless, the CID doesn't rush to judgment on these matters. If you are going to the club holiday at Luxor, you may run into him. Despite the past between you—one, I understand, that almost resulted in marriage—I urge you to be cautious."

How had he learned that she and Bret had discussed marriage? "Cautious of Bret? Absurd. As if I could have reason to fear him. He's saved my life a number of times. I'd trust him with my life now. This very moment."

"That's what I'm afraid of. Your trust may be your downfall."

She sucked in her breath. "How *dare* you, Inspector!"

He looked away to the blue delphiniums, their big heads nodding morosely in the breeze. "I'm sorry I must say these difficult things, Allison—"

"*Miss Wescott*, if you please," she gritted out. She wouldn't accept these insults about Bret. Cynthia was right. Julian Mortimer was—was tottering on a mental precipice, about to fall over. Well, he wouldn't drag her down with him. She wouldn't stop believing in Bret Holden. She knew him. She knew what it was like to be in his arms, to feel his kiss, his tightening embrace. She knew his allegiance to duty, to the CID. To—

Exhausted, her brain refused to go on.

"I'm sorry. I'll address you as Miss Wescott, of course."

"Maybe you're saying these things about him because you dislike him." The accusation escaped before she could stop it. She had told herself she would remain silent, but her emotions had gotten the best of her. She was afraid—for Bret, for herself…for their future.

"Dislike him?" His black eyes were guarded. "On the contrary, we were friends in England."

"Were you?"

"Your tone suggests otherwise. I wonder why?"

"Perhaps because Miss Walsh knows you quite well."

"Perhaps Miss Walsh has her own agenda and wishes to have you on her side."

"Then you deny knowing Miss Walsh in England?"

"I knew her, and Colonel Holden as well. I knew Neal Bristow, Paul Kruger—"

"It seems we're all becoming one extended, happy family."

"Not exactly happy, Miss Wescott." He looked at her, and she might have taken that dark, somber look for grief.

"Do you deny holding the colonel responsible for coming between you and Cynthia, for keeping you from attaining what you wanted most? Marriage to Miss Walsh?"

Julian's lean face tensed, and a line of white showed about his mouth. "She told you?"

"Yes."

"Well, unfortunately I cannot silence Cynthia from saying what she will, or keep her from filling people's minds with false impressions about my character. Certainly our past has nothing to do with what Colonel Holden has done. I do not make the decisions at the CID."

She'd made a mistake by saying that—his expression and tone of voice were clear evidence of that. Allison bit her lip, hoping she hadn't made matters worse for Cynthia and Lady Walsh.

"Colonel Bret Holden is suspected of selling rare treasures from one of the royal tombs in the Valley of the Kings. It is believed he stole the treasure, smuggling it into Berlin through the Berlin-Baghdad Railway."

No! She struggled to control her panic. Wasn't it what she had feared all along? *No, oh, no!*

Julian's voice was quiet again, calm once more, even kind, which made his accusation all the more painful. Somehow kindness and sympathy lent the impression there was truth to the charge.

"The colonel knows the ins and outs of the railway better than any of us. The CID hasn't gotten proof yet, but they believe it's upcoming. I'm sorry, Allison. I have no wish to see you hurt."

She shook her head and turned away, staring at the Residency without seeing its graceful and prestigious white walls. "I won't believe it of him, Inspector."

"Do any of us truly know others as well as we insist? Do we even truly know ourselves? How many times have we done something, said something we were ashamed of later, and we wonder in secret, 'How could I have done that? Said that? Whatever got into me?' When all the time, Miss Wescott, it wasn't what got into us, but what was already there, deep inside the soul, lodged like a root from a giant oak tree just waiting for the right season to sprout—"

"Stop it, Inspector!" She leaned forward in her seat to meet his dark, troubled gaze. "All your philosophical commentary doesn't change the facts. Bret is *not* a thief. He is a loyal British agent who has risked his life more than once for the honor of his country. And I don't care what the CID says, he wouldn't smuggle royal artifacts to get rich and ensure he is comfortable after the war. Because that's exactly what you're hinting at, isn't it? That he's gone sour on the war, on his country, and decided to do something for himself instead of the CID. Just like General Blaine! Like Sir Edgar Simonds! Like a host of other shiny red apples that look good on the outside but are rotten to the core!"

201

He sighed sadly. "Aptly put."

She stared at him bleakly. If only the accusations within her could be stilled as well. Bret *did* know the railway well. His dealings with it went all the way back to Carchemish, when she'd first met him before the war broke. He also had the map. The secret map taken from the sundial where Rex Blaine had hidden it before his death. As far as she knew, Bret had never informed the CID about the map, nor had he spoken of it to her father. She was sure that Julian didn't know about it. No one did, except she and Bret.

"What treasures is he accused of stealing?" She kept her tones neutral. "He has no treasures, that I know of. The baroness has Nefertari. Bret has nothing but his military wages."

"Actually, he may have a good deal more than that. In fact, it seems he has been accumulating wealth since before the war. You may be surprised to know this, but he's a somewhat wealthy man. His grandmother left him everything she had, which turned out to be a rather healthy sum."

It was the first she had heard of it, but it didn't matter. "I don't care if all he has is a shilling to his name, I believe in his integrity. In his honesty." She fought back desperate tears. "I love him," she whispered, more to herself than to the inspector. "I will continue to love him no matter what."

"Well." He tapped his pipe against his bottom teeth. "There's not much I can say to that, is there? Except he's a lucky chap." He paused, and Allison tried unsuccessfully to read the emotion on his face. With a shrug, he went on. "At any rate, the CID thinks the colonel may have discovered something of great import. Something that was so tempting that it brought his downfall."

Her gaze swerved away as a prick of guilt pierced her conscience. She wouldn't join the stone throwers by jumping to conclusions about the map.

Slowly she leaned back into the seat, feeling a warm breeze tugging at her hair. She fixed her gaze on Julian's pensive face. "There must be some mistake." She was somewhat surprised to find that she was more inclined to believe that now, regardless of the map and her fears.

"The CID doesn't think so. They have reason to believe an item of extreme value slipped past their noses on the train a few weeks ago. Though they are not prepared to say just yet where it was going."

"But do they have proof of his guilt?"

"No. None."

"Well, then!" She knew her smile was triumphant, but she didn't care. Of *course* they didn't have any proof. How could they? Bret was innocent! "All this is pure conjecture."

"No, not exactly. They have no proof, true, but I've heard that attributed to the colonel's cleverness rather than his innocence. Granted—" he waved an elegant hand—"they could be wrong. How glad I would be for that!"

Would he? She wondered. Would Julian Mortimer be pleased to discover Bret was unjustly accused? Or was he lying about his obsession with Cynthia Walsh and hoping to see Colonel Bret Holden humbled for taking her from him?

"In any case, the CID feels they can't take chances. So Bret's been relieved from his command until they know one way or the other. And your father will have much to say about it. Until he returns and turns off the heat, if he turns it off, Bret is in trouble, to say it mildly."

She knew her father used Bret as his "ace," as he often called him. She knew her father also had great influence on the CID and the London Office. Sometimes she thought he might actually work in the CID, that being chief consul was merely a masquerade. After all, such a position gave him audience with dignitaries he would otherwise never be able to meet. But it surprised her nevertheless to know the CID was waiting for his return to Cairo, or that Bret's future might depend on what he had to say.

A horrid thought materialized like a wicked genie from a bottle—what if something happened to her father? What if he never returned? *O God, grant that such a thing not be so!* But if it did happen, Bret might be left with little defense—an unenviable position when one was possibly facing the firing squad for treason! Did the enemy know this? Were they planning on it? Was it possible that this was their nefarious plan?

To destroy Bret?

A hundred torturous thoughts filled her mind until she found her fingernails digging into her sweaty palms. There was only one thing for her to do, only one way to find peace…

I'm going to Luxor. I'm going to find Bret one way or the other. And I'm going to help him prove his innocence, even if it means—

Even if it means—what? That she would leave with him for parts unknown? That she would never see her family or home again? She closed her eyes against the noon glare, feeling tiny beads of sweat break out on her forehead. To never see her beloved mother or father again…to never see Beth…? How could she even think such a thing?

Julian's voice was droning on as he played with the steering wheel and watched the Egyptian gardener digging and fertilizing the delphiniums. He knocked his pipe against the side of the car door to clear it, then replaced it inside his jacket.

"The danger is compounded where Bret is concerned because he knows how well the CID works." Julian's quiet voice went on, affording her little comfort. "From what I understand, he was quite high up in command."

"Yes, that's right."

"He knows agents in Berlin, Constantinople, as well as here in Egypt and in Arabia. Even in Jerusalem. No doubt about it, Holden is one of the best. He also knows who some of the enemy agents are."

Allison met Julian's considering gaze. Was he suggesting...?

"If he wanted to contact them," he went on, "he could. If he had something to sell, he might easily entice a foreign agent to risk meeting him in the Arabia Desert, far from anything except a few windblown tents of the bedouin. Believe me, Miss Wescott, the CID fears nothing more than one of their own cracking. 'Going bad,' they call it. When it happens, it threatens the whole team. Colonel Holden knows that, too. It could well be his way of getting even with a system he feels has treated him shabbily."

Allison fought the wave of nausea that threatened to overwhelm her. Julian had a quiet way of arguing that chipped persistently away at her defenses. That was the way Bret used to be. Chip, chip, chip...until the foundation began to crumble.

She tried to ignore her pounding heart. "I'm not so easily convinced, Inspector." If only her voice didn't sound so breathless, so desperate. "He has no reason to lash out at a system in which he believes so completely."

"Are you sure of that? He's very cool, very clever. And too ruddy smart for his own good. I hate bringing this up, but didn't your father pull the rug out from under him last December?"

Her gaze flew to meet his. Just how much did this man know? And where had he gotten his information? "Of course not. I don't know what you mean."

He looked pained. "I think you do, my dear. It's my business to know the business of the CID. Bret Holden wanted to marry the top man's daughter. And she wanted to marry him. But the boss wouldn't hear of it. Too dangerous, or so it was said. The good colonel didn't quite have the status the chief consul wants for his daughter."

Allison felt her cheeks burn with anger. "My father *never* said that!"

"Not in those precise words, I'm sure," Julian agreed, "but undoubtedly the meaning was quite clear to Colonel Holden."

She leaned her head back against the seat and stared up at the blue sky. A lone bird flitted overhead, its dark wings confident in their movements. Yes, if she would admit it, Julian was saying things that she herself had painfully considered on more than one lonely night after Bret had been sent from Cairo.

"I see by your grieved expression that you understand." Julian's soft voice wrapped around her. "I'm truly sorry to say these things, my dear. I wouldn't hurt you for the world, I hope you know that. But word has come from General Murray that the ship carrying your father has been delayed indefinitely. We don't know for certain when he will return to Cairo. And what he would have told you about Colonel Holden has been delegated to me. You're asked to avoid him in Luxor. Even, if possible, not to go."

She studied his face, wondering. Had her father somehow wired for Julian to talk to her? It was, after all, her father who recommended Julian to his new position, but she wouldn't make much of that. Not since Sir Edgar! Hadn't they placed Edgar in the Cairo police in order to trap him?

She sighed, struggling with feelings of unutterable weariness and defeat. "I'm sorry, Inspector, but I am going to Luxor on holiday. For Beth. And as for Bret getting in touch with me, he hasn't so far. I see no reason why he will in Luxor. You're sure he's there?"

"No, we're not sure of anything."

She looked at him, narrowing her eyes. "Yet you'll compound all these doubtful charges against him as though you know they're absolutely true."

"They are not my charges. They are the CID's. I merely pass them on to you. At the request of Sir Marshall."

"And we both know, don't we, that my father isn't in Cairo, so I've no way of double-checking your story."

He smiled.

"You know what they're doing to Bret? To his reputation? And if they are wrong, then what?"

"Yes, they know. And they assume he also knows."

She looked at him sharply. "What do you mean, he knows?"

He laughed, then sobered. "You're very quick, aren't you?"

She held her silence, and Julian shrugged.

"Colonel Holden knows the cost he'll pay."

She looked away, aching. Oh yes, the cost would be dear....

Please, God. Don't let it be true.

Allison turned back to meet Julian's penetrating gaze. "Have you any idea where he is now?"

"CID thought you might know."

"Since they claim to know most everything," she remarked dryly, "they should know I haven't seen him since before Christmas."

"They're hoping he'll contact you in Luxor."

She filled in the rest of what was left unspoken: They thought she might find out what Bret was doing. And report it to them. "Aren't they forgetting something, Inspector? Bret's inclined to think I broke off the engagement to please my father. That's why he hasn't taken the initiative to contact me. What makes them think he'll confide in me now?"

"They don't know for certain he will. But it's a possibility.

And you must understand that your cooperation may benefit the colonel. If he's innocent, there's nothing to hide."

She looked at Julian Mortimer for a long minute, wondering what he wanted from all of this, what really drove him.

"This is very painful for you," he said gently. "I wish it weren't happening. I wish it weren't needful, and most of all, I wish you weren't involved."

For some reason she believed him.

"What shall I tell CID?" His eyes were bright and watchful.

Her mouth tightened and she opened the car door. "Tell them I refused. I'm going to Luxor on holiday, Inspector. Nothing more. And if the colonel is as smart as I think he is, he's nowhere in the area. They are all wasting their time." She slid from the seat and stood, her legs weak from more than her hospital stay.

"I understand," he said quietly. "And you may be right."

She closed the door, and he started the engine, carefully putting on his hat. His voice sounded unhurried above the revving motor. "I'll pass on your decision. It may be I will join you in Luxor." He smiled. "I have a vacation coming myself."

"So soon? My goodness, they do treat you well."

Her wry comment wasn't lost on Julian, for he grinned at her and laughed.

Allison watched him drive away, then sighed and turned to face the Residency.

"Allison?"

She whirled, but it was only Doctor Howard walking toward her, frowning. His eyes crackled with disapproval. "I'm considering going to General Murray about the menace Julian is becoming to you and Cynthia Walsh. This intimidation and browbeating must be stopped."

He took hold of her shoulders, studying her face. "I'm just

leaving, but I can write you a prescription for something calming if you'd like."

She smiled. "No, no, Doctor, I'll be all right in a moment."

"Eleanor called for me. Beth isn't well. She refuses to leave her room."

"Oh no…"

"Rest easy, my dear, she's better now. I've given her some medication for her pining. The sooner that wretched trial is done with, the better off we'll all be. As for Gilbert," he stated impatiently, "all I can say is that the boy deserves a good beating. What did a sweet child like Beth ever see in him, beside his foppish good looks?"

Allison shook her head, weary to the core. "We've all tried to keep her away from him."

"Perhaps I should escort you into the house? You're looking pale."

"No, thank you. I'm fine. I don't want to keep you."

He shook his head. "I shouldn't have burdened you about Beth. You've enough to worry about. I'm afraid I couldn't help overhearing a bit of Julian's ridiculous rhetoric as I was leaving. I'd forget everything he said about the colonel. If any officer in the British forces is true blue, it's Bret Holden. I wouldn't, however, say as much for Julian."

She looked at him for an explanation. He seemed reluctant, then shook his head, obviously troubled. "Cynthia came to me about him. The poor girl's afraid of him. It was bad enough to have a man like Edgar Simonds sitting behind the desk as chief inspector. Now comes Julian, casting vengeful glances toward Cynthia Walsh. Really, it's all quite revolting. More ineptitude by those who should know better. Why don't they look deeper into the warped past of these fellows before they assign them? I tell you, I wish I could do something about it…if your father would arrive, a good many things could be swiftly settled."

"I wish he were here," Allison said, surprised to hear the catch in her voice. No, she was not going to cry. "I'm afraid for him," she whispered.

Spencer gave her a pat on the arm. "He's carefully guarded, you can be sure of that. You mustn't add to your worries, lest you end up like Beth."

"Yes, you're right. But Father's delay will be another disappointment for my mother." She gave the doctor a quick look. "How much does she know about the danger he might be in?"

"Knowing Eleanor, she probably knows more than any of us. I'm sure that's the main reason behind her troubled spirit these past weeks."

Allison looked toward the house, and Spencer patted his shirt pocket with nervous fingers. "I must be scurrying. It's trying indeed to have lost Nurse Phillips. She kept my schedule well arranged. I fear I've taken on too much. A good holiday at Luxor looms more enticing than ever."

When he left, Allison walked slowly toward the wide, stately front porch, stuffing her hands into her pockets. She quite agreed with Spencer: a reprieve at Luxor grew more enticing with each passing moment. She had told Julian it wasn't likely that Bret would contact her there, but that didn't limit her from doing some snooping on her own. Her steps quickened.

"I have a right to know what he's up to," she murmured. "And what has happened to that map."

THIRTEEN

ALLISON WAS SURPRISED WHEN MR. RAHOTEP arrived the following afternoon in a huff of nerves. He wrung his square, brown hands and vented his concerns as he moved about the drawing room, his flowing brown robe flapping about him. It seemed he had an excessive number of burdens and didn't know where to begin in expounding on them.

"I have been harried about all morning," he complained to her and her mother, "and through no fault of my own. Mr. Sayyid expects miracles. Yes, miracles!"

"Do sit down, Mr. Rahotep," Eleanor soothed. "A cup of Arabic coffee, perhaps?"

"Ah! But, ah! Madame, you are too kind! Yes, too kind. I should bless Allah thrice for such a cup and a tablet for my head. Yes, any tablet would suffice, Lady Wescott!"

Eleanor looked sympathetic as she gazed upon the man as he sank, short of breath, into a large, overstuffed chair, his sandaled feet just touching the floor. Eleanor went to give orders to Zalika to bring in an urn of coffee, then went upstairs to her room for a bottle of mild headache pills. Mr. Rahotep continued his complaint to Allison.

"I shall resign my duties. Yes, and move to Alexandria. Mr. Sayyid grows more demanding as the days pass."

"I'm sorry to hear that," Allison said as soothingly as she could. "What seems to be the problem?"

"Everything! Simply everything. I am now blamed for misplacing the list of interested buyers of the Blaine house. But I am positive I did not lose it, Miss Wescott."

Allison remembered Cynthia's concerns. "Is the list so important?"

"Important? To me, it was not. To Mr. Sayyid it was not. But suddenly it has become *extremely* important to the police. That Inspector Mortimer wants it. He insists that if it's missing, someone deliberately stole it! Or that I am holding back from him! And Mr. Sayyid is angry with *me*. He calls me inept! I should resign at once. Yes, at once!"

"But why? I mean, why would anyone go to such trouble to steal a list of names? Surely you know who they were? Can't you simply write them down and give them to the inspector?"

"That's just the difficulty, Miss Wescott. I have done so to the best of my memory, and I'm short five names! I am looked upon with grave suspicion now. And that, Miss Wescott, is where I hope you may come to my aid. You saw the list. Perhaps you could remember the five I have forgotten!" He pulled a rumpled list from his robe and handed it to her as Zalika came into the drawing room bearing the tray with coffee. Allison's mother, who carried a small bottle of tablets, followed her.

"Here you are, Mr. Rahotep. I'm confident this will make you feel better. Doctor Howard prescribed them for my headaches."

"You are kind, Lady Wescott. Too kind."

Allison was reading through the list of individuals, keeping her expression calm and indifferent. She handed the paper back to Rahotep a minute later, shaking her head.

"I'm dreadfully sorry. I barely glanced at the original list. I wouldn't know whom the individuals are that you've overlooked. As for these," she said of the list, "they're all strangers to me."

212

"They are from Alexandria and Fayid." He went on to cluck his tongue over his disappointment. "I shall keep trying to remember. In the meantime, I am here about a change in the club meeting at Luxor."

But before he could tell them what it was, Zalika brought in visitors: Spencer and Julian. At the sight of the inspector, Mr. Rahotep's brown complexion grew sickeningly pale.

"Hello Spencer, Julian," Eleanor greeted the two men. "Have some coffee, or would you prefer tea?"

"Nothing for me, Eleanor." Spencer shook his head. "I just stopped by to see how Allison is doing and to scold her severely for leaving Bulac without my knowledge." And he turned sharp physician's eyes on Allison as his brows twitched together. "You, young lady, should know better. I should have said something yesterday, but was so upset over Julian's badgering that my initial shock of seeing you gave way to other concerns. Julian, must you wheedle this young woman about the colonel?"

"You may call it as you wish, Spencer, but I am only doing my duty. I promise I won't be but a few minutes. I have one or two more questions is all."

"It's Beth I'm worried about," Eleanor said to Spencer. "She's not eating."

"I'd better see her while I'm here. I have a meeting with General Murray tonight. We play chess together." He smiled. "Perhaps I'll let him win this time. Now, where is Beth?"

Eleanor stood. "In her room. I'll bring you up."

"I must keep insisting you take her away from Cairo."

"Beth is leaving with Allison for Luxor on Thursday."

Mr. Rahotep jumped to his feet. "Ah! That is why Mr. Sayyid sent me. With the other troubling matter I'd almost forgotten! I was busy all morning making calls on the club members to give them their new itinerary. Here, Miss Wescott." He produced a sheet from his satchel and gave it to Allison.

"The baroness's assistant will not need to bring you to Luxor by way of a rented *falukka*, as first arranged. By the will of Allah a sudden, pleasurable change for all concerned has risen as mysteriously as the Nile overflows its banks!"

He smiled broadly, and Allison exchanged glances with her mother.

"What kind of fortunate change?" Eleanor asked dubiously, lifting a brow.

Rahotep hastened to explain. "The baroness returned to Cairo sooner than expected to meet her son, Paul. He asked her to voyage with him on *The Blue Nile*."

"The *steamer?*" Allison asked.

"Indeed. Exactly," Rahotep replied. "It would seem Paul wanted to turn the excursion to the Valley of the Kings into a Nile holiday. And the baroness, thinking the voyage advantageous to the enlightenment of the club members, has in turn managed to book passage on the steamer for all of the club members—at half price! Lady Walsh is particularly pleased, for now she will be able to join her daughter. She'll be comfortable on the steamer, where the meals are luxurious."

"So that's why Lady Walsh wants to see me," Spencer said wearily. "She'll be wanting to go with Cynthia. And no doubt she expects me to tag along to monitor that heart ailment of hers. Drat! I had hoped for some weeks to myself for a change, with nothing to do but let my beard grow and wear sandals. Now I'll need to escort Lady Walsh about, pointing out pyramids and other such spectacles. Naturally she won't appreciate them. She's already made the absurd comment that if you've seen one, you've seen them all."

Julian chuckled. "Looks like you've some work cut out for you, Spencer. So Lady Walsh isn't interested in the royal tombs of the great pharaohs? I wish there were less interest shown by Colonel Holden."

Allison stiffened and looked across the room at him. Why had he said that now, in front of everyone? Her mother looked embarrassed, and Spencer gave the inspector a scornful glance. Julian, however, stood with a debonair attitude, his expression calm. Interestingly enough, though, his eyes were not on Allison, as she'd expected, nor on Doctor Howard in response to his silent rebuke. Surprisingly, the inspector watched Mr. Rahotep.

That gentleman twisted his hands together. "Oh dear, oh dear, Inspector! Not more trouble on the black market?"

"Afraid so. Word came in to the office just this morning. A Kurd from Aleppo was found dead on the Berlin-Baghdad Railway. They think he may have been carrying a piece of great value."

"Smuggling?" Rahotep gasped.

"There's little doubt remaining. Still, we need proof before we can arrest those involved."

"I never would have believed it of Colonel Holden!" Rahotep looked unduly excited.

"Oh, *really!*" Allison jumped to her feet. "Such absurdity, Inspector!"

"Allison—" her mother began with a calm, albeit warning, tone. "The inspector is only doing his job."

"Is he?" she quipped, directing a glare at Mortimer. "You said yourself you have no proof, Julian. So why drop the colonel's name here?"

"It's true we've no proof, Miss Wescott, but we will." He looked back at Rahotep, and the Egyptian moved nervously about the ottoman.

"I've been thinking about the list of names, Inspector

Mortimer," he said, drawing a piece of paper from his robe. "My memory is woefully faulty. This is all I can come up with."

As Julian took the rumpled paper, Allison thought over what Julian had told them. A Kurdish man was dead on the Berlin-Baghdad Railway.... Bret had Kurdish friends in and around Aleppo and Jerablus.

"What makes you think this Kurdish fellow was carrying a treasure piece?" Spencer asked. "Aren't you rushing to conclusions? I can't imagine the Turks and Germans turning over any evidence."

Julian's gaze was confident. "The CID have their agents everywhere, Spencer. Whoever killed this man for the piece was in such a hurry to escape he blundered badly and dropped its cloth. They found it clutched in the Kurd's hand."

A look of understanding passed between the two men. What Julian had said must be significant, Allison realized. If only she knew why. Glancing back at Mr. Rahotep, she noticed that his own nervousness had seemed to ease. In fact, rather than fearful, she thought his expression had grown shrewd and watchful.

"Mr. Sayyid and the baroness have been able to arrange some morning lectures aboard the steamer," Rahotep announced. "All in preparation for our visit to the house of the esteemed archaeologist, Dr. Howard Carter, near the Valley of the Kings." All in all, so he assured them, the voyage by steamer would give them a memorable holiday.

"Beth will enjoy it," Eleanor told Allison. "I must say I feel relieved you'll both be in company of the club. The idea of you taking the voyage alone by falukka had me a trifle concerned."

"No need to worry, Eleanor, I'll keep stern eyes on them both," Spencer promised.

"We both will," Julian added with a smile.

Allison looked at him. "You're coming along, Inspector?" There was little welcome in her voice, a fact that seemed to amuse Julian, for his dark eyes laughed at her.

"I wouldn't miss the delightful excursion, Miss Wescott. Unlike Lady Walsh, you see, I happen to think every pyramid holds a new mystery, and every royal tomb, the possibility of unexpected treasure. All we need is a map."

She felt the heat rise in her cheeks and resisted the flinch that tugged at her in response to the comment. It wasn't possible. Julian couldn't know…could he?

"Well, well, a jolly time shall be had by one and all, or so it appears." There was a wry tone to Spencer's comment. "Only I shall remain the bored dolt when it comes to the pyramids. Well, I shall at least keep Lady Walsh company on deck, and maybe get in a bit of fishing."

"What about Omar and the rented falukka?" Allison asked.

Rahotep's fingers twitched. "No difficulty, Miss Wescott. No difficulty at all. Omar is naturally to voyage with the baroness and her son, Paul. And the owner of the small boat will be paid for his trouble. And now—" he set his empty coffee cup down, along with the bottle of tablets—"Most helpful, Lady Wescott. Most helpful. The headache has gone, and I feel much enlivened." With a last glance at the inspector, and a bow toward all, he hurried out of the drawing room, ostensibly to inform the other club members of the change in plans.

"And now, Spencer, I do wish you'd have a look at Beth," Allison's mother said.

"I'm confident the news of the Nile excursion will do wonders for her. This is the best thing to happen yet. I wish you'd come along with your daughters."

"I wish I could, but you know how I feel about Marshall's delay. I can't possibly leave without him."

"You can, but you won't."

"However you want to put it, Spencer." She turned toward the inspector, who stood quietly listening. "And Julian, please don't worry Allison more than necessary."

"I shall be exceedingly brief, Eleanor, I promise."

The door closed behind her mother and Doctor Howard. When their footsteps faded in the outer hall, Allison stood from the divan and walked over to the front window, looking out at the drive and the bright Egyptian sunlight, which beat relentlessly on the flagstone.

Not unlike Julian and his questions…

"I really don't have anything else to tell you about what happened at the Blaine house," she said without turning to face him.

"You didn't tell me you had seen the list of names. I learned about that from Rahotep."

She had promised Cynthia she would keep Mrs. Walsh out of it, but could she? *I shouldn't have made such a rash promise.*

"It didn't seem important. After all, what's in a list of names?" It was the same question Cynthia had asked.

"Probably nothing. But since Sayyid and his assistant were nervous about keeping it hushed up, naturally it triggered my interest. What did he tell you about it just now, before I arrived?"

"That he had probably misplaced it, but that you were making too much of it. After all, why wouldn't there be interested buyers in the Blaine house? Property is hard to come by. Once you've been here a few months you'll see that for yourself. And who knows?" She turned and looked at him innocently. "Maybe your name was on that list."

"Mine?" He smiled. "I have a very comfortable little room near my office. An older estate replete with murders doesn't interest me at all."

"I would think a man in police work would find murders very interesting."

"I have interests other than police work."

"Oh? You have aspirations to become a judge perhaps?"

His thin mouth twitched with cool humor. "No, dare I say it, Miss Wescott? I'm most interested in archaeology. Yes, a little trying, isn't it? But true."

She looked pointedly at his long-fingered hand. "That accounts for the ring, I suppose." She remembered now what it was that had interested her about it at Ezbekiah Gardens: the carving of the cobra-head god—the god that supposedly defended the pharaohs.

"It was rather unfair of you to link the latest black market smuggling on the Berlin-Baghdad Railway to Colonel Holden." Allison knew her stance was as stiff as her words, but she didn't soften either. "You sounded like both judge and jury."

"I suppose it did appear that way. I also made it clear we have no convicting proof yet."

"And that you think you will."

He sat down watching her. "About that list of names, Miss Wescott. It doesn't bring me pleasure to keep after you, but anything you could remember may prove important."

"Important to what? Discovering who stole the menagerie Sarah left me? Or to convicting Colonel Holden of smuggling rare treasure pieces?"

"They seem like unconnected events don't they? As you said, the pieces Mrs. Blaine left you were tourist stuff. We'll give Colonel Holden more credit than that."

"Which doesn't explain why someone knocked me out to steal them does it?"

"Was Lady Walsh's name on that list by any chance?"

His dark eyes held hers steadily, and she finally spoke to prevent the warm flush from flaring her cheeks. "I would certainly think so, since it was her name that was selected to purchase the house." She turned her back and looked out the window.

"I agree, Miss Wescott. That is why her name should have appeared first on the list which you looked at."

"I only got a short look at the list, the names were mostly unfamiliar, and that's why I can't remember who was first."

"But certainly you would have remembered a familiar name like that of Lady Walsh, especially if she were on the top of the list, is that not correct, Miss Wescott?"

"Yes, I would have remembered that."

She heard him sigh and stand.

"Anything else you would have remembered?"

"No."

"I shall take your word for it." She heard him move toward the door. He opened it and called back: "I'll look forward to seeing you aboard *The Blue Nile*. Good day, Miss Wescott."

The door closed quietly, and she turned and stared at it.

Allison was thinking of Bret and the map when, some twenty minutes later, she heard Zalika go to answer the front door. A few minutes later she heard Doctor Howard telling her mother that Beth was feeling much better, and that now he must rush to see Lady Walsh.

"I daresay most of her ailments are in her head," he said. "It's a shame she'll insist on the Nile excursion. Cynthia, poor girl, could use a few weeks holiday without her complaining mother pestering her."

"Odd," came Eleanor's voice as she showed him to the door. "I always felt it was Cynthia who did the spoiled pestering of Lady Walsh. I've yet to meet a more selfish young woman."

Doctor Howard laughed. "Perhaps she and the colonel are

suited for each other after all. I must say, people do surprise us. One thinks a certain fellow has character through and through, then suddenly something happens to make him snap. It's most disagreeable. Rather ruins one's opinion of our inestimable CID."

Allison stood there, feeling as though she were in a fog. She was aware of the front door closing and the sound of her mother's steps as she crossed the hall, then paused outside the drawing room.

"Allison? Can you come up and see Beth? She wants to talk to you."

"Yes, Mum, I'll be up in a minute."

"All right, but do hurry, dear. I've an appointment to keep with the wife of the American ambassador."

A short time later, when Allison entered her sister's room, Beth was up and parading about in a pink robe. Her long, dark hair tumbled loosely about her shoulders, and as she turned from the window, her face was flushed and her eyes were as bright as brown marbles.

"I'll need a pair of desert walking shoes. Did you ever get yours from the Blaine house?"

Allison grimaced. "I'm beginning to loathe that pair of shoes. They remind me of murder. Yes, I've got them. They're still in the trunk. Someone from *The Blue Nile* is to come for our baggage tomorrow. If you're hoping to buy additions to your wardrobe, we'd better do so this afternoon."

Beth mimicked Cynthia Walsh as she swayed across the room to her wardrobe. She leafed through her clothing, frowning as she did so. "Darling, I simply *must* have something very elegant to wear to dinner each night aboard ship."

Allison smiled ruefully, watching her.

"Mum says the steamer will dock at fancy places along the

Nile. And we'll be going ashore to dine and sightsee at scads of interesting places."

"Is that what you wanted to talk to me about? Borrowing some gowns?"

"Yes. The new one Mum has? The scarlet one? You borrow it, will you? Then I'll borrow it from you on the boat."

"Oh, no." She looked at Beth's dark hair. "If you want it, you borrow it. I look dreadful in scarlet, and Mum knows it."

"She won't let me wear scarlet."

"You have more gowns than I do," Allison said, "I should borrow one from you."

Beth seemed to lose interest in the topic. She turned her head to look at Allison. "There's something else I wanted to talk about." Her face was sober now. She sank to the edge of her bed, holding a yellow silk frock closely against her. Her alert brown eyes glanced toward the door where it stood open a few inches. She walked over, looking into the hall, then, apparently satisfied, shut it quietly and came back to face Allison. Her eyes held a familiar, enigmatic glow.

Allison sat opposite her on a large, pink velvet ottoman with white silk fringe. "Is it about what happened at the Blaine house?"

"Remember what I told you in the garden? About how Gilly didn't kill Sarah?"

So, they were back to that again. She didn't want to upset Beth by disagreeing, not when she appeared to be snapping out of her dark mood.

"Well," Beth went on, "I'm even more convinced he didn't do it. I haven't told everything to Inspector Mortimer yet. I told him I was hiding under the bed during the time someone knocked you unconscious and stole the box. He thinks I didn't hear or see anything."

Allison's heart began to beat faster. She leaned toward her sister. "You mean you weren't under the bed?"

Beth fingered the silk dress, her brown eyes downcast. "Oh it's true, I was hiding under the bed all that time. But I saw someone."

"You *what?*"

"That is," she hastened, "I didn't see the person's face. I saw the person's, well, their shoes."

Shoes. Beth had seen the intruder's shoes.

"Yes, go on." Allison forced a calm she did not feel into the words.

"He—that is, I assume it was a 'he.' Although I suppose a woman *could* have worn men's shoes, though she'd need to have big feet—"

"Beth! Please! Just get on with it!"

"All right! All right. He came right inside the room where I was hiding beneath the bed. Your old room, the one facing the front drive. I think he came up the stairs from the back of the house where you were, though I can't prove it. It's just a feeling I had, like he was there all along, even before you arrived. When I was alone in the house and went to sit in the garden, I now think he was watching me all that time from Marra's bedroom window. I get the creeps just thinking about it." She rubbed her arms and shuddered, glancing about as though he might emerge right then and there from beneath her own bed.

Allison drew in a breath and straightened. "Go on. What about his shoes."

"I was terrified! I could hear his furtive footsteps coming into the room, walking about, and stopping by the bed. But something seemed odd because he sort of, well, dragged his feet as he walked. Then I got a glimpse of his feet—and—" Fear flickered in her eyes. "I think I saw those old shoes before.

In Rex Blaine's office. They were *his* old desert shoes."

Rex Blaine's shoes?

"Isn't that odd, Allison? I was almost sure whoever it was would stoop and look at me. I kept praying and praying that Jesus wouldn't let him bend down. And he didn't! He went to the window, then turned and went out. Thank God."

"Yes, thanks to our heavenly Father," Allison whispered. She reached out to hold her sister, thankful she was safe. "Oh, Beth, God kept you safe. He is the God who is there. He's not with us only when life is sunny and pleasant, with apple pies baking in the oven, and when life is filled with hearth, family, and friends! God is with us when the mountains shake, the earth quakes, the waves roar, and evil may come to circle our house. When sickness robs us of strength, when those we love walk out on us. Jesus is there, through the worst of times."

Beth smiled and blinked. "I know one thing: he was with me then. And because he was, I think he'll be with me no matter what. That brings a lot of confidence, doesn't it?"

Allison simply smiled. Outside the window, a bird landed in the flame tree and began to sing. Almost, Allison thought with a pang, as though to affirm what they were saying. As they sat, Allison's mind began to wander back to when she had hidden from Rex Blaine beneath the porch at the archaeological huts in Aleppo. She knew exactly the terror that Beth must have felt. She reached over and took Beth's hand. "Go on. I think you have more to tell me."

Beth shook her head. "No, that's all. I just saw those desert shoes. Rex Blaine's old shoes."

"Shoes don't mean very much, Beth. Do you realize everyone going on the holiday to the Valley of the Kings will have a pair of expedition shoes like that? Even Mum has a pair."

Beth nodded, silent, seemingly lost in her thoughts.

"Well, if you didn't see who it was that came into the room…" Allison's voice fell off into the obvious: nothing could be proven. It was also safer for Beth if not everyone knew that she was hiding under the bed. Her sister's loud insistence that Cousin Gilbert hadn't murdered Sarah Blaine was dismissed as the frantic assertion of an overly emotional young girl who was in love. No one, not even Allison at first, had taken Beth seriously.

"Not that seeing a style of shoe proves who was wearing them," Allison said. "As you say, shoes are shoes." She mused, more to herself than Beth. "Like a list of names, it might mean something, then again, it probably doesn't."

"Well, it couldn't have been Sir Edgar sneaking about the house. I mean, he's in jail."

Now why did she bring up Sir Edgar?

"But it does prove something," Beth said. "It could have been someone else—someone other than Gilly—who murdered Sarah. And that someone is still searching for something in the house."

Lady Walsh and Cynthia? No, Allison could never bring herself to think of them as international spies or murderers. And there was the new information Beth had given her in the garden about Sarah putting up a struggle before her death. Clearly, that left out the aged and ailing Lady Walsh. Cynthia was young and strong, but Allison doubted the young woman had it in her to physically overcome Sarah.

"He must have thought he'd find what he wanted in the box of doodads Sarah left you," Beth was saying. She looked at Allison sharply. "You know what I think? Someone needed you there. They didn't want to waste time searching. You would lead them straight to the box. They were waiting, watching. And that's why I felt their eyes when I was out in the garden, before you came there and found me. Didn't you say you thought you heard someone?"

Allison was worried about Beth. She knew too much and wasn't afraid to speak her mind publicly.

"How long were you there before I arrived?"

"Maybe an hour. But I didn't hear anything, or see anything. But I had a funny feeling about Marra—I mean, about the room she stayed in. By the way, where is Marra?"

"Near Suez, working at the hospital. They expect a new German offensive there trying to cross the Suez." Allison was frowning. It hurt deeply that Marra didn't trust her over David. She had thought they were allies, friends who would never turn against the other. Marra's bitterness had come as a shock to Allison. It was a part of the young woman she hadn't seen before—at least, not directed at her. She had thought she knew Marra so well, but evidently she hadn't.

"Someone wanted you there," Beth continued. Her eyes narrowed. "Maybe Sarah didn't really leave you that menagerie. Maybe it was just a way to get you to lead them to where it was."

Allison's gaze rushed to Beth's. "Hmm! If that's true, then whoever knocked me unconscious and took it must be unfamiliar with the details leading up to Sarah's death."

Beth jumped up. "You see? I'm right, about Gilly, I mean. It's someone else. But clue me in, why do you say he's a stranger to the events?"

"I can't say for sure that he is. But finding the box in the storage closet should have been easy if, as you say, I was needed. Most everyone already knew the details of how Sarah and I found the broken cobra head there. They wouldn't need me to lead them to it. Well, it should be easy to find out if Sarah really left it to me," Allison said with determination. "I'll make certain I have a look at the will. If Mr. Sayyid was mistaken—"

"Or lying," Beth put in bluntly. "I don't like him. That distinguished beard he wears, for one thing, seems more like a mask than anything else. And that black turban is so foreboding and secretive."

"I'll tell Father to check the will when he gets home. And you can explain about the shoes and about Gilbert. He'll know whom to tell, whom to trust. Unfortunately, we're in a situation where we can't know. In the meantime, we need to keep quiet about our speculations. Outside ourselves, we don't know whom we can fully trust. Beth, you mustn't say a thing about having seen someone come into the room in that pair of shoes."

"Do you think he'd try to silence me?"

"I think it's been shown he isn't above silencing any of us." She touched her still bruised forehead. "Have you told any of this to Mum?"

"No, but—"

Allison waited in vain for Beth to explain. "But, what?"

Beth's eyes narrowed mysteriously. "Like you say, we'd better keep still. That attack on you in the storage closet,...it might have been worse. And Allison, I still think we can trust Julian. I think we should sit down with him and tell everything. When are we leaving on *The Blue Nile*?"

"Tomorrow afternoon," she said, disturbed by Beth's confidence in Julian. "I don't think we should say anything to the inspector. Not yet. There will be time enough on holiday, if it comes to that."

Beth's sharply analytical gaze came to rest on her face. "You don't trust him."

"Beth, you mustn't openly scrutinize people. With me, it's safe, but with others…"

Beth shrugged. "Everyone seems to have something to hide—oh, I don't mean you, but all the others. Even old Lady Walsh. I think they *want* Gilly to die."

"You're exaggerating, dear. Lady Walsh didn't even know Gilly. Anyway, I'm thinking about you. If you say it to the wrong person it might prove, well, dangerous."

Again, Beth shrugged, her brown eyes hardening. "It's true, though. Gilly's execution would protect the real murderer."

"Even if Gilbert is found guilty, they won't execute him anytime soon. There's time for us to bring all of this to Father when he comes home."

"I suppose. And a holiday on the Nile does sound fun and refreshing. I've *got* to get Mum to lend me her scarlet gown. About Julian, I think he's quite handsome, don't you?"

"Hmm? What did you say? Oh. Yes, I suppose he is that. Rather too dandified for my taste in masculine looks, but handsome. Look, Beth, before you get too friendly with Julian, there's someone else I want to discuss all this with while we wait for Father."

Beth nodded sagely. "Bret?"

Allison walked toward the door. "Yes. You'd better get your things packed. I'll do the same. Then we can go into town and do some shopping."

"Did Mum leave yet to meet that American wife of the ambassador? I'm going to try on that *too* darling scarlet gown."

Allison left her sister's room and walked down the hall to her own. As she entered, she was frowning. She was even more worried about her sister than she had expressed. There seemed little she could keep from Beth these days. That in itself wasn't disturbing because she didn't have anything to hide. But what if she did? How would she feel? How would someone else feel who did have something to hide? Someone, for instance, who was becoming convinced that little Beth—with her insistence that Gilly was innocent and with her snooping about and her attentive gaze—suddenly was becoming a danger to their secret?

She stopped, her hand resting on the doorknob. Her palm began to sweat. Her statement repeated itself in her mind: What if someone *did* have something to hide? How would that someone feel about Beth?

Allison's hand slipped from the doorknob. She heard Beth's light steps going down the hall to her mother's room to locate the new gown. Beth was growing up quickly. She was much cleverer than anyone had given her credit, but she was still young and sometimes full of fun and mischief. She didn't take the threat to her safety as seriously as she ought. And because she didn't, Allison knew she must protect her.

Her mother and Doctor Howard were right: Beth must be taken away at once. But it wasn't lost on Allison that many of the people who would be on holiday at Luxor were the same ones connected, even if only remotely, with the murderous events at the Blaine house—and Beth was convinced that one of them was a murderer.

PART II

THE NILE

In the day of my trouble I will call upon You,
for You will answer me.

PSALM 86:7

FOURTEEN

THE DECKS OF THE STEAMER *The Blue Nile* were crowded with passengers, including the fifteen members of the archaeology club. Allison, arriving late with Beth, found that most of the group was meeting below in the salon where trays of cool drinks were being served.

As she entered with Beth, Allison hardly recognized the tall man in a crisp short-sleeved white jacket and slacks who walked toward them briskly.

Was this the "Cranky Old British Doc"? Why, he didn't seem old at all. Allison had always looked on Doctor Howard, well—as a contemporary of her father's. Perhaps it had just been his attitude, for watching him now, relaxed and smartly dressed, he seemed rather...debonair. Allison blinked and stared at him. Doctor Howard couldn't have been much older than Julian Mortimer—who, like the doctor, had that certain appearance that she labeled a "benign thirtyish look."

Doctor Howard strolled up, his usual cryptic smile on his face, but his eyes were troubled. "I'm glad to see you've both made it. I was beginning to think your mother changed her mind about getting you two out of Cairo after this morning's news. I'm pleased to see she didn't. Makes better sense to send you on to Luxor. Especially now." He drew out his pocket watch and scrutinized it. "The sooner we sail, the better for us all. If one can depend on this crew, which is highly unlikely, we are due to sail in precisely four minutes." He glanced across the salon and his expression clouded.

Allison followed his gaze to Julian Mortimer.

"Rather surprising, the inspector being here, considering," Spencer remarked.

Considering what?

Before Allison could inquire, he anxiously moved off to speak with Julian. "I shall ask him about this apparent discrepancy in his job obligations, of that you can be sure!"

"What was *that* all about?" There was a puzzled knit to Beth's dark brows.

"I don't know. Odd, wasn't it?" She watched Doctor Howard walk up to the lanky inspector. The two seemed opposite personalities. Spencer with his cryptic mannerisms and his impatience with those who blundered in their professional responsibilities was as British as a strong cup of tea. Julian was suave, unhurried in speech, pensive about people and possibilities.

"Dreadful news, isn't it, Miss Wescott? Simply *outrageous!*"

Allison turned in time to see the little Egyptian, Mr. Rahotep, mopping his brow with a large, white cotton handkerchief and hurrying on his way, his sandaled feet clacking over the floor that smelt strongly of disinfectant. Quite bewildered over what the "news" could be, she turned toward the window, where a ruckus was coming from the Egyptian deckhands. She couldn't see anything from where she stood, but Beth was looking out and called over her shoulder, "They were hauling up the gangway and getting ready to depart, but then spotted another passenger."

Allison came up beside her in time to see the deckhands waving their arms wildly to halt the gangway from being lifted. A minute later, someone came running up the gangway, dropping his bags on the deck and reaching into his pocket for a small folder. A shock jolted through Allison as she watched

Bret Holden flash the folder for the captain to see, then pick up his bags and start inside.

A rush of excitement swept Allison, and she struggled to keep her heart calm. Bret! She certainly hadn't expected the good fortune of having him aboard! Could he possibly be going with the club to Luxor? There was so much to tell him! So many questions to ask! She bit her lip to keep from rushing out of the salon to greet him. Then the memory of their parting in December came to her.... Was he still angry?

She turned from the window as he entered the salon—and felt she hardly recognized him. Accustomed to seeing him in a spotless British uniform, sporting a Luger, and working dangerous missions for the CID, it was a bit of a shock to find him dressed casually in expedition clothes. He carried two bags and had a jacket slung over his shoulder. He looked as civilian as the rest of club—yet, even without his military dress, Allison thought he only looked more ruthless. Unlike Spencer Howard and Julian Mortimer, Bret could hardly be described as *benign*.

The salon fell silent as he entered. Allison turned to him, and his coolly observant once-over appeared to belie his ever having desired to slip an engagement ring on her finger.

"Hello, Allison." The greeting was a study in calm simplicity.

Her heart was thundering in her eardrums, but she affected a matching indifference. "Oh. Hello, Colonel."

"It's no longer 'Colonel,'" came Inspector Mortimer's voice. "Mr. Holden's a civilian now."

Allison could feel the tension between the two men—as, apparently, could everyone else. Lady Walsh and Cynthia, who had entered from another door coming up from their cabin, stopped.

Something flickered in Bret's cobalt blue eyes...something that matched the malicious amusement in his smile as he looked at Julian. "Hello, Julian. I didn't know you were aboard. After the news this morning, I would expect you to be out with the Cairo bloodhounds, searching."

There it was again, the reference to the *news*. What was going on? Allison found that she was gripping her handbag. She feared Julian would say something more to Bret that might anger him and took a step forward as though to end the discussion. Lady Walsh may have had the same concern on her mind for she moved forward, her walking stick thumping on the floor, and spoke to Allison in a rather too loud voice that seemed a bit shrill.

"My *dear* Allison, I am told some *ghastly* individual knocked you unconscious at the Blaine house! What a positively *dreadful* thing to befall you!" And she made a helpless little gesture toward both Julian and Bret. "I do hope those of you in authority plan to do something about catching the fiend? If attacking Allison wasn't enough, he made off with Sarah's little menagerie." She didn't wait for a reply but looked back to Allison. "Whatever possessed them to steal such a trifle do you think?"

Allison, still worried about a confrontation between the inspector and Bret, was at a loss for words. She was surprised when Bret quipped boldly: "He hoped to find another Egyptian treasure, like the Nefertari."

Now why did he have to go and say that? Allison glanced at him, irritated. *And in front of the inspector. It's almost as if he's daring everyone to go ahead and think him guilty of being involved.*

Julian seemed ready to oblige. "Interesting theory, Bret. One I hold to as well. Have any ideas who it might be?"

Bret dropped his bags on the floor and took a glass of refreshment from the Egyptian steward. He looked at Julian over the rim. "No. Not yet. I thought the young and brilliant new chief inspector might be hot on the villain's trail by now. Especially after this morning's news."

Doctor Howard stepped forward, looking impatient. "Yes, Julian, I was asking you that very thing before the colonel arrived. It does look rather bad for you, old man, to be taking a holiday now."

Julian relit his pipe with one hand. "Yes, it does, rather, doesn't it? But perhaps we expect the criminal to be on the same route to Luxor."

"I hadn't thought of that. Yes, I suppose he could. Great Scot, man! You don't think he's aboard this ship?"

"If Julian thought that," Bret said lazily, "he wouldn't have permitted the captain to leave the port. Isn't that right, Julian?"

"Spoken like a true CID man," Doctor Howard said. "Even if—" he caught himself, looking a bit chagrined.

Bret, on the other hand, looked undisturbed. "Even if he's been suspended under a cloud of suspicion?"

Doctor Howard looked genuinely embarrassed. "Sorry, Holden, I didn't mean—oh, well, you know very well I can't believe a word of it."

"No reason why you shouldn't." Bret's cynical reply was delivered with the ghost of a smile. "You'd be in good company. The CID believes it. And Julian, as well."

Allison felt angry and embarrassed at the same time. Bret seemed to be going out of his way to announce his guilt.

Cynthia left her mother's side and walked up to Bret. "I don't believe a word of it!" She made this declaration with a shake of her head, and Allison saw that every dark hair was in place beneath Cynthia's stylish hat. The creation, a white silk, most likely direct from Paris, gave the woman's model-like profile an elegance that Allison was sure everyone must notice. She touched her own hair to see if the wind had blown it.

"I think it's all nonsense," Cynthia went on. "Come, Bret darling, it's dreadfully hot and stuffy in here, and I should like something cool to drink. Then you can take me up on deck. We're about to sail."

Allison felt a pang as real as any stomachache when she saw the flicker in Bret's gaze as he looked at Cynthia. Cynthia, evidently taking that meditative glance as sign of victory, wore a faint, triumphant smile.

The heat burned in Allison's cheeks. She glanced at Julian. A vivid expression of anger hardened his otherwise aristocratic face, but the man's all-too-open dislike seemed as much for Cynthia as for Bret. Remembering what Cynthia had told her at Ezbekiah Gardens, she wondered whether the two-week voyage to Luxor would be a holiday after all. *If we weren't already sailing, I'd order my bags off and go home!* How could Bret oblige Cynthia? And in front of her! Should she feel humiliated or just plain furious with him? It was all the more galling because she had been the one to call off the engagement at her father's wishes, not Bret. Was he *trying* to hurt her?

Allison watched them go up on deck as Lady Walsh, who was beside her, said airily, "Oh, well, my dear, as they say, it's all likely to be a tempest in a teapot after it's come to a boil, about Sarah's stolen menagerie, I mean. There couldn't be *two* Nefertaris—even if the first one came from King Tut's tomb. And I've my doubts about that. Helga should be able to tell us at Luxor. She and that blond Count Roderick." Lady Walsh glanced about. "And where *is* Baroness Helga Kruger? Oh, well, she'll show for the dinner dance tonight. Between us, my dear, she's rather enamored with the count." She adjusted her pince-nez. "As for you, you're looking pale—a bit of a ghastly blue remaining on the forehead, too, but we'll all pretend it isn't there. You could use a little face powder, you know, to hide it.

Oh! I say, did you hear the news? My Cynthia and the colonel are getting serious again. Of course, I always expected they would when once he wearied of—" She stopped, as though she just realized whom it was she was talking to.

Allison felt the muscles tighten at the back of her neck. So Bret and Cynthia were "getting back together again," were they?

"Rather bold of him to show himself among us, considering." Lady Walsh spoke in a suggestive whisper, excitement in her tone. "But he's such a darling rogue. One would expect him to show up like this to see Cynthia, of course, once he knew Julian was on board. He's so protective of her. And of course Julian can be so odious at times. A rather strange fellow…sometimes he's so reserved, butter wouldn't melt in his mouth. Then again, at other times he's known to go into temperamental rages! I'm delighted Bret is here to keep my Cynthia safe."

Doctor Spencer Howard had walked up and looked at Allison with a hint of restrained sympathy. "You mustn't tire Allison, Lady Walsh. She's still recovering from that concussion."

"You're right. Terribly thoughtless of me. But really, Spencer, you shouldn't have said what you did to the colonel."

He looked bored. "Let's not get back to that. I'm afraid our club holiday is turning into a disaster before we even leave Cairo."

"But it does seem unlikely, Spencer, that a man of his disciplined stature would ever compromise his duty."

"There must be some mistake somewhere, yes, but he does seem a bit bitter about something.…"

Lady Walsh turned to Allison with an accusing glance. "Whatever ailed Sir Marshall to order the head of the CID to suspend him from duty? Was it Julian's doing?"

Spencer interrupted, looking only mildly interested. "Julian? Why do you think that?"

"Well, isn't it obvious, my dear fellow? I mean after all, we all know why Julian dislikes the colonel so."

"Do we?" The doctor seemed to disagree.

"Indeed. And he's determined to prove Bret is selling treasures on the black market."

"I wouldn't know," the doctor denied flatly, and Allison restrained a small smile. At least one person didn't seem to relish chewing on this line of gossip.

Lady Walsh tapped her cane impatiently. "Oh come, Spencer! Everyone has heard about it. It's all over Cairo."

"I don't listen to gossip, and neither should you. It's bad for your heart. I'm going to my cabin. How about you, Allison? By the way, where is little Beth?"

Allison hadn't seen her since she had called her to the window when Bret arrived.

"Probably gone down to our cabin."

"A good idea. We all should follow her example, I think. I'll see you and Cynthia at dinner, Lady Walsh." He looked at her, patiently now, all physician. "Be sure you take your medication, dear. You're terrible about missing your doses."

"Yes, of course I will, Spencer dear boy. Run along to your cabin. I shall be quite fine on my own until Cynthia returns. You too, Allison, run along. But I simply must insist, dear, that it was a dreadful mistake of your father's to suspend the colonel."

Doctor Howard shook his head and walked away.

"In time of danger and war we need men like the colonel to protect us," she went on to Allison. "German and Turkish spies are everywhere you know. After this visit to the Valley of the Kings, Cynthia and I simply *must* return to England."

Allison's face felt stiff from trying to hide her emotional upheaval. "Yes, I see what you mean," she commented, and excusing herself slipped away, but she didn't go to her cabin yet. The ship was sailing and she wanted a few minutes to herself before facing Beth. She wasn't likely to see Bret and Cynthia on deck, so she went up and found herself a spot on the other side of the steamer. She leaned against the rail, frowning.

Something about what she'd seen this afternoon in the salon just wasn't right. The scene between Bret and Inspector Julian Mortimer, Doctor Howard, and, yes, even Cynthia...it all had seemed almost—what? Deliberate? Performed? Contrived? As though it were meant to convince someone of something. Allison shook her head. But what? How many members of the club had been present? Eight, maybe ten. Who hadn't been there? Helga, Paul, Count Roderick, Gamal al-Sayyid—

She paused. No...Mr. Sayyid had been there, as had his assistant, Rahotep.

Why would Bret wish to sail with the archaeological club? Because of Cynthia? There was Helga Kruger, of course, his friend and ally in the CID. But with all the talk about his going wrong, it seemed likely that he would wish to avoid Helga. It couldn't flatter his ego to have those who knew him wondering if there was truth to the accusations made against him! Yet, he hadn't looked ashamed. If anything, he had looked...defiant.

She frowned, folding her arms and leaning against the rail. It was like Bret to meet criticism with a hard head and cynical rebuttal. He wasn't the manner of man to turn and run, but to stare down his accusers. For just a brief moment Allison allowed herself to consider whether Bret might be guilty after all. True, Julian could be hoping to ruin him because of

Cynthia, but what of her own father? Would he have requested Bret's dismissal if he thought him innocent? She stirred uneasily. Not when he needed Bret desperately in Baghdad and Jerusalem.

Her troubled heart pulled her in opposite directions; her tense gaze fixed upon the stately date palms growing along the bank, sliding past and shimmering in the heat. All around them were square-prowed sailboats, *falukkas*, with their massive triangular sails as tall and graceful as bird wings. A small breeze blew across the sun-baked deck as the steamer glided down the Nile on its way to Luxor, Aswan, and Elephantine Island, named for the large, dark, shiny rocks that resembled the wonderful beasts.

Allison's ship slipped by a British warship at anchor, a French frigate, an American merchant ship from New York, and some cargo ships risking German U-boats to haul desperately needed cotton to England. She remembered Bret telling her how Sir Edgar had smuggled cotton into Switzerland to sell to the Germans. They, in turn, used it to clothe their needy soldiers on the front in the fight with France and Belgium.

Smuggling…would Bret really risk such a thing for some personal goal? Or out of anger with CID—or with her father?

Of course, if Bret *was* selling treasures on the black market, the voyage to Luxor might bring him into contact with interested buyers. That unpleasant notion left her little comfort, for it could mean the buyer was someone in the club.

She didn't know how long she watched the ancient river slip by until she sighed and turned away from the rail. No use trying to make sense of things, not when she didn't have all the facts. She headed for her cabin, wishing as she walked that there was a breeze from the Nile. No such luck. The air was what her mother called *sticky*. Allison left the deck and went below to find her cabin.

Below in the long, white corridor it was hot and airless. She located cabin number 15 and found the door unlocked. Beth stood from where she had been sitting in a chair by the lower bunk when Allison came in. The change that had come over her sister was marked. Her face had lost its youthful color.

Allison moved quickly to her sister's side. "What's wrong? You can't be seasick."

"I've found out what the news was that everyone was talking about," she said in a low voice.

Allison paused. A premonition of disaster hovered. Did she even want to know? It was their father, it had to be. Something had happened to him. That was the reason Spencer had looked at her so sympathetically when she came aboard. What had he said? *"I'm surprised your mother let you come, considering the news."* Yes, it had to be her beloved father. But wouldn't her sister be weeping? Perhaps about Bret then?

"It's Cousin Edgar."

"Sir Edgar?" Allison repeated numbly.

"Allison, they say he somehow escaped the jail he was in."

Sir Edgar? Escaped? But how? "I don't believe it," Allison whispered, a chill running over her nerves. She had always been terribly afraid of Sir Edgar because he had reminded her of Sarah Blaine's husband, Rex. "How do you know this?"

"I met Helga's son, Paul, when I came down to our cabin. He was coming out of his own cabin, the next one down from us. He introduced himself and asked if I'd heard the news about my cousin. I said, 'You mean Gilly?' And he said, 'No, his old man, the inspector, the one who strangled Sarah Blaine—'" And Beth's hand went to her throat as she turned pallid.

Allison took hold of Beth's shoulders and lowered her to the chair, aware that her own legs felt weak. "Never mind about Sarah. We don't think he did that, remember?"

"But it wasn't Gilly I tell you!"

"All right, Beth, calm yourself. Whoever is guilty will be caught, you'll see. And if it's true that Sir Edgar escaped, they'll catch him."

Beth's brown eyes were apprehensive. "Will they? But while Cousin Edgar is running around loose, Inspector Julian Mortimer is taking a holiday on the Nile."

Beth's eyes narrowed suspiciously, and Allison looked away because she knew what her sister was thinking and she didn't want to confront the possibility.

"Allison? Do you think he's aboard *The Blue Nile*?"

"Don't be silly, Beth, how could he be?" She was irritated with herself because her voice quavered. "Of course he isn't aboard. Why Inspector Mortimer would have had Cairo police swarming all over the ship looking for him before the captain ever left the docks."

"Yes, I suppose…but don't you think it's strange? How Bret came aboard so late?"

Beth seemed to have noticed everything.

"Why do you think he did that?"

"I've no idea." Allison knew there was a tinge of coolness in her voice and smiled to soften the words. "Maybe he took too long to decide that he wanted to walk Cynthia on the deck in the Egyptian moonlight."

"Or maybe there's another reason. Maybe he thinks Sir Edgar's aboard, too, and doesn't want to take chances with your safety. So he came at the last minute, even if it meant risking Julian and the club members all thinking he's selling smuggled Egyptian treasures."

The idea that Bret came because he knew she was aboard softened her heart and mollified her hurt over his response to Cynthia. But she wondered if it could possibly be true. She remembered Lady Walsh's assertion that Bret had come to protect Cynthia from Julian's supposed revenge. That might be true. Julian *had* been angry when Cynthia had cuddled up to Bret, especially when they went up on deck together. But she didn't think Julian was the vengeful sort. Nor was she certain there was anything to the tale Cynthia had told her when they had tea together at Ezbekiah.

So, then, why *had* Bret come, looking as if the decision had been made at the last moment? Could it be because of Sir Edgar? Or because he really was involved in smuggling and selling treasure?

"I don't think we've any reason to fear meeting Sir Edgar." Allison tried to soothe Beth. "Surely they would have searched the ship before allowing it to leave. And why would he come aboard anyway?"

"I don't know."

"There's nothing aboard ship he'd want, nor any person he'd wish to deal with, especially with Inspector Mortimer on board. So you see, there's nothing at all to be worried about. By now Edgar has snuck out of Egypt and is on his way to Constantinople." Allison wished she could believe her own words.

"I suppose you're right. But it's a dreadful shock. And a bit embarrassing, too. I mean, he's our cousin, and everyone will be looking at us and wondering how we feel about the ghastly news."

Allison pulled off her shoes and went over to pour herself a glass of lemon water. "They can look all they want. It won't bother me. I'm going to rest before the dinner dance tonight."

"Sort of spoils everything." Beth shuddered. "I mean, what do we do if he sort of pops up?" She stood with a grimace, then stooped to peer under the berth.

"If Sir Edgar was under there, he'd have told us by now. And anyway, if he dotes on Gilly as much as I think he does, he's bound to be worried that his son is about to be convicted for several murders."

Beth's countenance fell. "Either Sir Edgar committed those murders or there's someone else working with him. And I'm not so confident he'd stay around Cairo biting his nails over Gilly."

"Well, he's *not* hiding beneath our bed. So let's get some rest before tonight. My head is aching. I suspect Bret will have a few answers when I speak to him."

"I'm glad he's aboard." Beth's usually gay tone was sober. "Julian, too. I like Julian," she added thoughtfully. "I could like Paul Kruger a lot, too." She frowned, pondering. "There is something about him, though…something kind of strange."

Allison tied the sash of her robe. "What do you mean?" She thought of her own meeting with Paul aboard the train.

"Well, when I met him coming out of his cabin he looked a little out of breath, as though he'd come from someplace else and was just pretending to come from his cabin."

Allison brushed her hair thoughtfully. "Did you see Helga?"

"No. Have you?"

"She must be aboard. She'll probably come with Paul tonight."

In the silence that followed Allison listened to the water slapping the side of the hull. Even though she hadn't commented when Beth said she was glad Bret was aboard, her heart agreed. She would see Bret tonight. He would explain everything to her then. She had a few things to tell him, too:

What did he think about her being knocked unconscious in the Blaine house when the box was stolen, the same box he knew had concealed the broken cobra head that Rex had hid there for Sarah to find? And just what was Bret doing with the map to a royal tomb in the Valley of the Kings?

Yes, indeed. The dashing colonel had much to explain.

The sun melted into the Nile leaving a blaze of gold and rose in its wake as the night sky came alive. Club members gathered in the salon to dine before enjoying an evening on deck under the stars, listening to the small band.

The salon was crowded with passengers when Allison came down with Beth to join the others. They were gathered at a large table where two guests were noticeably absent: Cynthia and Colonel Bret Holden. Allison glanced casually about. She finally saw Bret, but almost wished she hadn't. He came from the upper deck with Cynthia, who floated along beside him, a vision in a provocative crimson lace dress. Her arm was confidently looped through his, and a sultry smile was in her eyes as she looked up at him.

Beth moaned and whispered, "I *knew* there was a reason I don't like the name *Cynthia*. It conjures up an image that makes me feel inadequate. She makes her grand appearance in crimson lace that makes me look like a factory second." She sat with her elbows on the edge of the table, chin in hand. "And after all I went through to borrow Mum's red dress."

Allison had had one too many disappointments of her own to console Beth. Watching Bret smile at Cynthia made her stomach feel she'd eaten ship iron instead of flaky cheese appetizers. Sitting at the table now with her too simple cotton dress, Allison wished she could slip beneath the table. Where she looked merely presentable, Cynthia looked stunning. What was worse, she was turning her charm on everyone around her with what appeared to Allison to be astonishing success. Only Doctor Howard looked unaffected.

Lady Walsh was already seated, and Bret led Cynthia toward the two empty chairs beside her at the opposite end of the table from Allison and Beth. Allison's hand balled the napkin in her lap. Bret hadn't even noticed her.

Lady Walsh lifted her pince-nez. "Discarding the uniform has served you well, Colonel. I can't say I miss it at all." She turned to Doctor Howard. "They make *such* a handsome couple, don't you think, Spencer?"

Spencer Howard was busy adding some self-diagnosed bitters to his glass of ice water. Stirring vigorously, he frowned at the too short spoon. "I hadn't taken particular notice." He followed this caustic comment by looking at the indicated couple with raised brows. "Well, Colonel, I see you're making the most of your leave from this depressing war. Can't say I blame you." He grimaced as he drank his bitters. "Battle fatigue can lay you flat on your back just as surely as malaria. Splendid view up on deck though."

"Too hot and sultry, I'm afraid. I far prefer the Mediterranean Sea breezes and white sand."

Allison recalled how she and Bret had discussed going to Helga's Riviera retreat on Cypress for their honeymoon. She glanced at him, but his attention was on Cynthia, who was smiling at him as though they shared some little secret.

"Bret and I were just discussing buying Helga's Riviera." Cynthia beamed at those around her.

Lady Walsh's hand flew to her heart. "Oh, isn't that wonderful! So much better than that *ghastly* Blaine house!"

Stung to silence, Allison bit into her fourth cheese appetizer, but found it dry and tasteless. She glanced at Bret, but either he didn't want to meet her gaze or his thoughts were occupied. He was not smiling, and his gaze was directed across the salon at someone who had recently entered. A moment later, Inspector Julian Mortimer came to the table and took his seat. Allison was still trying to recover from Cynthia's announcement and hardly heard his polite greeting. She felt as she had when a bomb had landed too close to her once: dazed, unable to think straight. Only one thought rang out in her mind: *I must get through this dinner without humiliating myself or embarrassing Bret.*

As though to make things more difficult for her, Spencer remarked, "So you're interested in buying some Mediterranean property, Bret?"

"I've stayed at the Riviera before. Helga mentioned she might be willing to sell."

Allison was careful not to react. Where would he get such a vast amount of money? Julian Mortimer appeared to wonder the same thing. He held up a Venetian glass, from which he sipped a green, syrupy drink that looked like creme de menthe. At the mention of buying property on the Mediterranean, he swirled his glass and directed a particularly hard, analytical look across the table at Bret.

"The Riviera on Cypress?"

"Yes, Kyrenia. Ever been there?"

"Once, briefly. An admirable place with a dramatic view."

"So I thought. A good place to settle, far from the typical madness, with little more to worry about than collecting sea shells." A wry glint sparkled in his dark blue eyes.

Julian petted his curled mustache. "Ah! I may enjoy joining you there, Colonel. But it sounds a bit pricey for the likes of me. The baroness's property must be…quite valuable."

A brief silence descended around the table. Bret's gaze was maliciously amused. "It is, indeed. But you're too polite, Julian. Why not simply ask how a suspended colonel in the CID could get the funds for such a purchase? As you would know from searching through my files, I haven't been paid in a month."

Julian looked at Cynthia, as did Allison. The woman twisted the stem of her glass, her eyes like seething pools. It was written all over her face that she thought Julian was really trying to get at her, not Bret.

"I'm not prying, Colonel. It's sufficient that the CID is investigating your recently swelling bank account."

Swelling bank account? Allison glanced at Bret, then at Julian. How clever of Julian to drop the news of his being investigated to everyone at the table!

Julian was smiling. "In my humble position as mere chief inspector, subtlety has always served me well."

"Since subtlety prevents you from publicly pursuing the matter, I'll satisfy your curiosity," Bret said, but Cynthia turned toward him.

"You needn't accommodate him, darling. It's none of Julian's affair *what* we do, or where you get your money."

The resentment in her voice appeared to startle everyone at the table except Bret and Julian.

Allison twisted her napkin into a damp knot in her lap.

"Neal Bristow and I have plans to enter into business selling Egyptian artifacts," Bret went on. "Once I've begun, I'll have little difficulty earning enough to buy property in Kyrenia. Lady Walsh has kindly offered to give us a loan to get the enterprise started."

Us? Did that mean Bret and Neal? Or Bret and Cynthia? Allison glanced toward Lady Walsh, who picked up her glittering black fan and cooled her face, her guarded glance shifting to Julian. Allison thought she knew what was troubling the older woman—a thought that was confirmed when Julian remarked blandly, "You've been accumulating quite a bit of property recently, Lady Walsh. First, the Blaine house, and now the baroness's Riviera."

"I've no interest in Helga's Riviera," Lady Walsh snapped. "I'm doing it for my daughter. That should not disturb you, Julian, should it?"

"No, Madame, it does not," he agreed obligingly. "That is, not unless it is financed by the sale of artifacts that are actually Egyptian national treasures. If the CID had sufficient evidence of that activity, they'd have made an arrest by now."

"Thank you, Julian," Bret said, though too gravely. He watched the inspector over the rim of his water glass.

"No offense, Bret, you know as well as I, they have nothing on you that will prevail."

"Implying?"

Julian smiled. "Probably only that your temporary suspension isn't likely to go anywhere."

"What he means, Bret," Spencer said in a dry, friendly voice, "is that there will be a lot of stammering apologies when this idiotic investigation is over. They'll rush to welcome you back, making crippled excuses for suspending you." He shook his head with wearied forbearance. "Ah, the ineptitude of the bright boys in government. They ought to be out looking for German and Turkish spies instead of harassing one of their own."

"German spies?" Lady Walsh gasped. "How *appalling!*"

Bret spoke with a trace of bitterness. "Asking me to return once I've been forced to walk a bed of coals won't be as simple as all that. Risking my neck for the CID is a thing of the past.

251

The freedom of doing as I wish with my time, while living comfortably, is far more entertaining....Thank you, Cynthia," and he accepted the glass, lifting it to drink, while studiously avoiding Allison's questioning gaze.

He couldn't mean that. Why was he saying these demeaning things in front of everyone? And what of Julian? After trying to convince her of Bret's guilt and enlisting her aid to trap him, had he actually given up and changed his mind? Or was it to his advantage to convince Bret he no longer suspected him?

It was all absurd. She tossed her napkin on the table with an abrupt motion, angry with Bret for behaving this way in public. She had always respected his service in the intelligence department. She had fallen in love with the cynical but loyal and disciplined colonel, with the man whom she had once accused of being a "uniform without a heart." It wasn't until now that she realized how much his service for England meant to her. He was throwing it all away, making light of it....

Allison hated to admit it, but she didn't particularly like this new ex-colonel Holden.

The others around the table, however, did seem taken with his remarks. She glanced at Paul. He sat slouched in his chair, his boyish face cast in a sleepy countenance, but his eyes were bright and alert. Gamal al-Sayyid was stoically expressionless, but Allison noticed he watched with cool interest, and Mr. Rahotep's twitching fingers were crawling up and down his lapel, as usual.

"I, for one," Spencer declared, "can hardly criticize you for becoming bitter. A colonel, awarded a Victoria Cross for bravery, suspended on mere suspicions?"

"Poor rewards from a department that expects you to hazard your life," Paul agreed.

Julian's dark eyes flashed with unexpected temper. "Come,

come, gentlemen. In all fairness to the CID, and to England," he added crisply, obviously displeased with criticism of his government, "it can hardly be said that the colonel was temporarily suspended on 'mere suspicions.'"

"What he means to say," Bret said silkily, "is that the department is convinced their loyal agent has gone rotten to the core. I leave their conclusion to your judgment."

Allison could no longer keep silent. She leaned forward. "I must say, you're rather cavalier about all this, Colonel."

Bret lifted a brow and looked at her steadily for the first time. "Am I? My apologies, Miss Wescott. I will try to look humbled and beaten for you sake."

Cynthia smiled and lifted her Venetian glass.

Allison fought the anger that welled up inside her. "It seems to me you're in a grave and deplorable situation. I would think you'd find it the greater part of wisdom to avoid discussing it so—glibly."

"I'm grieved for having disturbed you." Bret's tone was dry, almost bored. "I overlooked the fact I'm in the company of the patriotic daughter of our outstanding chief consul, Sir Marshall. But there's no secret about why I've been stripped of my uniform. We do agree, however, that I find myself in a 'grave and deplorable situation,' as you so accurately put it. But considering it was *your* father who helped put me there, I'm sure you'd be the last to question his wisdom in the matter. You seem to accept his decisions concerning my unsavory character without much difficulty."

It was on the tip of her tongue to inform him that she'd given in to her father's wishes to keep Bret from being sent to France. But she held her silence. With the way matters had turned out, perhaps France would have been safer.

It was also obvious from the expressions of those present

that if anyone had any remaining doubts about his willingness to throw the CID overboard—and his relationship with her along with it—Bret had done a thorough job of eliminating them. The corners of Cynthia's mouth turned up as she looked down at her plate, and someone clumsily changed the subject.

Allison lapsed into silence, fuming. Beth reached over and awkwardly squeezed her hand for moral support.

The conversation was all about her but she wasn't paying attention until she realized that Spencer, who sat two chairs down from her, was leaning toward her, speaking.

"Any news about your young cousin, Neal Bristow?"

"No, I'm afraid not. It remains a matter of concern." That the tension in her voice was less about Neal and more about Bret bothered Allison to no end.

Julian turned to Bret. "If Neal hasn't arrived, how did you come to an agreement about your export business?"

In the momentary silence Paul Kruger reached into his pocket, then reached into the opposite pocket and drew out a silver cigarette case. He removed a Turkish cigarette and lit the end. "I can answer that, Doctor Howard. I was there in London with Bret and Neal when they discussed their business plans. You remember, don't you, Bret? We were having dinner with Simington, from the British Museum."

"Yes, about the reliefs found at Carchemish. A fair find by Neal." Bret smiled smugly.

"Well, the fact that you've both worked at professions where you've developed contacts in Constantinople and Berlin will enable you to find buyers," Julian suggested.

Bret's eyes were faintly mocking. "We'll wait until the war ends, Julian. We wouldn't want to get shot for treason. In the meantime, Helga offered to let us use her export shop in Old Cairo for storing certain items."

The export shop! Was it Allison's imagination, or did he deliberately startle everyone at the table? Even Cynthia stirred, and Lady Walsh fanned herself and said something unintelligible to her daughter, who began looking around about her mother's chair. Doctor Howard leaned toward Lady Walsh and said something, and the elderly woman nodded wearily. "Yes, but I seem to have misplaced it."

"Bret," Cynthia said with a gentle tone, "Mother's water glass needs refilling so she can take her medication. Would you be a dear and get the attention of the steward?"

"What a horrid evening. It's given me indigestion," Beth whispered to Allison.

They were halfway through the meal before anyone even thought to bring up the matter of Sir Edgar. It was never apparent to Allison who had mentioned him, but as the topic circulated, the guests at the large table eventually fell into an uncomfortable silence. Julian sought to ease Lady Walsh's concern for her safety.

"We have Cairo under watch," he told her. "Sir Edgar won't go far, not with his son facing conviction."

"Have you checked the Blaine house, Julian?" Spencer asked.

"First place we searched."

"I suggest you look for an accomplice." Allison ignored the interested glances that turned her way. "He couldn't have escaped on his own. It doesn't seem possible."

"Not suggesting one of us may have slipped him a key?" There was a hint of goading amusement in Bret's voice.

Allison looked across the table at him. His level gaze seemed to tell her to keep quiet about what she thought, but she was in no mood to comply with anything he wanted tonight. "I wouldn't know, *Mr.* Holden. I suppose any one of us could have arranged it—if the stakes were high enough." She knew what that flicker of molten blue in his eyes meant, but far from frightening her, it gave her a perverse sort of pleasure to know she'd gotten to him.

"He had outside help. It's obvious," Allison repeated to Julian.

"Nothing is obvious," Bret said flatly.

She looked at him. "It's *quite* obvious to me. Someone left him alone so he could escape."

"He was under guard," Bret countered.

"Then the guard was working with him," she insisted.

"The guard is dead."

"Then there's someone else who killed the guard, Colonel."

His eyes narrowed. "Heart failure, Nurse Wescott."

But her gaze refused to yield. "I doubt it."

Bret turned toward Doctor Howard. "Your opinion, Spencer?"

Spencer sighed. "It does sound like heart failure, yes. I had a few minutes with the physician who did the autopsy. A bit clumsy of the police, though, letting Sir Edgar walk out under their noses like that. If I didn't know of the incompetence of some in authority, I'd agree with you, Allison, that someone helped him." He looked down the table at her with his cryptic smile. "But as unlikely as it seems, he probably did walk out beneath their noses. Anything is possible with this police department—you'll excuse me for saying so, Julian."

Julian was tapping his pipe against his teeth and leaned forward now, looking at Allison. "Sir Edgar was able to get the keys from the guard when he had the attack. Rather fortunate for him, I agree, but there you have it."

"I'm still inclined to think he had help. The question is—"

Cynthia gave a shriek, and Bret pushed back his chair and

stood, helping her to her feet and handing her a napkin to blot her skirt.

"Oh, my dress!" she cried. "I can't imagine how that happened. The glass just tipped, and I—"

"You'd better go down and change at once, or it'll soon be ruined," Lady Walsh said. "Give it to the steward to have cleaned."

"Yes, yes, I think I'd better."

"In the meantime we can all go up on deck," Lady Walsh said decisively, using her walking stick to push herself up from her chair. "I hear the orchestra. Spencer, I'll need your assistance up those stairs. Do run along, Cynthia."

The others dutifully followed Lady Walsh's lead and stood. Allison glanced about at the varied faces. "If you'll excuse me," she hastened, "I think I'll go back to my cabin. It's been a long day and I think I shall turn in early. You can stay up till eleven, Beth, if you think you'll enjoy the music."

"Yes, do come up dear," Lady Walsh offered. "And Allison, do take care of that ghastly concussion. We'll see to Beth."

"Yes, please stay awhile," Paul said to Beth. He looked at Allison. "I'll see her safely back to your cabin, Miss Wescott."

Beth looked surprised but flattered by his attention, and agreed she might stay for a short time.

As Allison walked away, she overheard Bret saying: "If you've got a few minutes first, Paul, I'd like to discuss Carchemish with you."

"The digs? Certainly. One moment, Miss Beth, please."

Allison glanced back. Bret and Paul were walking from the table toward an open window. Bret's voice came clear: "Neal sent me a report on the latest findings on that lamp—you've probably heard Helga mention it. The conclusions are inconclusive. We've a buyer, but I would like to hear what you think of it first...."

257

Allison entered the stuffy corridor below, still burdened over Bret. How could he behave so disrespectfully?

Cynthia was already standing in her cabin doorway in her robe, the lace dress in hand, giving curt orders to the stoic-faced Egyptian steward. He left with the gown, and Cynthia's door shut resoundingly behind her. Allison watched the steward disappear, then retreated inside her own cabin. How had Cynthia spilled her glass?

Well, it didn't matter. Actually, Allison was grateful for the excuse to escape what was fast becoming a wretched evening. Out of sorts, feeling miserable, she pulled off her shoes and dropped them with a clatter. She thought about her own actions, of how she had angered Bret.

She tensed, hearing the slow turn of the doorknob to her room. How had the stylish Cynthia already managed to ready herself? As the door pushed open, Allison turned, prepared to tell Cynthia she wasn't going to the dance.

Bret entered, motioned for her silence, then shut the door, sliding the bolt through the lock. He turned and faced her.

"You've a good deal of explaining to do!" she whispered heatedly.

He took hold of her arm and propelled her across the cabin. Below the window, he turned her round swiftly to face him, then pulled her into his arms. "But why waste the few minutes we have together?"

She tried to twist free. "What's wrong? Do you have to rush back to dear, darling Cynthia?"

"Retract your claws, darling." His arms tightened about her waist, and Allison fought against the dragging, warm tide that washed over her at his nearness. "It's quite impossible to satisfy your too inquisitive mind, not in so short a time." He held her in a comforting prison from which she couldn't escape, even had she wanted to. She felt herself starting to weaken. Her head fell back against his arm, and he was looking deeply into her eyes....

Suddenly she was filled with a heart-thumping urgency that demanded her arms go around him, that her lips respond willingly as his head lowered. Her senses swam as they kissed, and she reveled in the feel and taste of him.

"That—" he whispered into her hair a minute later—"was to convince you I haven't forgotten...not that I wouldn't forget if I could. I didn't forget you in London before the war, so it's not likely I've forgotten you since December. And a few minutes with Cynthia in the moonlight isn't likely to cure me, either." He lowered his head to hers again, but his words echoed hauntingly in her mind..."*a few minutes alone with Cynthia in the moonlight.*"

The image came rushing in with the full impact of a London downpour. She stiffened and with a gasp of anger wrested free, backing up shakily. "You—you *dare* think you can spoon with her in the Nile moonlight, while you've ignored me, then—"

"Now do you see why it's awkward for you to be here on the ship?"

"Oh! I can *see* why!"

"You only think you do. That's the ruddy luck of it!"

"Your arrogance is unbearable!" Her breath was coming in gasps. "At the table tonight—the way you behaved!—then you come here. And you think all you need do is kiss me—and tell me you haven't forgotten me either. *December*—that's how long it's been since I've heard from you. This is *May!*"

"My dear," he stated with belabored patience. "It was *you* who permitted Daddy to come between us in December, all with the dreadful idea of waiting until the war is over. We must wait until the posies bloom again and the bluebird sings in the apple tree. Daddy hasn't said yet what our options are if Germany sustains the war and blows up all the apple trees. There won't *be* any blossoms. The sun may not shine again. Without posies and bluebirds twittering in the apple trees, who gets married? After all, things have to be right, and we must wait for peace in the world. I suppose it's fairly obvious that our relationship is doomed."

Her hands clenched in frustration. "You needn't be sarcastic. You're being unfair. It was a mutual consent to wait and you know it. It was you who disappeared from Cairo."

"Again, thank your father. And I don't call coming to a decision in my absence *mutual*. Then again, maybe I don't have anything to say about it?"

"He threatened to send you to—"

Swiftly his hand closed over her mouth. He glanced toward the door. If there had been a slight creaking, the lapping water covered it.

They stood there, neither of them moving for a minute, then Bret walked to the door and listened, while Allison stood, her eyes riveted to the door.

He must have been satisfied, for he came back, his eyes burning with emotion. "I shouldn't have risked coming here. Your presence only increases the danger around you."

"Danger? What danger? On the boat? Sir Edgar couldn't be aboard—"

"Of *course* he isn't aboard. Danger from another, equally deadly viper."

She swallowed. "What do you mean?"

His mouth twisted as he looked down at her. "That was an exceptionally brilliant tidbit of detective work you did earlier at the table about Edgar. Brilliant and infuriatingly unwise. Were you out of your mind talking like that in front of the club?"

She winced. It had been a mistake, she knew that now. "Everyone knows Sir Edgar couldn't have escaped on his own," she whispered defensively.

"Everyone did *not* know, but they do now," he said dryly. "You've just told ten people *you* know someone helped him escape."

She moved uneasily. "What if I did? It's probably true."

"Of *course* it's true!" His whisper came like a crack in the silence. "Ten people," he repeated. "And there isn't *one* of them I'd trust enough to turn my back to in the storage closet at the Blaine house." He lifted his hand, frowning when she flinched. His fingers came to gently massage her forehead. "I was rough on you tonight at the table....It was necessary...." His jaw flexed. "You know, Allison darling, you can be very exasperating sometimes."

Her eyes searched his. "You don't mean that you think one of them—?" She couldn't say the frightening words, couldn't voice the thought that someone among them had been at the Blaine house, had attacked her, struck her unconscious, and taken the box.

"Probably." His frankness was brutal, but he watched her steadily. "And helped Edgar escape, too."

"Surely not!"

"And if that isn't enough, I could give you a few more bits of information to make your blood chill, but I won't. With that in mind, darling, you were about to pose a very nasty question to that group until I stopped you by ruining Cynthia's dress."

"*You* did that?"

"What were you going to say at the table after you announced someone helped Edgar escape?"

She wrapped her arms about herself as though cold and

glanced toward the door again. "It's obvious, isn't it? The CID helped Edgar escape. Just the way they brought him here from Constantinople in the first place. They expect to learn something by letting him get away."

"Wrong. The CID did *not* help him escape. But whoever killed Sarah Blaine did."

"What?"

"Someone arranged it through the guard, then killed him so he wouldn't be able to identify who had hired him. That's the way this individual works—anyone who knows his identity is silenced." He took hold of her, this time protectively. "Now do you know why it was dangerous to speak as you did tonight? Especially after what happened to you at the Blaine house. Julian told me you may have gotten a glimpse of who it was."

"Julian...told you?"

"Yes, Julian. And don't make anything of that. Tell me, did you see this person or do you have any idea whom it might be? Even if the idea at first seems absurd to you, tell me."

She ran her hands through her hair, shaking her head in frustration. "No, I—I can't remember anything, Bret. It's as though my mind has blocked it out. But why are you involved if you've left the CID?"

"Don't you know? I would think you could guess. Naturally I don't want you placed in more danger. It's too much isn't it, to expect me to completely change because I've been suspended?"

She stepped back, bumping into the edge of the table. Bret moved closer, keeping her there. "It's likely the others guessed what you were about to say tonight, even as I did. They're not as empty-headed as they appear. For that matter, I suspect they guessed why your speech ended with the wet dress! But they're not certain I'm the one who caused the stir. Anyone sitting close by may have done it, even Cynthia herself or Lady Walsh.

Look, the ship docks tomorrow at the Flamingo Hotel. We're all to get off for the day and leave again the next morning. I want you on a train back to Cairo."

She threw up a hand, moving away from him. "I can't go back now. I promised my mother I'd bring Beth to Helga's boat."

"What a ruddy mess! If only you'd followed your original plans, things would be less complicated for me now."

"Because of Cynthia?" she half accused. "You'd prefer I didn't see you together, is that it?"

His eyes narrowed. "Yes, that also. Because of a great many things. I didn't know Cynthia was aboard. It came as a surprise, but for quite different reasons. I expected Helga to be aboard. With you present, it makes matters ruddy difficult!" He walked up to her. "So you won't go back?"

"It's impossible, Bret, please understand. I promised I'd care for Beth. She's gotten herself ill over Gilbert. A holiday at Luxor is necessary."

"As you wish. Just don't be crushed when I don't live up to your expectations."

"What do you mean?"

"I think you know. I'm selling Egyptian artifacts out of the country and making money doing it. I'm accused of master-minding an incident on the Berlin-Baghdad Railway. You heard Julian and your father. You know what the CID thinks about me. I wouldn't want to disappoint them. Since you won't leave, you'll need to be disappointed, too." With that, he turned and went out as suddenly and silently as he had arrived.

Allison collapsed onto her bunk and sat with her head in her hands, emotionally exhausted. He hadn't denied it. He only wanted her gone so she wouldn't see what he was doing. His words ran round and round in her heart.

~ ~ ~ ~ ~

The black hands on the little porcelain clock with the pink rosebud reached 10 P.M., and still Allison did not go up on deck. Alone among the string of empty cabins, with everyone at the dance, or seated in deck chairs enjoying the orchestra, she could make out the strains of the lovely music. Bret was with Cynthia, but it no longer mattered, she told herself, because he belonged to her. They would work out matters between them, somehow. At the moment, she trusted him and nothing could change that.

The music changed unexpectedly, a strange arrangement that conjured up emotions of the Arabian Desert in her mind. She began to think of the Valley of the Kings, of Helga's houseboat, and of the club expedition. Bret didn't trust the ten club members who had sat around the table....

Her gaze traveled about the modest cabin with its simple table and chair, to the wardrobe, to her blue trunk sent along at her request from the Blaine house. It was a mistake to have done so. She should have given orders to send it to the Residency since there was little inside she could use now other than the sturdy leather walking boots.

She found the small trunk key in her handbag and went to unlock it. Lifting the lid, she searched through sundry garments until she found the boots at the bottom, beneath the small Christmas present she had meant to give Sarah.

She paused, staring at the package. Reaching down, she removed the gaily-wrapped package, now crumpled. The squashed red silk ribbon reminded her of a wilted rosebud. Sadly, she made to lay the package aside—

She stopped, staring. What was this? She turned the package over in her hand. What had happened? She had bought

Sarah a novel, but though it was the same Christmas wrap, what Allison held in her hand now was too thin and light to be the same gift.

Her eyes widened. Someone had opened the package, removed the book, and inserted something else, then replaced the wrapping in a hurry.

Her hands shook. Who could have done it? And had they done it recently? Or at the Blaine house, before—

Before Sarah was murdered?

She looked up at the ceiling of the cabin. The music had ceased. It was suddenly horribly quiet. She held her breath and heard the water lapping against the sides. Was the hull creaking? Her gaze swerved, frightened, to the door. Someone was out there, and this time she felt sure it wasn't Bret.

The light was shining in the corridor. She could see it beneath her door. Only a dim lamp burned inside her cabin. She could see a moving shadow—someone *was* outside her door!

She stood, fighting the fear that wanted to overpower her. *Lord, help!* The desperate prayer brought her a sense of peace, enabled her to think more clearly. Had she locked her door after Bret left? She didn't think so. She had been too overwrought. She inched her way softly toward her door just as she saw the knob gently turning.

The key was in the lock, and, holding her breath, Allison reached shaking fingers to turn it, but as she did, voices and footsteps sounded from farther up the corridor. Passengers were coming back from the dance. Allison heard furtive steps rush away. Quickly she turned the key and leaned there, steadying her nerves.

The voices of the passengers were garbled as some took the more forward cabins. Doors opened and closed; more footsteps walked past. Then all was quiet again.

Allison was still clutching the Christmas package. Now, with the key in her robe pocket, she waited a minute longer. Assured that whoever had stood outside her door would not be able to enter, she moved to the table and chair. She turned up her lamp and removed the ribbon. On deck the intermission ended and the orchestra music began again, haunting, drifting across the Nile.

With trembling fingers, Allison unwrapped the package. Would she find something that would give her answers? Or something that would only make the nightmare that much more terrifying...?

FIFTEEN

ALLISON PULLED AWAY THE RED CHRISTMAS wrapping—and something fell out. She reached down to retrieve the papers that had fallen and turn them over. A handwritten letter from Sarah Blaine!

Quickly, she scanned the neatly penned words.

Dear Allison,

If I return alive tonight this letter won't be necessary. I will meet with a German agent that Rex knew who uses the name "George." That is not his real name, of course, but a mockery of our king. After much searching of my conscience I've come to a rather late decision that I cannot go on like this. I am telling you the truth; I must do what is right "for such a time as this," when our nation is at war and thousands of lives are in the balance. Your Christian character and patriotism have inspired me to at least one good deed for England. I cannot undo the tragedy and death already done by Rex, but I can refuse to do something even worse.

Yes, worse!

I can't explain everything, there's so little time. I did not feel so strongly against cooperating with Sir Edgar until I read the information that I was supposed to pass on to George. I was not supposed to open the envelope Edgar gave me, but after I learned what it was, I became frightened beyond words and was sorry that I had arranged the meeting. But now, to my dread, there is no way to undo it! Tonight, soon now, we are to meet. If I can convince George that I made an error in calling for him—I may survive. If so, I will come back, retrieve this letter, and burn it. But if not, I want you to know the truth.

I knew Rex was selling classified information to a German agent, whom he called "King George," but I never expected he was involved in murder! Please believe that I had no idea what his plans were when he went to the huts in Aleppo to find you. I thought Rex looked on you as a daughter, that no matter what political beliefs he held, he'd never allow them to master him. I suppose I was quite naive. I've learned that what a man believes he becomes—that we cannot divorce our actions from our worldview.

Rex always told me that if anything ever happened to him, I was to wait a few months, then look in the sundial. He wanted me to leave for Constantinople, taking the railway to Berlin. He left the broken cobra head in my menagerie box and said that some treasure was within that would make me a very rich widow. To this day I don't know what it is. I've been too afraid to go there!

Sir Edgar Simonds discovered through Professor Jemal that Rex was selling information to the enemy, and he came to me recently boasting of how he'd come across sensitive information while serving as chief inspector. He says it's more valuable than anything Rex ever sold, but Sir Edgar has no idea who Rex's superior is or how to contact him. That's where I came in. He insisted I contact him, and if I didn't, he'd arrest me for murdering Neith. I've never met George before, but

Edgar was right, I do know how to contact him. George can be reached through Mr. Galli's son-in-law. He works at the merchant shop in Luxor.

I'm so afraid I can't think straight! Edgar brought me the information tonight. But Allison! I've looked at it—and I can't put it into the hands of the enemy. If I do, I'll betray those I care about—you and Marra, Bret and David, and all the rest of the British Tommies. I don't feel the way Rex did about politics. No matter what happens when I meet George tonight, I simply can't tell him!

I haven't much time. I've burnt the information so George can't get it from me, but I'm afraid that my attempts will not stop him in the end. George may have been alerted to something important and keep trying to get it. He may go to Edgar himself. That's where you come in, Allison. You must know what the information is so that if anything does happen to me, you'll know what you must do.

The Foreign Office in London must be warned. Secretary of War Kitchener must not sail for Russia for his secret meeting with Czar Nicholas. Germany doesn't know he is sailing—but Edgar knows the itinerary. George would give anything to obtain this. If he succeeds, he'll pass it on and it could eventually reach the U-boat commanders in the form of an order to torpedo Kitchener's ship. Your cousin Neal is a British agent working with Colonel Holden. And Neal may be on that ship as Kitchener's aide. You see why I can't cooperate with George tonight? Everyone on that ship will go down in the icy sea. I wouldn't have that on my conscience for any amount of money. Even if I must die, I want you to know that your godly character and patriotism at Kut have affected me.

I'm leaving this letter in the Christmas present. No one will think to open it and look inside. Thanks for the book, Allison. I hope I live to enjoy it. I'm really sounding sacrificial, aren't I? You should see me writing this letter! You've never seen such a coward, shaking like a leaf.

Remember, if anything happens to me, if I don't come back from the meeting with the mysterious George, tell Colonel Holden. He'll know what to do. Don't trust anyone else, not even Marra nor David. I'm sure they are true, but who knows anymore? There is one other person you can trust with your life, Helga. Bret and Helga. No one else."

"For such a time as this,"

Sarah B.

Allison gripped the letter. Her eyes shut tightly. "Oh, Sarah…if only you'd told me sooner. I could have supported you—I could have gone to Bret!"

Her heart beat loudly in her eardrums. A German agent had killed Sarah. Her hand formed a fist. That explained the dreadful news Beth gave her about Sarah being beaten to death. Allison was growing more afraid with the passing moments.

Beth was right. There *was* someone more dangerous and ruthless than Gilbert and Sir Edgar, and Edgar had pressured Sarah to contact him. And now, Sir Edgar had escaped. What if he was somewhere on board? No, she tried to reason herself into calmness. They'd have found him by now. The steamer was searched before setting sail. But why was Julian aboard? And Bret? Did they expect Sir Edgar to contact someone in the club?

And George—did they know about him? Her mind rushed to what Bret said earlier: "I wouldn't trust my back to any of the ten seated at the table."

She must speak to Bret tonight. She must tell him about the assassination attempt on Secretary of War Kitchener.

Allison folded the letter and looked at it, trying to think, but anxiety held her in its clutches. Should she burn it? No…no, Bret must see it first. He might glean something from Sarah's words that she had missed. A little dazed, she tried to rewrap the Christmas paper, to cover the letter, but the wrapping was too wrinkled and her fingers were clumsy. She could hide it again, but what if the enemy knew about the letter? Though Allison couldn't imagine Sarah telling anyone, nothing was impossible. No, she wouldn't leave it in her cabin.

The Christmas paper—she must burn it. It might cause suspicion if someone noticed it. She found a box of matches and struck the flame, holding it to the paper, then the silk ribbon. The ribbon burned, but left a gray ash remnant that still showed the weave. She brushed it all onto a piece of scratch paper, crumpled it, and stuffed it inside her handbag to throw away.

She dressed quickly, placing the letter inside her bodice. She closed the trunk lid, relocked it, and then went to the door. She paused, listening. All was quiet in the corridor. She would need to seek out Bret at the dance. But what would Cynthia think? It might draw too much attention. He might ask her to waltz—she shook her head. No, after their meeting earlier she didn't think so.

Beth! She'd get Beth to waltz with Bret, to tell him Allison had to see him again, tonight. There was no time to lose. When did Kitchener intend to leave on his voyage? What if his ship had already left Dover?

She locked the cabin door and hurried silently along the hot passageway. As she rushed up the steps to the salon she heard the popular refrain from an American war song drifting to her on the cooler air.

Inside the salon she found several club members seated on a circular divan, sipping refreshments and discussing archaeology and the Valley of the Kings. She paused. Did she look frightened? She tried to affect a casual behavior lest the others notice her agitation.

Cynthia and Lady Walsh were there, as were Bret, Doctor Howard, Paul Kruger, and Professors Blackstone, Allerton, and Beasley. Miss Cook from New Zealand and several students, mostly French and Egyptian, also had gathered from the dance floor above. Julian was noticeably absent, as was Beth. Mr. Rahotep sat alone, a few feet away from Allison, scribbling notes in a brown leather folder. He looked up and saw her before she entered the salon. Standing quickly, he came toward her.

"Miss Wescott, you found your cabin in order and the voyage comfortable?"

The round-faced Mr. Rahotep was smiling broadly, his velvety, dark eyes alert and bright.

"Oh yes," she assured him, "My cabin is fine." She made to join the others when he cleared his throat and added in a low, secretive tone, "Most surprising and unfortunate incident at the Blaine house. That you are strong enough for this rigorous holiday ahead of us is fortunate." He bowed and gestured toward two chairs across the salon near an open window. "Er—you will sit a moment, Miss Wescott?"

He wished to talk, but what about? She glanced toward Bret and then smiled at Rahotep. "Yes, that would be pleasant."

He walked with her, and Allison sat down next to the potted leafy palm. A late evening breeze blew in from the Nile, and while it wasn't exactly refreshing, it was more pleasant than the stuffy cabin.

Rahotep's eyes darted about the salon like a nervous swallow, and Allison had the impression he was watching for someone. Since most everyone in the club was already seated in the corner lounge, she suspected he was keeping an eye out for Mr. Sayyid. Perhaps his employer frowned upon him talking too much to the guests.

He wrung his long fingers. "It is that I feel very bad about your injury, Miss Wescott, responsible, perhaps."

"Oh, you mustn't feel that way, Mr. Rahotep. The responsibility rests solely with whoever knocked me unconscious." She smiled faintly. "Somehow I don't think it was you."

"True, true," and he flushed a purplish color, making Allison ashamed she had been so glib. "Yet, I feel as though I should have accompanied you upstairs to get your trunk." He glanced toward the entry door again. Had Mr. Sayyid rebuked him for leaving?

"There was no need, and you were busy. Please, think no more about it. Have you, um, found the list?"

He looked at her, wide-eyed. "The prospective buyers? No, no, very trying. But you! I trust you found your trunk undisturbed."

"Undisturbed?" What an odd thing to ask.

"I hope all was in order. The police can move like water buffalo. They did not damage anything? Break the lock on your trunk, or—?" and he spread his hands.

With all that had happened, the man's sudden interest in her trunk made Allison nervous. She glanced toward the club members engaged in conversation across the salon. If only Bret would come to speak with her...

As though he'd heard her silent plea, Bret said something to Lady Walsh, then took her empty glass and brought it to the nearby sideboard, which was laden with an array of refreshments. Bret took a leisurely amount of time refilling his coffee cup and Lady Walsh's glass of iced water.

Allison felt sure he had come close to listen to her conversation with Sayyid's assistant. She would play along with Rahotep's questions to see how close to the truth they would come. She raised her voice slightly. "No, nothing of mine was damaged. There was nothing of value inside my trunk from the Blaine house. But I can't help wondering why someone would wish to steal the box with Mrs. Blaine's menagerie."

Mr. Rahotep nodded, glancing often toward the steps to the deck where the orchestra was playing another popular American song. He seemed unaware of Bret's proximity. "Yes, yes, very odd about that box, wasn't it? You believe there is no value to those little items. Nothing like the great find of Queen Nefertari?"

"I'm sure they've no real monetary value."

For a brief moment he started, then fumbled, "Yes, of course, of course. No monetary value."

"Taking the box must have been a mistake," she continued with a deliberate frown.

His quick eyes met hers, and she was sure she saw a shrewd alertness in their depths. "I, too, am of that belief. I told Inspector Mortimer so. Someone believed a chance for great wealth was within reach, that there was another Nefertari to be found, another Ramses perhaps."

"Yes, perhaps, and yet, how would they know Mrs. Blaine left the menagerie to me in her will? It seems they were waiting for me to reveal its location. I had no idea she'd left it to me until Mr. Sayyid told me about it when I went to Sarah's house."

His fingers pitter-pattered along the lapel of his somber, black tunic. "Ah, I see you are very astute, Miss Wescott, very astute. It is puzzling, so I have thought, too. I've been thinking much about it since we set out on this Nile voyage." He cleared his throat and glanced toward the door. "I was talking to Miss Cook, who told me an interesting thing."

"Miss Cook?" she repeated.

"Yes, the museum secretary. She handles many matters. She helped Paul Kruger arrange this voyage for the baroness. A tragedy she did not come. You see—" and he leaned forward intently—"the contents of Mrs. Blaine's will was known some weeks ago."

Startled, Allison frowned. "But I only learned Sarah left me the box on the same afternoon I went to the house."

"That is it—that is what I am saying. Most peculiar...for Mr. Sayyid dictated a letter informing you nearly three weeks earlier. Miss Cook, who handled the matter for him, confesses she must have made a mistake. She found the letter, you see, on the museum floor behind her desk the morning you received it. It must have dropped when the boy came to deliver the mail. Yes, that is what she says." He lowered his voice. "I say all this to show there were others who did know that Mrs. Blaine left you that menagerie. It actually seems you were the last to find out." Allison wanted to glance at Bret, to see his reaction, but she was afraid of drawing Rahotep's attention to him. She forced a wry smile and touched her forehead. "Well, I certainly was in the wrong place when whoever wanted the menagerie entered the house, wasn't I? But his plans were all for nothing, so it seems."

He perked up. "Meaning, Miss Wescott?"

"Meaning that whoever was waiting for me to lead them to the menagerie must now be disappointed. Instead of a pot of

Egyptian gold, my attacker found some inexpensive pieces from Mrs. Blaine's travels around the East and India."

"Yes—" he scratched his chin—"Yes, I see what you are saying. Yes, I think they will be very disappointed. Has he learned perhaps, as you British say—that he was duped?"

"But that rather implies someone tricked him into thinking the box was important."

"So, yes, so, yes, I suppose it does. You do not think someone—say, Mrs. Blaine—wanted him to think the menagerie was important when there may have been, perhaps, something else of real importance elsewhere?"

The letter!

Even as the realization hit her, Allison kept her expression blank, hoping it was believable. She spoke slowly to keep her voice casual, though her heart was pounding. "Something else? Real importance? What else could there be?"

Julian Mortimer appeared in the salon with Beth at his side. Rahotep saw him, stood quickly, and removed his handkerchief from his pocket to mop his brow. "I see what you mean, yes." He answered her question, but his nervous eyes were on Julian. "It was only a fleeting thought. But yes, I see it could not be." He rushed his well wishes for the night, saying he hoped the heat would not be troublesome to her sleep. She thanked him, and rose to walk with him across the lounge toward the others. Bret, too, returned to Lady Walsh with her lemon water.

Julian walked up to Allison, smiling. He was meticulously garbed in dinner black, a single white camellia on his lapel. His sleek, oiled mustache glistened and his watchful dark eyes studied her face, then Rahotep's.

Allison fanned herself with the dance flyer, all the while nervously aware of Sarah's letter, tucked safely—or at least she

276

hoped so!—inside her bodice. She had to speak to Bret!

Julian bowed his head. "A delightful evening, Miss Wescott. I looked for you on deck tonight. I was hoping you might come up and enjoy the orchestra with Beth and me. I hope you don't mind that I borrowed her company for a short time from Paul Kruger." Not waiting for a reply he turned to Rahotep.

"Well, Rahotep, I've news that should make this excursion more cheerful for all of us, especially you. I realize Mr. Sayyid has been displeased with your misplacing the list of prospective buyers for the Blaine property."

Rahotep opened his mouth to say something, but must have thought better of it and remained silent.

"The list showed up this morning. I intended to mention it sooner, but with the goings on it slipped my mind until this evening at dinner when Bret brought up the matter of buying the baroness's Riviera. One of our Cairo policemen found the list."

"You found it?" Rahotep repeated, sounding almost astonished.

Allison glanced at the others who were seated nearby on the divans. Julian had spoken so clearly that she was sure everyone heard. Silence enveloped the group as though they were now honed in on the inspector's words.

What, she wondered yet again, *is so interesting about that list of prospective buyers?*

"This is great relief, Inspector," Rahotep said. "Miss Cook and I searched the museum office inch by inch."

"You were both searching in the wrong place," Julian said amiably. "We found it quite by chance while searching the Blaine house. Either you or Mr. Sayyid must have dropped it while you were there."

"Astonishing. I believed I gave it to Mr. Sayyid. Perhaps—

perhaps he dropped it when he left."

"Yes, perhaps." Julian smiled.

In the silence that followed Julian's cryptic comment, Spencer asked: "Where is Helga? I haven't seen her since I arrived on the steamer."

"Unfortunately, she remains in Luxor, awaiting the Egyptologist," Paul answered. "Count Roderick was to have arrived to look at the queen, but something must have detained him. So Mother thought it wise to wait for him there." Paul looked at Allison. "I hear you and Beth will be staying on the houseboat."

Allison nodded, wondering at his use of the term "the queen" for the funerary treasure piece of Nefertari. He made it seem as though the thing were alive.

"Yes, the baroness invited us. Mother will come down to join us as soon as my father returns to Cairo."

"Why not go to the archaeological huts nearer the Valley of the Kings?"

"Because of me," came Beth's unexpected reply. "It was all a plan to get me out of Cairo for the rest of Gilly's trial." Beth's animated gaze darted about the table. "I'm sorry, everyone, but I loathe archaeology. And I wouldn't have come if I knew I had to stay in the huts and attend those long, dull lectures. So Helga arranged for the houseboat."

Before Allison could try to smooth over her sister's blunder, Paul turned to her, and his smile was understanding. "Indeed, you need not apologize, Beth. We all understand you are distraught over your dear cousin. Grief and fear often rob us of appreciation of even the deeper things of life."

The deeper things of life? Allison glanced at Bret. He wore a vague smile, as though ironically amused.

In the silence that momentarily enveloped the table, Beth

appeared to have recovered from her outburst and had the grace to blush at Paul's implication that her disinterest was more a reflection of her state of mind than a commentary on the scholarly content of the upcoming lectures. Paul began to lecture Beth on the profound "spiritual mystery" in the construction of the pyramids, implying that they were to be looked upon as "shrines of knowledge." His disdainful superiority reminded Allison of their meeting on the train—and of the niggling sense of distrust she'd felt toward him from the very beginning.

As he expounded the virtues of archaeology, his voice grew almost feverish and his attitude became nearly trancelike. Those listening grew silent, and Allison frowned. Paul spoke about ancient history as though it were happening now.

"The pharaoh's funeral rite is full of splendor. The coffin, the royal mummy, is carried in somber procession from the mortuary temple in Thebes. We follow…in the daily path of the sun. We ascend over the top of the Theban cliffs, down into the Valley of the Kings to the royal tomb, facing the western horizon. Our path brings us toward the setting sun. During the funeral the pharaoh enters the horizon and withdraws in death, then is united with Amon, the sun god, and passes into the evening underworld with the setting sun. We enter the tomb, passing through the tunnels, the corridors, they're called. The sun's path and the death of our pharaoh and the accession of his successor are all represented in similar terms.

"'King Tuthmosis III went up to heaven;
He was united with the sun disk;
The body of the pharaoh god joined him who made him,
When the next morning dawned
The sun disk shone forth,
The sky became bright,

King Amenhotep II was installed on the throne of his father.'

"The funeral is like a play—following the journey of Amon. And we, the priests, make certain the funeral rites coincide with the astronomical calendar. Our ceremony of burial is theological in nature, created to hinder national disaster because of the death of the god-king. At the heart of our ceremony is the monument of the royal tomb itself, and the mummy of the pharaoh. So we see why there was such a great effort to build these tombs! Ancient Egypt's religious order—indeed, its very identity—was based on Amon, which became the embodiment of the pharaoh and his throne, which affected the religious mind that made the pyramids in the Valley of the god-Kings!"

Paul looked at each of them, the triumphant smile on his face seeming to imply he'd just accomplished something notable and now awaited his crown. His pale blue eyes were bright; his face was flushed with excitement.

Silence held everyone. Allison looked at Bret and saw him tapping his chin, watching Paul with a seeming casual air—but she saw the intensity in Bret's eyes.

"Great Scot!" Spencer managed at last. "You positively unnerve me. One would think you were some ancient temple priest from Karnak yourself, leading us all out to sacrifice to Amon!"

Paul turned his golden head. "Why that's it, naturally, Doctor. It's all a spiritual exercise." He set his glass down on the table. "Do I take it, sir, that your venture here among us is merely to enjoy the Nile breezes and escape the crowds of Cairo?"

Spencer's brows shot up like the fur on the back of a cat. "You may take it so, young man. You might as well know I don't share your viewpoint about archaeology at all. Seems rather bizarre to me. I'm afraid I don't see the point of turning a simple search for historical facts into some mystical mythological discovery. Absurd, really."

"Oh, dear," Lady Walsh said, her hand at her heart. "I think I do feel a spell coming on, Cynthia dear. My powders—are they in my purse?"

"I'll look, Mother...."

But Paul merely shook back a swatch of golden hair that had fallen onto his forehead, as though ridding himself of a bothersome insect. "In my opinion, Doctor, archaeology would do well to treat the tombs and pyramids of Egypt with the respect they demand. After all, they still contain the greatest spiritual mysteries of the ancient past."

"Do you suggest the Valley of the Kings is holy ground?" Spencer scoffed. "Nonsense. It's a place where death reigns."

"Death has reigned in all the world, from Adam until now," Allison inserted. "Only Christ has gained any victory over it. It is not the sun god, but the Son of God that defeated sin, death, and the grave. Only Christ has been resurrected from death. Did the gods of Egypt have any power over the true God when his servant Moses announced to Pharaoh each of the ten plagues against all of the false things that the Egyptians worshiped?"

"Oh, dear! Oh, dear!" Lady Walsh said. *"Must* we discuss these unpleasant subjects? So serious, so depressing. Cynthia, darling, do hand me the plate of sweetmeats."

Paul seemed oblivious to both Allison's statement and Lady Walsh's attempted detour. "The robbers of the royal tombs are robbers of truth. The pharaoh's treasures and the mummies should be left unmolested."

"Poppycock!" Spencer waved a dismissive hand. "They belong in museums for all the world to see, to enjoy."

"And in the private collection of the kaiser?" Paul's question was laced with anger.

Allison's tensions spiraled. Why didn't Bret say anything to end all this? Did he want to hear it? She might agree that the conversation was unmasking personalities, but it could lead to trouble between Spencer and Paul.

"I think," Gamal al-Sayyid said too calmly, "that both Mr. Kruger and Doctor Howard hold a measure of truth to what they say about Egyptology. The thoughtlessness of some archaeologists has resulted in the permanent loss of great finds of antiquity; robbers of temples have torn out the heart of ancient Egypt and carried it away to adorn the private collections of Europeans and Easterners alike."

"Ah!" Paul's eyes shone with deep satisfaction and he looked at Spencer as though he had won the argument.

"On the other hand," Mr. Sayyid continued studiously. "I do not think, Paul, that your mother would agree with you about treating the royal tombs and pyramids as spiritual discoveries—"

Paul broke in. "Yes! Helga is now in Luxor with the funerary piece of the queen. Such an antiquity, pulsating with life, should be returned to its proper place in the royal tomb of Ramses—where it belongs, before—" he stopped.

"Before the curse of the pharaoh strikes?" Beth's question was hushed, as though she was even afraid to voice it.

"Perhaps," came Paul's quiet agreement. "Before Wadjit, the guardian cobra god, strikes us all."

"Preposterous!" Spencer barked out abruptly. "You're frightening the child, Paul."

"You may mock, Doctor, but there are stories about the curses…and not all are nonsense."

A tiny, splintering crash interrupted. They all turned toward Lady Walsh, who had stood to her feet. Her face was ghastly pale, and she was staring straight ahead, as though astounded by what she saw in her mind's eye. Her glass of lemon water had slipped from her hand to shatter on the floor. She gasped, reached for her throat, then collapsed to the floor in a heap of gray organdie.

"Great Scot!" Spencer pushed his chair aside and rushed to kneel beside her.

Cynthia gave a small cry, staring down at her mother wide-eyed. Immediately the salon was humming with voices and activity. In that brief moment Allison saw Doctor Howard moving to comfort Cynthia; saw Bret rise and move to Lady Walsh, kneeling beside her on one knee, looking at her without touching anything.

Julian's lean frame moved like a sleek tiger to the low table in front of the divan, where there were a number of drinking glasses. He was snapping orders at everyone: "Don't touch those glasses! Nobody move! Is that clear?"

The change in his voice, the sudden, dreadful implication of that order, brought a look of consternation to the faces of those gathered there.

"Well, Doctor?" Julian demanded.

Spencer turned his head and looked at the grave-faced Julian with a frown of disbelief. Then he looked with pity at Cynthia. "Heart failure is my preliminary guess." He paused, as though loathe to make the declaration. "She's gone."

There was silence again—a terrible frozen silence that surrounded the group. Nothing was heard except the music from the orchestra. Paul Kruger, tensely pale, shot a glance at Bret, who turned to Cynthia. She gave a sob, and Miss Cook, a woman in her forties, went to console her.

"But she can't be—dead." Cynthia's words were choked with a stunned grief. "She—she was just here! Where did she go? Where did she go?" She turned, stricken, to Paul. "It's *your* fault. You, with that foolish talk. You—*killed* her!"

Paul stepped backward as if she had slapped him. Bret moved toward Cynthia, reaching out to grip her arm and give her a shake. "Snap out of it, Cynthia."

She looked at him, then broke into tears. "Oh, Bret!"

He took hold of her, comforting her as she sobbed against his chest.

Allison sank, weak-kneed, into a chair. Julian came to lay a wiry hand on her shoulder for a moment, as if to sympathize, then walked back to the low table where the glasses were still in place. She saw him gazing down, studying each place where the others had sat around that table only moments before. By now the captain of the ship had been notified, and Allison watched as he came hurrying into the salon with his chief officer.

"I'll need to wire ahead to the authorities at Asyut," Julian told him. "I've a colleague there. The police will want to come aboard and ask questions before we can journey on to Luxor."

The inspector released Spencer from the room—after, of course, the chief officer had searched him. "Fetch your medical bag from your cabin," the inspector commanded, and Spencer hurried away.

When he returned, the chief officer took the medical bag and opened it, peering inside.

"Nothing that could be the poison but a bottle of bitters, Inspector." The chief officer held up the bottle.

Spencer endured the indignity in silence, making no comment when Julian told the chief officer to take the bottle for safekeeping. "Just a precaution, Spencer."

"Of course. I would be disappointed if you did anything else, Inspector. I would also advise confiscating the purses of the ladies present." He turned to Bret, inclining his head to the still sobbing Cynthia. "Please, would you escort Cynthia to her cabin?"

Bret nodded, then glanced at Julian. "Miss Cook...?" he inquired, and Julian nodded.

"Of course." He turned to the older woman. "Would you be so kind as to accompany Miss Walsh?"

Miss Cook nodded, and followed the others from the room. In a short time Allison and Beth were allowed to leave as well. But Paul was ordered to stay, as were Mr. Sayyid and a shaking Rahotep.

Allison walked to Julian. "Why are we being detained at Asyut? Lady Walsh surely died of heart failure. Everyone knew she had a condition. Doctor Howard's been treating her for months."

Julian turned burning, dark eyes upon her but made no reply.

"What else could it be?" she insisted in a whisper. "Who'd want to harm Lady Walsh?"

"You'd better go to your cabin," Julian told her, and Allison was surprised by the gentle quality of both his tone and his gaze. "Try to sleep, my dear. There's nothing you can do. You've been through enough."

Allison searched his face. Lady Walsh must have died of a heart condition. She *must* have, she thought desperately. Because it was Bret who had brought that glass of lemon water to Lady Walsh. Her eyes involuntarily strayed to the sidebar where the various refreshments were kept. Julian glanced there, too, as though he knew what she was thinking. He turned to the chief officer and gave a quiet order. "Don't let anything be touched or removed. And you'll have to seal off the entire salon until we dock tomorrow morning at Asyut."

Allison and Beth started from the room, only to be halted

when Julian said, "Beth, can you stay a few minutes?"

Allison turned quickly to stare at him, and he smiled reassuringly. "Don't worry, Allison. This has nothing to do with Lady Walsh."

She watched as Julian took Beth's arm and led her to a corner where they could speak alone.

Someone had covered Lady Walsh's body with a blanket. Allison, afraid, went down to the cabins. She had to talk to Bret....

She entered the steamy corridor and saw that Miss Cook was just leaving Cynthia's room. The woman looked strained as she adjusted the spectacles on her pug nose, which was dotted with sun freckles. Her pale, almost colorless eyes looked through Allison as though she didn't see her. "Is there anything I can do to help?" Allison asked.

"What? Oh, Allison! I'm sorry.... No, I don't think so. Miss Walsh is all right now. Both Doctor Howard and the colonel are with her." Her thin brows lifted. "I don't think she wants our company. She demanded I leave. She's rather a loose-witted girl, isn't she? I don't know how she'll survive on her own. Probably spend herself into penury. They say she hasn't got the money she believes—or pretends." She shook her head. "I can't see how Lady Walsh could buy the Blaine house *and* the Riviera if their funds are low. Oh, well, it's none of my affair. A sorry thing to happen like that—and so suddenly. Just as Paul Kruger was into that *ridiculous* and overly emotional dispute about curses——" She stopped, as if catching herself, then adjusted her spectacles and straightened her bony shoulders. "Well, I'm off to bed. Is this your cabin?"

"Yes."

"I'll be in cabin twelve if you need me. Colonel Holden is in ten. Doctor Spencer in eleven. Good night." She walked down the corridor, while Allison looked after her.

So Bret was in ten. That was good to know. It would be better if she weren't noticed by anyone asking to speak with him alone. It might look as if she had something to hide. She could wait in his cabin instead. They could have their meeting, she could turn Sarah's letter over to him, and no one would ever have cause to speculate about their conversation.

Glancing down the corridor to make certain she wasn't being watched, and hearing voices in Cynthia's cabin, she hurried past Spencer's cabin, then Miss Cook's, where she heard the woman moving about.

How will I get in? she thought, biting her lip. She needn't have worried. The door to number ten had been left ajar, as though Bret had dashed inside for a moment, then rushed out again.

She pushed the door open carefully and peered inside, just to be certain Bret wasn't there. The cabin was empty. She slipped inside, closing the door quietly behind her. Her eyes scanned the neat cabin. Bret's bags had been unpacked and his clothing put away. There was an empty coffeepot and a cup on the table.

She listened for footsteps outside in the corridor. The paper on which Sarah had written her information rubbed against her skin in an irritating way, reminding her of the heavy burden she carried.

Soon she would be able to turn that dark burden over to Bret. Soon he would hold her and soothe her raw and painful emotions, as he had comforted Cynthia over the loss of poor Lady Walsh.

Sharp emotion stabbed at her, and she pushed it way. She wouldn't be jealous over his kindness to Cynthia in such a moment.

She moved to sit in a chair but couldn't sit still for longer than a minute. Naturally, Bret would be late. He wouldn't leave Cynthia until he was certain she was calmed down. Allison stood again and paced, listening hopefully for the sound of his steps, but instead she heard something quite different; her heart, whispering a warning...

What if you hear words of darkness and not light?

As she paced quietly on the rug, her gaze drifted to a book Bret had left on the side table. Her nerves on edge, she picked it up. How little she knew of the private life of the man she loved! What was he reading? She turned it over and smiled. Archaeology, of course. But no—the book was on ancient Egyptian religious beliefs, the myriad of gods: Osiris, who found the Nile sacred; Heka, the frog-headed goddess; the scarab beetle, Apis; the black bull; insect-gods; the sky goddess; the sun god, Ra; Amon...the list went on. As she turned a page, a piece of paper fluttered to the floor. She picked it up, intending to replace it inside when the drawing caught her eye.

She looked at the woman Bret had sketched. She was garbed in ancient Egyptian dress, lovely and haunting, with wide, black-rimmed almond eyes. It was Queen Nefertari, and it wasn't...

Bret had meticulously altered the features into the unmistakable face of Cynthia Walsh. Waves of shock washed over Allison, threatening to suffocate her. This was not a simple drawing. It was far too intricate, far too...emotive. No, this was a drawing that showed a troubled mind...a soul that was possessed by the woman depicted there—for across the woman's head was written a simple, chilling title:

Queen Cynthia.

SIXTEEN

ALLISON SAT STARING AT BRET'S DRAWING of Cynthia for unnumbered minutes before backing out the door. As she neared her own cabin, Doctor Howard stepped into the corridor from Cynthia's room. "She'll be asleep soon," he said to Bret, who followed him out.

They peered down the passage and saw her, but Allison didn't speak to them. Instead, she went inside her cabin, closing and locking her door. She leaned against it, hearing them walk past. One of them paused momentarily. Bret? Her heart pounded, then relief swept her when the steps walked on. A door shut, then more steps sounded as someone went up on deck.

Probably Spencer. He would need to inform Julian of his preliminary diagnosis for the cause of Lady Walsh's death. Tomorrow when the ship docked at Asyut, the authorities would be called in. Julian would want to ask them questions. And Bret...

Bret had given that glass of lemon water to Lady Walsh.

A few minutes passed before Allison noticed she was still holding Bret's drawing of Cynthia. Oh no! He was sure to notice it was gone! She reached for the door handle, then stopped. It was too late now. She couldn't bring herself to return it to him. If she confronted him now, it would place them both in an awkward and miserable situation. He would be angry, accusing her of snooping, which she hadn't meant to do.

Even worse than his anger, though, was the prospect that

he might admit his fascination with a woman he denied being in love with. Of course, he could deny the drawing was even his. Had it not been for his behavior recently, she could easily talk her heart into making some excuse about the drawing because she so desperately wanted an explanation…and not the obvious one.

She couldn't bear to look again and see the proof of Bret's fascination with Cynthia. She folded the drawing and clumsily stuffed it inside her handbag. Pressing a hand to her forehead, she felt sick and miserable. The scratching of Sarah's letter inside her bodice only added more weight to her dilemma.

She thought about Bret leaving the CID. It wasn't just Julian who had warned her, but her own father had requested that Bret be placed on suspension. Bret's words tonight, the drawing, the map he had not reported…all seemed to indicate he had changed. Or could it be that she was seeing the true Bret Holden for the first time?

As she stood there, her heart resisting the evidence that continued to weigh against him, someone entered the passageway, walking softly, pausing every few feet. The footsteps were creeping past her door down to one of the other cabins. When they began to fade, Allison carefully opened her door a crack and looked down the corridor. Cynthia either had not taken her sedative or it hadn't started working yet. Nor did she appear as heartbroken as she had earlier.

She stopped in front of cabin ten and tried the door. It opened readily. Bret stood there, clearly visible, his jacket removed, his white collar loose at the neck. He said something to Cynthia, and she threw her arms around him. He embraced her with a kiss, drawing her into his cabin. The door shut.

Allison stared, her knuckles pressed against her mouth to

silence the wounded sob that struggled to escape from deep within her soul.

She closed her door and covered her ears. She couldn't bear the thought of hearing—or not hearing—Cynthia's stealthy footsteps as she returned to her cabin.

Allison went to her bunk and fell on it, feeling Sarah's letter again. She tried to pray, but no words came. Where had she gone wrong with Bret? Had God intended her to marry Wade all along? There were no simple answers to the devilish whirl-wind that had her trapped within its force. She grabbed her pillow and placed it over her head, gripping the ends as her tears ran freely.

"Believe" the notes had said. But she could not.

Trust in God, trust him, trust him—her aching heart echoed, and she wasn't even sure she could do that.

The door to Allison's cabin opened and someone came in, walking up beside the bunk. Through the pillow Allison heard the muffled words: "Allison? Are you sick?"

It was Beth.

"I simply can't believe what happened to Lady Walsh. Julian is questioning everyone. I heard Spencer say something about poison—I'm afraid. You don't suppose Sir Edgar's on board do you? Maybe he killed Lady Walsh. Allison? Are—you awake?"

She didn't answer. Not even when Beth gently touched her arm, or when she moved away and Allison heard the door to her cabin close.

They docked at Asyut the next morning. Allison didn't go up for breakfast but pleaded a headache. Spencer sent powders to add to her tea and a note suggesting she stay aboard and rest instead of subjecting herself to the ordeal of luncheon ashore with the club.

The steward brought a bowl of fresh fruit from Julian, and a note was enclosed:

Unfortunately it's necessary to be detained at Asyut while those who were present at Lady Walsh's death are questioned. I will be working with the authorities here, and if everyone cooperates, we should be over this in a few days and be able to continue the voyage toward Luxor. I've arranged a room for you and Beth here at the Flamingo Hotel. With all that you've been through recently, may I suggest that you take the day to rest and recuperate? I won't need to question you until last, per- haps tomorrow over dinner?

Julian

Neither Spencer nor Julian knew it, but she had been up since dawn making plans, and now she had come to a deci- sion. Yes, she might meet with Julian over dinner tomorrow and trust him with Sarah's letter...if only she could be quite certain it was the right thing to do. The fact he was chief inspector meant little after Edgar's deception. Besides, Sarah had made her directions explicit: Trust no one except Bret and Helga.

Allison swallowed the black tea, which was almost as bitter as her thoughts. Her confidence in Bret had been shaken. He had become a stranger who had wounded her, and she must avoid further damage. There was no time to waste mourning the loss of the man she thought she'd loved. There would be a thousand bitter tomorrows in which to do that! Right now, lives were at risk. If she wasn't sure about Bret, that left Baroness Helga Kruger.

Now that Allison had decided what to do, she would waste no time in carrying it out. The delay at the Flamingo Hotel worked in her favor. She would go on to Luxor alone to find Helga and turn over Sarah's letter. Helga would know the right person to contact. Allison had thought of wiring her father, but he wasn't in Cairo yet, nor could the wire service be trusted. No, she must go on to find Helga in Luxor. *I can make it,* she told herself, gritting her teeth. *With the Lord I can survive, even without Bret if it's God's will.*

Beth returned to the cabin after breakfast, and Allison drew her aside. "What I'm telling you is important, and you must promise to keep it between us."

Beth eyed her with concern. "Sure I will. You've been acting strangely since last night."

"Once we're in the hotel it's crucial I leave without anyone knowing. I'm going on to Luxor alone."

"They won't let you go, you know that. Even if Julian didn't stop you, Bret would. Or the local authorities."

"That's where you come in. Make excuses for me at luncheon. During that time I'll slip out the back. There's a train from here to Luxor, and I must be on it."

"But why, Allison?"

"I need to meet with Helga before the club arrives."

"That still doesn't answer my question. Why is it so important for you to leave?"

Allison considered how much she could safely tell her sister. She trusted Beth, but she didn't want to place her in a position where she might accidentally let something slip.

"Remember what you told me in the garden at the Blaine house?"

Beth became cautious. "Yes."

Allison tried to appear confident so Beth wouldn't spread fear to the others. "I'm sure now that you were right. There is someone else. And the only person I dare trust at this time is Helga. She'll know what to do about it."

"I don't understand your reasoning, but I'll accept it. At least let me come with you."

"I can do this faster on my own. As soon as I get there I'll wire you at the hotel to let you know I'm safe."

"What about Bret, and Julian?"

Allison set her jaw and shook her head. "Only Helga. She's there, probably on the houseboat waiting for Count Roderick. Will you cover for me? Make any excuses you can to give me time."

"You know I will, but I'm afraid! If the killer is still loose, then what if he follows you?"

"He won't. There's no possible way for anyone to know what I'm going to do unless you let it slip."

"Oh, I won't, but what if Bret comes to the room—"

"He won't." Allison's reply was flat and unemotional. "If anyone else comes make some excuse."

"But if Spencer thinks you're that ill he may insist on seeing you."

"Tell him anything! Avoid him, don't answer the door, anything. All I need is a day's head start."

"All right, I won't let you down, but I'm still afraid."

Allison squeezed her hand. "We'll pray before I go. We'll commit our tomorrows to God's sovereign care and purpose. And Beth, when the club is allowed to proceed with the voyage, I want you to wire home instead. Tell Mum something's come up and you're taking the train back to Cairo. Should father arrive, tell him to contact Helga and me at once."

Beth nodded, pulling at her hair. "All right, but I'd rather go with you. You may need help."

Allison managed a smile, but it faded. She was remembering Cousin Leah going into the desert to meet her contact. Allison had been in the same position as Beth was now. What if something went wrong? Even if it did, the future belonged to God. Nothing took him off guard.

Beth searched her eyes. "What's happened between you and the colonel?" The soft question was filled with concern. "I noticed he had hardly anything to say at breakfast. And he left early, without even speaking to you."

Allison went blank. "You know as well as I that our marriage was called off last December."

"Yes, but there was always the future."

"He's changed his mind. And so have I. Now, if you'll forgive me, I don't care to discuss Colonel Holden. Listen, that's the whistle. We can check into the hotel now—and remember, you're to say nothing of this to anyone."

Beth nodded, her eyes somber. "I won't. I promise. Let's go. Julian's arranged our room. He said it's on the first floor near the garden."

Allison moved to follow her sister, wishing the ache in her heart would ease. *Where will it all end, Lord?* She forced away the tears that threatened to overflow. *What does the future hold for us? For me...without Bret?*

Part III

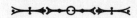

VALLEY OF THE KINGS

He lies in wait secretly, as a lion in his den.

PSALM 10:9A

SEVENTEEN

THE SUNSET COLORS OF RUBY AND AMBER boiled, filling the horizon above the great Theban hills standing opposite the Nile. Behind the high, rose-colored limestone cliffs was the Valley of the Kings, shrouded in purple dusk. Cut deep into the cliffs were the royal burial tombs, containing a series of doors and intricately chiseled passageways leading down into the largest chamber that guarded the royal sarcophagus—the gold coffin that held the mummy of the Egyptian pharaoh.

Alone, as planned, Allison had arrived earlier that afternoon at the train junction. She'd hired an Egyptian donkey boy to bring her to Helga's houseboat, which was moored somewhere between ancient Thebes and Luxor on the bank of the Nile. She found the houseboat near an ancient burial barge, which was tied close to several great pillars—remnants of a temple to the sun god Amon.

Allison glanced about, her gaze resting on the surrounding hills. With the stillness of the night, she could almost see the area as it had been hundreds of years ago, in 1570–1320 B.C. It was then, during the eighteenth dynasty of the New Kingdom Pharaohs, that young, dead King Tutankhamen had come down the Nile on a funeral barge. In her mind's eye, Allison could see the Egyptian temple priests carrying him, in somber pomp, up to the hills above the Valley of the Kings for burial.

A shudder passed through her at the thought that she would spend the dark night in this place, aboard Helga's boat—a structure that creaked and moaned and groaned, while the water gently tapped at its hull.

Even so, Allison was surprised when she saw the houseboat. From the way Helga had described it in her letter, she expected a rundown fishing boat with chipped white paint. Instead, her first look brightened what otherwise had been a fatiguing and emotionally distraught day. A large, square, house-shaped cabin with small, evenly spaced windows took up most of the deck. A blue fringed awning offered shade to the forward section of the deck, where some chairs and a table faced landward, toward the Theban hills and the Valley of the Kings. A walkway encircled the large cabin, and there were some pieces of ceramic pottery sitting about where flowers must have grown.

The sun had set, and night settled quickly. As a warm, moist breeze twirled the fringe on the tattered awning, the emollient smells of the ancient river, of hot rocks and sand, saturated Allison's senses. Her footsteps made a hollow sound on the wooden deck as she walked to the small door in the middle of the cabin. The outside lamp was there, bolted to a wooden table. She found the box of matches and lit the blackened wick. Light showered down upon another piece of pottery: the sly, toothy crocodile doorstop she had been told to look for. Allison stooped and reluctantly slid her hand into its mouth, between the teeth, to locate the key Helga told her would be there. Instead she felt a note.

Now what? She would need to get inside through a window—

She pulled out a folded piece of paper. A message from Helga? She brought it to the deck lamp to read. It was dated two days earlier.

Helga,

I am sorry to have missed our scheduled appointment at the club huts. The train was delayed three hours
at Aswan. I have gone ahead and settled in at the club
compound. If I do not hear from you by Monday, I will
come back to the houseboat. My assistant and I are most
anxious to see Nefertari.

V. Roderick

Then the count had arrived at last. But where was Helga?

She frowned. It seemed rather strange the German count
would apologize for being a few hours late on the train from
Aswan but make no mention of being more than a week late
for his original meeting.

Had he arrived when Helga had expected him, she would
have been able to join Paul and the rest of the club on the voyage. Not that the cruise on the Nile had turned out to be a
pleasant one! Had Beth been right when she told her that
Julian mentioned poison? She must have been wrong. Who
would have wanted to harm Lady Walsh?

Pushing such thoughts from her mind, she turned to the
task of finding a way inside the houseboat. On a whim she
reached for the door handle and discovered, to her surprise,
the door was unlocked. Had Helga been here? If so, why hadn't
she found the message from Count Roderick?

Inside the houseboat, Allison found a lamp near the door
and lit it. Bringing the lamp with her, she moved from room to
little room, lighting every lamp she could locate. Soon the foreboding darkness had fled. The half dozen rooms were aglow
with golden flickering lights that added encouraging life to the
too silent boat.

With light all about her giving her courage, Allison toured her surroundings, pleased with the nice-sized front sitting room. It was furnished with a long, comfortable-looking divan in sea-green damask. It was pushed up against a walnut-paneled wall. Several chairs faced each other, with a large fringed ottoman in the center and an assortment of useful tables and utility lamps set about. The room was empty of clutter and swept clean, but Allison had a notion that someone had been here recently.

Helga, of course, she scolded her nerves.

She toured the small dining room, and a still smaller kitchen with two hatches—one leading up to the roof where one could sit and enjoy the evening hours sipping tea, and the other going down into a storage area below the floor.

She stooped, set the lamp down, and opened the lower cover, grimacing as stale air reeking with odors assailed her. She leaned over and plunged the lamp into the inky space— the light revealed a bundle of cooking wood, some old tarps, dusty crates, and tins of fuel. There was dust on the wooden steps and what appeared to be some recent scuffmarks, as though something had been dragged below.

Well! I'm not going down there.

She quickly closed the hatch and stood, glancing about for something to set on top, to hold the cover firmly in place. There was a box of outdated archaeological journals in the corner, and she dragged it over the hatch, then brushed her hands clean.

Next, she toured the sleeping area in the rear. There were three small rooms, the larger—which obviously had been Helga's—was attractively decorated, with a comfortable-sized bed and a cupboard that filled one entire wall and was full of drawers. To her surprise she saw that Helga must have decided to stay on the houseboat after all. Various articles of clothing, all expensive and clearly "Helga Kruger" in style, were strewn all over the bed. A satin robe—rather out of place in the desert, but nonetheless typical of what Helga would wear—was there as well. The covers were still drawn down, and the pillows showed evidence of having been slept on.

Relieved, Allison smiled. *Thank you, God.* Helga was here. Finally Allison had found a strong, dependable friend. She was not alone with Sarah's letter or with the frightening possibility of "George" somewhere about. Since Helga was here, there would also be some food in the pantry and the makings for tea and coffee. Allison could use a cup after the long and arduous journey by train.

Helga must also have brought along her assistant, Omar, to do housekeeping. Where he was now was anyone's guess. As Allison turned to leave, she noticed the curtains on the window were missing. Odd! Helga's bedroom drapery would naturally be of the same good quality of heavy damask that she had used throughout the houseboat. Why would she have a window without drapes? Anyone could see inside.

She walked slowly to the window, holding the lamp high as she peered out into the darkness. She saw nothing except her own frightened reflection in the glass. Where had the drapery gone?

Quickly she left the room. There were more important things to worry about than absent draperies. The two other bedrooms were smaller, hardly more than a cubicle large enough to sleep in; the hanging cupboards had barely enough room to store one's shoes and clothing. Still, one of these would do well enough. Both rooms were unoccupied...Allison frowned, thinking for a moment. Then she shrugged. Omar must be sleeping off the houseboat.

As expected, she found food in the pantry, but not nearly the quantity—nor quality—she would have expected Omar to arrange for Helga. There were a few tins of corned beef and tongue, an unopened bag of ground coffee, and a tin of tea and biscuits. She grimaced; she loathed tongue. Perhaps Omar hadn't come after all and Helga was on her own. That might account for the odd selection of goods. With a shrug, Allison went to find a pan and put the water on to boil for tea.

The evening wore on. She'd finished her tea and the half-eaten tea biscuit sat beside her empty cup on the dining-room table. The rhythm of the river, as old as time, gently rocked the boat. The clock reminded her with each tick how late it was, how Helga should have returned by now.

Helga must *come*, Allison argued with herself relentlessly. *Perhaps she went to the Valley of the Kings and found Count Roderick at the club huts. If so, it's likely they had dinner together and Helga stayed on to discuss archaeology with him. All quite normal.* If that were the case, she wouldn't see Helga until tomorrow. She might as well go to bed. Come morning, Helga would arrive. Allison would turn the letter over to her, and a great burden would be taken from her.

She brought her two bags to the rear of the houseboat, to the room nearest Helga's. As she proceeded to put her things in the cupboard, the night sounds on the Nile filled the background of her mind...croaking frogs, the whoosh of water, the slight rocking of the boat, the inevitable creaking wood, and the nasty pitter-patter of little rat's feet beneath the floorboards.

Allison glanced nervously toward the front of the boat and was about to slip into bed when she remembered she hadn't locked the front door when she arrived. She'd been in too much of a hurry to light a lamp.

Walking in her stocking feet through the other little rooms, she went to slide the bolt through its catch. As she did, she heard another sound—but this one didn't originate from the Nile. Footsteps. Not outside on the walkway, but on the roof. She glanced up at the low, wood-paneled ceiling. She'd forgotten all about the hatch leading to the roof! Had Helga been up there all along, sitting in one of the chairs? She almost laughed. The baroness must have fallen asleep in a deck chair and had just awakened. Or maybe it was Omar up there cooking his supper on an open fire, enjoying the evening stars.

Or...

Allison's mouth went dry. Or maybe it was Sir Edgar. Maybe he had escaped and come here, waiting for the mysterious George. But even as the fingers of icy fear tightened around Allison's heart, logic forbade quick conclusions. There was no reason for Edgar to come here. He didn't know who George was. Besides, why would Rex Blaine's German contact be here in the Valley of the Kings?

No, it could be anyone up there, even an Egyptian peasant who had thought the houseboat empty and decided to temporarily claim it for sleeping quarters.

She moved away from the front door, looking at the ceiling, following the direction of the footsteps. The steps went to the kitchen, and then to the hatch. She quickened her steps. *Lock it!* her mind screamed at her. *Until you know who it is, slide the bolt into place!*

She ran silently through the dining room and into the kitchen, brushing past the table. She hurried to climb the ladder to the hatch in the roof. *Hurry!* each beat of her heart warned.

Then her gaze riveted upon the bolt—for it was lifting out of her reach.

The door opened, and Allison froze, halfway up the steps, her breath sucking in as she met an all-too-familiar ice blue gaze.

EIGHTEEN

><del>⊶!⟨⟩⊷⊙⊶⟨⟩!⊷</del>

BRET STEPPED THROUGH THE HATCH, his desert boots sounding confidently on the steps. As he came down the stairs, his jacket inched aside, and Allison caught a glimpse of the Luger in his leather shoulder holster.

"The train must have been slow." He gave her a disarming smile as he glanced at his watch. "You're late. I expected you by four o' clock. I fell asleep waiting. Pleasant breeze on deck though."

A wash of warm relief splashed over her, but it quickly heated to frustration. "You nearly frightened the wits out of me!" She looked around for something handy to throw at his smug face. Nothing was within reach but the half-eaten tea biscuit.

Oh, well, better than nothing.

She flung it at him, and it hit him with a satisfying thud square in the chest.

Those aristocratic brows arched. "Temper, temper, darling. You should be glad to see me. I promise to be on my best behavior, and," he added airily, "to protect you from a very nasty German agent who is at this minute on your trail."

Her breath caught in her throat, then came out in a huff. "Here? After me?"

"Always lock your doors when you're alone, my love. If you'd been careful, you wouldn't have needed to come running to bolt it at the sound of my footsteps. Make certain of security first thing." He remained on the steps, gazing down at her, but his smile had faded.

"Are you—" She met his eyes in disbelief—"Are you telling me you *deliberately* walked loudly so I could hear you?"

"Yes. If you insist on involving yourself in intelligence work, I need to give you a few pointers. If I were Lady Walsh's murderer, your mistake would have cost you your life." His glance swept her. "I suppose you didn't bring the gun I gave you, either."

"No, I left it in Cairo—" She stopped, her lashes squinting into displeasure.

"Another jolly mistake."

"Quite. Because if I had one right now, I might want to use it on you!"

His brows creased into a frown, and he scanned her face. "Yes. I think you would. Especially after peeking out your cabin door last night and watching me give Cynthia a brotherly kiss good night."

Brotherly! She felt her face go hot as the viper of jealousy bit into her heart. So he had seen her. "I don't care to discuss Cynthia with you." She turned and walked into the sitting room.

"I can explain what happened, if you let me." His tone, as he followed her, was as smooth as ever.

"Don't bother," she replied in the same tone. "I don't want to hear it."

"Just like a woman. Saying you don't want to hear, when all the time you can hardly contain your curiosity."

"Maybe I don't want your excuse, though I'm sure you've come up with a good one. You're very good with your 'role-playing,' Bret, and I have no desire to be deceived."

"I'd think you know me well enough to have seen through my latest façade." He spoke in a quiet, pensive tone.

"This time I do."

"Do you think so? Then my *role-playing* is very effective, indeed. So much so that even you believed it. And I thought you knew me, Allison."

"I do now, and I'll never trust you again."

He caught her arm and spun her around to face him. She was surprised to see hurt and frustration reflected in his blue eyes. She hadn't actually meant what she'd said. She'd just struck out, wanting him to know how hurt she was and that *he* was responsible. Her wounded heart had pushed her to say more than she really believed.

O Lord, forgive me! Quick shame washed over her. How easy it was, in the midst of hurt, to forget the One who owned her!

"Bret, I—"

His hold was gentle, but his expression was almost desperate. "Please don't ever say that again. Don't say you can't trust me."

"Then tell me the truth!" Her breath came in painful gasps. "You want me to trust you? Oh, Bret, I *do*, despite everything. But I want to be trusted, too, by you. What are you keeping from me?"

He closed his eyes for a moment, then opened them and stared at her. "All right. You'll have it. Though it could cost me my neck with the CID." His gaze held hers. "You ought to have guessed, Allison. I'm on assignment."

Yes, she had thought of that. And yet, she must be certain. "You're on suspension," she protested in a dry whisper. Fear coursed through her. Seeing Bret with Cynthia had nearly undone her. The very thought of him with any other woman, of losing his love…

No, she wouldn't even think about that. He was here. He had come to her because he knew she had seen him with Cynthia. He wanted to explain. She'd never known the enigmatic Colonel Holden to explain himself before. Surely that was proof that he cared deeply…wasn't it?

"I'm not on suspension. It's part of a tactic to snare an agent. A German agent, one who is quite powerful and far too effective." His blue eyes softened, and he reached up a lean finger to tenderly touch her cheek. "Don't you know by now that you're the only woman in my life? That you occupy my thoughts…my heart. Don't you know that the only thing that could keep me from your side is my duty to my country?" He cupped her chin with a warm hand, and a small smile tipped his lips. "Trust me, Allison. *Believe.*"

She drew in a startled gasp. *Believe.* Was he saying—? "It was you." The whispered words were a statement, not a question. His smile deepened, and tears stung her eyes. "I thought you were gone—"

"I was there, always. Watching over you as best I could. Asking you in the only way left to me to have faith in me."

The warm, midnight blue eyes drew her heart into his. "I do." She whispered the words around the lump in her throat. "And I always will, until the very end.…" She closed her eyes as confusion swept over her. "But it's so hard when you're not near, and when Julian Mortimer believes you've turned traitor."

He went still, but held his silence.

"Well?" She opened her eyes and looked at him. "What about Julian? He insists you've betrayed your country. He came to me and asked me to help the Cairo police prove your guilt."

A flicker of wry humor touched his mouth. "Very thoughtful of him. I'll need to inquire more carefully regarding his motives next time he and I meet." He shook his head. "I can't discuss Julian with you, darling. We'll talk about us, even about my work, but I'm not willing to risk anyone else. You accused me of playing a role, and that's exactly what I've been doing—but it is one I didn't want and I told your father so."

Allison stared at him. "When did you meet with Father?"

"Before he left Cairo. But when I learned what my next mission was about, what was at stake and who it was we were after, I couldn't say no. I knew it meant risking your trust, Allison, but I hadn't counted on you actually being present when I played my part. It was…disconcerting—" His smile seemed directed at himself more than anything else—"and very frustrating, especially when I needed to entertain Cynthia. You can't imagine the skill it takes to focus on another woman, all the while pretending that the woman I'm madly in love with isn't sitting at the opposite end of the table."

His words surrounded her, warming her heart. She took his hand and held it tightly. "But what has my father to do with your assignments?"

He contemplated her for a moment, then took both her hands in his. "You said you wanted me to trust you, to show you how much I respect you? Very well. Your father is my immediate superior."

It was a good thing the divan was immediately behind Allison, for she sat down hard. "So I was right. I wondered if Daddy might be in the CID, if he was using his government office as a cover."

"Sometimes you're too smart for your own safety," Bret said dryly and sat down beside her.

"Yet I never dreamed he might be directly over you."

"Why do you think I didn't want you coming to Luxor? You'd see me at my worst. Can't you understand how I felt? My frustration? I was torn between my duty and my heart. I still am, if you must know—" He broke off with a muttered exclamation. Heaving a deep sigh, he ran a hand through his thick hair. "I shouldn't be breathing a word of this to you."

"My heart is sealed—" His gaze came to meet hers, and she

smiled—"as are my lips. But, Bret…" She hated to bring it up, but she had to. "I don't understand. About Cynthia…"

He tapped his chin, leaning back against the divan, watching her with a moody glint in his eyes. "That was the role I balked at the most. It was one thing to be stripped of my uniform, to show bitterness toward the CID, to be accused of smuggling. But behaving as though our broken engagement had set me on the rebound with Cynthia was…irksome. And yet it was, unfortunately, necessary. I had to convince her everything that was being said about me was true, that I really had been suspended and so was out to get even, and set on getting rich in the process."

Her gaze dropped to his lips. "Did you enjoy it?"

His eyes narrowed. "Enjoy what?"

"You know!"

One brow lifted. "I haven't the dimmest notion what you mean."

But when she looked at him, she saw his eyes grow warm. Encouraged by what she saw reflected in those blue depths, she affected a pout. "I think you're trying to gain time, Colonel. Did you enjoy kissing the elegant and beautiful Miss Walsh?"

He tipped his head to the side, pursing his lips, looking for all the world as though he were seriously considering the question. Then, as though suddenly coming to a decision, he shook his head firmly. "No, no I'd say not. It was strictly business. Rather tedious, actually."

"Oh, come! You *did* enjoy it."

All teasing gone, Bret leaned forward. He took her hand and enclosed it gently between his. When he spoke, his voice was low and sure. "No, Allison, I didn't. How could I when all I could think of was you?" He lifted her hand to place a gentle kiss at her wrist, and her breathing caught in her throat at the contact. His gaze came back to hers, and she saw only sincerity there as he went on. "It didn't matter that we had set our engagement aside, I still felt as though I was betraying your trust. Why do you think I'm here now? When I realized you'd seen me with Cynthia, I knew what you would think—" Pain showed in his eyes—"and I couldn't bear letting you go on thinking it was true. That's why I went along with the delay in our engagement. Had you been wearing my ring, I couldn't have gone through with it."

She watched him steadily, searching his face. This was the man she knew. Here, beside her, was the Colonel Bret Holden with whom she had fallen in love.

His gaze rested on her face. "Well?" His tone was gentle. "Go ahead and ask."

She shook her head. "No. It isn't necessary."

"I think it is, darling, because you may be in love with me, but you don't completely trust me. And the infuriating thing is, I fed your mistrust. That's why I've decided to give up my work, at least certain aspects of it, when you become my wife."

"Are you sure I will be your wife?" There was a painful catch in her voice, because at the moment, *she* wasn't sure it would ever happen.

He reached and brushed a finger against her cheek. "Oh, yes. I have no doubt. Because you see, my dear, I can't imagine going on without you. I know the Lord meant us for each other. You're the most precious thing God has brought into my life, after the gift of salvation, and I don't intend to lose you."

"Oh, Bret…"

He met her eyes without flinching. "Cynthia did come into my cabin. We talked. I made certain that the conversation continued until the sedative knocked her out. I carried her back to her room. On the way back I stopped outside your door. I

313

wanted to explain, but I couldn't. It wasn't until we docked the next morning and you didn't come down to breakfast that I knew I had to risk telling you what I'm doing. If I didn't, I'd lose you—" He broke off, and looked away for a moment. Then his eyes came back to hold her gaze. "I could accept a lot of losses in my life, Allison, but you are not one of them. And so I came. And if your father knew, my suspension would be real when I get back to Cairo."

She swallowed and looked at him. What he said was true. *Believe*, the notes had urged her. And she did. With all her heart. Perhaps she always had...Still—

"I believe you about Cynthia, and yet I still have questions about what you're doing."

"I was afraid of that." He kissed her wrist again, then sank back against the divan with a sigh. "Anything you say, my darling bulldog." His eyes twinkled at her huff. "But if you expect this to go on into the wee hours of the morning, I'd like some coffee. Does Helga have any?"

She smiled, realizing she felt lighter than she had for days. Weeks. Months. "Yes, there are some large cans."

"Good." He took her hand and pulled her up—and then into his arms. He held her close, burying his face in her hair. She clung to him, fighting the urge to weep against his solid shoulder. After a moment, he stepped away. "I needed that far more than I need the coffee," he said with a smile. "Thank you."

She nodded, speechless, and he reached for her hand, leading her into the kitchen. "You know what? I'm hungry, too."

She laughed. "Sorry, there isn't much food." She pulled out the matches to light the small cookstove to start the water boiling. Bret leaned against the wall, arms folded.

"I'm all yours, Allison. Ask away."

"Well, to start with, what are you doing here?" She struck a match with shaking fingers. "Is it true, what you said about an—an agent trailing me—ouch!" She burned her finger, dropping the match.

Bret took the matchbox from her and lit the flame under the coffeepot. "All true."

She took that in. "Why else did you come?"

"Same reason you're here. Looking for Helga."

"What makes you think I came looking for her?"

"Of course you came hoping to find her. You wouldn't have stolen yourself away if you hadn't."

He knew too much. "And you and Helga?"

"We were to meet here two weeks ago." He stared at the extinguished match and scowled. "For some reason, she hasn't shown up. I was told she would be on the steamer." He tossed the match away and looked at her. "We both know what happened there, so we're back where we started. Where is Helga Kruger? I wish I knew!"

She thought back to the dinner that night in the salon. "Paul and Mr. Sayyid both said they'd gotten a message saying she would be on the ship. Did she send one to you?"

"That's what got me worried. I haven't heard from her, yet she knew it was urgent for us to meet. If she had intended to contact anyone other than Paul, it would have been me. Instead, it was Sayyid." He repeated to himself, "Sayyid...I wonder about him, yet his record is clean. And Rahotep asserts the man is pro-British."

"You don't think Mr. Sayyid was lying last night at dinner?"

"If he was, I can't figure out why. He has nothing to gain. He'll have a lot to explain to Julian if it turns out he was lying."

She wanted to ask him about Paul, but decided to wait. "But Helga is here, just like her message said. Her clothes are in her bedroom. I saw them."

"Yes, I noticed them when I arrived. I got here about an hour before you did."

"How? If you were on the train with me?"

He smiled. "Quite regrettable, that trouble your donkey boy had with his animal. Ah, well, donkeys can be remarkably uncooperative creatures, can't they?"

"Yes, the poor beast had something wrong with it, and—" She broke off as sudden realization dawned. She pinned him with a look. "You told the boy to take his time."

"I needed that extra hour." He grinned. "Hope it didn't cause you too much discomfort."

She crossed her arms. "No, but I should have known. *Suddenly* the donkey was well again and moving at a good clip." She chuckled.

He was looking at the kitchen curtains. "Those drapes in the bedroom…"

She looked at him anxiously. "Yes, it's odd. What do you make of it?"

"I'm not sure. The boat was empty when I came here two weeks ago," Bret said quietly. "Helga wasn't at the huts then, either. David told me she was returning to Cairo to meet her son, then planning to sail back here with the club."

"So *that's* why you were aboard the steamer."

"Partly. I told you some of my other reasons last night. I knew *you* were aboard. And I admit I was upset. Your presence meant I'd need to play my role with you sitting right on stage. The idea was troublesome—and embarrassing, if you want to know."

She turned, wide-eyed. "Embarr—" she broke off, blinking

at him. "I've *never* known you to be embarrassed about any-thing."

His expression clouded, the teasing humor gone. "It embar-rasses me to pretend I was kicked out of Intelligence, that I'm selling stolen treasures on the Berlin-Baghdad Railway, and that I want to go around kissing Cynthia when someone far more wonderful—" His eyes focused on her mouth—"and *kissable* is just down the corridor in cabin fifteen."

Pleased warmth filled Allison, and she felt her face flush. She turned to occupy her time counting out the tablespoons of grounds, which she poured directly into the coffee water. "Go on."

"Go on?" The laughter was back in his voice. "What are you, an agent? I hope you won't hold my hand over the fire until I talk." She looked at him quickly and found his eyes sparkling with humor. He held up his hands in a gesture of surrender. "All right, for you...anything. What else do you want to know?"

It was on the tip of her tongue to ask about the map he'd found in the sundial, but for some reason she didn't. "Why are you looking for Helga?"

"You should know part of the answer to that. You're one of the few people I've told who she is. As to why I want to see her now, I can't explain that yet, I'm afraid."

"This 'big fish' you're hoping to catch—what's his name, do you know?"

He tilted his dark head and gave her a sideways glance, as though wondering whether she really expected an answer. "Be reasonable, darling. Do you think I'd risk your safety by telling you that? It's crucial his identity remain in the dark. He'll elimi-nate anyone who finds out about him. I'm confident he would have killed Rex Blaine himself before letting him return with

Sarah to England. Rex was useful to him only as long as he served the cause faithfully."

"But how did you know I was coming here?"

"I followed you," came the smooth reply.

"On the train? How is it that I didn't see you?"

He smiled wryly. "I didn't *want* you to see me."

"How did you manage to get away from the Flamingo Hotel without Julian stopping you?"

"Same way you did," he said, too casually. "We'll both have some explaining to do to the Cairo police when we get back."

"Except you have a bit more. After all, you were the last person to handle Lady Walsh's lemon water." She glanced toward him. "I saw you at the sideboard filling her glass when I was talking with Rahotep. By the way, did you overhear as I intended?"

"Yes, well done, and quite interesting. But you needn't worry about Rahotep. He's a friend of mine. As for Lady Walsh's lemon water, it isn't true that I was the last one to handle her glass. I set it on the table before I gave it to her. Any one of us could have moved it, since the glasses were within easy reach on the table."

"Are you suggesting one of them put poison in her water?"

"I'm not suggesting anyone in particular. I'm just pointing out that I wasn't the sole handler of her glass."

"Then the others are not under suspicion? Mr. Sayyid, Rahotep, Paul, even Beth, were up on deck listening to the orchestra."

"Not that simple. Just minutes before you came into the salon they were all there, with tinkling glasses of their own. And every one of them left his or her glass behind on that table before going up to the dance."

She stared at him. "Which means the poison could have

been in any of those glasses—but—" She stopped, frowning.

Bret concluded gravely. "Yes, you're right. Someone must have exchanged glasses when heads turned at your entry."

She shuddered. It was a horrid thought to believe her arrival had given someone the opportunity to poison Lady Walsh!

"But, Bret! Who would want to? I mean, she didn't threaten anyone. She was an elderly society woman!"

"Not really. She was more than she appeared. Or maybe I should say she was 'less than' she appeared. But I'll let you in on a secret: that dose of cyanide wasn't meant for Lady Walsh."

"Not meant for—?"

"We think she picked up that glass by mistake."

"Then whom was it meant for?" She poured the coffee slowly to avoid disturbing the grounds. "Me?"

"No. No one knew you were coming back up to the salon. It was meant for me."

She sucked in her breath. "But—" She stopped as the reality of what he suggested began to make sense. "Then someone knew your suspension from the CID was a ruse?"

"I don't know for sure, but I don't think that was the reason. I had everyone pretty well convinced." His smile was wry. "Even you, unfortunately. But I think there was a different motive, one completely divorced from the ugly business of espionage. A reason quite off the track, one having to do with something even more ancient than betrayal. Jealousy."

"Jealousy?" She looked at him, her mind spinning. Who would be jealous of Bret? Especially jealous enough to want him dead?

"What is it Solomon said in Proverbs, 'Jealously is as cruel as death'? Whatever the cause, it's devious. Rather unnerving," he said dryly, drinking the cup of coffee. "I'm used to facing

German Lugers or being chased across the desert by enemy soldiers. But drops of cyanide in my lemon slush seems rather unsporting."

Allison leaned against the cookstove, feeling weak. What if Bret were dead instead of Lady Walsh? She remembered how quickly the poison had acted. One moment the woman had been sitting there well and talking, the next she was gone.

Allison's hand went to her throat.

Bret set his cup down and came to her, taking both her hands in his. "It's all right, darling. I'm here, as difficult to handle as ever. I shouldn't have told you. I'm telling more than necessary to convince you to trust me again. You see how desperate I am?" Frustration filled his eyes and voice. "Loving a woman changes everything for a man. I'm doing what I'd never have done two years ago, or even a year ago. I'm discussing secret information. I'm even more convinced this is going to be my last assignment. But I will tell you what stands out to me with this poisoning. When the cyanide ended up killing the wrong person, someone wanted to make me look guilty."

"Why do you think that?"

"Because the scenario fits with everything else we believe about this person."

"We? Who is working with you?"

Again, he gave her a hesitant glance. "Rahotep, for one."

"Rahotep! What else do you believe about this case? What scenario fits?"

He shook his head. "Enough questions. Now it's time I asked *you* for some information."

Allison uneasily brushed a strand of hair from her neck. She would need to decide about Sarah's letter. Should she tell him…? If she truly couldn't trust him, then she might as well surrender any notion of ever being his wife. Marriage was built on trust, as well as love. Love was no problem—her love for Bret filled her every pore—but trust...? That had to be earned, to be built slowly, one brick upon another. Trust was what formed the foundation for the relationship.

She was sure Bret was telling the truth about Cynthia...

But what about the drawing? an inner voice whispered.

Something held her back from voicing that question. Like Sarah's letter, it would remain in the shadows until she was ready to risk everything again. And she wasn't there yet.

He had lifted a tin of tongue from the cupboard. "War rations...Is this all there is to eat?"

Allison produced a tin of corned beef and tea biscuits and held them out. "Your choice, Colonel."

"I hope this isn't a sign of days to come. You do cook, don't you?"

She smiled.

"All right." He tapped the tin of corned beef. "Considering I'm half starved, I'll try it. Where's the opener?"

Allison handed it over. "When father talked to you about this assignment you're on, did he tell you that I brought up the subject that we wanted to marry on Christmas eve?"

She saw the curious look in his eyes. "No. Did you?"

She explained the scene with her father. "In the end, he threatened to have you transferred to France before we could go through with it. And, of course, I didn't need to tell you I'd changed my mind because he told you."

"He told me you agreed to call it off at his wishes." His eyes darkened. "Looks like he used thumbscrews on us both—" He drew a deep breath, then sighed—"as well as some common sense. He was probably right about waiting. It's not something I want to think about, but I could easily not come back from one of these missions. I admit, though, I wasn't so much thinking of that but how much I loved you and wanted you."

She had to clench her hands behind her to keep from rushing to him and throwing her arms around him.

"I thought you were pulling back just to please your father. The idea upset me. I wanted to be first in your allegiance. A bit selfish, perhaps."

"No, a husband *should* be first."

He smiled, his eyes teasing her. "I'll remind you of that sometime in the future." He sobered. "So I went ahead and agreed to the mission. Which is what your good father wanted all along. Marriage to his daughter would have interfered. The mission was dangerous, and he knew it. But I did insist he was to explain everything to you when the mission was completed. I didn't realize I'd need to do it sooner." He grimaced. "As I said, I hadn't counted on you being aboard the steamer."

"And neither did my father. You know, don't you, that even David thinks you may have cracked and gone wrong?"

Bret scowled, but it wasn't clear if it was over what she had said about David, or the smell of the corned beef he'd opened. "I need to convince my friends if I expect to convince the enemy. David will learn the truth, even as you have. I'm not worried about what he thinks right now, but what *you* think of me is important. Vitally so." He set the tin down suddenly and turned toward her. "I've come to realize how essential your trust is to me, Allison. Do I have it?"

Her heart reached out to him. "You know I love you. Even when I didn't trust you, down deep, I did. Does that make sense?"

"Yes," he said softly. "I understand what you're telling me. The man you believed in didn't fit the part I played, but while it confused you, deep in your heart you still wanted to believe in me."

"Yes, oh, yes Bret, I do love you."

"Yet I didn't ask if you were in love with me. I asked if you trusted me. Because now it's *my* turn to ask for the truth." He caught her gaze and held it. "Are you still trying to decide if you can trust the man you're going to marry? You don't think I'm about to sprinkle cyanide in your coffee?"

"That's not amusing."

"I agree, but the reality we're living with happens to be brutal. We're both in danger right now, you know that as well as I. You have, as you say, come here to find Helga, but I know you too well. You didn't come because you were anxious to see her and talk about old times, or even about archaeology. You could have waited two weeks and come with the club as first intended. No, something happened last night, something that made you risk coming at once. And alone. As much as you were upset about Cynthia and Lady Walsh's death—that's not what brought you here. I want to know what did, Allison."

"First, there's a few things more I must know about Paul Kruger. How much do you know about him?"

He didn't appear surprised by her question, though Paul had been far removed from their discussion.

"I know about him. He claims to be Helga's son. I met him in Europe over a year ago. We both were trapped in France, trying to get through to London."

"Yes, he told me. He said the soldiers with you were all dead, that his motorcar had been shot up, and that you and he got through together. He seemed to think well of you, as he should, if it's true."

"Did you doubt I'd gotten him safely through?"

Surprised, she scanned his face. "After getting Wade out of Kut? No. By the way, any news of the soldiers trapped there?"

"Kut surrendered," came his bitter reply. "Most of the men

died on a forced march across the desert."

"Oh no…I'm sorry, Bret."

He refilled his cup. "How's that corned beef coming?"

She got up from the table and went to the stove. "I'm afraid it's starting to burn."

"I thought so. I can smell it. Maybe it's just as well. Come, I've had enough of this smelly little room. Let's get comfortable in the sitting room. It's going to be a long night." And he caught up the tin of tea biscuits and the coffee, and propelled her through the rooms to the sea green divan.

She plopped down, then looked at him. "Do you have a photograph of me?"

"Why do you ask? I carry your image in my mind and heart."

"Paul Kruger—if that's his real name—told me—"

"Wait." He held up a hand. "If that's his real name?"

"Well, we don't know for sure, do we? I mean, the only one who would know for certain is Helga. And since she hasn't arrived yet, who is to know?"

"And no one can remember seeing Helga in person since your mother met her at Ezbekiah."

"So she told you about that?"

"Your mother, my dear, unlike Marshall, happens to think jolly well of me."

"Yes, but he adores you—as his expendable ace."

"A matter soon to be permanently remedied. Let's get back to Paul Kruger. Something you said alerted me. When did you see Helga last? And I don't mean all these tokens we keep running into, like letters, wires, clothes strewn on the bed. Have either of us actually seen Helga in person since a month ago in Cairo?"

Allison was suddenly rigid. "No. I haven't," she whispered.

"David and Marra delivered a letter from her some weeks ago when I was at Zeitoun. In the letter Helga suggested Mum and I use this houseboat to get Beth out of Cairo for the remainder of the trial. You know all about that. Helga was to show up at the museum the night the club auction was held, but I didn't attend. I was recuperating from the incident at the Blaine house."

"Sayyid said Helga didn't show. She was reportedly here in Luxor. Then except for your mother, no one has actually spoken to her for a month."

Allison's skin tightened at the back of her neck. "You're not suggesting Helga can't be trusted?"

"I'd never suggest that about her. She's risked her life too many times."

"Then what are you getting at, Bret?"

"I'm not sure myself." He gazed off, his expression unfocused. "I expected her to be here tonight. If she doesn't show by tomorrow, it's time I checked out the archaeology huts. And if she isn't there…" He didn't finish.

He didn't need to. Allison moistened her lips. "But surely she must be here, because I must—"

His cool, suddenly analytical gaze drew back to her. "Yes?"

Allison forced a bland face. She stood and smoothed her dress. "Her clothes are in the room. Even her fragrance lingers…she's late, is all."

Bret was noticeably silent, and Allison's eyes involuntarily swayed to his. His expression told her he suspected her of keeping something back. She made an airy gesture and paced.

He leaned there, studying her, and his gaze became disconcerting. She looked away.

"What of the letters, the wire sent to Paul and Mr. Sayyid? They've all come within the last ten days."

"All true, but need I point out that anyone could have sent those wires?"

"But—why would they want to?"

"Or the letter you say Marra brought you at Zeitoun. Was there anything in it that wasn't common knowledge? Anything that any one of us couldn't have written?"

Allison grew breathlessly still. Any one of them...Marra, David, Bret...

"Do you still have the letter by any chance?"

"No," she whispered, watching him.

His jaw flexed. "Why are you looking at me like that? Do I need to deny I wrote you the letter to lure you here?"

She shook her head and turned away. The way he said *lure you here* gave her a shiver. Did he think someone else had wanted to lure her here? She turned toward him suddenly. "Is that what you think? I was lured here? But how can that be? Unless someone wanted Beth, too—" She sucked in her breath. "Beth! She's alone with the club members at the hotel!"

"Don't worry about your sister. She's safe with Julian."

"Julian! You trust him?"

"What makes you think I wouldn't?"

"Cynthia. She said you and he were, well, enemies."

"Ah yes, she would....When did she tell you that?"

She explained about the strange meeting she'd had with Cynthia at Ezbekiah Gardens. "She was afraid of Julian because of their failed romance. She claimed he was still rather, well, obsessed by her."

"Obsessed?" He turned sharply toward her.

"Well, yes, something of that nature." She shifted uncomfortably. "Julian not only wished to get even with her by making something out of her mother's interest in buying the Blaine house, but she said he blamed you for coming between them in London."

He shoved his hands in his pockets. "Interesting tale, but totally exaggerated. I didn't come between them. I've told you before, I didn't chase Cynthia in London. The truth was, when we met, I didn't want to become enamored with any woman—" he arched his eyebrows at her—"*including* you. Cynthia and Julian had already ended a romance that he claims went nowhere but in circles. I gathered he was glad to break free of the cycle."

"That's not what Cynthia says."

"As for that list of prospective buyers she's made so much of, Julian eventually learned that Sayyid gave her mother first choice over the others simply because he thought he was getting a better offer, with the money going to the museum and the club. The list sounds much like Cynthia's red herring. She was out to muddy the waters, or maybe to see how much you knew."

"You mean you don't think one of those interested buyers wanted the house to search for something important?"

Bret leaned forward to the table and poured coffee into his cup. "There was something important, all right. There still is. Yet no one on that list knew about it, including Lady Walsh."

"How can you be so sure?"

"Julian showed me the list. There was no one on it with any connection to Rex Blaine or espionage. Or, for that matter, with smuggled Egyptian treasures. Lady Walsh wanted the house for the reason Cynthia told you. It was to be a wedding present," he finished dryly.

"Along with Helga's Mediterranean hideaway?" Her tone of voice matched his.

He looked at her. "Let's not get into that. If you had suc- cumbed to my ardor last Christmas, we'd be safely snuggled away there now, listening to the waves on the beach."

She folded her arms. "And instead of disappearing from Cairo without so much as a word, you might have come to me and at least told me you were going on assignment. Then all would have been nicely understood and settled."

He smiled. "I did send you word, remember?"

She refused to give in to the smile that twitched at her lips. "The flowers were nice—"

"And the notes."

She gave in and smiled. "Yes, and the notes, though they caused me no end of deep thought and confusion."

His aristocratic eyebrows arched. "Is there someone else in your life who would send you such things?"

She pondered that. No, for all that she was blessed with good friends, she couldn't see any of them—not even David or Wade—sending her the flowers and notes. If she'd thought about it clearly, without fear clouding her mind, she would have known it was Bret reaching out to her.

"No. No one."

"Well, then. Let's call a truce and get back to business. Yes, someone was looking for something at the house, and it wasn't Sarah's menagerie. And they didn't find it. Sarah was a smart woman. Much more so than we gave her credit for. She wanted someone to think she had left you something in that menagerie. So she left it specifically to you at the last minute. The CID found a letter in her bedroom drawer. It was in this note that she left you the box. It was signed, dated, and wit- nessed. All legal."

This was the first she had heard of such a note. Mr. Sayyid had never told her. "Witnessed by whom?"

"Marra."

"Marra!"

"Marra signed it the afternoon of the murders. We asked her about it recently at Suez. She says she went along with Sarah's request and then forgot about it. It didn't seem important. But it was. We know that now because of the menagerie being stolen. Clearly someone expected to find what they were looking for inside. But they were disappointed."

"Sarah led them on a wild goose chase."

"Exactly. But she used you to do it. She set you up as a target, which upsets me. Someone, the agent I'm after, thinks she left you important information." He watched her. "Did she, Allison?"

Allison plucked at the collar on her bodice, her eyes drifting toward the door. "Do I hear footsteps? Helga?"

"No, the wind. You're changing the subject again."

Her eyes rushed to his. She flushed. "Why do you say that?"

His gaze drifted over her thoughtfully. "I've been doing some thinking about things, and I don't like the conclusions I've been forced to come to—because they include you and Helga."

Bret might suspect Sarah left her something, but it was clear he didn't know what it was. She must either trust him and turn the letter over now, or wait for Helga. She agonized as the silence grew. Finally, pinned under his vivid gaze, she blurted out: "But Helga is here. Her clothes!"

"Yes, her clothes," he repeated thoughtfully, tapping his chin.

"Then she must be at the archaeology huts or with Count Roderick."

"What do you know about Roderick?"

"Very little. When I met Paul on the train a few weeks ago

he told me the count was the expert called who'd been in to study Nefertari. And that reminds me. What about the—"

"Don't change the subject. I know what you want to ask about, the ruddy map. We'll talk about it later. I want to know about Roderick."

"I know very little except what Paul told me." She reiterated what he had said about his life in Berlin and about the count being friends with the family. "Not with Helga so much, but her husband, the baron, who helped to sponsor the Berlin-Baghdad Railway."

"All true, but the man traveling with Baron Kruger when the train crashed in the mountain pass in Bulgaria was not Victor Roderick. The Baron was killed, but the stranger survived. He's the agent I'm looking for."

"You don't know who he is?"

"I have an idea, but no proof."

"Are you hinting that all was not what it seemed in the train crash that killed Helga's husband?"

"I don't know. Everyone is under suspicion at the moment. As for Roderick, I don't have anything on him. The CID confirms what Paul Kruger told you on the train. That the count despises Kaiser Wilhelm, and that he's pro-British. But that doesn't prove anything. Naturally he would have an excellent cover."

"He left a message in the ceramic crocodile for Helga," she told him. "I'll get it for you. It's right over here on the table. I was going to give it to Helga when she came home tonight."

Bret studied the brief message far more carefully than she had.

"Does something bother you about it?"

"No. I can easily check the train from Aswan to find out when it arrived, and we've been following Roderick's itinerary from the time he arrived in Cairo in December. You say you found this in the crocodile by the door?"

"Yes, when I looked for the house key. It wasn't there, but I suppose you have it. That's how you got in."

"No, I had a key of my own made the first time I was here. But I did open the front door for you." He smiled. "The letter from Helga—she told you the key would be in the ceramic?"

"Yes. At first, Omar was to come with me. We were to travel by falukka—" She brightened suddenly. "That must be it. Omar has the key and he's out, so he took it with him."

"Maybe. Time will tell. In the meantime—" He scowled at the tin of dry tea biscuits.

"I'm sorry I burned the corned beef. There's always the tin of tongue."

He caught her gaze, and she smiled and offered him another biscuit. "They're really quite good," she said lamely. "Didn't your Granny ever teach you to dunk them in your tea? Like so...here, take a bite."

"Thank you, no. Let's get back to Paul Kruger. So Helga isn't around to disclaim Paul as her son. Interesting you thought of that."

"You mean you didn't?"

"Yes, but if you did, I'm thinking the agent has also."

"Mr. Sayyid appeared to accept him as her son. Unless he was just assuming it was true, having no cause to question it."

"Maybe," he said again. He was quiet for a moment too long, then he stood. "On second thought, I'll have a try at that tin of tongue. Can you handle it while I look around a bit, or do you need me to open it for you?"

Allison stood and smiled into his teasing gaze. "I think I can handle it." She left the sitting room. Once alone, she made her way more cautiously through the shadowy dining room, past flickering candles into the kitchen.

She heard the front door shut softly. She shuddered over the turn of events, then went to open the tin of tongue. Did he really want this, or was he keeping her occupied for some particular reason?

She held the tin in her hand and listened to the Nile frogs. A breeze had developed in the last few minutes, and the boat moved gently, the water making odd sounds against the hull.

Bret still hadn't answered her question about giving her photograph to Paul Kruger. Had that been deliberate? She closed her eyes, fighting a desperate sob. If only she knew what to do....

But all she knew right now was that she was confused, and until that changed, she would wait to tell Bret about Sarah's letter—and about the mysterious German contact, George.

NINETEEN

IT WAS AT LEAST AN HOUR BEFORE BRET returned. Allison met him as he came in the door. "Where did you go?"

"The village. I recognized the donkey boy who brought you here from the junction. I wanted to ask him a few questions. He tells me Victor Roderick arrived a few days ago."

"Then the message he left for Helga is genuine."

"It looks that way."

She was almost afraid to ask. "And has the boy seen Helga?"

"He insists she's been here on the boat, but he can't remember when he saw her last."

She sank to the divan with relief. "There! You see? We're worried about nothing. She's most likely at the huts with Count Roderick, sipping tea and having a lively conversation about archaeology!"

Bret didn't deny it was possible, but his expression was grave. Had he hoped the donkey boy would say Helga hadn't been here after all? But no, that didn't make a bit of sense. He said he had come to find her, even as she herself had. Unless—her mind stumbled over a terrifying thought and refused to go on.

She sat in silence, watching Bret. He was seated across from her, the tasseled ottoman between them. Deep in thought, he found a pencil and notepad from Helga's desk and started writing something—or was he sketching?

Allison held her breath when he glanced at her, then back to the paper, the pencil moving carefully.

"Bret?" she breathed tensely.

"Hmm?"

"Do you have a photograph of me?"

He kept his eyes on the paper. "You asked me that earlier."

"And you didn't answer."

He smiled. "A strange question. Why are you suddenly interested in photographs and drawings?"

"Drawings? I don't think I mentioned a drawing. Why? Do you sketch?"

"Where would I get a photograph of the beautiful Allison Wescott?"

"Neal had one. You may have seen it." She paused as another thought nudged her. "How strange that we haven't seen Neal since you were with him in London. Like Helga."

His pencil stilled, and he looked at her for a long, silent moment. "Are you connecting the two disappearances?"

"Of course not."

"We know where Neal is, Allison. He's with Kitchener. As for the photograph, yes, Neal had one. We talked about you in London. He wanted to know what I thought of you." He smiled. "I told him I was trying not to think of you at all."

Allison leaned back deeper into the back of the chair. "And Paul was with you?"

"Yes, he was with us."

"Did you show Paul the photograph and advise him to look me up when he came to Egypt?"

Bret snapped the notepad closed, and the corner of his mouth tipped. He deposited the pencil in his pocket. "No. Neal showed him your photograph." He tossed the notepad onto the ottoman and stood restlessly, hands in pockets, beginning to pace. "Photographs…I wonder…"

Allison had a fleeting impression that, for all of his seeming distractions, Bret was on the alert. Her teeth chattered, and she clamped her jaw and glanced toward the door and window drapes. The heavy damask curtains were drawn shut. The lamp flickered on the wood panel wall. The frogs outside croaked; the boat creaked. Allison sat stiffly, chewing her lip.

Even though she wasn't sure that she trusted Bret completely, she would rather be here with him than alone.

"What are you wondering?" She watched Bret carefully. "What about Paul? What about photographs?"

He stopped and looked at her, as if debating something in his mind. "I wasn't thinking of Paul. Or of photographs. That word you used earlier to describe Julian Mortimer's continued interest in Cynthia…he had an 'obsession' with her, you said. Interesting you would choose such a description."

"It was Cynthia who first used the word, when we were at Ezbekiah Gardens. You don't agree with the assessment?"

"I could be wrong. About a lot of things, actually. But Julian doesn't come across as a neurotic victim of a doomed love affair. He's too practical. The idea of someone being obsessed with Cynthia, though…that is thought provoking. It would require a certain personality type…" His voice dropped, and it was almost as though he was talking to himself. "Yes, that could very well explain the drawing."

Allison stood slowly, her eyes going to his. "Drawing?"

He looked at her, seeming startled to find her standing there. He gave a brisk nod. "A drawing of Cynthia. I found it on the steamer after Lady Walsh died. It was pressed between the pages of a book." His eyes darkened, and Allison had the impression the discovery had not been a pleasant one. "It was an odd drawing, as though the artist was totally enamored with her. When you mentioned Paul just now, asking if I'd shown him your photograph, it got me to thinking again about that drawing."

Allison snatched the notepad from the ottoman. She must know. Her face flushed. She looked at him, surprised. "This is just a drawing of the rooms in the houseboat."

He frowned, hands on hips. "It helps me to think. What did you think it was?"

She laid the notepad down and turned toward him, her eyes searching his. What she saw mirrored there filled her with relief and joy—this was Bret, her Bret, the tough, practical, cynical, and thoroughly wonderful man with whom she had fallen in love. "I have something to confess," she whispered.

His eyes narrowed. "Yes, I thought you might. Suppose you start confessing."

"Wait a minute."

She turned and went to her bedroom to find her handbag. Removing the drawing of Cynthia, she returned to the sitting room where he was waiting for her. She stood before him, meeting his considering gaze steadily.

"I went to your cabin last night to talk to you about something important. You were still with Doctor Howard in Cynthia's cabin. I, well, I picked up the book thinking it was yours. This fell out."

She handed him the drawing of Cynthia.

He took it, watching her. "So that's where it went. I was wondering why someone didn't take the book with it." He paused. "Ah, I see. You thought I drew this? That I was obsessed with Cynthia?" He looked at her, his midnight blue eyes irritatingly amused.

"Well the book *was* in your cabin. And you must admit you were behaving odiously all evening." She sniffed. "You even promised to buy her the Riviera. And hinted you might be selling archaeological pieces and smuggling them over the Berlin-Baghdad Railway."

He laughed and came toward her, but Allison backed away, bumping into the chair. He caught her and drew her into his arms.

"That was Julian hinting I'm a thief. If I recall, I said I was quite respectable and everything I was doing was legal. Do you think I convinced them?"

"Convinced whom?" she murmured, not quite able to think clearly with him so near, his arms firmly around her waist and shoulders.

"Whoever intends to contact me about getting Nefertari, and—" He lowered his head to meet her eyes—"the little map we found in the sundial." He smiled. "Remember?"

"So you *do* still have the map. You haven't given it to the CID."

"Ah, my sweet, how you love jumping to conclusions. It's that suspicious, untrusting nature of yours! What makes you think I haven't told the CID?"

She studied his face, saw the teasing laughter in his eyes. Reaching out a hand, she traced the scar along his chin with her finger. "Well, then, have you told them, or not?"

"But of course I have. Your father knows all about it." A slight smile tilted his lips. "Do you think I'd keep something like that from them? I'd soon be hung."

"So it's all a ruse, being suspended, being accused of keeping back information and selling treasure."

"All part of my assignment."

"But Julian said—"

"Julian, the dear old fellow, is doing his job, helping me tempt a certain individual to come out of the mist and remove his or her mask."

"To try and buy Nefertari?"

"And the map." He drew her closer until she rested against

his chest, then whispered next to her ear. "I promise you, my love, if I ever buy a Mediterranean Riviera, there will be only one woman to share it with me. If I'm obsessed with any woman, it's an enchanting war nurse who has an infuriating habit of being in the wrong place at the wrong time."

She pulled back to protest, but the words died on her lips. The look of pure tenderness on his fact took her breath away. She blinked—and his smile broadened.

"I'm not always in the wrong place," she finally managed.

"Indeed, not." The soft words floated around her, and his gaze was fixed on her lips. "Right now, for example, I'd say you're in precisely the right place. I'd like to keep you there indefinitely." He pressed a soft kiss to the side of her face. "Forget the Riviera—" A second kiss was bestowed upon her nose—"This creaking little houseboat meets my needs perfectly, as long as you're in it."

She touched his face and felt the tears of happiness that his warm words brought to her eyes.

"And that, my darling Allison, is why I must be careful and settle for a simple good-night kiss." His warm lips met hers— for one, all-too-brief moment, everything else faded away. Nothing existed but the two of them and the love they shared.

When he drew back, they both were breathless. Bret steadied her, then released her and stepped away.

"It's time you got some rest," he told her gently. "And I have a few important things to do before morning."

"You're leaving?" She didn't relish the thought of being alone on the boat.

He leaned in the arch of the doorway for a moment. "I won't be far away. Good night, darling, and don't worry. You'll be safe tonight. I can guarantee that much."

She watched him leave, then closed her door quietly.

～～～～～

Allison awoke, her room dark and the hour unknown. The houseboat was astir with small, muffled creaking noises. She lit a candle and looked at her clock. She had been asleep for two hours. She assumed Bret was somewhere inside the boat, or he may have decided to sleep on the roof in one of the lounge chairs. The night was warm and the moon had set, and the Nile breeze churned the short cotton curtains on her window.

Suddenly Allison went still, all her senses focusing with alertness. Were those footsteps outside on the walkway encircling the house? Relax, she scolded herself. It's just the wind. Or was it...?

Allison sat up, listening intently, then drawing a sharp breath. The noise was coming from inside the boat!

She listened, then caught the sound again—it was as if boxes or crates were being moved. Was it Bret? What was he doing? What was he searching for?

She threw aside the light coverlet and groped about the foot of the bed for her robe, then went to the door and opened it a crack. All was dark except for a faint gleam of light coming from one of the other rooms.

Helga's bedroom?

Lighting a candle, Allison slipped from her cubicle and padded barefoot down the hall.

No, the glimmer of light wasn't from Helga's bedroom—it was coming from the kitchen. The door was open a crack, and she could see a lamp glowing on the wooden table used for preparing chopped meat or vegetables.

"Bret?" she whispered as she entered the kitchen, but he was nowhere to be seen. The hatch up to the roof was open, and she climbed the wooden staircase and came out on the top of the houseboat. The stars were a brilliant white in a soft, black sky. The Nile shimmered like a silvery ribbon, and night birds swept low along the bank where tall, dark silhouettes of palm trees and rushes stood. Far in the distance her eyes could make out what she knew to be the Theban hills and the royal tombs.

The breeze threatened to squelch the tiny flame of her candle, and she cupped it with her hand, glancing about the deck chairs for Bret. They were all empty, nor was there any sign that he had been here. The wind blew her hair and sent the hem of her wrapper billowing. She turned and started back down the stairs.

The kitchen loomed warm and stale, the one lamp glowing on the table. Then she heard a muffled noise. Her eyes darted to the open hatch leading down to the storage room in the hull.

So that's where Bret was. What was he doing down there?

Allison knelt by the open hatch and grimaced at the hot, unpleasant odors seeping up. She could see a faint glow of light coming from the recesses of the hull.

She climbed down the wooden steps.

She looked around, able to make out a stack of crates, and—

Her breath sucked in and she nearly dropped the candle. There, in front of her, she saw the outline of a royal Egyptian sarcophagus! The lid had been lifted, and a lamp was glowing eerily at the head, suspended on a chain. Someone was standing there, looking inside, and when he moved back she saw that it was Bret.

"Stay where you are." The softly spoken warning was filled with raw emotion.

She swallowed, her heart thudding in her throat. "What is

it?" she managed around the choking fear. "Who is it? Who's in there?"

He shut the lid and came quickly toward her, and while she couldn't see his face, she could feel the tension in his grip. Her hand shook so that the candle fell with a tiny crash, and the flame extinguished.

"Oh, Bret—" She clutched him, and his arms held her so tightly it was hard to breathe.

"It's Helga," he whispered against her hair. "She's wrapped in the drapes from the bedroom."

A sob of horror escaped her.

"Steady, Allison."

His deep, calming whisper surrounded her. She bit her lip to keep from making any sound and opened her eyes. The glow from the lamp seemed brighter now, and the sides of the sarcophagus glinted of gold and silver.

Bret's hands squeezed her arms briefly. "Wait for me upstairs. There's something I need to do."

She began to climb, but her trembling legs would not cooperate. She nearly sank to the bottom step. Strong arms caught her, and Bret held her again for a moment, letting her lean into him. His strength and confidence sustained her, and she stepped away.

"All right now?" The question was tender.

She nodded, still unable to speak, and slowly climbed the ladder.

Poor Helga. Tears slid down Allison's face as she stepped into the kitchen, and in a flash her shock gave way to anger. Who had dared to kill her? The fiend, the evil, diabolical fiend!

She was seated in the dark sitting room, trying to keep her knees from shaking, when she heard Bret in the kitchen. A moment later he came and sat with her in the darkness, his arm around her protectively. She laid her head against his chest, taking solace in the steady beat of his heart.

The inevitable croaking frogs filled the night.

"Who did it, do you think?"

He didn't answer, and she sensed his hardened anger. He had liked and respected Helga Kruger; she'd been his friend as well as a comrade in the CID.

"It—it couldn't have been anyone in the club." She shook her head, dazed, needing to make sense of this horrible happening. "They're all at the Flamingo Hotel."

"She's been dead some time." Bret's terse comment was filled with rage, and Allison knew he was angry that he hadn't been able to protect Helga.

"Why would anyone kill Helga?"

"She was taking a great risk coming here, and inviting the archaeology club. She was working with me on this assignment—" He broke off, and when he spoke again, his voice was hoarse. "And it cost her life. We allowed everyone to think she had Nefertari."

"What! You mean she didn't?"

"No, but we even arranged for Victor Roderick to be allowed into Egypt by way of Constantinople to look at it. It was meant to be a trap."

"For Count Roderick?"

"No, for a German agent. Unless, of course, Roderick *is* the agent." He looked at her. "The agent we're after was Rex Blaine's superior."

Allison's breath tightened, and she remained silent, watching him.

"The man is clever, but we've learned he has an Achilles heel: an obsession for Egyptian antiquities. He's been a buyer on the black market at Galli's shop in Old Cairo since before the war. We're sure he's the one who was dealing with Professor Jemal. Which is why we're certain he knew about Nefertari and the map. Helga's club has been a cover for spies from its inception, thanks to her contacts with agents working in Cairo, Constantinople, Berlin, and London." He paused and looked at her. "Remember that diamond that came loose when Sarah dropped the doll?"

"At Galli's shop, yes."

"We think even that treasure was meant for the man I'm trying to contact now. But we underestimated him. We didn't think he'd unmask himself to Helga until the club arrived. We figured that was his cover for being present."

"But—why would he arrive early?"

"He must have thought he could get her to turn Nefertari over to him, which tells me he's grown more cautious. He didn't want to show himself as an archaeology lover on holiday this year."

Allison fixed her gaze on Bret's face, illumined in the moonlight coming in through the windows. "You don't think Helga gave him Nefertari, do you." It was more a statement than a question.

Bret shook his head. "She didn't have it to give. We thought it safer. We were wrong." He looked away, his jawline tense and clenched. "I'm beginning to see a pattern in the way this man works."

"What do you mean?" Allison wished her teeth would stop chattering.

"I think this is the same man who killed Sarah. Both women died the same way."

Allison closed her eyes to block out the horror of what Bret was saying. *Oh, Helga…I'm so sorry!*

"Which tells me he's the agent I want, if that makes sense to you."

"It does," she whispered. "Anyone who sees him must die to protect his cover. His name is George. King George."

Bret turned sharply, bringing her face toward his. "How did you know that? Who told you? Even knowing that name places you in danger!"

"I'll explain soon. But first there's something I must know. You said Helga was working with you, that she didn't have Nefertari. Then who has it?"

"I do." She heard the pain in his voice. "When the agent contacted Helga, she was to send him to me. I was to be here with the club. My new position as a rogue agent has been well established, thanks to Julian and your father. Even our broken relationship helped. You could no longer consider marriage. You couldn't trust me. And I was back with Cynthia and suddenly wealthy, talking to Helga about buying her Riviera. At least," he corrected bitterly, "that was our plan. It didn't work. He came to Helga all right, but apparently he came before the chess pieces were all in place. The club hasn't even arrived yet and she's been dead for weeks! She must have insisted that she didn't have Nefertari, that I had it—" He broke off, looking away. "But he killed her anyway."

"Yes, because she knew he was George."

"And, like Sarah, once you've met with him and know he's a German agent, you must be eliminated."

"But—" Allison stood—"that means if you play to his obsession with Nefertari, you, too, will know who George is."

"Yes." There was a tinge of cool satisfaction in the confident assertion. "And he'll need to eliminate me as well. Only this time it will be the other way around. George—" Bret's eyes glittered with a steely determination—"is a dead man. But if my

344

guess is right, he won't contact me yet. Not until he's certain I have the treasure and the map. He's cautious. He's still not sure whether I've turned on the CID or not. I'll do some more convincing when the club gets here."

"How?"

"Roderick is here to see Nefertari. All I need now is the members of the club—one of whom we suspect is George. If we're right, then when I produce Nefertari and mention the map, he won't be able to control his greed. He'll risk contacting me. And when he does, King George will lose his head."

"But who will go through with the club holiday with Helga and Lady Walsh dead?"

"I'm afraid no one is grieving over Lady Walsh. The club members hardly knew her, and only those with a sense of propriety will find it necessary to want to call the trip off and return to Cairo."

"But—Helga!"

"That, unfortunately, is the ruddy part of it. There's only three people who know she's dead. You and I and George. You and I won't tell anyone yet. Neither will George. His eye is on Nefertari and whatever it was he expected to find in Sarah's menagerie. He may suspect you have something that Sarah left behind." His gaze held hers. "That's why I came here. This is the last place you want to be alone."

She looked at him, her breath caught in her throat. His hands took hold of hers and squeezed them reassuringly. "Allison, I've got to go through with my original plan. Helga would want me to...now, more than ever."

She buried her face in his chest. He held her tightly, and she felt his lips brush against her hair. When he spoke, his voice was rough. "Helga must remain buried in the sarcophagus until all this is over."

"It's—it's dreadful!"

"Yes, but look at it another way. Her body is only an empty shell now. And in this life she had great respect for antiquity, so what better place to leave her buried than in a royal Egyptian casket? Someday we'll see she has a Christian burial."

Allison looked at him, and her worry must have been clear on her face, for he reached out to touch her cheek gently. "Don't fret, Allison. I know you weren't close to Helga, but I was, and I can tell you with confidence that she was a believer in Christ. We don't need to grieve for her. She's with the Lord. What I must do is stop George from killing again."

"Yes—" He was right. Allison knew it. She thought of the ship that would carry Secretary of War Kitchener and Neal toward Russia. So many innocent people were on that ship— and if they didn't stop it, they all would die when a German U-boat targeted the ship for destruction.

Bret went and struck a match, lighting the lamp. The flame sputtered, then flared up. Allison saw his intense expression and that his fingers shook slightly as he watched the smoke rising from the blown-out match. He muttered something under his breath, then looked at her.

"I can't have you here, in the thick of the danger, Allison. But whether I like it or not, you're already deeply involved." He clenched his jaw. "If I found you dead, like Sarah and Helga, I don't think I could take it."

Her heart breaking at the pain in his eyes, she rushed to him. She wrapped her arms around him, not sure which of them was trembling most.

"I'll be all right, Bret. God will watch out for me, I'm sure of it." She looked up at him. "But there's something you need to know. I came here looking for Helga because I had to."

His eyes smoldered. "Tell me what you came here to discuss with Helga."

"Turn your back." She spoke softly, glancing to see that the curtains on the window were still tightly drawn.

"Do what?"

"Turn your back." He did so, eyes narrowing, that familiar, slightly cynical smile on his face. "What are you going to do, clobber me from behind? Maybe I've underestimated you. Maybe *you* are George."

"Very amusing." Allison quickly unbuttoned her bodice, removed the letter, and rebuttoned the robe. She drew in a breath. "All right, you can turn around now."

He did, brow lifted. "Your buttons are crooked."

"Never mind. Here. If I hadn't caught you kissing Cynthia I'd have given this to you on the steamer." She handed him the letter. "It's from Sarah."

He took it, bringing it to the lamp. "Where did you get this?"

"I found it in the trunk I left at the Blaine house in December. Sarah was clever about hiding the letter. She unwrapped a Christmas present I had stored away to give her, exchanged the gift with her letter, and closed the wrapping around it. She must have left the book out to draw my attention."

"When did you find this?"

"On the steamer. As I said, I intended to give it to you, but before I could Lady Walsh was killed. Then I went to your cabin to give it to you, but I found the drawing, and well—you know what I thought. Besides, you'd been behaving so suspiciously, nothing like the Bret Holden I knew at Kut. I was beginning to think you really had turned traitor. When Sarah warned me in her letter to say nothing to anyone but you or

Helga, I was left with only one option."

He nodded. "You weren't sure about me, so you did the only thing you knew to do. You risked your life to come here and look for Helga. Yes, I see how it was."

He opened the letter and stood by the lamp, holding it to the light, while Allison sat down in the chair beside him. She felt cold, as though it was a chilly, rainy night in London.

When he had finished reading, he stared at the paper for a long moment—then he struck a match and held the letter to the flame. Allison watched it burn and shrivel into soft gray ash. Her eyes came to his.

"We can't take any chances," he said simply. "I'll need to get this information to CID at once."

"How can you without returning to Cairo? The wires aren't safe. That's why I didn't use them."

"True. But I've other means." He paused reflectively. "This matter about Edgar complicates things."

"You think Edgar will come here looking for George?"

"No. He wouldn't know George was here...not unless George contacts Edgar—" He stopped. "Of course! I should have thought of it."

"Thought of what?"

He looked at her. "George must have murdered Sarah, not over Nefertari but for the information Edgar wanted to sell. I'll wager it was George at the house, as well. He must have had some idea that Sarah left you something important." His brow creased. "Either the information, or—" He stopped, and in the lamplight she saw his jaw tense—"or his identity."

She drew away. If the agent thought she knew who he was, then he would seek to eliminate her just as he had Sarah and Helga. Alarm sang through her, but Allison did her best not to let it show. The last thing she wanted to do was add to Bret's concerns. "He must not think I know anything." She laid a calming hand on Bret's arm. "He had opportunity to kill me when he knocked me out and took the box."

"You're assuming your attacker was George. I don't think so now. This changes things."

"Why don't you think George was the one at the Blaine house?"

"For the reason you just mentioned. He wouldn't have taken any chances and left you alive. No, it must have been someone else. Someone unaccustomed to brutality."

Allison watched him nervously. He seemed to know something he wasn't telling her. She drew a steadying breath. "Then George has someone working with him."

"Undoubtedly. Which means I can't risk sending you back to Cairo on the train. He may follow or he may have someone watching you."

She knew why Bret was frowning: he didn't want her to go with him to the huts to meet Count Victor Roderick.

"I'll be safe with you." She forced cheerfulness to her tone.

"Now that George knows Sarah didn't leave the information in the box, he has two choices; confront you, hoping you have brought it here to Helga, or go for the man willing to sell the information to him in the first place."

"Sir Edgar," she said with a shaky intake of breath. "But Edgar doesn't know who George is. That's why he needed Sarah to make that initial contact."

"Which is why George may contact Edgar."

"But if George must choose between taking a chance that I have the information or going to Edgar—won't he opt for the surest thing? Sir Edgar? Mightn't they both be far from here by now?"

"I might think so, except for one very important thing." He

looked at her. "George won't leave Egypt without the treasure. Greed, you see, will bring about his ruin. And a certain obsession. The two, together, have set the trap that will be the king's undoing."

Allison hugged herself. "Can—do you think a man like that could be obsessed by several things at once, and well, sort of get them mixed up in his mind?"

"You're thinking of the drawing of Cynthia?"

"Yes, I was."

"If I could identify the artist who drew Cynthia as Nefertari, I think we would have our agent."

The thought of someone sketching Cynthia Walsh as Nefertari, of the way the two must be mixed up in his mind, made Allison's skin crawl. "What if his obsession leads him to go after Cynthia?"

"I don't think we need to concern ourselves with that angle."

"Why not?"

"Because I believe he already has. The infatuation is mutual."

She stared at him astounded. Such a thought had never entered her mind. "Cynthia is in love with George?"

"Not in love, no. I doubt she knows the meaning of loving someone. She's selfish. She cares about Cynthia and what she thinks will make her happy and satisfied. Anything or anyone that detracts is a burden. She's irresponsible. Whoever George is, I'm willing to wager he's promised her riches and excitement and no responsibility for the unpleasant things of life. He's promised her an escape as he coddles and coos her."

She watched Bret closely, surprised that she felt no satisfaction at hearing his quiet, unemotional unmasking of Cynthia's weaknesses. If she'd still held any doubts to Bret's feelings about Cynthia, his cool assessment of the woman removed them completely. "You know her so well," she commented, surprised.

"I knew what she was like the first few weeks after I met her."

She stared at Bret, and a wave of gratitude filled her heart. *I really don't need to fear losing Bret.* The realization resonated throughout her. *Not even to a woman who is wealthy and glamorous. He's not taken in by such things. He wants something deeper.* She felt her lips lift in a glad smile. *He wants me.*

"And George," he was saying thoughtfully, almost to himself, "is the one who interests me now. I keep telling myself the answer is clear, if I could break past the barrier that has me blinded. What kind of man would become obsessed with Cynthia? What does he see in her besides the obvious?"

"He must see his ideal of Nefertari."

"True."

"What else are you thinking?"

He sighed and leaned back. "Maybe I'm wondering if someone who is physically unattractive would be more inclined to overestimate her because of her outward beauty."

Allison found that she was sitting stiffly on the edge of the chair. "That would leave out Julian."

"Yes."

"And Paul Kruger."

"Yes." Bret's gaze came to rest on her, and Allison's fingers moved nervously along the lace at her collar. A strange sensation inched up her spine.

"But that's quite impossible, Bret. You said she was infatuated with him as well."

"I said she was enamored with what he could give her."

"But we both know she's been infatuated with you since the two of you met in London."

351

"Do we?"

"Well, yes, of course we do. It's been evident in her actions anytime she's been near you."

"What if I told you she's an exceptional actress."

"Actress! Cynthia?"

"Lady Edith Walsh was no more a true Lady than the diamonds she wore were genuine. The Walshes once had money, in England, but Edith's husband had made some bad investments before he died. Mrs. Walsh learned she was nearly penniless. Still, one thing she and Cynthia had was the ability to convince others that they were rich. Mrs. Walsh hoped to catch Cynthia a wealthy husband, and they put on quite an act at times. It turns out that buying the Blaine house was beyond Mrs. Walsh's means. Did you notice how gloomy Sayyid behaved at dinner that night?"

"Yes…" She thought back. "But I thought he was worried about Julian discovering he had committed some impropriety in selling the house to La—Mrs. Walsh."

"No, he had discovered she wasn't as wealthy as she pretended. If I was worried about anything that night it was about Sayyid growing suspicious over the pretense of Mrs. Walsh lending me money to go into the export business with Neal and buying the Riviera. As for Cynthia, she really is an actress. She worked in the theater in London for a season, and the critics commended her performance. She should have stayed there. Her search to locate a rich husband has led her to the cliff's edge. I suspect she became involved with George by accident, but his devotion to her, and his promise of great wealth, most likely have led her to fit in with his schemes. There is something to the saying that opposites attract, but more often than not a man and woman of like character will find in the other an image of what they believe themselves to be. That's not always the case of course, but with Cynthia and George, I'd be surprised if they weren't drawn together as magnets. She found her selfish ego adored; and he found his pound of fleshly beauty, his Nefertari."

Allison thought about Bret's words, and nodded slowly. "And little by little she found herself moving over to his side, his way of seeing the war and life."

"Indeed. To Cynthia, carting off the Egyptian treasure has convinced her she'll find a life of luxury and entertainment. She likes to have her amusements, whatever the cost."

"Were you playing your role with Cynthia on the steamer so you could learn how much she knew about George?"

"We thought she might be involved in something unpleasant even before Sarah was murdered. It was part of my assignment to find out for sure. It wasn't until I found the drawing that I became convinced of it. The more time I spent with her, the more I was sure that something she said or did might give away who George was."

Allison was on the edge of her seat. "And did you?"

He tapped his chin, musing, looking off at the window with its drawn drape. "I didn't at the time because my mind was set on the kind of agent I expected George to be. But the truth, I think, is beginning to emerge from the fog."

"And Cynthia was trying to learn whether or not your suspension from the CID was real."

"No doubt about it. The questions Cynthia rather naively put to me were actually George's." He stood and walked about the little room as Allison listened to the creaking boat.

"Cynthia." She struggled to take it all in. "I never would have guessed—" She looked up, pursing her lips. "Except…"

Bret stopped pacing and looked at her. "Except?"

"There was one time when I thought I saw her where she

shouldn't have been. At the time I didn't think much of it, but now, I wonder."

She had his full attention. He sat down on the divan beside her, his gaze intense. "Explain."

Allison thought back to that morning at the Residency when she had returned from working with Oswald Chambers at the Zeitoun camp. "Actually, there were several odd things about that day."

Bret's hands closed tightly about her shoulders as he turned her to face him. "Yes, go on."

She told him that when she had entered the house she heard her mother arguing with the foreman about the redecorating. "But when I walked into the ballroom, no one was there."

"Arguing you say? Your mother hardly seems the type to make a scene with the foreman."

"You're right. I hadn't thought of that."

"You didn't see the foreman?"

"No, and I learned later that they were already out to lunch." She looked at him. "I saw Beth in the window of my father's office, at least I thought it was her. She was dressed fashionably.... I thought Beth had gotten into mother's wardrobe again."

"When was all this? Before you went to the Blaine house for your trunk?"

"Yes, but there's more." She told him about seeing someone in the delphiniums, and about seeing who she had thought was the servant clearing the luncheon table.

"It turned out that the servant had the day off. The maid insisted no one else had gone to the table."

"Ah. That would account for the missing letter of course. Someone wanted to learn rather badly what Sayyid had told you about Sarah's will. They couldn't waste time searching the house for it, so they waited for you to unwittingly lead her to it."

"Her!"

He nodded. "Cynthia. Whom else could it be? That accounts for your nearly winning that wrestling match until she got hold of something and knocked you unconscious."

Suddenly images flooded Allison's mind, and she stared at Bret, wide-eyed. "That's it."

He tilted his head. "What?"

She brushed a hand over her eyes, disturbed to see it trembling. "I knew there was something about the attack that I couldn't recall, something that kept nagging at me. I remember it now." She met his curious gaze. "I felt my attacker's face, and it shocked me—because my mind insisted I was touching Beth! And I just couldn't accept that possibility. There was one horrid moment when I thought she might have gone over on Gilbert's side and was trying to do something to help him, even if it meant turning on me. But Bret! There was something else. Mother found something in the delphiniums when she went there to cut some flowers for the hall table—a leather pouch. It was empty. She must have thought it belonged to the gardener, as did I. Especially after it was taken, but now—"

"What kind of pouch?"

"Tobacco. I could smell it. But it *couldn't* have belonged to the gardener because if Cynthia returned the letter, and then went on to the Blaine house to wait for me, she must have taken the pouch, too. But why?"

He stood, alert now. "I can think of one good reason. Because it was incriminating to George. He must have dropped it there, but that raises a curious question as to why he was standing in the flower bed"

Allison's gaze held his. She stood, fighting the weakness that threatened to overtake her. "Because he had been there earlier, perhaps, meeting with Cynthia. The person I saw—it must have been George. He was searching for his pouch!"

"And when he didn't find it, he came back. He found Cynthia there, scolded her for daring to show up at the Residency and drawing attention to him."

Allison felt sick. "He came out of the dining room, and I told him my father wasn't back yet from his voyage to the Dardanelles. He wasn't looking for my father or my mother. He'd come from an office he knew was empty—except for Cynthia, who was hiding in there. I saw her step back from the window. And—oh Bret!" Horror filled her. "He had luncheon with us, and all the time he was looking for that pouch."

"He must have hung around in the garden after your mother went back to the house and retrieved it. Either that, or Cynthia did." His somber gaze met hers. "So now," he said quietly, evenly, "we know who George is."

"I can't believe it of him." She sank to the divan. "I can't believe Spencer Howard is a murderer."

"It makes sense, and it accounts for the way Helga most likely died."

"How did she die?"

His expression grew even more grave. "My best guess is cobra venom."

"A cobra?" she choked.

"No, only its venom. Neatly and precisely administered by a quick injection from a needle."

Of course. As a doctor, Spencer was well acquainted with giving injections. Still...she frowned. "But he couldn't have given Helga an injection. She would never have stood for it."

"Look, darling, he wouldn't need to give an injection, not the way you're thinking of it with that nurse's mind of yours.

356

I've seen it done before. In India."

India...Spencer had come from Bombay when she first met him near Kut.

"A needle can be placed on the end of anything, including canes and umbrellas. The trigger mechanism dispenses the poison rapidly by releasing a spring. The weapon is as concealed as it is lethal."

Allison's breath sucked in. "But Spencer never showed interest in Cynthia."

"He wouldn't. His public image has been carefully created— the dour and cryptic doctor who is impatient with the blundering of government and military. He was also clever enough to mask his obsession for Egyptology. Remember Paul's overdone speech on the burial of the royal kings?"

"How could I forget? He was dreadfully morbid."

"And Spencer went out of his way to distance himself from anything Paul said. He must have hoped to make Paul look guilty, and Paul didn't help with his behavior. If I hadn't already known he was Helga's son, I might have suspected him. His knowledge of Egyptology clearly made him suspect. Now I'm sure he was trying to impress Sayyid with his knowledge, hoping for a position in the museum."

"Yes, I can see how that could be." Sudden alarm shot through Allison. "Bret! If Spencer actually is Rex Blaine's superior, Beth may be in danger! She told me she hid beneath the bed at the Blaine house when someone came into the room—but she saw the man's shoes. She said they looked like a pair of Rex Blaine's old desert trekking shoes. If there's any chance Spencer knows she was there, he may well think she recognized something about him."

"Don't worry, darling, I made certain Beth is safe under Julian's care before I left. And if Spencer Howard wanted to silence her, that must have been his reason for wanting to get both of you here on the boat. So he used Beth's trauma over Gilbert's trial to convince your mother to send you both."

Allison recalled with cold fright how Spencer had come to visit Beth several times after the incident at the Blaine house, always insisting that their mother send them away from Cairo. "When he came to the Residency, he must have been trying to find out if Beth recognized him. If she had, he would have known by the fear showing in her eyes when left alone in his presence."

"Exactly. And she would have confided in someone. Most probably you. Spencer knew that. So he was watching both of you carefully. Beth didn't think it could be Spencer, so she wasn't afraid around him. That saved her life. And yours, too, at Bulac Hospital. But he kept you under constant watch, waiting to see if something stirred in your memory, and if you had shown the slightest sign of suspicion—well, I'd rather not go into that."

She straightened. "Bret, you were there, in my room."

His eyes met hers and a small smile tipped his lips.

"It was you, wasn't it? And you left another of the flowers?"

"I couldn't let you endure such a thing alone, now could I?"

She shook her head. "It was more than that, wasn't it?"

He sighed. "So much for pure romance, eh?" When she didn't smile, he nodded. "Yes, I came because I wanted to watch over you."

"Because you suspected Spencer?"

"Because I didn't wholly trust him." He smiled gently. *"And* because I wanted to be there with you."

The look in his eyes and the warmth in his voice enveloped her, melting some of the chill that had been seeping into her during their conversation. "I'm glad you were there."

His eyes darkened. "I wish I'd been there sooner. At the Blaine house."

Allison's eyes widened again.

"What?" Bret asked, and she shuddered.

"After I was attacked, when I left the house and collapsed on the road, Mother said she came looking for me with Spencer and Mr. Sayyid. She mentioned that Spencer had nearly run me down. You don't suppose—?"

Bret's eyes flickered. "Yes, he probably hoped to run you down in what looked like an accident. I heard about that from Julian. Sayyid mentioned the incident to him."

Allison swallowed. "'My times are in Your hand,'" she quoted from the Psalms. "Thank God nothing can destroy us in this life unless he allows it."

Bret cupped her chin and planted a tender kiss on her lips. "You're right. And I thank God every day he kept you safe."

"Do you think Spencer knows about me now?" She looked toward the door. "That I have Sarah's letter."

"Yes." Bret's whispered response was sober, and his gaze moved swiftly toward the back of the houseboat. Suddenly he stood, alert, listening. "He knows now." His eyes came back to hers, and his expression was grim. "And if that sound is what I think it is, he's here."

Allison's trembling hands flew to her mouth. "O Lord, be with us. Protect us. Keep us from evil."

She felt Bret's steadying iron grip on her arm. Her eyes lifted to the ceiling; she heard the same terrifying sound of muffled footsteps that she had heard when Bret came in through the hatch on the roof.

"Lock the hatch," she choked, but he squeezed her arm encouragingly.

"No. This is it. What we've planned for and waited for. He

doesn't know I'm here. He thinks you're alone." His hands gripped her arms tightly. "Can you handle this, Allison?"

She wanted to scream. She wanted to turn and run madly, but his steady gaze offered confidence and strength.

"I'm here, and I'll protect you." Bret's promise was filled with a quiet confidence. "If I wasn't sure I could stop him, I'd never risk you." He reached under his shirt, and his Luger emerged.

Allison thought of Sarah facing Spencer alone in the garden...of Helga, brave and patriotic, facing him alone here on the boat...of Helga's body below in the sarcophagus—and Allison's strength rallied. These women had given their all for their country. Could she do any less?

She nodded, then looked quickly toward the kitchen. The hatch was opening. He was coming down the ladder.

"Let him talk," Bret whispered. "Just like Gilbert did."

Her heart fluttered when Bret's hand reluctantly let go of her and he slipped into the shadows of the room. Alone, Allison stood rooted to the floor of the houseboat. Her heart was beating so fast she felt breathless; her hands were sweaty and cold. She bit her lip and clenched her hands together behind her, staring intently through the small doorway that led toward the kitchen.

The candles flickered with the breeze coming from the opening. The brighter lantern cast shadows on the wall. She could hear footsteps coming quietly. He left the kitchen, then came through the dining room. She could see his form now as he paused. He must have seen her standing there. A horrid thought flashed through her mind: what if he didn't bother with words? What if he just shot her from where he stood?

But no, he wouldn't do that, he couldn't. He wanted the information Sarah had left her. And he wanted Nefertari. His plan would be to get what he wanted from her, then dispose of her in the same way he had the others. Then he would go to meet Bret at the huts when the club arrived. He would have some plausible reason for why Allison was missing, just the way Helga was. And if Bret hadn't come tonight, no one would know the truth but God, the Judge of all the earth. "Shall not the Judge of all the earth do right?" Abraham had asked. The answer was a resounding yes!

Spencer Howard would meet his judgment for murder, and Cynthia would answer for the selfish greed that had turned her to cooperate with a murderer and a German agent.

Spencer walked toward her slowly, glancing about them, his expression cautious. Was it possible he knew Bret had left the Flamingo Hotel?

Her blood turned cold when she saw the cane in his hand. It sounded on the floor as he drew nearer, as though the sound bolstered his courage. His pensive gaze came at last to rest on her. "So you managed to get here on your own."

It was time. She gripped her hands together tightly and gave him and imploring look. "S-Spencer, what are you doing here? Did you come alone? Where are the others?"

He stood still, staring at her, and every fiber of her body screamed to turn the other way and run. Instead, she put a hand to her chest.

"You nearly frightened me to death creeping down the hatch, Spencer. Why didn't you come to the front door?" She looked past him. "Is Julian with you?"

"Don't move!" The snarled command snapped her to attention. "There's cobra venom in the tip of this cane, and you're just a step away from it." His smile was ugly. "Ingenious idea, isn't it? It has served me well on a number of occasions. Works wondrously! So quickly! One quick jab, a squeeze of this handle, and the hidden needle injects deadly venom into your system. It worked well on the Blaine woman and the baroness." His expression darkened as he studied her. "You stupid little fool, had you any sense you'd have stayed out of this! I gave you every chance! I didn't want this, but you kept meddling, you and Beth both."

"Beth!" The startled word slipped out before Allison could stop it.

"Oh, don't worry over your empty-headed sister," Spencer said disdainfully. "She's hale and hardy. Though the only reason I didn't kill her is that she didn't recognize me. I knew Julian and the colonel already suspected me, but they had no proof—and I couldn't give them any by silencing her, now could I? Or you, for that matter. Though I do confess I was tempted to do so at the Bulac Hospital. Now—" he gave a heavy sigh—"I've no choice."

"But—but I don't have the information you want."

His cold smile emerged again. "So, you've given up playing at not knowing who I am, have you? Just as well. Such games get tedious. As for not knowing anything, you're lying. The Blaine woman left you a letter. She mentioned it to me before I killed her." His smug smirk turned Allison's stomach. "She was ready to tell me whatever I wanted to know by the time I got done with her. But I could never find the cursed thing. I thought it was in the box, but she was cleverer than I thought. It was in your trunk, wasn't it? How stupid of me not to have opened that Christmas gift."

"I don't have it. I gave it to Julian before I came to find Helga."

He shook his head. "Nice try. But I know better. You came here to give it to Helga because you didn't trust Holden or Julian. Sadly, our dear Helga is dead. If you look below you'll find her. I silenced her a month ago. She was croaking too much, like a noisy frog! I discovered she had sent a wire to Bombay asking about my record. I knew then that she must be silenced. She'd learned who I was—"

"George." Allison's whisper was hoarse.

Spencer smiled. "And now you have that unique privilege as well, so it seems." His expression darkened. "How typical. You and those like you all seem to think you know so much. You dabble in history, in archaeology, and think yourselves so wise." A glazed, faraway look came over him, and his tone softened, as though he was talking more to himself than to Allison. "I've watched them come so many times, those idiot tourists who like to fancy themselves in love with the land. But I know better. They haven't the capacity to truly appreciate the ageless mysteries to be found here."

"And you do, I suppose?" The caustic comment was out before Allison could stop it.

Spencer's eyes came back to rest on her, and he sneered. "Yes, as a matter of fact, I do. But then, I wouldn't expect you to know that." He sighed. "What a pity. You seem to hold so much promise, but you're really no different than they. I'll be doing the country a service by removing you." His smile was ugly. "Which I will have to do, as I'm sure you realize."

"I—I won't say anything." If only the terror in her voice were a pretense—

He laughed. "Ah, but the patriotic little nursing angel would rather die than keep so wicked a secret. You're much too noble, Allison. And so I've no choice—" He broke off suddenly. She saw his eyes stray from her momentarily and a muscle in his cheek twitch. Allison tensed, but did not dare follow his gaze. The coffee cups! The plates of food! Clear evidence that someone was with her! She must draw his attention away—

It was too late. His eyes flashed with hatred. "Bret is here!"

Spencer started toward her, bringing the cane to her throat. She froze, staring at the tip that was now mere inches away.

"Don't move, Holden! Not one step!"

Bret had come up behind Spencer from the shadows of the divan, his Luger pointed at the other man, but he halted as he was told. Spencer's cold smile broadened.

"Pull that trigger and Allison is dead, too. Is that what you want? Alas, I thought you wanted Cynthia! You fooled me well. So well in fact that Mrs. Walsh was insisting she marry you. Nothing must come between Cynthia and me!"

"Or Nefertari?"

At the mention of the funerary treasure piece, Spencer's cheek twitched again. "What do you know about it?"

"I have it," Bret said calmly. "Here, on the boat."

"You're lying. Helga had it, to meet Roderick."

"It was too risky to leave her alone with Nefertari. As her death proves. I arranged to have it with me."

A fine sheen of sweat broke out on Spencer's forehead. "You're lying again, Holden, just like you've been lying all along. And you're not suspended from the CID."

"But I do have Nefertari with me now. I'm willing to bargain. The piece for Allison."

Spencer licked his lips, then narrowed his gaze. "I can't let her go now. She knows too much."

"Then the three of us must die together. I'll kill you if you squeeze that trigger. Then who will get Nefertari? Julian, is my guess. He'll end up with Nefertari and Cynthia. Is that what you want? His arms will hold her, his lips will kiss her, and the two of them will be rich and comfortable in Constantinople."

Spencer gave a low curse.

Bret smiled coolly. "Just turn Allison loose and you can have both Cynthia and Nefertari all to yourself. We both know your work as George is over now anyway. You could never return to Cairo and continue your practice in the British military. I can arrange for Cynthia to meet you on the Berlin-Baghdad Railway."

"You'd never do that, Holden. You're too much the CID man for that!"

"I would do it for Allison. I want her as much as you want Cynthia and Nefertari. We'll keep it a little secret between us, and we'll go our separate ways. We both know the war will go on whether we live or die. Why should the three of us be found here dead when there's a reasonable way out? We'll let the heads of government fight their own war."

The sweat was now dripping from Spencer's face. Allison glanced at the tip of the cane and tried to silence the loud pounding of her heart in her ears. "Bret is right, Doctor Howard," she whispered. "I'll go with him, and you leave with Cynthia."

"I have Nefertari," Bret said again. "Would you like to see her? She's right over there in my satchel. She's been there all along—in Cairo, on the steamer, and here now, tonight. You can go see her for yourself."

"I'm not a fool. The moment I move from Allison you'll use that Luger on me."

"Then I'll open the satchel."

"Slowly…one step a time."

"Not unless you also move a few feet away from Allison."

"I'm not taking this cane away from her throat."

"Then you'll not have Nefertari."

"All right! But she stays where she is. She doesn't move an inch."

Bret looked at Allison and as their eyes met, she felt she

understood the message they contained.

Bret slowly opened his satchel and removed an object wrapped in cloth. He looked at Spencer.

"Go ahead," Spencer urged. "Remove the cloth."

Bret unwrapped Nefertari. The moment the Egyptian image caught the glow of the lamp, glittering in golden splendor, Spencer sucked in his breath. In that split second, Allison threw herself to the floor, rolling toward the divan. The house-boat reverberated with the blast from Bret's Luger. Spencer cried out as the bullet struck his hand, and his cane fell to the floor. Allison surged forward, grasping it and moving quickly to the other side of the room.

There was a brief scuffle as Bret threw himself into Spencer, knocking him backward into the wall and delivering several vicious blows to his stomach and jaw. Soon Spencer was dou-bled over on the floor, gripping his bloody hand, and bitterly cursing Bret. Nefertari lay between them, cold, lifeless, and glit-tering.

"It's all over, Spencer."

"It will never be over. This is only the beginning. You stopped me, but I'm one small fish in the pond. You haven't stopped the kaiser and you won't stop the U-boats. It's already too late for Secretary of War Kitchener." He glared at Allison. "And for Neal!"

Bret grabbed him by the front of his shirt and yanked him to his feet. "What do you mean? Talk! Or you'll soon be munching your teeth."

Spencer spat in his face.

Allison winced and turned her head as Bret laid his palm across Spencer's face, smashing his head backward against the wall. "Talk."

Spencer spat blood. "Go to Hades, Holden. You and England both!"

Bret backhanded him again. "Talk."

Spencer gave a harsh laugh. "It won't matter, you know. It's too late. The ship Kitchener and Neal are on is a graveyard. It's already been sent to the bottom of the icy Atlantic!"

Bret's hand tightened on his shirt. "You're lying."

"Am I? Then how did I know about Kitchener's secret voyage to Russia to meet with Czar Nicholas? How did I know Neal was onboard as one of his aides?"

Allison took a step toward Spencer, searching his glazed eyes for confirmation. "Yes Bret, how does he know?"

Bret's jaw flexed angrily and his hand dropped from Spencer. Spencer's grin was pure evil. "I'll tell you why, Colonel. Because I *did* arrange for Edgar Simonds to be released from prison. We arranged for him to meet us on the road to Aleppo, and he came because he thought we also had Gilbert. Edgar didn't need to sell the information anymore, he was only too willing to spill it for free once my men had abducted him and brought him to the Berlin-Baghdad Railway. He talked all right. And when they were through with the blubbering dolt, they tossed him from the moving train like a bloated bag of rotting potatoes. Kitchener's dead. England, dear Merry Old England, is without the brilliant secretary of war. We sank your precious ship on May 5!"

Allison's hand went to her mouth. Her eyes closed and hot tears spilled down her cheeks.

For a moment Bret didn't move, and then as Spencer laughed and sank into the chair, Bret lifted the Luger steadily. Spencer grew still and cautious.

"I think you're telling me the truth for once in your life,

Howard. And I'm sorely tempted to put a messy hole through your heart. But CID will want the pleasure of a little chat with you first. Before they're through, you'll reveal the names and whereabouts of your German sympathizers."

"You underestimate me, Holden."

"No, I've never done that. It's you who have underestimated England. It won't be Gilbert Simonds that hangs for the murder of Mrs. Blaine. You'll answer for that, as well as for Helga and the chauffeur."

Spencer Howard's hot gaze mocked. "They can only hang me once. But you've forgotten the French official who recognized me from a meeting with Edgar Simonds in Bombay. I'm disappointed in you, Colonel. I eliminated him in the garden."

"And Mrs. Walsh."

Spencer's smile faded.

"What do you think your beloved Cynthia will do when she learns you dropped cyanide in her mama's glass?"

Spencer's rebellious attitude crumbled. "Edith was an accident."

"Oh, of course she was. You meant that little present for me."

Spencer's mouth shot down violently. "Yes! My one mistake, Holden, was not putting an end to you after you killed Rex Blaine."

"When Cynthia learns you murdered her mother, she'll despise you. For a bit of leniency in her sentence, she'll tell everything she knows about you to British Intelligence. Think about it. You've lost her love, and Nefertari. Forever."

Spencer's shoulders sagged a little as he fell back against the chair, but Allison could find no sympathy for him in her heart. The coldness within her was echoed in Bret's command: "Get up, Howard. You and I are making a train trip back to Cairo."

TWENTY

THE HEADLINES BLARED FORTH the shocking news: "Kitchener and Staff Perish at Sea; Lost on Cruiser, Perhaps Torpedoed; England Suspects Spies."

Allison read the story in hushed silence.

LONDON, Wednesday, June 7, 1916

Bound for Russia on an important military errand, Earl Kitchener, the British war secretary, and his staff were lost off the West Orkney Islands Monday night by the sinking of the carrier *Hampshire*. Whether the warship struck a mine or was torpedoed by a submarine is not known, according to Admiral Sir John Jellicoe, commander in chief of the Grand Fleet. Jellicoe's brief official report to the Admiralty gives the only published facts about the catastrophe, which by its suddenness has stunned the entire people of Great Britain.

Earl Kitchener was going to Russia at the request of the Russian government. He intended to land at Archangel, visit Petrograd, and visit the Russian front. His mission had chiefly to do with the supply of munitions for Russia, but an official statement issued last evening said that he was to have discussed important military and financial questions with Emperor Nicholas.

Several weeks had passed since the night on the boat, and Allison still hadn't seen Bret again in Cairo. But to her surprise two unexpected visitors had arrived one morning a week ago to see her and were waiting in the parlor when she came down.

A woman turned, her blond hair catching the light from the window. "Marra," Allison cried, going to embrace her friend. "What are you doing here? How good to see you!"

"I'm on leave," Marra said cheerfully, her eyes twinkling. "So is David. We arrived two hours ago. Sit down, you look as pale as a ghost—or around these parts, I suppose I should say as a mummy. Looks like I missed out on all the excitement on the houseboat."

"I assure you, you're fortunate that you did."

Marra grinned. "I had better things to do. I have a big surprise for you." She held out her left hand, wiggling her ring finger where a diamond wedding band sparkled and danced in the window light.

Allison gave a delighted laugh and hugged her. Marra laughed, too.

"Congratulations!" Allison told them, and David grinned.

"Could you ask for any greater proof of my courage?" he quipped, and Marra stuck her tongue out at him, then turned back to Allison.

"We've been married a whole week! Imagine. A honeymoon in the desert among the troops. We're both being sent to Palestine in a few weeks. That's another reason why I came. You had said you'd be coming with us to the field hospital."

"Yes, yes." Allison smiled, trying to keep all her facts straight. "I expect to do so just as soon as I hear from Bret. Father says he'll be moving out in August to join General Murray." She took Marra's hands. "Now sit down, tell me all about it. How did you and David get back together? And how did you find a rabbi to marry you and—"

"We didn't," Marra said boldly. "The chaplain married us."

Allison stared at David, and he shrugged. "No, we're not Christians, but I confess I've been interested in reading the epistle called Hebrews in your New Testament. So who knows? Maybe God is trying to tell me something, eh?"

Marra threw up her hands. "Anyway, David came looking for me at Suez. He said all the right things, and well, here we are. Mr. and Mrs. David Goldstein."

Well, there were many things left to celebrate after all! Allison's smile broadened. There were many blessings for which to give thanks to the God of all mercies. Marra and David's happiness warmed her heart with renewed hope.

Marra and David had left after a wonderful visit. They returned to the military camp life and settled into the ongoing dreary business of war. Now that both Allison's father and Beth had arrived home safely, the Residency was busy with the comings and goings of foreign dignitaries, ambassadors, and military officers. Allison had heard from her mother that Cynthia had been detained and was to be returned to London for questioning by the government. Cousin Gilbert's sentence had been changed from the murder of Sarah Blaine to the murder of Professor Jemal Pasha, which still meant he would receive the death penalty. There was no word about Doctor Spencer Howard, but his end was sure.

As for Paul Kruger, Allison heard he had been offered the position he had wanted in the Cairo Museum. But upon learning that his mother had been killed in valiant service to England, he declined the position and offered himself for service to the CID.

The most surprising bit of news was that Julian had been working closely with Bret all along. Allison discovered this when Julian came to call at the Residency—not to see her, but Beth, in whom he had taken an interest recently.

"Bret and I are brothers." Julian delivered this astounding tidbit to Allison and Beth as they sat munching cookies and sipping tea in the parlor. Allison and Beth both stared at him, stunned, and he laughed. "Not blood brothers, I admit, but we were raised in Charles Spurgeon's Boys Orphanage. Bret was adopted by his Old Granny, as he calls her, but Granny turned out to a be a wealthy woman, as her will later proved. Cynthia found out about that before Bret did."

"But what about the things you told me in the motorcar that day when you brought me home from Ezbekiah," Allison protested. "You certainly didn't sound like a brother, or even a friend."

"Did you meet someone after I pulled away, someone who almost immediately appeared to greet you?"

She hesitated. "Spencer."

"Yes, I saw him there. And it was an opportunity to let him overhear every word about Bret and Cynthia."

Beth looked at Allison with a smile. "Julian was once a Shakespearean actor in London. That's how he met Cynthia."

Allison turned to Julian, relief washing over her. "Then you didn't—I mean, I don't want to sound as though I'm prying, but your obsession with Cynthia was merely stage theatrics?"

"I was drawn toward her once, but it was never as serious as she implied. We drifted apart soon after she spotted Bret. I knew what she was by then. Cynthia made you think I was still bitter over it when you had tea together. She admitted coming here to the Residency one evening to see you to learn where Bret was. Spencer followed her and was enraged that she would risk coming here without his orders. They met in the garden near the gazebo."

"The blue delphiniums." Allison nodded. "He must have dropped that tobacco pouch then. But what was Cynthia doing inside the house with him when I arrived from Zeitoun?"

"From what we've been able to determine, Spencer blamed her for losing his pouch. He couldn't think where he had left it and knew it was a dangerous risk. She had come back looking for it."

Beth leaned forward, her brown eyes bright with interest. "Was Bret right that it was Cynthia who waited for Allison to lead her to Sarah's menagerie?"

"She admits it. It was also Cynthia who came into the bedroom where you were hiding. She had seen you arrive, watching you from the room Marra had slept in. She had taken off her heels so that she could walk silently, and when she entered the bedroom she was wearing a pair of Rex Blaine's old walking shoes."

"So that's why Spencer never tried to silence Beth. He knew she couldn't identify him because it was Cynthia who had gone into the room," Allison said.

"Why did she come to that room?" Beth wondered. "Why didn't she just stay hidden?"

"That window faces the drive, and she wanted to see where the chauffeur was parked so she could avoid him when she left. She didn't know at the time that Spencer had killed him."

"Did he tell Cynthia why he had?"

Julian considered Allison's question. "No, but he admitted to Bret that the chauffeur had seen him walking up through the trees. He had to avoid being identified as being anywhere near the Blaine house."

They lapsed into silence, and Julian saw her looking at his Egyptian ring. "A gift from Mr. Sayyid when I first arrived as the new Cairo inspector." He smiled. "It's the only piece of Egyptian art I own. Before I leave Cairo I shall collect a few more prizes." And he looked at Beth.

A faint, pink flush on Beth's cheeks told Allison that she might not be at all averse to the notion.

Zalika came into the parlor then and smiled at Allison. "Sir Marshall and Miss Eleanor want to see you in his office."

Allison left Beth and Julian together and went to the other side of the Residency to her father's office. She entered quietly, shutting the door and glancing about uneasily. Was there more bad news about the war?

Her gaze was caught and held by ice blue eyes filled with tender amusement. Bret! Her heart danced as she looked at him. He was immaculately dressed in his colonel's uniform again, and she returned his smile as his warm gaze flicked over her with appreciation. Her mother stood beside him, looking as contained and elegant as always.

Her father walked toward her, giving her an affectionate hug. "Hello, Daughter. What's this I hear about you and our new assistant director of the CID?"

She noticed her father's eyes twinkle and was about to ask what he was up to when what he'd said hit her. She stared at her father. "The...what?"

"Assistant director." Her father's smile was smug. "Only makes sense, you know. The lad is more than qualified—"

"Yes, of course—"

"Besides, can't have him gallivanting around on dangerous missions when he has a family to think of, now can we?"

She looked from Bret to her father. "A—family?"

"Your father has a tendency to rush things, darling." Bret smiled indulgently.

"Well, not such a rush, I'm sure. You're to have a June wedding, so I should think a family isn't so far off. A year at the most, eh?"

Allison looked from her father's smiling face to her mother, who laughed with delight. Slowly Allison turned to face Bret. He started to walk toward her, and before she knew what she was doing, she was running to meet him. He opened his arms to her, and she was in his embrace. Before their lips met, she was vaguely aware of her mother taking her father's arm and walking with him out onto the open veranda where they stood together, arms about each other.

"But *this* is June," Allison breathed, hardly daring to believe what she'd been told.

"Yes." The lazy smile Allison had come to love so well crossed Bret's handsome features. "So it is. Today is June 25, to be exact. Do you know what that means?" His arms squeezed her.

A smile of pure joy filled her face. "We have less than a week to arrange for a June wedding, complete with orange blossoms." She frowned suddenly. "Bret, will you be happy?" At his questioning look, she went on. "Not being in the field, I mean? You love it so—"

"Not nearly so much as I love you." His smile was tender. "Will I be happy?" He pressed a kiss to her cheek. "How can I not? I'll still be involved with CID, just in a way that will be a bit safer and won't take me away from you. So I'll have both the work I love and the woman I adore." He kissed her other cheek, then looked deep into her eyes. "And that, my dearest love, is enough to keep me happy forever."

Her heart full, Allison lifted her face to his. Never one to need too much coaxing, Bret took full—and very satisfying— advantage of the action.

They held to each other, lost in a world all their own as they became a part of the warm stillness of the June afternoon. From below in the garden the fragrance of soon-to-be wedding blossoms drifted up with the sweet, cheerful promise of bird song. And two valiant hearts beat together as one in praise to the God who had joined them.